Praise for R

'A *Devil Wears Prada* for t
Glamour

'Rosie Nixon's comic take on Hollywood and
fashion is a gem'
Stylist

'Absolutely riveting, and so true!'
Joan Collins

'This is a must read for *Devil Wears Prada* and
Shopaholic fans!'
Adele Parks

'A brilliant and funny insight into the circus of
show business and fashion by an author
who's seen it all herself. Loved it!'
Martine McCutcheon

'Funny, showy, but also poignant, this is a
fashionista's dream book'
The Sun

'Acerbic, glamorous fun'
Daily Mirror

'A stylish, fun read, I absolutely loved it!'
Jackie Collins

'Captivating, glamorous and laugh-out-loud funny!'
Giovanna Fletcher

Rosie Nixon is an author, broadcaster and coach. She is the author of four novels and one non-fiction collection. After a long career in women's magazines, latterly as the award-winning editor-in-chief of *HELLO!* magazine, Rosie now enjoys a portfolio career and is a qualified life coach. In 2024 she founded Rosie's Reinvention Retreats, a series of day retreats supporting midlife women through career, business and wellbeing transformations, enabling them to realise a more fulfilling way of life.

Having previously held senior positions at women's glossies including *Grazia*, *Glamour* and *Red*, Rosie regularly uses her wealth of experience in the media as a mentor and brand consultant. Rosie is a proud ambassador for the charities Wellbeing of Women, Wellchild, and the anti-FGM charity Educate Not Mutilate. She lives with her family and two cats in Surrey.

Also by Rosie Nixon

Fiction
The Stylist
Amber Green Takes Manhattan
Just Between Friends

Non-Fiction
Be Kind

bad influence

Rosie Nixon

HQ

ONE PLACE. MANY STORIES

HQ
An imprint of HarperCollins*Publishers* Ltd
1 London Bridge Street
London SE1 9GF

www.harpercollins.co.uk

HarperCollins*Publishers*
Macken House, 39/40 Mayor Street Upper
Dublin 1, D01 C9W8, Ireland
This edition 2025

1
First published in Great Britain by HQ,
an imprint of HarperCollins*Publishers* Ltd 2025

ISBN: 9780008273446

Set in Sabon LT Std by HarperCollins*Publishers* India

Printed and bound in the UK using 100% Renewable
Electricity at CPI Group (UK) Ltd

MIX
Paper
FSC™ C007454
FSC
www.fsc.org

For more information visit: www.harpercollins.co.uk/green

For Bella and Poppy
Be brave, bold and unashamedly you.

'Fashion is life-enhancing, and I think it's a lovely, generous thing to do for other people'
Dame Vivienne Westwood

PROLOGUE

Dear Destiny,
Can you ever know that someone is truly yours?

So asks one follower by the initials AG this week, and the simple answer is: no. I hope this hasn't cracked your heart in two. Let me explain:

Dear AG – If you are in a relationship and concerned whether the other person is as committed to you as you are to them, or you are questioning your own commitment to a long-term relationship, firstly, may I strongly suggest that you do some work on yourself. This kind of question reveals a deep insecurity and a lack of trust that is likely to make any suitor catch the first bus out of your area. Secondly, you need to get out there and enjoy having a full relationship without fear. Thirdly, remember that no one can actually climb inside anyone's brain, so it's impossible to know if they are truly yours, all you can do is trust them – until they show you otherwise, which might be never or might be tomorrow. Work with factual information, AG, because guessing about a person is the road to ruin. And be thankful they can't climb into your mind either – that really would be the death of nearly all relationships, wouldn't it? AG, you must believe in your ability to love and be loved in return.

Best of luck,
Dear Destiny

CHAPTER ONE

It was 2.15 p.m. on Saturday and I'd just popped to the loo after lunch with Mum in Peter Jones, Sloane Square. I was sitting on the toilet, having a quick scroll from Instagram to WhatsApp to Gmail, when I saw it there. I read the email three times, because I couldn't believe it was real. Then I jogged all the way back to our table from the ladies'.

'You'll never believe it.' I grinned at Mum. My forehead was sweating lightly. I knew this because my mother was looking up there, rather than at my lips.

As it turned out, no, she could not believe it, in fact it made no sense to her at all, because she had no idea who Mandy Sykes was.

This was hugely frustrating for me. I mean, gah! *What planet does she live on?*

I'm sure I don't need to tell *you* that Mandy Sykes is the biggest thing to have hit the internet since Kylie Jenner's lips or Prince Harry's todger. Following her bunion operation last year, Mandy's right foot gained the highest *ever* number of likes on Instagram and spawned its own TikTok account, which swiftly paved the way to an eponymous range of bunion correctors to 'Cheat feet into wearing the heels you deserve!' Heels by Mandy Sykes, of course.

Where have you been, mother dearest?

We were in Peter Jones because Mum was trying to cheer me up.

She wanted me to play her personal stylist and source a mother-of-the-bride outfit for her to wear to my sister Lucy's wedding. Less because she actually wanted this service from me, more because she thought it would be a good distraction from the fact I was being made redundant from my job in the visual merchandising department at Selfridges.

So here we were, in ladieswear, on this busier-than-usual afternoon. The novelty had worn off on both of us.

'Yellow is definitely *not* me,' Mum stated, turning her nose up at practically all of the spring/summer collections on the floor.

I tutted loudly. 'It's more mustard than yellow. Won't you just *try* the dress, so we know for certain that it's not you? Mustard is a good colour for you. Mustard is bang on trend – and that's the brief you gave me, if you remember?' I pulled out my phone at this point and began scrolling to find the WhatsApp message in which she had commissioned me to find her, and I quote, 'an on-trend wedding outfit'.

She brushed the phone away.

'It's just now that I *see* the options, I don't know if I could actually wear them.'

I sucked in my cheeks. I've had way more disingenuous clients in the past, but there's something about being related to one that is next-level difficult.

'And one hundred quid minimum for a dress?' Mum was complaining. 'This is scandalous!'

'How about a print?' I offered, guiding her from one concession to the next. 'Prints are huge this season.'

Mum fingered a price tag. 'Three hundred and fifty pounds!' she exclaimed loudly, turning her head for dramatic effect in the hope of catching the eye of a kindred spirit to back her up.

'I thought you wanted to get something special, Mum – you're the mother of the bride. Believe me, you'd pay a lot more for bespoke. And you told me you wanted to look *fashionable* at this wedding.'

'Prints are ageing and yellow is for WAGs,' she replied as if the matter was closed. 'I want to look age appropriate.'

'WAGs,' I scoffed. 'Very Noughties.' *It's like shopping with a teenager!*

'The only thing that feels appropriate right now is for me to disappear,' I muttered, looking hurt.

'Oh, don't be silly, Amber. It's just that after all these years, I like to think I have *some* idea about what suits me.' We walked on.

'So why are we here, if you don't really want my advice?' I asked belligerently.

She ignored me. We both knew the whole thing was a ruse; a way to build our relationship. After the three months I had spent with Rob in New York, I had felt distant from Mum, as though we couldn't just pick up where we left off anymore. An unspoken Sahara Desert appeared between us where she didn't really understand my world and I felt estranged from hers. Plus, getting made redundant had hit my ego hard. The truth was, I felt like a failure. Even though I tried to tell myself I didn't want to be a window dresser forever, so to see it as an opportunity, I was worried about the future and what I would do next. Plus, not having a steady income would affect Rob's and my plans to buy a flat together. She had suggested the girlie trip to 'cheer me up', but it was having the opposite effect. Being with my decisive, high-achieving lawyer mother was making me feel even more inadequate. A partner in a prestigious law firm, with no plan to retire any time soon, Mum seemed so capable of anything she put her mind to. *Sometimes it's hard to believe I came from her womb.*

I sucked in my cheeks as Mum squinted at her mobile phone. *What could be more important than a whole floor of new season collections?*

'Is it a work thing?' I probed.

'It's your father,' she said, not looking up. A serious expression fell across her face. 'I forgot to tell him to take the steak out of the freezer.'

I puffed out my cheeks and then slowly released the air inside. I thought about all the times when I was sixteen and I could be so frustrated, so *disgusted*, by things my mum said that I would storm off in a huff. It was a shame I couldn't get away with petulant behaviour anymore. Adulting is hard.

'Okay, Mum.'

Things improved marginally once we found Ralph Lauren and a sale rail containing a dress almost identical to a navy-and-cream one she wore to the last family wedding.

When I reminded her of this fact, she muttered, 'At least I already have a matching hat. Anyway, if not the wedding, maybe it will work for the hen do? I'm going to need something for that too. It's quite Parisian, don't you think?'

I bristled at the mention of the hen. 'It's quite plain, to be totally honest. But if you like it . . .'

There was something I needed to tell Mum today, but so far there hadn't been a right moment; probably because there was no easy way of saying it.

She tried on the dress and the twelve was too big and the ten too tight. I breathed a sigh of relief – which was more than she could do in the ten – and then we both decided we needed some time out. And a cheese scone.

In the café, I snuck a look at my phone. I had been expecting something to come through from my boss at Selfridges, Joseph, about my redundancy package, but I found a very different email – one that was infinitely more welcome. And now that I had this email in my possession, I wasn't going to let a failed shopping trip dampen my mood.

While Mum went to the loo, I phoned Rob. *He'll know how big this is.*

'Mandy *who*?'

My heart sank. Clearly, he hadn't been looking at Instagram every five seconds for years, like me.

I googled a photo and sent it to him as a reminder.

'Oh *her*,' he conceded. 'The one with the bunion. She's epic, isn't she? That's great news, baby, it could be perfect timing! Shall I cook later? We'll have to stop splashing out on takeaways. I'm near Sainsbury's?'

I had a quick re-read of the email. It was short, but to the point:

Dear Miss Green,

Ms Mandy Sykes is looking for a UK-based personal stylist. We wondered if you would be interested in coming for an interview? Ms Sykes will be in London on 1 March and can see you at Corinthia London. Please let me know as soon as possible if you can meet with Ms Sykes and her team with regards to this position.

Best wishes,
Julie-Ann Morris
Agent to Ms Mandy Sykes

It took me a nanosecond to decide if I was interested. With no job, no takeaways for the foreseeable, and the renewal of my mobile phone plan coming up, this email could be the answer to my prayers. It was also, as of now, my only option. A pang of worry about money was lodged in my mind, like a heavy rain cloud. My life-savings would cover my share of our rent for the next few months but that was it. I hadn't been expecting to be made redundant.

'Efficiencies are being made across the company,' Joseph had told my co-worker Shauna and me when he called us into a meeting yesterday morning.

'The graffiti's off?' Shauna jumped the gun, assuming he

was referring to our proposal to involve the hottest street artists for the summer shop windows.

'I don't just mean the graffiti idea has been slammed – although it has.' Joseph avoided eye contact with us. 'I mean they have asked all managers to look at efficiencies in other areas too.'

We sat in silence for five seconds. I knew it was five because I counted as the second hand moved on the wall clock.

'Are you trying to tell us we might be out of jobs?' Shauna asked. I could always rely on her to be direct.

'Nothing is concrete yet,' Joseph continued awkwardly. 'But I've been asked to make you aware that your role is at risk of redundancy and, at about six p.m. today, the company will be sending out emails to certain individuals, either confirming the redundancy or offering an alternative role for you within the company. I'm sorry for this news.'

Shauna flicked her nails in the way she did just before she was about to blow up.

'When you say "certain individuals", do you mean both me and Amber, or just one of us?' Her brow was furrowed. 'I mean, I'm assuming you wouldn't be telling us this, if we weren't getting the email?'

Joseph stroked his chin, the way he did when he was anxious about something. 'You'll find out soon enough,' he replied.

'Are they mad?' Shauna scoffed. 'I mean, do they *seriously* think it's possible for you to manage the window designs on your own? They have no idea—'

'It's hard to swallow, mate, but the reality is that physical sales have been impacted by AI and online systems, making it easier for people to shop from home,' he said. 'The lack of footfall in the store is having an impact on all aspects of retail – including the window displays.'

'Great, so we're going to be replaced by AI?' Shauna said scornfully.

'Enter the robo-stylists . . .' I muttered, backing her up.

'We're not there – yet,' Joseph replied calmly. 'But there's been talk of digitising the windows. I didn't even get the David Koma display approved, and I only got him to agree to do it because he's a friend.'

'I'm good with digital,' Shauna piped up seriously. 'Did you see my last TikTok?'

Joseph continued calmly, 'Listen, I know it's a shock, it was for me too. But try not to panic. Please keep an eye on your inbox and I'll support you however I can through this process.' He had obviously been heavily briefed by HR not to go into any detail. Though I was pretty sure that being in the at-risk category didn't sound promising.

Sure enough, I got the email later that day, just as I set foot on the down escalator at the Bond Street Tube station. It stated that my role had been made redundant and there were 'regrettably, no other openings within the company' for me at this time. I texted Shauna to see if she had received the same email and she replied immediately, *No babes – I'm sorry.* It was crushing for my confidence, but, as Rob reminded me over a bottle of wine that evening, after all the fun and excitement of styling the Angel Wear fashion show in Manhattan, going back to work as a shop window designer hadn't been cutting it for me for a while. I missed styling real people instead of mannequins.

'Maybe this will turn out to be a good thing?' he had offered, green eyes shining. Rob's ability to look on the bright side was one of the things I loved about him. 'You'll get two-months' pay to tide you over while you find a new job. And I'm sure that won't take you long. You're Amber Green, stylist to the stars, *dahling*!'

'Former stylist to the stars,' I corrected him, morosely.

So, right now, eighteen hours later, as I waited for Mum in Peter Jones, this email felt like I'd been thrown a life jacket. *It would be amazing if I could secure a job immediately. Then I might be able to afford a few new outfits from the two-months' pay.* There was a new fire in my fingertips as I replied to the email.

Dear Julie-Ann, thanks so much for getting in touch. I'd love to meet up! Just let me know what time suits Ms Sykes and I'll be there. Kind regards, Amber Green

I instantly regretted the fact I'd made myself so available. Enthusiasm had probably knocked a zero off my potential salary. I'd never been good at stifling excitement. If I was likened to a punctuation symbol, I'd be an exclamation mark, no question. I could never be as aloof as all the moody full stops you see decorating the front row at fashion shows.

In a panic, I realised I hadn't given Julie-Ann my mobile number, so I sent her another email adding my mobile, plus

Instagram and TikTok handles, just to cover all bases. The show of excitement had likely shaved another chunk off my salary, but was totally and utterly authentically me.

With a cheese scone sitting like a kettlebell in my stomach and Mum looking jittery after two cups of coffee, we decided to abort the shopping trip and go home. She had some partially defrosted steak and a legal case to check on, and I wanted to discuss the email with Rob.

We parted company on the Bakerloo line with a stiff hug and a promise to do this again because it had been so lovely. *Neither of us is good at lying.* As the train pulled away, she urgently mouthed at me: *See you next Friday for Nora's birthday, don't forget!* And then a text came through: *Sorry for being a shitty client, you are wasted on me. That Mandy will be lucky to have you. Good luck – go for it. Mum.*

This made me smile. It was as close as I would ever get to a compliment. I hoped 'That Mandy' might feel the same.

As I continued my journey back home to Kensal Rise, I became curious about who had recommended me to an agent of Mandy Sykes. The fact the email referred to a 'position' made me think it was more than an ad-hoc enquiry about styling Mandy for the occasional event. My immediate thought was Mona Armstrong, the notorious celebrity stylist, and my former boss, whom I assisted during one memorable awards season between London and Los Angeles three years ago. Mona wasn't known for being particularly generous when it came to good deeds, especially for ex-assistants, so it was unlikely to be her, unless she had an ulterior motive, which was plausible.

Maybe I had met one of Mandy's entourage during that whirlwind circuit? I couldn't recall who. Or perhaps Mandy had read about the Angel Wear show, during those incredible few hours last autumn when I had found myself trending on Instagram. Maybe she had made a note?

Then it clicked. It might be Poppy. As in Poppy Dunn, the actress. Just before Rob and I spent three months in New York last year, I bumped into Poppy, sat in Mandy Sykes's car outside Selfridges, as she waited for her mega-famous friend to return to the vehicle after emptying half of the Hermès concession. Poppy and Mandy shared an agent at one point, when Poppy was trying to break America, so she was the only certain link to Mandy I could think of. I had come to her fashion rescue a couple of times during those three crazy months in Manhattan, so she owed me a favour. Yes, it had to be Poppy. I looked up and whispered into the lighting on the stuffy Tube carriage. *Thank you, Poppy, you're a total babe.*

When I made it back to our flat, Rob was already home. I call it 'our' flat, but it wasn't so long ago that I shared this place with my best friend Vicky, before Vicky moved to Los Angeles and stayed there with her film director boyfriend.

At least Vicky will understand how big this is.

I was itching to call her, but it would only be eight a.m. in LA and Vicky was not an early riser.

'So, were you successful in making over London's most fussy client?' Rob asked. He knew my mother sufficiently well enough that he was allowed to make derogatory comments.

'Don't be stupid,' I replied. 'I was always going to fail.'

'Did she buy *anything*?'

I sighed. 'Nope. We should have gone to a gallery or a matinée, she wouldn't have had to suffer all my bad suggestions then. I mean, can you believe I had the audacity to suggest she try wearing a shade of yellow?'

'Not very her.' He smiled.

'She'd have looked great, if only she'd given it a go. And it's bang on trend.'

He smirked. 'Did she at least buy you lunch?'

We were interrupted by my phone buzzing. Lucy.

'Amber, I've been waiting for you to call. How did it go with Mum?'

I paused. I knew full well what she meant.

'Am?'

'I'm here. I literally just walked through the door.'

'So, did you do the deed?'

My silence told her the answer.

'Oh Amber, this is the *only* thing I've asked you to do so far. And, as my maid of honour, you kind of have to do it. We only have eight Eurostar tickets and I've invited everyone. I can't tell one of my best friends that they can't come anymore. It's only a couple of weeks away. What are we going to do?' The 'we' made me flinch – such a friendly but loaded word.

'I'm sorry, Luce, there wasn't a good moment,' I replied, feeling irked that my main duty as maid of honour appeared to revolve around delivering bad news, rather than knocking back champagne whilst giving a second opinion on the wedding flowers. Lucy seemed to have conveniently forgotten that I had successfully steered her away from the horrendous tulle wedding gown, which came with a stitched-in suspender-belt, that she would have ended up in if left to her own devices. Surely that was a big tick under my MOH duties? Telling the excited mother-of-the-bride that she was barred from her own daughter's hen do shouldn't be a prerequisite for the role, if you ask me.

'Perhaps we should just get another ticket?' I offered, meekly.

Lucy recoiled. I could sense it through the phone.

'No,' she said, measuredly.

She was right, of course. But I was angry that she had let Mum believe she was invited, leaving me to do the dirty work.

Lucy could be bossy at the best of times, but her wedding run-up had been a marathon – and there were still four months to go. I felt horribly disloyal even thinking it, but I wasn't looking forward to my own sister's hen. To compound matters, she was also starting to make noises that the Pronovias gown I helped her choose – *and* at a fifteen per cent discount, thanks to my fashion connections – was giving her nightmares because she thought it made her back look like she 'wrestled for a living'. Naturally, being a stylist, I was to blame for this imagined situation; when in reality the champagned-coloured sensual 'mermaid' gown with rippling sequined effect, plunge back, and a neckline with exquisite beaded edging, was going to make the most breathtaking bridal look for the bride who insisted she couldn't wear white.

'Don't panic. I'll talk to Mum in the next couple of days,' I muttered, to get her off the phone.

'Okay, great, let me know when it's done.' She sighed. 'And don't forget Nora's birthday next Friday. Come any time after six as she's having a party with her school friends first. Expect a sugar high, but it would be lovely to see you. I'll save you some cake.'

'Of course,' I said. 'I'll be there.'

When I had hung up, I pulled my sweater sleeves down over my hands and sucked in my cheeks.

'She's going to be devastated,' I said, flopping onto the sofa beside my boyfriend. 'Rob . . .?' I said, louder.

'Not wedding drama again?' He was squinting at his laptop.

'You need to get your eyes tested. How do I phone Mum and tell her she's not going to her daughter's hen do?'

'Get it over with. Blame a mix-up over numbers, it'll be done by the time I've made you a mug of tea.' He leant forward and passed me my phone from the coffee table.

'Thank Christ for that!' Mum exclaimed once I had broken the unfortunate news that due to a computer glitch somewhere between here and King's Cross, we seemed to be one Eurostar ticket short for a sold-out train, and, as maid of honour, I didn't want to have to ask Lucy to let one of her oldest friends down, so it was either her or me.

'*Please* don't tell your sister, but I think a Paris hen do is more for you lot, rather than me,' she said, sounding upbeat.

'Are you absolutely sure, Mum?'

'Darling, I've never been surer. To be honest, I'd much rather stay at home. I was going to talk to you about it today, but there wasn't a good time.'

'Thank you for being so understanding,' I added duly. 'Lucy feels terrible.'

'That's one outfit we can scratch off the list,' she added jovially. 'You must be relieved.' Her tone was friendly, as she alluded that she might not have been the easiest customer today.

'It's no bother, Mum, honestly.' I smiled. 'But I still wish you'd tried the mustard.'

Being a lawyer, Mum was used to keeping it professional in smart suits and dresses, but this was a big family event. It was such a wasted opportunity! Things like this pained me, deeply, on a visceral level, like the thought of chewing cotton wool balls or watching Rob eat a peach.

Buoyed by telling Lucy the good news that we were going to Paris without mother in tow, and redeeming myself as her wedding attendant, I decided to ditch cooking and go with Rob for a date-night dinner of snacks and wine. 'We may be broke, but you're worth it,' he had declared, and as usual we opted for our local, The Chamberlayne.

Nico was behind the bar. He was always a comforting sight, having been pulling pints and shaking cocktails in The Chamberlayne for as long as I'd lived in the area. He'd been witness to more than a few 'spirited' evenings I'd had in here with Vicky – and there was that disastrous night with Rob, before we were together, when I fancied him like crazy and managed to slag off his current girlfriend before drunkenly toppling off my bar stool and twisting my ankle. Luckily, there wasn't much about my behaviour that could shock Nico – he claimed to have 'seen it all'. But none of it went outside of these four walls. He'd merely wink and flash his wide, warm Italian smile the next time I saw him.

'If only he wasn't gay,' Vicky would lament, almost every time we had come to the pub and shared a lock-in with Nico. 'I mean, do you think he'd *ever* fancy me?'

I didn't need to order before a glass of white wine was placed on the bar in front of me, and a pint for Rob.

'Table or bar, you beautiful pair?' Nico asked, looking across at the half-empty space. It was nearly seven p.m. and by eight on a Saturday evening, most of the tables would be taken.

'We'll grab that one please, mate.' Rob gestured to a cosy spot.

'So, tell me properly about this email,' he said, when we'd ordered a carb-tastic array of bar food to nibble on, plus the cheese croquettes, which made me salivate just thinking about them.

I pulled out my phone and located the email. Reading it aloud made it even more real.

Please let me know as soon as possible if you can meet with Ms Sykes and her team with regards to this position.

Best wishes,
Julie-Ann Morris
Agent to Ms Mandy Sykes

I added a flourish to the last part, to accentuate how big this was.

'So, what are you going to do?' Rob asked.

'Durr!' I replied, staggered. 'Seeing as I'm currently unemployed, coupled with the fact I miss the fun of putting clothes on humans, rather than shop window dummies, I've emailed her back to say I'm interested already – it's a no-brainer. But there is a chance this email has gone out to lots of other, more established stylists so I'm trying not to get my hopes too high.'

Rob sniggered.

'What's so funny?'

'I was just remembering how you were ecstatic to get the Selfridges job after assisting Mona Armstrong, precisely for the opposite reason – you were sick of actual people, their crazy demands and showbiz nonsense,' he said, smiling endearingly. 'Mannequins were appealing.'

'You've got a point. But clothes look the same on those dummies – they don't come alive like they do on real bodies. I miss people, their energy, and, most of all, their stories.'

'There were some *crazy* stories,' he observed. 'It wasn't all about bringing clothes alive, it was the reverse sometimes. Remember Liv Ramone, who preferred to go naked rather than wear any of the outfits you carefully sourced? And the fact you ended up styling a six-foot-four drag queen in an Angel Wear diamond bra? That wasn't a standard day at the office.'

'I know, I know,' I giggled, 'but it was brilliant. They were

proper fashion moments. I love the power of bringing out
the best in people . . . and I guess I miss the drama of it all.'

'Be careful what you wish for,' he warned.

Rob had a point. I had been so caught up in the excitement
of celebrity, it nearly cost us our relationship. I bristled as I
recalled how I let my obsession for building an Instagram
following take over my life.

Yet there was something so tantalising, so alluring, about
the prospect of being a personal stylist to a personality
as big as Mandy Sykes. It could turn my career around.
It would show Joseph and the Selfridges bosses. The fact
Mandy's agent had taken the time to write to me personally
was such an ego boost.

'I could start a new career as a personal stylist with a job
like this,' I enthused. 'And I would get to know Mandy, what
suits her shape, her personality, rekindle my relationships
with top designers to reinvent her look, help to bring out
the real her – I'd love to get to grips with the fiery Latino
side of her that the tabloids like to spin as if it's a negative.
I'd love to see her really *own* her heritage, her curves – the
real her. I could be so creative again.'

'*If* Mandy is up for the journey,' Rob reminded me.
'What does Vicky think?' he asked after a pause.

It was a question I often asked myself at life junctures,
big or small. Like when Rob asked me to move in with
him. Vicky told me to go for it. Or, the time when Joseph
was being unreasonable at work, expecting me to stay late
without any extra pay for the second time in a week – just
like he had the week before. *What would Vicky do?* 'Tell

him, no! What are you, fashion roadkill? No overtime pay, equals no extra time. Tell him you have boundaries. End of.'

I could always rely on Vicky to tell it straight. When Mona offered me the chance to go and work for her in LA, it was Vicky whom I got drunk with the night before and who stayed up all night to help me pack my suitcase. No way was she going to let me miss that plane, even though it broke both of our hearts to end such a special era of flat-sharing together.

Vicky was the best of BFFs. She always had my interests front and centre, and was the only person who could be completely honest with me – brutally, at times – but she could do it in a way that still made me greatly admire and love her. (And, by the way, I did get the extra pay from Joseph.)

I sat back in my seat. 'I haven't had a chance to speak to her about it yet,' I told Rob, feeling the urge to FaceTime Vicky immediately but restraining myself, seeing as I was on a date night with my boyfriend, not my long-distance best friend.

Vicky had come between Rob and I once before, when she rocked up unannounced on the doorstep of our tiny sardine-tin bedsit in Williamsburg, New York. That was all in the past, but I still felt a wariness about putting her advice ahead of his too often.

'I reckon she'd tell you to go for it, don't you?' Rob lifted his hand and stroked my cheek, as if reading my mind.

'Probably. Do you think I should?' I asked, gently capturing his fingers on the side of my face and holding them there for a moment.

'Of course, beautiful.' He smiled. 'Just as long as Ms Sykes doesn't have you on her private jet every other day, so I never get to see you.'

'Well, now I just have to hope that Julie-Ann Morris, Agent of Ms Mandy Sykes, gets back to me. I gave her literally all my contact details, save my NHS number.'

He laughed and, as the dimple appeared on his left cheek, I marvelled at how lucky I was to have him.

The following day I FaceTimed Vicky and she confirmed what I suspected.

'This is the most exciting potential job I've ever heard – you've got to get this!' she squealed. It seemed that living in Los Angeles, and regularly doing her weekly shop at Erewhon next to Hailey Bieber, had done nothing to dampen Vicky's excitement about the power of celebrity. 'Surely you've checked her Instagram recently?' she asked. 'She wore the most heinous white body-con monstrosity to a Taylor Swift gig. Two words: camel foot. If she was meant to be a white witch, she could have cast a better spell over her wardrobe.'

I laughed.

'No, seriously,' Vicky continued. 'I mean I'm all for body positivity, I think she's got a shape to die for, but she *needs* Amber Green in her life. Never mind her bunions, you need to save her front bottom, Amber. This is a fashion emergency!'

I was belly-laughing into the screen now, instantly reminded of why it was friendship at first eye-roll when

Vicky and I met on the first day of university in Brighton. We've been BFFs ever since.

Since that day, Vicky and I had probably shared over a million eye-rolls, sniggers behind hands, and knowing looks. We once nearly wet ourselves at a British Airways check-in desk when we tried to explain, in heavy French accents, that she was nominated for the Palme d'Or at the Cannes Film Festival, as we tried to blag an upgrade to Nice. When the woman behind the desk pointed out that the festival finished last week, and the flight was full, award-winning directors or not, we were forced to retreat to the back of the queue, blushing and Vicky muttering, 'Sacré bleu, les Angleses est trop rude,' as we joined the snaking economy line that almost reached the French border anyway.

Little did we know then that one day Vicky would be living in the movie industry capital, Los Angeles, with an actual film director boyfriend. *Talk about serendipity!* I felt a pang. I missed my partner in crime. But perhaps an opportunity like this, working with an American star like Mandy Sykes, might mean I could see her more often. The pluses were stacking up.

CHAPTER TWO

On Monday, mid-afternoon, which was early morning in Los Angeles, an email arrived from Julie-Anne Morris. The fact she had placed me at the top of her week's to-do list had to be a good sign.

> *Dear Amber,*
>
> *Many thanks for the swift response. Ms Sykes and her team will be in London this coming Thursday through Monday. She can see you at 10am Friday 1ˢᵗ March at Corinthia London. Please confirm.*
>
> *Regards*
> *Julie-Ann*

With no job to go to next week, save an allotted time to clear my desk on Friday afternoon, I didn't have to think twice.

When the day of the interview came around, I felt inordinately nervous.

Just because I've come across many famous people in my

styling career so far, my friends and family tend to assume I'm cool as a cucumber, nonchalant even, when it comes to being in the presence of someone in the public eye. Although I have mastered the art of not actually fainting when in the presence of showbiz greatness – let's gloss over the time I briefly passed out at a Hollywood premiere, back in the days when I was styling the actress Beau Belle (the LA sun combined with a sugar dip was to blame) – they couldn't be more wrong. When I see a superstar in the flesh, I still get a quickening of the heartbeat, and an adrenalin hit akin to the one time I shoplifted something (for the record, it was a travel-size dry shampoo from Boots when I was fourteen).

Yes, although you would never guess it, as I have calmly smoothed the VPL on a celebrity's rear or inserted some chicken fillets to enhance a well-known cleavage, most of the time, I'm screaming *this is amazing!* inside my head.

Today was no different.

As the Tube neared Embankment station, my pulse started to rise. In a matter of minutes, I would be a few feet away from Mandy – *the* Mandy Sykes – and didn't my sweaty palms know it.

At Baker Street I had opened the mindfulness app I downloaded earlier that morning. By Piccadilly I had closed it again because I couldn't concentrate on the instructions, and by Embankment my heart was beating like a drum in my temples.

On the short walk from the Tube to the hotel, I was shaky with nerves. My phone lit up with a stream of good-luck messages from Vicky.

You got this! Followed by, *Don't leave until she offers you the job*, and a further, *Americans don't do subtlety. Tell her how much you want this job. MAKE her give it to you!*

I battled with my internal voice. *What if I can't do this?*

A message from Rob came through: *Good luck, baby. Just be you!*

Just be me.

Fashion has been in my blood for as long as I can remember. There is a family legend that, aged four, I refused to sit on a sofa next to my cousins for a photo, because I was so offended by the apricot colour of the sofa and how it clashed with my red dress. When I was six, I styled my own angel costume for the school nativity, complete with glittering tiara and long, cream lace gloves, both discovered in our local Oxfam. By the age of eight, I had assembled a huge dressing-up box, and unsuspecting playmates became my clients, as I delighted in transforming them with a mohawk wig, a silk pyjama top, or some of Mum's old sunglasses and beaded necklaces. I revelled in their delight at the big 'reveal' moment, when they were allowed to look in the mirror. It's fair to say that from a young age, I had grasped the transformative power of clothes, but I had no idea yet of how this would set me up in my working life, because, truth be told, I always saw myself as a fashion fraud.

As I progressed through my awkward teenage years, I became less confident in dressing myself, but very interested in clothes worn by other people. When it came to shopping, I worshipped at the altar of charity shops and vintage stores, especially the ones in well-to-do areas like Notting Hill and Hampstead where you could regularly pick up designer seconds for a fraction of the price. There was something compelling about an item of clothing or piece of jewellery that came with its own story – the circle of fashion was a beautiful thing to me. I was all about the hunt for a bargain, or a killer accessory to reinvent an existing outfit, and always something that would suit my mum, dad, sister, or friends, before myself.

After uni, I got my first proper job in luxury retail when I literally stepped into Vicky's shoes when she vacated a role as store assistant at Smith's, the famous designer boutique on South Molton Street in London, and it was there that Mona Armstrong and I crossed paths on one of her visits and she offered me a role as her assistant.

Yet throughout my journey with clothing, I have come to learn and appreciate first-hand that you can dress a body in the finest, most exquisite clothes but they will do absolutely *nothing* for them until the person inside is able to shine too. And that's the part I love the most.

I suppose you could call me a therapist-stylist. This was why the shop window dummies I once craved, after working with some challenging personalities, were losing their allure. And I missed the human connection of styling a person to help influence them to become their best self.

I looked down at my classic black loafers and flared black trousers, which I had teamed with a crisp white boyfriend-style shirt, untucked, and biker jacket. I had styled the outfit with some gold jewellery, not much make-up and my hair back in a low ponytail, because it looked smart that way. It was a sharp yet safe look. No star likes being out-glammed by their stylist – our job is to make the client feel like the only person in the room. But now I felt a tug of regret, hoping Mandy wouldn't think I looked too casual. I wondered if I should have worn something borrowed, to give us a talking point around sustainability, the buzz word in fashion.

It was too late now. My mind could be its own worst enemy.

I pulled up the collar on my biker. After a month of eyeing it up in the All Saints concession in Selfridges, having this job interview had given me the incentive to blow a large portion of my March salary on it. So I ordered it online, even paying for express delivery to receive it in time.

You've got this, Amber. You look great.

When I let the lady at the front desk know who I was there to see, she lowered the tone of her voice.

'Of course. I'll let Ms Sykes know you're here. Can I get you some water?'

She was being extra nice to me and I was under no illusion why – the cost of the Royal Penthouse Suite was probably more per night than I used to get paid in a month.

'Mr Marquez is going to meet you out of the private lift,' she said, beaming, and a porter appeared from nowhere to show me up.

Jose Marquez. Before he got together with Mandy, the tabloids portrayed him as a suave events promoter on the make. He was a regular on the Hollywood club and bar scene, regularly pictured with his arm around a celebrity, wearing a black T-shirt with a large gold necklace around his neck. He was mildly famous by association. Since he married Mandy two years ago, in a blaze of publicity, a *People* magazine cover, and a stat-breaking TikTok Live, he had become Mr Mandy Sykes: husband, manager, bodyguard, handbag holder. Mega-famous by association. Being married to one of the biggest personalities on the planet meant leaving your ego at the altar. I wondered how this had affected him. Whether he begrudged the fact his own career aspirations had been put on hold; and how the dynamic worked behind closed doors.

As the lift stopped, I had a few seconds to compose myself before Jose appeared. I recognised him immediately, his face a daily occurrence on my Instagram feed since Mandy had become a celebrity over here, as well as in America. Although in good shape, he was smaller than he seemed on screen, and older looking than I imagined. He couldn't be much more than five-foot-eight and was of a stocky build, a firm belly pressed against his black T-shirt, olive skin, forearms with visible veins, and flecks of grey in his wavy black hair, which was tucked loosely behind his ears.

'Hola, you must be Miss Green.' He grinned and a gold tooth at the side of his mouth glinted in the light. His smile was so wide and teeth so perfectly straight and white, I could be looking at a poster in a dentist's waiting room. He had a husky voice, a hint of Spanish to his American accent, and when he reached out to shake my hand, his were baby soft with neat, manicured nails. As we shook, I noticed a lively look in his eyes. His hair was slightly damp, or perhaps gelled. He smelt fresh, like he hadn't long been out of the shower. A medium-sized diamond stud in one earlobe sparkled.

'It's great to meet you. Please, call me Amber,' I replied, trying to sound as calm as possible.

Jose looked over his shoulder as he ushered me through the door to the suite and down another corridor. For a fleeting moment I wondered if he had expected me to arrive with my agent. Not that I had one at the moment – my days of having an agent had come to an end when I left New York – as I hadn't been actively seeking styling work.

'I hope you live up to the hype,' he said, smiling.

I squirmed. *Pressure*.

As Jose led me through the entrance foyer and into an elegant lounge, my eyes searched the room, wondering where Mandy was. The floor was white marble, an open fire crackled on one side of the room, though on a double-take I could see it was actually a video of one on a flat-screen television. Opposite it, through another doorway, I could see a spiral staircase, at the top of which I presumed the bedrooms must be located.

Jose was standing beside a large window now. Casually he flicked a switch and the blinds clicked into life, slowly gliding upwards to reveal stunning views of the river Thames snaking through the city – the London Eye across the river was lit in shades of pink and purple, Westminster to the right, and the city was to the left, distinguishable by the gleaming angled panes of The Shard. It was a breathtaking sight, putting a new spin on the city I had called home for my whole life. I felt like a tourist looking out from this privileged perspective.

When I looked at Jose, he returned a friendly smile. It might be a cold, grey wintry day out there, but in here it was warm, cosy, and comfortable.

'We've not been up long,' he explained, feeling the need to justify the reason the blinds were not open already. 'Jet lag's a killer from LA.'

'I remember, it's always worse in this direction,' I replied, still looking out, entranced by the vista.

'Did you have to travel far today, Amber?'

'Oh no,' I said, his gentle tone putting me at ease, my breathing steadier. 'I live in London, just a Tube ride away.'

'Born in the sound of the Bow Bells?' he asked, doing a bad imitation of a Cockney accent.

'Good knowledge.' I smiled. 'But no, I'm a North Londoner, born and bred in this city though.'

That piqued his interest. 'Very rare. I haven't met many true Londoners,' he said. 'Mandy's just finishing up in the "spa".' He made air quotes and I followed his gaze to a closed door across the other side of the hallway.

Spa in their room? This really is another world.

'Take a seat.' He pointed to a cream armchair positioned smartly beside another. As I sank into it, he chose to perch on the edge of the sofa on the other side of the glass coffee table. As he moved, I got another strong whiff of his fresh, musky scent. There was something weird about being alone in a hotel suite with a man I barely knew. With my back to the windows now, I busied myself looking at the artefacts on the shelves around the fake fireplace – mostly big design books, a vase stuffed with white roses, and some gold shell ornaments, gleaming in an unsentimental, luxury-hotel way.

'Would you like a drink – water, juice, Nespresso?'

He wasn't an unattractive man; just *very* groomed. If Rob was here, he would have smirked at the way Jose referred to Nespresso as though it were a type of drink, like tea.

'I'm good, thanks.' I reached for my reusable water bottle and pulled it out of my bag. 'Got some water.'

It occurred to me that it was unusual to have such an intimate meeting with a big celebrity – most superstars come with a gaggle of assistants, but there was no entourage present.

Perhaps the fact it appears to be just the two of them is encouraging?

A couple of long minutes passed. My mouth became dry, so I took a gulp of water and my throat gurgled as I swallowed.

Jose smiled, letting me know he heard. I felt my cheeks redden. If Vicky had been here she would have giggled too, but the uncomfortable silence made me nervous.

'Are you sure I can't get you a Nespresso?' he asked, maybe looking for a reason to do something. 'Or a tea? I know you Brits *love* your tea?'

Massive stereotype there, Jose.

I grinned innocuously: 'Thanks, but I've had my coffee for today.'

Before we were plunged back into silence, the door handle across the hallway turned and we both jumped, like guardsmen, to our feet.

Encased in a fluffy white robe and hotel slippers decorated with a large gold C, Mandy, at first glance, looked more like a regular spa customer than an international megastar, but when she lifted her arm to shake my hand, the gigantic pink diamond on her ring-finger told a different story. Her nails, immaculately painted with a pale, iridescent polish, made it look as though she had ten oval-shaped pearls at the end of her digits.

Her chestnut hair was scraped back off her face in a ponytail and she was barely wearing any make-up, except for false eyelashes, which were long and thick. Her olive skin had the fresh glow that only an expensive facial can give. *She is as spellbinding as she is in photos.*

'Excuse the gown, I didn't have time to change,' she commented, extending her hand. 'You must be Amber.'

We shook and her hand felt warm and soft. It seemed oddly formal given the informality of her clothing. 'I figure *you're* the woman to tell me what to wear today.' Her voice carried a lilting flow that was both soft and friendly, yet there was an edge to it.

'That's right.' I smiled nervously, unsure whether she was joking or not.

'Did Jose offer you a drink?' She gestured to him, perched on the sofa arm again.

'No, I mean, yes, but I'm okay.' I sensed Jose was going to be in trouble if he hadn't.

'You don't like champagne?' she enquired.

It's only ten o'clock.

'You're hesitating,' she quipped. 'That means, we should

all have champagne. The rosé, Jose, please. I always fancy a glass after a massage, it seems to get into my system quicker – you know?'

'Yes,' I replied, instantly feeling a little silly for saying so, when it was absolutely *not* something I could relate to. *If Vicky could see me now.*

I wondered if she was testing me. 'Thank you, but I don't drink while I'm working.'

Her glass charged, Mandy led me up the spiral staircase into the heart of the suite, the master bedroom and dressing room. On the way up, she delivered my instructions.

'Formal interviews don't reveal raw talent,' she said, 'so I thought we would do a dry run – I'll give you the scenarios, and you choose what I should wear. Like a game. Only not.'

I was glad she walked ahead, because she couldn't see the panic on my face.

'Of course,' I replied calmly. Concentrating on not tripping up the stairs, I noticed the famous floral tattoo decorating her ankle come into view.

There was so much about Mandy that was familiar, even though we had only just met. I wondered if I would get a glance of her bunion scars.

Extensive online research last night reminded me that Mandy had been famous since she jumped to fame at age fifteen, catching the judges' attention as 'one to watch' on the final season of *Star Search* in 1995, where she won over the audience as much for her charisma as her singing talent. She was the daughter of two immigrants – a mother from Mexico and father from Jamaica. Mandy's parents and their families travelled to the United States in pursuit of a better life, well before they met working in the same life insurance sales office in Gainesville, Florida.

When Mandy was young, the family had moved to California for their only child to attend school, and when she got a place at the University of California, Santa Cruz to major in American studies, Mandy decided to put her singing aspirations to one side, to become the first person in her entire family's history to entertain the idea of a university degree. She was almost ready to graduate in 2002 when *American Idol* came calling. Encouraged by friends to give it a go, Mandy queued for seven hours to attend the first audition. In a story which is now Hollywood folklore, one of her high heels became lodged in a drain as she neared the front of the queue, so she did her first audition in one shoe. This enabled her to create an impression with the judges, and Mandy ended up making it through round after round, becoming a runner-up on the first series.

'Mandy was born with ambition,' her father had regaled to E! News in a biography of his superstar daughter's life.

Drama camps, singing lessons, a dialect coach, and her early experience on *Star Search* had grown her confidence as a teenager, and although she missed out on the top spot on *American Idol*, it served her well as more reality shows and brand endorsements quickly followed, and Mandy became a household name.

Over the last twenty-three years, with various talent management agencies, she underwent a number of reinventions as popular culture moved with the times –

there was a stint as a TV actress, a small movie role in a medium-budget comedy where she played Ben Affleck's former girlfriend, and cameos in a number of music videos. But it was on social media and her eponymous YouTube channel that Mandy found a lucrative, natural home and captured the hearts of a legion of loyal American fans with her roller-coaster love life, pneumatic style and curvaceous looks. After a series of broken hearts, when she finally met her 'Prince', Mandy and Jose live-streamed their wedding, and the moment Jose lifted the veil to kiss his new bride became 'the most defining image of 2020', according to *Variety* magazine. It was the fairy-tale ending her story had been waiting for, only that was five years ago now. Since then, only the bunion operation had come close to the stats she once achieved, and there were only so many times she could blame the algorithm for a dip in popularity when brands began to question her star power.

I imagined it was time for Mandy's team to explore opportunities in different parts of the world, hence London had been identified by Julie-Ann as a good place to start.

'Obviously I only have a capsule wardrobe here today,' Mandy said, gesturing to the expansive walk-in closet which was half full. The dressing room in itself was as large as my whole bedroom and plenty big enough to hold any normal person's wardrobe, for their entire life. It was so large it also housed a Pilates reformer machine – one of those beds that looks more like an instrument of torture, or a large sex toy.

Our worlds were so far apart, the amount of money it

took to stay in a suite like this was barely comprehensible to me. Yet I had to put this to one side – to make her see me as an equal, at least when it came to style – if this was going to work. I took a deep breath. *You've got this, Amber Green.*

I was beginning to feel quite hot, so I took off my biker jacket and set it down on the floor.

'Here,' said Jose, handing me a hanger. I had barely noticed him join us in the room.

I hung my jacket and slipped off my shoes, instantly feeling better in bare feet on the cream carpet.

'There is plenty to work with here,' I assured her, 'you have great taste.' The second part wasn't quite true but, in this moment, I needed her to like me as well as respect my judgement.

My eyes darted from one thing to the next: a couple of patterned kaftans; three Hermès bags and a host of clutches; a row of formal dresses made from stretchy body-con fabrics, in vibrant colours that would make anyone stand out in a crowd; and a more sedate section of black, white, and neutral items. To the left were at least ten shelves containing a range of shoes. Mandy was definitely not a flats person, or even a walking one – none of her vertiginous heels looked capable of taking the wearer much farther than a few steps from car to venue to seat. But then again, Mandy was experienced at high-octane glamour. *Maybe she can run a half marathon in them.*

I turned to her and said brightly: 'I can see you love fashion, Ms Sykes.'

'Call me Mandy, please.' She smiled. 'You've got that right.'

Rule Number One of winning a celebrity's favour: flattery. Though they might try to tell you differently, celebrities thrive on compliments – it's their equivalent of chocolate. After all, fame dies without adoration.

Mandy had turned away and was rifling through a drawer of body-con undergarments.

'Spanx, Skims, Intimissimi . . . I've collaborated with them all,' she said, as she artfully opened her gown and wriggled into a pair of sculpting mid-waist nude briefs, and then she dropped the gown and put on a matching bralette, keeping her back to me the whole time.

'I loved your campaign with Skims, you looked incredible,' I gushed, grateful for all the Insta-stalking I did last night.

'That was fun. Kim Kardashian is *such* a doll.'

She's warming to me, I can feel it.

Jose was now sitting on a chaise longue in the bedroom, a vantage point close enough to observe and record my progress, but not to interfere with the rapport we were building.

'Okay, chica, scenario one,' Mandy announced, turning around to look me in the eye. 'It's the amfAR Gala dinner, Cannes. What do I wear, stylist?'

'You have two minutes!' Jose called from the bedroom, before pushing a button on his expensive timepiece.

Feeling the pressure, I felt glad I hadn't accepted any champagne. My pulse rate began to soar, and my hands felt clammy. I hadn't yet eaten this morning – maybe I should have accepted a second coffee. It didn't help that the *Countdown* theme tune was giving me an ear worm.

I sucked in my cheeks in an effort to pull myself into sharp focus. *You got this, Amber, you got this.* I had listened to enough self-improvement podcasts to know that your inner voice should be your greatest champion. *You can do this. Focus.*

AmfAR Gala.

What the hell is amfAR when it's at home? Some kind of gathering of long-lost Americans?

Deciding against coming clean, I deduced that whatever it was, it was bound to be glamorous because it was a gala event at the Cannes Film Festival – which had to mean chic evening wear suitable for the French Riviera.

I set to work, strumming a row of gowns hanging on the centre rail in the closet. For a moment I paused to closely examine a delicate black ruffled gown by Dior, marvelling over the craftsmanship of the tiered chiffon with lace trim. It was a definite contender, but black struck me as too sombre for Mandy to make an entrance in sun-soaked Cannes. Continuing down the rail, I was drawn to a stunning silk scarlet gown with a plunging neckline and soaring split. With its low back and delicate straps, it would hug her curves and be sure to make Mandy stand out from the crowd.

'This is a showstopper,' I announced decisively. 'It's so striking you can let it do all your talking – I would keep your hair and make-up simple and minimal, just a smoky eye is enough. For accessories, some diamond earrings and a tennis bracelet – we could borrow some jewels for an event like this. A simple gold sandal would be best to set it off.'

'Ah, my Jessica Rabbit dress.' Mandy smiled, giving me the sense that I had chosen well. 'I wore it to a benefit in Venice last year, maybe you remember.' I smiled reassuringly, unsure whether the fact she'd worn it before was a good thing in her mind, or not.

'Oh, and sunglasses, mustn't forget those!' I said cheerily, picking up a chic pair of large round black Chloé shades from a menagerie of accessories she had laid out on the dressing table. 'The red carpet will most likely open in daylight, this being Cannes, and the sun doesn't set until nine p.m. in summer, so you don't want to be squinting at the paparazzi. It's chic and the perfect finishing touch. If you wanted to take a clutch, I'd suggest this miniature gold one, to tie in with the sandals,' I added, lifting a tiny box bag from a nearby shelf.

'Time!' Jose yelled over my shoulder, signalling my first test was complete.

Neither of them gave much away about how I had done, but as I wasn't being handed my coat, I assumed okay.

I wondered whether Mandy would try the outfit on, but instead, she nodded approvingly as I hung up the one complete look, on the side of the closet.

She walked towards a section containing drawers. Again, she stood with her back to me as she emptied the drawers, turning to produce a handful of beachwear accessories from behind her back like a magician, then she grabbed some underwear and placed it all in a pile on the floor.

'Scenario two. I've been invited aboard a top movie director's yacht in Saint-Tropez for the day. We'll lunch at Club 55. What do I pack?'

I sprung to life, all of my past experience returning in a heartbeat as I skilfully began sorting the jumble before us into accessories, underwear, and beachwear, because the first thing a stylist needs is order. Surveying what was at my disposal, I then began putting some looks together. Without really thinking about it too hard, I instinctively reached for a Dolce & Gabbana leopard print bikini and a gold mesh cover-up. I pulled the items together, mentally picturing them looking smoking hot on Mandy.

Then a minidress from Zimmermann caught my eye – made of linen, it would keep the wearer cool on the hottest of days, and the light and airy fringe detailing around the bottom ensured it was attention-seeking enough for lunch at the hottest table on the beach.

'It can be worn with simple tan sandals, or dress it up with wedges,' I explained. 'Two looks sure to get the director's attention, whilst keeping his wife onside at the same time.' I smiled, aware that Mandy's natural assets would overshadow most women in the blink of an eye.

'Love it!' she cheered.

I felt my shoulders drop; this was becoming fun.

Mandy had moved out of the closet area now and into the bedroom, where I noticed another person had joined us. There was a man younger than Jose, and he was sunk casually in an oversized armchair, looking at his phone.

'This is my brother-in-law,' Mandy informed. 'He got in from Miami this morning.'

The guy looked up from his phone briefly to acknowledge me, more as a courtesy than with any real interest.

'Ciao.' He picked up a plate of croissants from the table next to him and offered it to me. 'Croissant?' His eyes sparkled.

'Oh, no thanks,' I replied. 'Pleased to meet you . . . um?' I looked at him blankly, panicked that his name had gone in one ear and straight out of the other.

'She didn't tell you my name,' he responded, reading my mind. If I wasn't mistaken, he had a smug smile on his lips. He spoke perfect English and if it wasn't for the Latino lilt I would think he was an entitled British upper-class brat. There was an awkward moment as we caught each other's gaze – a fleeting appraisal – before quickly looking away. His clothes smelt of money, a Ralph Lauren logo on his T-shirt, and a pair of box-fresh Nikes on his feet, that I'd bet were limited edition.

'Seriously, where are your manners?' Mandy said, swiping a croissant from the plate and nibbling it. Flakes of pastry instantly fell onto her chest, into her bosom cleavage and onto her dressing gown.

'Where are *yours*?' he teased. He turned to me. 'My name is Jimi.'

I took him in; it was impossible not to stop what I was doing and absorb him for a second. He had a thick, curly mop of dark brown hair, flecked with sun-kissed, caramel-coloured highlights. His wide face was framed by strong, defined cheekbones. He had deep brown eyes, the colour

of shiny conkers. The sharp, zesty aroma of his aftershave
floated around us and made my nostrils twitch.

*Christ, he is ridiculously good-looking, and he smells
amazing.*

I felt a pang of something, which I tried to convince
myself was just hunger. *A hunger for what, I am not quite
sure.*

With her free hand, Mandy brushed the bits of croissant
off her chest before waving for my attention.

'Amber,' she said, then swallowed, snapping me back
into the room. 'We're onto outfit three.' She fixed me with a
stare. I wondered whether she and Jose had pre-planned the
scenarios or if she was making them up on the spot. 'Let's
say I'm doing some editorial for a luxury fashion magazine,
and they want to shoot me on Necker. How would you style
me for the front cover?'

I paused. *Necker.* She didn't mean the sugary fluid inside
a flower, it had to be Necker Island – the idyllic private
paradise owned by Sir Richard Branson. I'd read about it
before.

'Presumably we're talking resort wear, if you mean
Necker Island?' I asked to double check.

For a moment she looked indifferent. 'You tell me, you're
the stylist.'

'Resort wear it is,' I muttered and walked back into the
closet. I felt so much more comfortable surrounded by
clothes than people.

'Two minutes. Go!' Jose called after me.

I paused.

'Would you mind if we stop the timing element, please?' I asked. 'It's just that I'm feeling quite flustered by the added pressure.'

I stopped. *Has that really just come out of my mouth?* They both looked stunned. *What would Vicky do now?* I took a deep breath and continued, 'I mean, I know that none of us have all day to be doing this, it's just that, in the real world, I'd always ensure we aren't scrambling for an outfit in a short space of time. I need to give the clothes, and the wearer, an opportunity to speak to me.'

'Clothes *speak* to you?' Jimi asked, the corners of his mouth turning up.

'It's just a turn of phrase,' I replied, determined not to let my nerves show. 'I believe the best styling is a marriage of personality as much as picking out a nice-looking outfit. I want to give Mandy the best choice, based on her needs for the event in question, and I do this most effectively when I don't feel flustered.' I smiled at the end, an attempt to lighten the mood.

'You feel flustered?' Jimi folded his arms across his chest.

'She just told you she did,' Mandy responded, whacking his knee.

She then turned and gave me an encouraging wink, saying without words that not many people had the courage to stand up to Jose like I just had. To be fair, I was on the seventh day of my menstrual cycle, which helped. I got the impression she was warming to me.

'Fair enough, Amber Green. Forget the timer, let's see

what the clothes have to say. Take your time,' Jose said. He glanced at Mandy, who was looking at the side of his face.

Jimi couldn't resist another wry smile, but it was clear I was now in the driving seat.

'You're welcome, and thank you,' I replied.

My mother had installed a politeness in me that kicked in when it needed to.

Once more my fingers began running over the garments on view.

It was much easier to let my actions take the lead, as I sifted through a symphony of kaftans, my fingers moving like a conductor artfully guiding an orchestra of fabrics. I held up a few bikini top and bottom combinations, before settling instinctively on a Missoni swimsuit, the distinctive multicoloured zig-zag design and deep, plunging neckline making it an iconic, timeless piece. This style had a stark black trim, giving it a modern edge that would add some drama to a tropical backdrop.

'This will create an enviable silhouette for a magazine cover,' I said, holding it up for Mandy's approval. 'How do you feel about this one?'

'It's brand new,' Mandy replied. 'I saw it on Mytheresa yesterday and had it shipped. I love it.'

'You have an excellent eye.' I smiled. 'I'd team it with the matching maxi dress, they do one that you can have buttoned or open, to show off your curves. I could call it in from their press office for the shoot. I know the girls there. Your hair would look great pulled back into a slick bun for this, add some gold hoops, a glossy lip, kick back in a hammock and you'll rock the front cover. Bare-foot fashion at its best. Or killer heels on a jetty – the outfit would work either way.'

'Sold!' Mandy shrieked. 'I love the sound of this! In fact, I wonder if they have the maxi in stock now – we're off to the Maldives tomorrow to film some content.'

I took this as my cue to go one step beyond.

'Let me see if the PR team will arrange a loan for you. I'm sure I can make it happen.' I had no idea in that moment if I *could* actually make it happen, but I was sure as hell going to try if it might get me this job, whatever this job, actually was.

I fumbled to find my phone in my bag on the floor. A missed call from Rob, which would have to wait. I noticed it was already gone eleven, the last hour had flown past.

Trying to look as cool and calm as possible I began scrolling through the contacts on my phone – I knew I still had many of my styling contacts in there and believe me, when I was working for Mona, I needed *everyone* on speed dial.

Missoni.

Missoni.

Missoni.

Nothing was coming up.

Perhaps sensing my panic, Mandy came over and placed a hand gently on my back.

'No problem,' she purred. 'It can wait.'

I sat back and placed the phone back in my bag, relieved.

'Sure. Well, if you'd like me to follow up, just say the word.' I wasn't going to press the issue.

I stood up and hung up the Missoni swimsuit and gold hoops next to the other two looks, and we both stood back to admire the three outfits together.

'I like the way you've curated these, it's different,' she remarked. 'It feels fresh.'

'I'm glad you think so,' I replied. 'In fact I think we could push things even further, if you're game. I think we could really put you on the map as a fashion-forward personality.'

'You're right. Beachwear is one thing,' Mandy said, pulling a strand of hair that had stuck to her peachy lip gloss, 'but I need to know if this leopard can change her spots.' She glanced sideways at Jose. I had a strong suspicion that they were silently weighing up whether to tell me something. 'Imagine, for a moment, that we're moving to the UK,' she continued, her eyes widening. 'How would you suggest I evolve my style of dressing?'

'Well, I mean, wow, that would be exciting, of course. I—' I began to reply, but Jose interjected, perhaps he was annoyed she'd said too much.

'Which brings us neatly onto the fourth outfit,' he stated. 'It's London Fashion Week, the weather is god-awful British rain, Mandy's got four shows back to back. What does she wear?'

I paused for a moment. My experience of one particular fashion week came back to haunt me and I felt my palms become tacky again. I'd attended New York Fashion Week in a Manhattan heatwave, and the Michael Kors show was the scene of a career-defining moment, when I inadvertently exposed the super-stylist Lola Jones's alopecia. The episode taught me a lot about social media and the power of one ill-advised post – how it could go viral in a split second. I was very, *very* lucky that this particular post was an innocent mistake – I had no idea that the top of Lola's head was in the photo, let alone that she was struggling with a hair loss condition. I would *never* have posted a photo with her in it if I had. Within minutes, some trolls had spotted it and before you could say 'stop the world I want to jump off' my image went viral. Fortunately, something positive came out of it in the end because this went on to become one of the trending fashion week news stories for all the right reasons. Instead of hiding away, Lola chose this moment to speak about her condition with a view to supporting other alopecia sufferers and made the news agenda globally. Plus, I gained thousands of new Instagram followers in the process. *Phew.*

For Mandy's next imagined styling assignment, I was ready. *You're not fooling me. No way, Jose!*

'Is this a trick question?' I smiled.

They both stared at me, puzzled.

'Dressing for London Fashion Week,' I said confidently. 'Well, it all depends on which shows you'll be attending. I mean, are we talking Burberry or Harris Reed, perhaps Roksanda, David Koma, or Julien Macdonald?'

Mandy shrugged. 'All of them?'

She clearly wasn't wise to London Fashion Week etiquette, where celebrities showed their fierce allegiance to one or two fashion houses, rather than appearing beside every catwalk, along with the fashion press.

'Whoever you want to see – and we would work together on who aligns best with your brand – the etiquette is you wear that designer. If I was your stylist, you could trust in me for that. I would arrange with the fashion designer's team that you sit front row at the show, and we would borrow a current look from the collection. If for any reason they won't lend, we would work to build a relationship. All this takes time and a strategy.'

'A fashion strategy. I love the sound of that, darling,' Mandy cooed. Her face lit up as she looked across at Jose in an *I told you so* way.

I loved the sound of it too. I just hoped I could come up with one. Although Mandy didn't strike me as a natural fit at London Fashion Week, I instinctively felt she would be fun to work with, and there were bubbles of excitement in my stomach – a sensation which had been absent in my working life for a while.

I took this as my podium moment – the chance to leave her with something powerful, in the form of a few choice words that would hang in the air long after I had left the room, in a bid to win me this job.

Think Best Actress Oscars speech, Amber. Move over, Emma Stone, I've got this.

'Mandy, I would really love this opportunity to work with you,' I began, nerves kicking in as I held her gaze with mine. It was the first time I'd noticed what an exquisite, pure shade of aquamarine her eyes were. 'Not just because I think you are a fantastic personality, but because I believe we have an incredible, once-in-a-lifetime opportunity here.

You see, I don't just love fashion – it goes much deeper than that. I really believe in the power of fashion to influence how the world perceives you.' Mandy looked intrigued, so I took a deep breath and continued, 'This isn't new. Sartorial choices have been on the front line of communication since ancient times – just ask the ancient Egyptians, where practically every colour, accessory, and garment a Pharaoh wore had meaning – but it has never been more important in modern times than now. Today's online world is crowded with unsolicited opinions, and how you present yourself is a form of art. It has *never* been more critical to let your authentic self cut through the noise and shine through. Your wardrobe is one of the things you have within your control. Mandy, I want to help you step into not only some fabulous clothes, but to create stories with them – stories the world will fall in love with because they are one hundred per cent authentic to you. To help spread influence in a really good way.'

I stopped. I had surprised myself with the reference to the ancient Egyptians but felt relieved that not even Mandy could have a hotline to Cleopatra to check out the details.

I looked searchingly at the couple for a response.

'Wow. Thank you, Amber,' Mandy said after a beat. 'I can see how much this role would mean to you.' I nodded sagely in response. 'And I'm glad you've said all this, because I wanted you here to discuss the whole of me.'

'The whole of you?'

'Not just what I wear, but what it all means.' She paused and I wondered if she meant she was looking for a ghost writer as well. 'I meant that figuratively,' she clarified. 'What I'm trying to say is, I like your idea of storytelling. Fashion is about invention and fantasy. I'm looking for a stylist just like *you*, Amber.'

She looked me straight in the eyes. She had now fully shed the cold demeanour I first witnessed. She appeared interested.

We smiled at each other slightly awkwardly, before she added, 'Thank you for today. Jose will see you out.'

I glanced longingly at the open bottle of champagne she had left on the side, wishing I could take it with me. Turning down a free, cold glass of Veuve Clicquot was criminal in my book, but this was my signal to depart, and I had my desk to clear at Selfridges today.

I reached for my bag and Jose gave me a curt nod as he held out my coat the way waiters do, and ushered me towards the stairs. I glanced across at Jimi as I bade Mandy goodbye. He raised his hand casually but didn't open his mouth. He seemed arrogant.

Jose was at the door of the suite.

'We'll be in touch,' he said, opening it.

'Thank you so much, Mr Marquez, I really enjoyed meeting you both.'

'It was a pleasure, Amber.' Jose smiled. This time it didn't feel as though he found me slightly amusing. Instead, it was a smile which acknowledged I'd done a good job. 'We'll call Julie-Ann today and she will be in touch.'

Then he stretched out a soft, manicured hand and I held out my sweaty palm to meet it. Taking it, he moved his face to the side of mine and gently kissed the air on either side of my cheeks. 'Ciao, bella.'

I was taken aback to be getting a kiss after an interview, but supposed it was the Latin American way.

And he does smell so good.

As I exited the Corinthia and began walking up Whitehall towards Trafalgar Square, on my way to the Tube, a black taxi pulled up at the traffic lights beside me. At first, I thought my brain was playing tricks, but when I blinked and looked again, I could clearly see that it was covered in the tagline for Mandy's YouTube channel, which was currently smashing audience figures.

Why is it that when you want something really badly, the universe shoves it right in your face?

'What Mandy wants, Mandy gets . . .' it said, in big bright-pink text, next to an image of her in a crisp white shirt held together over her chest by just one button. She was looking at the camera seductively, a coy smile dancing on her glossy lips, which were partly obscured by her raised forefinger, held lightly against her slightly parted lips in a pose which suggested Mandy had lots of secrets. Her long mane, with caramel highlights, was tousled to perfection and blew out away from her face, thanks to the close proximity of a wind machine or hairdryer being held just out of shot. I had been on enough photoshoots to know there would be a whole team of people just shy of the camera, each with a role to play to ensure every aspect of a publicity photo was perfect. Collar up, no unsightly creases, shimmering tan on every visible morsel of flesh, baby hairs smoothed with lacquer.

The taxi pulled off revealing a further image of Mandy emblazoned on its back, this time she was waving. 'See you soon, England!' said the pink wording.

See you soon. I hope.

I crossed the road and into the Embankment underground station. As I glided downwards on the escalator, my phone rang. I hurriedly pulled it out of my bag thinking it was probably Rob wanting to know how the interview went, but to my delight it was an American number. Could it be Julie-Ann already? 'Hello?' I answered. The little bars indicating the level of reception were dropping by the second – three-two-one. 'He-llo!' I repeated. 'Can you he—' It went dead. *Damn you, reception!*

The end of the escalator was still a little way off. Panicked, without thinking straight, I turned around and began charging back up the escalator, my bag flying out to the side, knocking into people on the way past.

'What the hell are you doing?' shouted one man.

I knew immediately this was a bad idea, but I was committed to climbing the downward moving stairs now, and I had to make it to the top if only to save face. Panting, I strode upwards, taking the wide steps one by one, each steeper than the former.

'Twelve, thirteen, fourteen . . .' I reached the top, my legs shaking and my finger already on the little green 'phone' icon. *Please answer, please answer.*

'Hi, Amber.' It was Mandy. 'Thanks for calling back. I wanted to discuss something,' her voice purred as I caught my breath.

My heart was beating hard and fast.

'Hi, Mandy. Is everything okay?' It was a challenge to speak. I was so out of breath. Surely, I hadn't just risked my life on an escalator for the sake of Mandy asking whether the Missoni PR office might gift her the new resort collection? *You wouldn't believe how many celebrities ask for freebies from their stylists, often putting us in the tricky position of having to beg someone on their behalf. It's Awks with a capital A.*

'There is something about this potential position that we didn't discuss,' she said.

She's right about that – the salary.

'Julie-Ann will want you to sign an NDA before I can disclose the full details. I can't say much, but – between us – I'm coming to the UK.' My mind flashed back to the 'See you soon, England!' line on the back of the taxi. It made sense that UK streaming platforms and e-commerce sites would want to get in on the cash-cow that was the world of Mandy Sykes.

'That's great news. Do you need someone to get you ready for some promotional activity?' I probed.

'Honey, it's not just the publicity I'll need dressing for – I'm actually moving to the UK, so I'll need my stylist with me twenty-four/seven. So, I'm asking if you'd be open to joining my in-house team and move in?'

I dropped my bag to the floor.

'Move in?' I repeated.

'Ah-huh.'

'Oh wow.' I tried to take it in.

From the corner of my eye, I noticed a Tube attendant waving at me. I turned away, pretending not to have seen him. I needed a moment to process what Mandy had just said.

'So, are you offering me the job?' I clarified. 'And is it based in London?'

'Well, I can't say much, but it's definitely somewhere in the UK,' she replied. 'It's a secret location. And yes – I'd like to offer you the job of being my personal stylist. You'll join my glam-squad-in-residence.'

I breathed an audible sigh of relief. In the last couple of years, I had lived with Mona in Los Angeles, and then in our basic New York studio, so I didn't fancy moving back to America, not now that Rob and I were properly living together.

The Tube attendant was right in front of me now. 'Excuse me, madam, but you're causing an obstruction. I need you to decide if you're going down, or coming through the ticket barrier. Which is it?'

I mouthed at him in response, *Two seconds!*

'I can't see that being a problem, Mandy,' I replied, without having a moment to properly consider the words tumbling out of my mouth. 'Count me in. Thank you.' I paused. 'Oh, and the salary – are you able to—'

'Excuse me, madam, but I need you to move along,' said the man, more frantically this time. 'Not in two seconds. Now!'

'Great news!' Mandy trilled. 'Welcome to the team, Amber Green! We'll finalise the details from the Maldives and then you can meet my A Team. I'm sure you'll get along great.'

'Thank you, Mandy.' I beamed.

'Julie-Ann will give you a buzz about all the other details,' she replied.

I had forgotten how averse celebrities can be about discussing important points like salary and start date.

'No problem, I'll speak to Julie-Ann. Thank you!'

A voice rang out from the station's Tannoy: 'Would the woman with the bag on the floor currently obstructing the downward escalators please vacate the area? See it. Say it. Sorted.'

'Sorry – I mean, sorted!' I shouted at no one in particular, as people turned to look at me. Then I stepped back onto the downward escalator, my head spinning, heart pumping – and a big smile spread across my face. The timing could not have been better.

The train carriage was busy, but I never minded being on the Tube – to me it was a place to observe fashion in action, spot trends and marvel at how people decided to present themselves to the world; it was a place where you didn't know if someone was rich or poor by looking at them. In fact, many of the wealthiest people in this city cared little about gaining status through the labels in their wardrobes. In my observation, through working in fashion, many of those with the least to spend liked to wear a branded item like a designer cap or tote bag. It always fascinated me how people used the currency of fashion to tell their story.

I wondered what conclusions people might jump to if they studied my clothing; if they would have any inkling that I was a personal stylist. And not just any stylist because, as of two minutes ago, I became the stylist to Mandy Sykes, A-list celebrity.

Well, perhaps more C-list, depending which gossip site you subscribed to, but still.

As I looked around me, I tried to process the conversation I had just had with Mandy. This was a dream job for me. Sartorially speaking, there was so much potential. There was still the small matter of my salary to be discussed, as well as the details around what 'moving in' with Mandy actually entailed, but I imagined Julie-Ann would soon be in touch and this kind of role was much better than earning nothing. It was likely to be a rise on my paycheque at the store. The headline news was that the feeling in my stomach right now was akin to the time I found a vintage Mulberry handbag grossly under-priced in a charity shop, so I took this to be a good sign.

As I sat on the Tube, I WhatsApped Rob and Vicky in tandem. *I've got the job!!*

Rob messaged back immediately. *Amazing! Well done, baby, what did she offer you?*

Fortunately, my reception faded again before I could reply to that one. I'd make it a priority to email Julie-Ann the second I re-emerged from the Tube.

Nora's birthday dinner was going to be fantastic this evening, because there was so much to celebrate.

I caught the eye of a small, older woman squashed into the corner of the carriage not far from me, her deeply tanned face ingrained with lines that held thousands of stories. We smiled at each other. Perhaps in her brief assessment of me, she recognised my excitement.

As I left the carriage, she whispered something and pressed a piece of paper and a sprig of heather into my palm. In that second before the Tube doors closed behind me, I had nothing to give her in return but a big smile.

On the platform I opened and read the handwritten words on the piece of paper: *Don't just exist – live.*

She would never know how much the words resonated with me. Mandy had handed me an opportunity to participate in life; to feel something new. Whatever the salary, I knew I had no choice but to take it.

On the platform, I looked down at the sprig of dry heather in my hand and snapped a photo of it. As I ascended the escalator at Bond Street, I uploaded the image to Instagram, with the caption, 'Don't just exist – live'.

It would be my new mantra. I liked the phrase so much, I even added it to my bio. Most of all I took the gift as a sign that everything was going to work out.

I had been asked to clear my desk at Selfridges today and now I was feeling good about it. As I left the Tube station, I dropped a five-pound note into the hat of a busker. Paying a kind act forward felt like the least I could do. Then I did a full three-sixty twirl around a lamppost, and I didn't care who noticed.

CHAPTER THREE

I had been working as a window designer at Selfridges, on and off, for the best part of two years, and I couldn't really blame my tall, handsome, charming boss Joseph 'don't call me Joe' Davies, for putting me in line for the redundancy instead of Shauna. He had been kind enough to grant me the chance to take a sabbatical for my Manhattan adventure. Besides, Shauna deserved to stay. I mean, she was prepared to spend a whole weekend making four hundred miniature origami swans when they were required for a Swan Lake-themed Christmas window. I had to hold my hands up – I could never be that committed, let alone that good at origami. Shauna lived and breathed the window-dressing life. A life that she took great delight in sharing with her three thousand strong TikTok following – a niche, yet dedicated community in which she extolled the highs and lows of her busy working life.

Entering the office today I already felt like an imposter. Ideally, I would creep in unnoticed, grab the stuff from my desk drawers (mainly Pret cutlery, Tampax, and chewing gum) and leave. But it was never going to happen with Shauna around. She was up and out of her seat and flinging her arms around me the second I appeared.

'Babe, this is horrendous. I'm so sorry!' she announced, trying her hardest to feign sympathy and failing. She shoved a Tupperware box in front of me. 'Have a Mars bar slice. Approximately one thousand calories per piece. I guarantee you'll feel better.'

'I'm not into emotional eating,' I responded, the smell of milk chocolate hitting my nostrils in a tantalising way. 'But I am hungry.' I lifted one out and held it to my lips, ready to take a bite.

'Wait!' she yelled, putting her hand on my arm to stop the slice just short of my lips. Her long fingernails decorated with little diamanté jewels on the ends dug into my leather jacket, while with her other hand she artfully lifted her iPhone and snapped. 'TikTok opportunity!'

And there it was: me, lips parted, eyes wide, chocolate slice just shy of my open mouth, uploaded to TikTok and Snapchat simultaneously, complete with a salivating dog GIF and the hashtags #workOG #bae #missyoualready #solongamigo #ambergreen.

'Thanks, Shauna,' I mumbled, appreciating the sugar hit. 'I'll miss you, too.'

Joseph peeked over the top of the large screen on his desk and stood up. 'Hey, Amber.' He came over, ready to embrace me too.

'It's okay, no one's died,' I said. 'No need to hug it out. I'm honestly fine.'

'It's shit and I'm sorry.' Joseph hung his head. 'We'll do drinks, right?'

'Sure,' I commented noncommittally.

Tempting as it was to brag about my job news to them today, I was sensible enough to know that I had better wait until everything was agreed in writing before I made it public, and there was still no official word from Julie-Ann.

As I threw away most of the contents of my desk drawers – and put the spare knickers, box of Tampax, deodorant, and array of business cards I might need one day, plus a stash of unused Post-it Notes into a bag – my hand was never far away from my phone, as I checked my inbox precisely every three seconds. *An email from Julie-Ann would be very welcome right about now.*

Fridays can mean a lot of different things to people every single week. There can be special Fridays and insignificant ones; Fridays so full of fun that I have not wanted the night to end. And ones when I have been very happy to say sayonara to the working week. Fridays with a bottle of wine, TV, and the sofa. Fridays with girlfriends, Fridays with family, Fridays alone, and Fridays with Rob. It's the day I generally enjoy the most in the week. The evening in which I regularly eat a family bag of Maltesers, and the night Rob and I nearly always have the best sex. But what about this Friday?

Right on cue, a new email appeared. It was from Julie-Ann.

Today would be remembered as the Friday I left Selfridges for the last time as an employee – and walked straight into a new job.

CHAPTER FOUR

The email from Julie-Ann was a job offer – a three-month contract to be Mandy's in-house stylist during her time in the UK. When Julie-Ann said 'in-house' she meant it literally. As part of the deal, I was required to move into the mansion which Mandy and her entourage would be inhabiting for the full twelve weeks. During which time, they would document her life on social media and for her YouTube channel, work on brand endorsements and generally raise her profile this side of the Atlantic. After signing an NDA, I was informed that the house was in Surrey – a suburb just outside of London – which felt reassuringly close to my home with Rob. But here came the catch: *This is an exclusive agreement whereby you will work full time for Mandy for the full twelve weeks, and not be permitted to see anyone outside of the house, aka your 'work family', for the duration of the contract, to ensure complete confidentiality. For the avoidance of doubt, this includes your spouse or significant other. Holiday days must be reviewed and agreed in advance and your contract is subject to termination without notice if necessary.*

Yikes.

The salary was better than my pay at Selfridges had been,

plus it included accommodation, food, a few expenses, and a very appealing bonus of the same amount again, payable once the twelve weeks were fulfilled, to serve as an incentive. With Rob and me saving for a deposit for a flat together, the bonus was a huge plus.

My role was to dress Mandy daily, for all engagements taking place both within the house and on location. Plus, there might be a trip abroad. It was going to be like styling a photoshoot every single day. It sounded exciting, different – a once-in-a-lifetime opportunity. And the fact my job at Selfridges no longer existed, there was little risk in accepting a short-term contract because it wasn't as if I had any other job prospects at this moment. The only negative was three months without Rob. I wondered how he would feel about me moving out of our flat – and his entire life – for that period of time. It would be hard, but there was no rule about FaceTiming and phone calls, and when you broke twelve weeks down to eighty-four days, it didn't feel too long. *Did it?* Plus, it would be worth it for the bonus at the end; it was the kind of sum that would add a huge chunk to our savings for a flat. It might actually make our home-owning dream a reality. Rob had to agree it was worth it. I decided to break the news to him this evening.

After years of 'living in sin' as my mum and dad called it, raising their daughter, Nora, out of a matrimonial home, Lucy's boyfriend of ten years, Rory, had finally done the right thing – in my parents' eyes – and proposed. He did it on Lucy's birthday last October over dinner at a fancy Japanese restaurant in central London.

'Very flashy for Rory, do you think something's up?' Mum had excitedly fished over the phone, while she was babysitting for Nora that evening. In retrospect, I'm sure she was in on it, as we discovered Rory had done the traditional thing and asked for Dad's approval to marry his daughter the weekend before, and there was no way Dad could keep that secret from Mum. Sure enough, when they arrived home that evening, Lucy was sporting one of Nora's toy rings on her wedding finger. Rory was far too sensible to purchase a diamond without seeking Lucy's approval in advance, knowing how fussy my sister was. This was the person who would not enter a coffee shop until she was sure they sold her preferred brand of oat milk and the beans were a hundred per cent fairtrade.

'Lucky I said yes, or he would have ruined my birthday forever,' Lucy remarked dryly, as she retold the story to me with her trademark cynicism over FaceTime the following day. She may have tried to sound cool, but I could see the excitement ripple from the upturned corners of her lips to her eyes as she began to visualise what their wedding might be like. She told me Nora was already plotting what the bridesmaids would wear – herself as the chief, naturally.

By the time I arrived at Lucy's house this evening, I had fully convinced myself that this job was my destiny.

Nora opened the door, dressed head to toe as Harry Potter.

'Hey, Harry! Don't put a spell on me!' I pretended to hide behind my hands.

'Don't laugh. Anyway, I'm not Harry. I'm Nora!' the

little girl replied, sounding cross. 'Grown-ups are so stupid sometimes.'

'Nora Potter,' I said, undeterred. 'I'm sorry.'

'I can wear what I like,' she commanded indignantly. 'It doesn't change who I am, you know.' She threw the glassless round spectacles onto the floor.

'Of course you can – and you are perfect as you are,' I said, marvelling at how strong-minded she was. Nora was my kindred spirit. I set my bag down and crouched, taking Nora's hand, the one that wasn't clasping a wand. 'Are you going to invite me in then, birthday girl?'

'Do you have a present?' Her eyes fixated on the canvas bag over my shoulder. I greatly admired her directness.

'Of course I do. Would you like it now?' She nodded in response. 'And by the way, you can dress any way you want to. Do you know why?'

'Why, Auntie Nana?' *Nana* was Nora's nickname for me, since before she could properly speak. It did nothing for my street cred, but I had learnt to love it.

'Because it makes life much more fun. And do you know what else?' She looked at me, wide-eyed, with such innocence, it made my heart swell. 'If you feel happy, then you will make other people smile too – that's the most special thing.'

'Yes, Nana,' she said. She picked up the glasses and put them back on her nose. 'Can I have my present now?'

I took it out of the bag and handed it to her, then she turned and marched me into the house.

Six months on from Rory's proposal, the July wedding

date was drawing closer and wedding planning was a constant topic of conversation in our family. Lucy and Rory were having a registry wedding followed by a meal and big party for all their friends at a country hotel with a marquee in the garden, not far from my parents' house in north London. Mostly on a Sunday evening, a flurry of WhatsApp messages would come from Lucy or Rory, asking for final names for the guest list and sharing dilemmas such as whether to have champagne or prosecco. Then there were questions from Mum about additional outdoor heaters and there was even a thread about the type of seat cushions they should choose for chairs in the ceremony. Until now, I had no idea that a wedding could have so many components – the thought of getting hitched seemed like an administrative nightmare. I was under no illusion that today's gathering for Nora's birthday wouldn't soon turn into a meeting to finalise the additional jobs we should each take on to help. My sister's penchant for delegating had not gone unnoticed by me.

Lure them in with the promise of cake and then – pounce!

I was feeling nervous about what Lucy might expect of me. Being in PR, she had never been shy of straight talk and lists. Arranging her hen do and associated matters was already taking up a lot of my time, yet Lucy was one of those people who believed nothing could *ever* be as busy or important as raising a child, so it was taken for granted that I, being childless, had an abundance of empty hours at my disposal. Hours in which I could assist her.

I walked into the kitchen to find my family assembled

around the kitchen island, picking from a depleted bowl of Wotsits and the remains of some crudité and sandwiches, presumably leftovers from Nora's birthday party earlier in the afternoon.

Lucy was holding a mug of tea.

'Children's parties are a special kind of exhausting,' she said, and pulled me in for a hug with her free arm. 'It's been intense.'

'Present from Nana!' Nora cooed, tugging at the ribbon tied around the gift.

'Did you bring wine by any chance?' Lucy asked. 'I meant to ask you to stop by the offie.'

'Don't worry, I'll go,' Rory chipped in. 'I could do with some air.'

'Couldn't we all,' Lucy muttered under her breath.

'Evening, Amber, lovely to see you as always.' Rory gave me a peck on the check as he passed, and grabbed his keys from the side.

'First things first, something for my favourite niece.' I smiled, cutting the ribbon on the gift for Nora and leading her to the sofa in the lounge area of the open-plan kitchen. 'I literally cannot believe you are now seven years old.'

She ripped off the paper to reveal a palette of child-friendly make-up and a set of nail polish in a unicorn vanity case. The kind of gift that was my ultimate wish at her age – but not one my own parents ever granted. 'It's make-up, Mama!' Nora squealed. 'This is the BEST present ever! Thank you, Auntie Nana!' And she flung her arms around my neck.

'I'm so happy you like it,' I said through a steady stream of sloppy kisses planted square onto my lips. 'What are you going to put on first?'

From the corner of my vision, I noticed Mum's eyes roll.

Leaving Nora happily exploring a cacophony of eyeshadows, lip glosses, and cheek blushes, I went back to the breakfast bar to join Mum and Lucy who were now picking at a bowl of crisps. Mum was nursing a glass of wine.

'How much have you two had?' I asked.

'Not enough,' replied Lucy. 'Rory will be back with more in a minute.'

I felt like a child in a toy shop with my news buzzing around my head, I was so desperate to tell someone. But in my mind, I had decided to wait until Rob arrived before sharing it.

'How did it go at work today?' Mum asked.

'Depressing,' I replied. 'To be honest I'm glad to be out of there. Shauna was trying so hard not to gloat it was embarrassing.'

I managed to dodge answering any further questions, because I spotted an open Colin the Caterpillar cake box, a few remaining pieces inside, the white chocolate Colin head in there too. I fingered it, pulling the chocolate towards me, ready to help myself. Being with family made me behave in a way I never would at a friend's house. *No airs and graces. Everything that's theirs is mine.*

From nowhere, Nora helicoptered towards me at speed. Like a wild animal pouncing on its prey, she artfully glided across the tiled floor, skidding to a halt on her impressively fast pink socks.

'Nooooo!' she screamed, arms outstretched.

Then, using the breakfast bar to bring herself to a sharp standstill, she shouted urgently, 'Stop! That's the best part! Don't eat the head – it's mine! It's MY birthday and I was saving it!'

'Okay, okay. Don't panic!' I dropped the head and raised my arms like it was a hold-up. 'It's all yours.'

'Do you think I could steal you upstairs for a minute?' Lucy said, coming up beside me, to save me from Nora's wrath.

I followed her up the carpeted steps from the hallway. I loved Lucy's house. After a recent refurb it was the kind of cosy, tastefully decorated family home that made you feel like everything was going to be okay. It had curtains with pelmets and framed family pictures on the walls. The pale greys, greens, and cream were nurturing and calm. I wondered if I would ever be this grown-up.

Lucy sat on the side of her king-size bed, her eyes drifting to the wardrobes to her right. The doors were closed.

'Are you okay?' I asked.

'I'm fine,' she whispered.

'Are you sure?'

She glanced sideways at the wardrobe. 'Well, I do have a bit of news.' She stood up and opened the final door of their white wardrobes.

A sinking feeling gripped my stomach as she laid down the wedding gown, still in its protective case, across the bed.

'You hate it.' I pre-empted. 'You can be honest with me, sis, I'm a big girl now.'

'It's not that—' Her voice trailed off. 'It's more that it's not going to fit me.'

'Lucy, it's fine. I know the team at Pronovias really well. We can arrange a visit and have it altered, it's not a problem,' I said cheerily, putting my arm around her shoulder. 'It's your wedding dress – it's got to be perfect.'

She bit her bottom lip. 'I don't think that will cut it, I'm afraid. I mean it's *really* not going to fit.' Her eyes were glassy. 'I'm going to be a pregnant bride. A heavily pregnant bride.'

My mouth dropped open. I flung my arms around her. 'Wooooww! I never would have guessed that one!'

Lucy being pregnant was big news. When she gave birth to Nora seven years ago at home, the first words she said as I arrived a few hours later to meet my new baby niece were, 'If I ever so much as *think* I will do this again, please remind me of this moment – and shoot me.'

To be fair, Nora's birth was traumatic. After a prolonged labour, she finally arrived by forceps on the sofa at Lucy and Rory's flat, after the planned Zen water birth Lucy had been prepping for couldn't go ahead safely because Nora was a large baby and was basically stuck. Things had progressed and it was not safe to move Lucy to hospital for an epidural, so an emergency team came to her. After a ripped perineum, several stitches, a lot of swearing, and Rory fainting later – Nora finally arrived, screaming and very cross with the world, like a little red gargoyle, all nine pounds of her. It didn't seem possible that our petite Lucy could produce such a large baby. Lucy didn't even have any photos from the very first moments of holding her baby, because Rory was out of action. 'The front room looked like an abattoir – no one needs to see this,' she told me.

'And I'm spitting because the hypno-birthing course was a total waste of money. Money we could have spent on a night nurse.' Then she burst into tears. 'It's only been a few hours and I'm already a shit mum because I hated my birth and I'm absolutely gutted that my fucking fanny is never going to be the same. My life is over!'

'Of course you're not!' I had dutifully protested, reminding her she was due a painkiller. I took the bundle of new life, who smelt of malted milk biscuits, and held her tenderly in my arms.

'Isn't it amazing?' I murmured, enjoying the comforting feeling of Nora's warm little body next to mine. 'You created this perfect human.'

Lucy sighed.

'You did the best you could possibly do for her, Luce,' I continued. 'She's here and she's healthy. You shouldn't punish yourself for something so out of your control. I love you both very much.'

Nora gurgled, wrapped her tiny hand tightly around my little finger and stared back at me with a mixture of milk-drunk bemusement and total adoration. I'm sure we cemented our special bond at that moment.

Time was a great healer for Lucy. Gradually she was able to talk about the birth without breaking down in tears and she was a brilliant, devoted mum, but still, it was a lot, and I could understand why she and Rory had decided to stop at one.

'We count ourselves lucky' was how they looked upon it. And that was that. Until now.

Lucy and I sat on her bed chatting for a while longer.

'It was a total surprise,' she said. 'I honestly thought I was bloated.'

'Have you told Nora?'

'Not yet, she'd never forgive me for stealing her spotlight in her birthday month, and I didn't want to risk her blurting it out at school until we'd had a chance to tell you all. But now I'm three months gone, I will soon.'

'I'm going to be an auntie again!' I exclaimed.

'I think my child loves you more than me most of the time.' Lucy smiled.

'Anyway, how are you feeling?'

'Apart from morning sickness, I'm okay. I'd forgotten how bad it was with Nora. I'll bet there's another head-strong little girl in here.' She ran a hand over her stomach.

'Will you find out the sex?'

'I don't think so. Rory says there are few genuine surprises left in life, so why not let this be one.'

'And a massive control freak like you is happy to go along with that?' I smiled at the side of her face.

'To be honest I've been feeling too green to argue. We'll see, but for now, I don't have a huge urge to officially confirm my gut instinct that it's a girl.'

'We're going to need to find you a new wedding dress

then,' I said. 'But don't worry, I'm sure Pronovias do a maternity line. I'll sort it.'

Lucy hung the gown on the outside of the wardrobe and unzipped the bag, some of the champagne-coloured fabric immediately spilling out, shimmering sequins catching the light.

'It's a shame. I absolutely love this gown. I felt amazing in it.' Lucy took a final look at it. It was the most unwedding-y bridal gown I could find – on her orders – and it really was stunning.

The doorbell rang, making us both jump.

'It doesn't matter if he sees it now,' Lucy remarked. 'Come on, let's go back down and find you some wine.' She steered me towards the stairs again.

'Sorry I'm late. We met in the off-licence.' Rob was standing in the hallway with Rory. 'Happy birthday, Nora!' he called out, but Nora was still too busy devouring another mouthful of leftover cake to notice.

'Jesus, Mum, were you not keeping an eye on this?' Lucy asked, moving forwards to detach the little girl from the cake box.

Mum looked up from her phone. 'Sorry, darling – work stuff.'

We might have been together for two years now, but Rob still had the ability to put butterflies in my stomach, just like when I first clapped eyes on him in the Smith's boutique when he was making a TV show about Mona Armstrong. He had an undeniably, classically good-looking face, symmetrical features, sandy hair, green eyes, teen-pin-up qualities that had not diminished with age. *I'm lucky to have him.* I kissed him on the cheek, and he wound an arm around my waist.

'So – what's the latest?' Rob asked.

Everyone looked at me expectantly.

'I got it.' I smiled.

'Got what, darling? The bridesmaid dresses?'

'No, Mum. I had the interview today – for the stylist job for Mandy Sykes.'

'Mandy who?' Dad appeared beside us.

'Mandy Sykes. She's a celebrity. A big one. I got offered a job as her stylist.'

'Oh wow – have you accepted it?' Lucy asked.

'Not quite. I mean, yes, I probably will, but there are some parts we need to discuss.' I looked at Rob. We stared at each other for a beat. I didn't want to do this in front of my whole family. 'We can talk about it later. But it feels like perfect timing, given I'm unemployed.'

'Sorry if this is a stupid question,' Dad piped up, 'but who exactly is Mandy Sykes?'

'She's one of the wealthiest business stars on social media,' I replied, feeling my skin prickle. Somehow inserting the word *business* made me feel as though he was more likely to approve.

'I follow her on Instagram,' Lucy said supportively. 'She's massive. Think the Kardashians meet Housewives of Beverly Hills.'

Dad looked blank. 'Does this mean you're needed in LA again?'

'No, she's moving here – to Surrey,' I said hurriedly.

'From the Hollywood Hills to the Surrey Hills, I can see what they did there.' Lucy smirked.

'Still no idea, so sorry,' said Dad. 'Is anyone else peckish?'

'I'm starving,' said Rob. 'Here, I come with crisps.' And he pulled out two large packets from the carrier bag he was still holding and headed towards the kitchen.

I was glad of the change of subject, it gave me an opportunity to speak to someone more on my level. I padded over to Nora, who was now busy in a corner working on the Barbie house she'd been given for her birthday.

'Do *you* know who Mandy Sykes is?' I asked her in a hushed voice.

'Who?' she whispered back, conspiratorially. 'Is this a secret?'

'No.' I looked over my shoulder, suddenly feeling a bit pathetic for seeking validation for my career choices from a child. 'I'm just interested in whether you know who Mandy Sykes is.'

'Mandy who?' She looked at me blankly.

'She's on the internet and in lots and lots of magazines,' I said. 'She's very famous.' Still nothing. 'And she's on YouTube.' *Surely, I've hit a nerve there.*

'Kids YouTube?' Her eyes lit up. 'Can we watch, Auntie Nana? Let's watch? Pleeeease?'

She made a grab for my phone.

'Nice try.' I slammed my hand across the screen before she could reach it. 'It's not watch time. Don't worry. I just thought you might know about Mandy Sykes because she is a very, *very* big celebrity.'

'What's a celebrity?'

'Forget it.'

'I can ask Mummy?' she replied helpfully, eyes widening.

'No, no, it's fine. Forget it.'

I put my phone down in the kitchen and plonked myself on the sofa next to Rob, dying to tell him Lucy and Rory's news, but not daring while Nora was still up.

'How are you feeling about everything?' He put a hand on my knee.

'Okay, I think. But they definitely want me to move into the house with Mandy and her husband.'

'For how long?'

'Twelve weeks. There's a big bonus at the end,' I continued. I shuffled in my seat, building up to the part about not seeing each other.

'How much of a bonus?'

'The salary all over again. It's a huge incentive.'

'Wow. That will help with our savings,' he said excitedly. 'The timing couldn't be better, right?'

'The timing is perfect, but there is one other thing,' I continued nervously. 'They will literally own me for three months. And that means we won't be able to see each other.'

'What, not even on your days off?'

'It doesn't sound like I'll get many days off. She sounds paranoid about confidentiality.'

'So, I won't be able to touch you or kiss you, for three whole months? One quarter of a year?'

'That's right. And I'll miss you, obviously. It won't be easy, for either of us.'

He turned to look at me. 'Do you really want to do it?'

I nodded. 'Styling Mandy this morning reminded me of who I used to be. It's my passion. My reason for being. Besides' – I sighed – 'I might not get offered an opportunity like this again. It's literally fallen into my lap at just the right time.'

'It hasn't fallen into your lap – you've worked for this, Amber. You won this job, and you deserve this opportunity.'

'Plus, the bonus – think of the bonus,' I said.

'It sounds like a no-brainer.' Rob smiled. 'We can FaceTime and WhatsApp, I assume?'

'Of course.' I nodded. 'It's not like I'm going to Wandsworth Prison, and it's not forever.'

Then he leant into the side of my face and whispered in my ear, 'We'll have to come up with some innovative ways to feel connected then. And I'll keep the bed warm for you.'

I wrapped my arms around his neck and pulled him in for a kiss on the lips.

'Snog!' Nora pointed at us and giggled.

'Cover your eyes!' Rob called back.

'Julie-Ann wants to know my answer today, they mentioned a few other stylists they could see if I can't do it,' I told him.

'You'd better let her know then.'

As I stood up to locate my phone, I heard it ringing from the other side of the room. I saw Nora reach for it on the breakfast bar. Before I could stop her, she had chimed into it, 'Nana's phone!' and then laughed hysterically.

'If it's Auntie Vicky, tell her it's your birthday!' I called, motoring towards her. Vicky often rang me from LA around this time on a Friday, for a quick check-in ahead of the weekend.

'Auntie Nana says to tell you I'm seven and we had caterpillar cake!' the little girl squealed enthusiastically, before adding, 'What? Hello?'

I got the impression it wasn't Vicky on the other end and whipped my phone out of her hands. 'Give that back to me, you cheeky caterpillar,' I said, retrieving the sticky device. 'Hello?'

'Is this the right number for Amber Green?' asked a clipped American voice on the other end.

'It is, this is Amber.'

'Oh, hiii. It's Mandy Sykes.'

'Mandy, hello! I do apologise,' I said in my best English. 'I'm just with my niece. It's her seventh birthday, as you may have gathered.'

'We have a little,' she paused, 'fashion emergency. I'm hoping you can help?'

I felt my face heat up. 'What kind of emergency?'

Rob's ears pricked up across the room and he looked at me quizzically.

Okay? he mouthed.

I shrugged.

'A major event has come up for tomorrow. BAFTA are throwing a lunch for key talent. I'm amazed I've been invited and, obviously, I want to be there.' She paused. 'We were meant to be on a plane to the Maldives, but we've delayed the trip and I have nothing, and I mean *nothing* to wear.'

'Nothing to wear,' I repeated slowly. My mind flashed back to the hotel closet stuffed to bursting with designer clothes.

'Can you find me a gown? I need to make an impact. Consider it your trial period. If you can get to the Corinthia with some options first thing tomorrow morning, I'd really appreciate it, Amber.'

There was only one answer. 'Yes. Of course, Mandy, please text me your sizes and I'll get on the case.'

'Great, you can meet some of the team then too. You are officially onboard, I take it?'

'Absolutely,' I purred. 'I'll be there.'

As I ended the call, I noticed that my family had fallen silent around me, as they wondered what kind of emergency required someone to text their sizes before it could be acted upon.

My bladder felt like it was about to burst so I dashed to the loo.

On the toilet, knickers around my ankles, I noticed my heart was galloping. *What have I agreed to do?*

My phone pinged into life with a WhatsApp from Mandy sending me her clothes sizes.

I scrolled onto the email icon to check whether Julie-Ann had been in touch, a contract for me to sign would be useful right about now. And I hadn't known the offer was dependent on a 'trial period'.

Before I had pulled my knickers up again, registering that Mandy's sizes were pretty much identical to my sister's, I was struck by a flash of inspiration.

Returning to my family, when Rob innocently asked Lucy how the wedding plans were coming on, and Lucy sighed in response, I was glad to have a valid excuse to leave before dinner and swerve a logistical discussion about hotels in close proximity to the wedding venue. After a quick word with my sister about needing to get home to prep, and a big hug as I congratulated her on her news again, I bundled myself into an Uber.

On the way home, I glanced across at the Pronovias gown folded carefully onto the seat beside me. It was proof that one person's fashion fail, could be another's movie-star moment. It was a risk, but given the time limitations, it was a gift – and the only chance I had.

CHAPTER FIVE

I squinted at my bedside clock. Seven a.m. already.

Rob rolled over and flung a heavy arm across my body. My sleepy brain computed this as a wordless, neanderthal means of trying to make his woman stay in bed a while longer. I pushed my bottom into his side, making him sigh woozily and hold me a little tighter. His feather tattoo was clearly visible on his upper arm. I shifted my position to gain a better vantage point and tenderly ran my finger over it, the black ink slightly raised on his skin. I often did this when we were dozing in bed, finding the fine lines of the image a comforting presence on his body. I had noticed the tattoo poking out of his T-shirts a long while before we started dating, adding an extra layer of intrigue to him, making him even more attractive as my mind fantasised about whether I might get to kiss him one day. And when I finally did, in the middle of a crowded pavement on London's Oxford Street, it was as tender and sweet as I had hoped. I fell for Rob hard and still couldn't quite believe that I had actually, somehow, made him mine.

I pushed myself against him again, more firmly this time, testing how awake he was. Rob had taken one for our team, staying at my sister's house after I left yesterday. I imagined the wedding chat had been off the scale.

'Morning, handsome,' I whispered when he stirred.

'You're not leaving,' he muttered sleepily, eyes still clamped shut, his arms tightening their grip around my waist.

'I am, I'm afraid. I've got to get over to Mandy. It's a work day for me, remember?'

'Oww,' he murmured.

'How was the rest of last night?'

'Rory got the whisky out,' he croaked. 'He told me their baby news, I'm chuffed for them. Whisky is never a good idea, but we had to get away from all the wedding chat between your mum, dad, and sister. Your dad was really into it. I think he might have volunteered to make them a floral arch to get married underneath. He might regret that this morning. Lucy has a *big* vision. And she was the only sober one by the end.'

'Eek, poor Dad,' I said. 'Anyway, the whisky explains your breath this morning.' I recoiled as he tried to kiss me on the lips.

'Hey, not even a peck before you go?' he complained. 'I did you a favour last night remember.' He prodded my side jokingly. 'God knows what you would have been roped into if you had stuck around. I heard them discussing who could make 150 miniature bags for wedding favours at one point. I can always give Lucy a quick bell and tell her that y—'

'Stop!' I put my finger over his mouth. 'That's enough from you, Mr Walker. Save your kisses for when I get home, and when you've brushed your teeth. I think you should take advantage of the fact you can get some extra kip, while I have to drag myself into town. I cannot be late for Mandy Sykes.' I said her name theatrically, the novelty of the words coming out of my mouth not lost on either of us.

I had spent the rest of last night at home cobbling together the bits I had available to make up my stylist's 'kit' ready to take to the hotel this morning. In a bum bag, I gathered a miniature sewing set swiped from a hotel room a few months ago, some tit tape, gel implants to enhance her cleavage, though I doubted she would need this, plus scissors, bulldog clips, pins in a pin cushion, and some Body Blur – my secret weapon to smooth the skin for a glossy, even, photo-ready finish. A quick trip to the twenty-four-hour garage ensured I also had plasters and wet wipes. My experience in the styling world taught me that you can *never* be too prepared. You wouldn't believe how much damage a spiked heel through a delicate silk organza gown can do, or the drama a bust zip can cause, and it always seems to happen at the last minute, just as a client leaves their hotel room, or steps from a car to the red carpet. That kind of panic isn't pretty, I assure you. It's ugly, it's dark; it's a situation you need to fix – fast – and then you have to pray there's no lasting emotional damage to the celebrity, on top of the physical distress that might have been caused to a one-of-a-kind designer-creation. Styling is stressful.

In our small kitchen, a pan of cold pasta and pesto was sat on the hob in a flood of starchy water, which had developed a thin milky film across the top. The fridge was humming, and our miniature dishwasher hadn't been turned on overnight. Dirty mugs that had built up during the week lay in the sink unwashed. A packet of crumpets was open on the side, I saw them at the same time as a passing fly, and I watched as it took a pit stop on top of one. We might have had an excuse for living in a pig sty when we actually had a micro pig called Pinky as a pet for a short while, but since Pinky was rehomed while we were in New York, now there was no excuse. The evidence here all pointed to the fact that Rob must have got home very late and *very* drunk last night.

Rob and I still hadn't mastered the ability to successfully delegate household chores between us. The early days of our dating had been characterised by working all day, eating out, ordering Deliveroo, drinking in pubs, going to parties, and generally avoiding the shared grown-up responsibility of looking after a home together. It had been a heady time, lust-filled and fun. Talking about how to descale a kettle, or whose turn it was to clean the oven, wasn't on the agenda, even if we knew how to do either of those things. *Why don't they teach you this stuff at school?*

In New York we had both been so busy working, we didn't have to deal with domesticity in any detail. Besides, we, like everyone else in our block, pretty much lived off burritos-to-go from our local deli or Taco Bell.

Looking at the state of things now, I wondered if it was time to get more organised at home. I reassured myself that we weren't complete slobs because the place would look a hell of a lot worse without me having bought a bunch of tulips from the supermarket to decorate the kitchen table, and the throw I had found on a Portobello market stall recently had made a big difference to the sofa. I was good at up-cycling vintage finds and styling our home. It's just neither of us was very good at noticing when the washing-up liquid was running low. I shrugged. It was messy, but it was *our* mess, and I wouldn't have it any other way. In a funny kind of way, I thought I might miss Rob's untidiness when I moved in with Mandy and didn't have to see it every day.

I thought of Mandy waking up in the luxury of the Corinthia penthouse, no doubt encased in a cacophony of plump white duck-feather pillows and crisp, sweet-smelling sheets, a silver-service trolley on order with fruit, pastries, and coffee. A world away from my surroundings. We might live in one city but the disparity in living arrangements among its inhabitants was something I could never fully get my head around. I had witnessed so much of this polarisation between the haves and have-nots in my line of work. It never ceased to stagger me when I witnessed someone blow thousands of pounds in a couple of hours on the shop floor, and in the same breath enquire about getting on the waiting list for the latest Louis Vuitton bag. *Where did all this money come from?* Yet just metres away underground on the Tube, there I was being gifted a piece of heather by a woman who looked as though she hadn't washed for a while. It wasn't right.

I made myself a coffee in my reusable cup, put on my boyfriend jeans, a white T-shirt, an oversized grey wool blazer, and gold chain and rings – my go-to look when I didn't know what to wear – then scooped up the bag containing the gown, popped over to give Rob a kiss on the cheek, and left the house at 7.30 a.m. on the dot.

I can't believe I'm actually doing this.

'I hope she thanks you for this!' Rob called out as I closed the door.

When I arrived at Corinthia London, I was ushered straight up to the penthouse floor. Jose met me at the door again.

'Amber!' he greeted me warmly, like an old friend. 'Glad you could make it.' I thought about saying that I didn't really have much choice but decided against it. My straight talk had been tolerated the first time, but I wasn't sure how far I could push it.

After the obligatory kiss on each cheek, he took me through. This time the suite was busy, I felt several pairs of eyes immediately turn my way.

Ushering me ahead of him, Jose announced me to the room. 'The team is complete! Everyone, this is Amber Green, Mandy's new stylist. She's part of the live-in squad.'

'Hi. Jimi. We met before,' said the dashing man with cheekbones you could slice ham on. He had the kind of looks that actively made me feel uncomfortable. This time he seemed more friendly, holding out a hand to shake mine. 'I do all of Mandy's social media. I'm also a DJ.'

'And our personal trainer,' Jose added, slapping his brother on the shoulder.

'Do you work out, Amber?' Jimi asked, deep brown eyes sparkling.

'Um, yoga, sometimes,' I lied.

'Great, you might enjoy the Pilates too then,' he said.

Jose indicated to a petite woman with corkscrew curls standing on his right.

'Hi, I'm Lola, hair and make-up,' she said. 'Nice to meet you, Amber. I'm not live-in, but I'll be in and out of the house a lot. This is going to be so much fun!'

We didn't have time to get to the other two people in the room, as the clip-clop sound of heels on a marble floor grew louder. Mandy came into view down the central stairs, wrapped in a low-slung dressing gown. Her breasts peeked out like perfectly round scoops of ice cream nestled inside a waffle cone.

'Morning all!' she exclaimed. 'How is everyone?'

There was a murmur of 'good' and 'great' around the room.

'You all think you've arrived, don't you?' she said, eyes narrowed. We looked at each other nervously. 'Well, you have!' she declared, smiling broadly. 'You've reached the final stage of the selection process. Well, except for you, Jimi. You've always been here. Within twenty-four hours we're going to have contracts signed and you can start the day after that. We will move into the house tomorrow. Welcome to the world of Mandy Sykes!'

'Yeah!' cheered Lola, enthusiastically, the only one to make an audible response to Mandy's address. The rest of us Brits needed longer to warm up.

The fact that Mandy seemed to think I could start in two days' time was worrying – I was hoping I might have at least a week to get my life straight and make the most of being with Rob. I made a mental note to add that to the growing list of items to be discussed with Julie-Ann, who hadn't yet emailed my contract.

'Action stations, gang! Just because the cameras aren't rolling today, doesn't mean we can slack,' Mandy trilled, glancing over her shoulder at the youngest-looking member of the party who was descending the stairs behind her.

'This is Blair, my personal assistant. They will show everyone where to put their stuff and I'll meet you all upstairs.'

I looked around me to see who else she had been referring to, before realising that Blair was the 'they'. They had appealing, symmetrical features, shoulder-length brown hair and wore a pair of flared trousers covered in purple diamonds, black nail polish, one gold crucifix earring and a vintage Rolling Stones T-shirt, like a modern-day Harlequin-meets-emo, with a dash of Harry Styles.

'Please make us aware of your pronouns so we're all clear from the off,' Mandy added, before clattering up the marble steps once more, the heels and dressing gown combo grating on me. Blair shot me a smile before mouthing *Hi*, and scurried upstairs behind her.

Out of the corner of my eye, I spotted someone who looked as though they felt as out of place around here as me.

'Hi,' I said.

'Hi, I'm Coco,' the slender woman replied. 'Nutritionist.'

She had white-blonde hair in a short pixie crop and elfin features.

'Amber. I go by she and her. I'm brand new here – when did you start?' I asked.

'She and her as well,' Coco replied. 'Today's my first day too.'

'How are you finding things?'

She raised her hand and whispered behind it. 'Weird. But it always is at first, isn't it? I just need to get to grips with the plan.'

'I wouldn't know,' I replied. 'I've not done anything quite like this before.'

We exchanged a timid smile in mutual acknowledgement that this was not a normal job.

'You've never been in-house before?' she checked.

I shook my head wondering what I had agreed to when a jolly butler opened the door and delivered a tray of pastries into the room.

'Good morning. Something to brighten your day!' he announced. 'They're straight out of the oven, there's plenty to go around.'

An aroma of freshly baked, buttery croissants and pains au chocolat filled the air, it was delicious. I realised I was starving, having missed dinner last night. I instinctively moved towards the tray.

'Sorry, but no.' Coco intercepted the butler as he was turning to leave. 'These are not for now,' she said firmly. 'I ordered a fruit plate and crudité platter with hummus. We'll take that first.'

She was polite, but deadly serious. I wondered how many times Coco had done this before, suspecting this wasn't the first. Her bossy tone reminded me of my sister.

Coco must have seen the crushed expression on my face because she immediately offered an explanation. She aimed it at the butler, but it was clearly for all of our benefit. 'Two things: one, always eat fruit and veggies first. Carbs come last. It stops insulin spikes and keeps glucose in check. And two, we don't turn to food as comfort to escape our feelings.'

The butler looked deflated as well as confused. 'Sir, it was very lovely of you to offer these baked goods to "brighten" our day,' Coco continued, 'but we don't need food to regulate our emotions, thank you.'

'Of course. Apologies. I didn't mean to offend.' He bowed his head. I wanted to go over and give him a hug. *He was only being friendly! And I would have loved a croissant.*

'No offence taken,' said Coco, softening a little. 'It's just that so many people are unaware of how emotional sensitivity can affect their eating habits. If Amber here really wants a croissant, then she should have one – not to improve her day, she knows she can look within herself for that affirmation – but just because she fancies a croissant. This is how we learn to regain control over our health and life. Are you with me?' She looked at me.

'Absolutely,' I said gravely, wondering whether Mandy was about to get this spiel too, as I'd noticed the butler had a second platter of pastries which was presumably for upstairs.

'It's no problem at all, madam,' answered the butler. 'I'll

go get the fruit and crudités immediately. Shall I take away the pastries, or would you like me to leave them for later?'

'Leave them for later, thank you,' she said to my relief. She turned to us. 'Don't panic everyone, I'm not a food Nazi, but I do feel that if we're all going to be living together, and I'm keeping Mandy on a nutritional plan, then we should all contract to adopt the same healthy rules. Believe me, it just works better this way and makes things manageable. It also enables me to do the job I've been hired to do.'

'I'm in,' added Lola. 'I can't wait to sample your nutritious dishes when I'm in the house.' *Easy for her to say.* I felt a spike of envy that Lola wasn't going to be subjected to this every day, like the rest of us.

'Me too, and bravo for highlighting that food should not be used as a reward,' said Jimi.

'That's great.' Coco nodded, pulling her hands into a prayer position. 'Excited to connect with you on this, Jimi. Look, it doesn't bother me if any of you want to keep a secret crisp stash in your room,' she added. 'But it won't help Mandy. And we are all here to help Mandy. Isn't that right?'

'That we are,' I said gravely. 'The croissants can wait.' I gave her a tight smile and hoped she couldn't read my mind which was currently screaming: *GET IN MY TUMMY, YOU SEXY CROISSANTS!*

Little does unsuspecting Coco know that I am the person who thought complex carbohydrates was a topic I must have missed in maths, and has Dairy Milk on Subscribe and Save from Amazon. I crossed my fingers behind my back and hoped Coco wasn't being completely serious about subjecting us all to whatever nutritional plan she had in store for Mandy.

Blair came downstairs again. They seemed friendly and asked me to get the clothes ready for Mandy in the dressing room, before they directed the others to assigned areas of the suite, where everyone was asked to set up for our boss. Lola – also she/her – was instructed to start on Mandy's hair and make-up first. So, we all began, cautiously, carefully, like worker bees in the wake of our queen, doing the things we were each trained to do.

I unpacked the gown in the same closet I'd spent the morning in just yesterday, relieved to have a private space in which to prepare. Yesterday already felt like a long time ago. Carefully unfurling it from the protective case, I was thankful the shimmering champagne-coloured Pronovias gown looked even more glamorous, and much less bridal, than I remembered. It was sexy, cut low around the chest, and skin-tight to the knee, where it flared out dramatically, creating a stunning 'mermaid' tail shape.

Knowing it was always best to have more than just one option for a celebrity to try, I pulled out the scarlet silk gown from Mandy's existing wardrobe, the one which caught my eye during the interview process, and also the black ruffled Dior dress, in case Mandy felt that recycling one of her gowns was a more understated look for a classy event like this. If she loved the Pronovias mermaid dress as much as I hoped she would, we could even save it for another big event.

Keeping one eye on the clock, I rifled around in her underwear drawer for the perfect body-contouring pieces to wear underneath each gown, and selected a few options of sandals to compliment the looks, lining the shoes up neatly in a row to the side of the gowns like sentry guards. The rail full, I stood back to admire my work, visualising Mandy wearing each outfit, before picking out some pieces of jewellery to finish off each look.

Mandy came into the room about an hour later. Hair and make-up had run over – as it always does – and having helped myself to two strong Nespressos I was feeling wide awake. Mandy looked extraordinarily glamorous for ten a.m. on a Saturday, her deep skin glowing and her big hair bouncing with curls as light as candy floss around her shoulders. To my delight, she made a beeline for the Pronovias.

'Oh wow – look at this!' she exclaimed, pulling the side of the gown out from the rail, to admire the sparkling sequins adorning the fabric from top to bottom.

'She's special,' I agreed.

'Ahem – *she* could be non-binary,' Blair astutely pointed out, flicking me a look.

'You're right. I'm sorry,' I replied.

Mandy fixed her eyes on the dress. 'I love this! How did you find it so quickly?' She turned to me.

'I was able to call in a favour,' I stammered, thinking it was only a half-truth. 'It's perfect for a daytime event and will look great with your cream sandals. I thought the shell clutch would make a fun addition. I love how the big

sequins overlap one another to create the scale-like effect –
and it reflects the light, see?' I gently moved the delicate
fabric under a spotlight to illustrate. 'That's why it's named
the mermaid dress.'

'Sold!' She beamed, making my heart swell.

When Mandy tried it on, the dress fitted perfectly. Even
Jose joined the appreciation, telling her: '¡Qué guapa! ¡Te
ves espectacular!'

Which, I assume, is a compliment.

The only person I hadn't managed to engage with for
any length of time during the morning was Jimi. He spent
most of his time with Jose, setting up a bespoke Pilates
reformer machine in the bedroom, and adjusting various
sized straps around two shiny black inflated balls – a
contraption I heard him tell Lola was 'the biggest fitness
trend to hit Hollywood'. To me they looked more like
sadistic instruments found in fetish clubs.

When my work was done, I collected my kit and it was
air kisses all round for the goodbye.

'Thank you for this opportunity, Mandy,' I said to her
as I prepared to leave. 'I'm really excited about working
with you and understanding more about how you like to
be styled.'

She looked at me for a moment and I wasn't sure how
she was going to react, but then her expression revealed a
kindness I hadn't seen before.

'Me too, Amber. I can see I made a good choice in you.
Don't let me down.' I admired the way she skilfully cloaked
a threat in a compliment.

'I won't,' I vowed earnestly.

'I was thinking, we could discuss fashion strategy in the cryotherapy chamber at Harrods next week,' Mandy said, like this was perfectly normal. 'I find it helpful to have a distraction when I'm trying to stop my brain from freezing.'

'Sure,' I replied. *I have absolutely no idea what I've just signed up for.*

CHAPTER SIX

By the time I got back home, I had, at last, received an email from Julie-Ann detailing my official offer from Mandy, along with confirmation that ideally she would like me to start the day after tomorrow, on Monday, 10 March. I didn't foresee an issue with this, given my current status as unemployed, although I was a little rocked about packing up and leaving Rob so soon. I grounded myself by deciding to focus on the bonus. Seeing the figure in writing gave me reason to stop by the Co-op and pick up a bottle of prosecco for Rob and me this evening, because it made me feel certain I was making the right decision in rolling the dice on this new chapter.

Rob was busy making a full English when I came through the door; the smell of salty bacon hit my nostrils and made them tingle. This house was definitely not signed up to Coco's 'vegetables first' principle. I felt relieved that whatever the nutritionist had in mind for us in Surrey, was going to stay firmly in Surrey.

'Baby!' Rob beamed, pleased to see me. 'Come and join my hangover lunch – there's plenty.'

He flung both arms around me lovingly.

'Mmm, you smell much better,' I said, wrapping my hands around his neck and pushing my hips inwards to meet his, instantly comforted by his familiarity.

'I had three extra hours of sleep after you left.' He smiled. 'I feel reborn.'

I looked over his shoulder approvingly. 'And you tidied up. Is there black pudding?'

'For someone who claims to be mostly vegetarian, you had better keep your black pudding habit to yourself, Miss Green.'

'You know all my dirty secrets,' I replied, teasing his lips apart with the end of my tongue. 'Hmm you taste of bacon. Cook's perk?'

I let myself go, pulling him in for a proper slow, sensual French kiss.

He smiled into my lips when we moved slightly apart. We looked at each other for a moment longer than necessary. I liked to do that sometimes, to take him in. As I saw the sexy, slouchy Saturday Rob, I wondered which version of me he was seeing today.

'So how did it go?' he asked, when we moved apart.

'Really good. Mandy's wearing Lucy's wedding dress to her event today.'

'Wait – what?' His forehead crinkled.

'Yup, I'm not quite sure how I pulled this one off either.' I grabbed a piece of cut baguette and added an extra dollop of butter on top, before tossing it into my mouth. I hadn't eaten anything bar a couple of sticks of celery and some raspberries at the Corinthia. There had been no time for the pastry course, plus I wanted to make a good impression on Coco. 'But trust me – it works.'

He filled two warm plates with scrambled egg, bacon, a spoonful of baked beans, fried mushrooms, and grilled tomatoes, plus two slices of black pudding, declaring, 'The full monty.'

We sat at the small dining table in our kitchen.

'There's going to be a nutritionist living in the house with us, and she seems militant, so I had better make the most of this meal. It feels like the last supper. Which reminds me' – I paused to chew a mouthful of delicious egg and bacon – 'Mandy wants me to move in on Monday.'

'As in, the day after tomorrow?'

I nodded and tried to assess his gaze, which looked disappointed.

'I wasn't expecting it to be this soon either, but Mandy moves fast. I suppose the sooner I start, the sooner I'll finish though,' I offered, as a softener. And it was true.

He nodded sceptically. 'Yeah, I guess. I just thought we'd have a bit longer to get used to the idea.'

Knowing I would need to spend most of the following day packing for my three months away, I needed to use this time to talk about what was going on with Rob too.

Since he had started as a director at Serious Global – the TV production company with the world's worst name – Rob had seemed less enthusiastic than ever about his line of work. The television world was having a difficult time. Following a boom in commissioning, and career highs like the Angel Wear documentary Rob had directed in New

York, things had cooled off and fewer shows were being made. It wasn't a reflection on his skills, but a market trend – audiences were becoming less loyal to streaming platforms and commissioners had had their budgets cut. Rob's most recent pitch, about the inside world of influencers and their relationships with fashion brands, had failed to make it past the development stage because of the extortionate fees the influencers required to consider taking part in it – they could simply upload a sponsored image of themselves relaxing in their garden sporting some new sunglasses for ten times the money Serious Global could offer.

It meant that, as a stop gap, Rob had been seconded to a less senior role assisting the production of the long-running daytime reality show called *Bag a Bargain*. The problem was that the show was currently in the middle of a media storm following the dismissal of one of its lead presenters, whose extra-marital relationship with a much younger colleague had recently been revealed via a photo sent to *The Sun*, thus making front-page news across three continents. To be fair, 'Bag Another Woman' made a really good headline. It didn't help that said presenter was also one of the stakeholders in Serious Global.

None of this looked particularly great on Rob's CV, so he had taken a pause on applying for other roles while this played out. Unsurprisingly, it was getting him down.

'Did you get a chance to chat to Rory about your work last night?' I asked, feeling glad to have a level of food in my stomach that made me feel human again.

'Not really, Rory seemed too preoccupied with his own work dilemma,' Rob replied.

'Oh, really?'

'Yeah, it sounds like your sis has designs on taking over the PR world, so Rory may look at reducing his days when the baby comes.' He paused. 'You Greens are strong women.' He looked across to me, his green eyes shining, yet I couldn't quite work out whether it was in awe or contempt. He was hungover, so I decided to give him the benefit of the doubt.

On a practical level, I hoped that my news about the bonus might cheer him up. 'Anyway, The Divorcee had Girl Friday over last night,' Rob offered between mouthfuls of food. 'You slept through it.'

'And did they get to fourth base?'

'Yes, twice, they kept me awake.'

Damian, known affectionately to us as The Divorcee, lived in the flat above ours, and the paper-thin ceiling did nothing to muffle the sounds of him having sex with his girlfriend, whom we nicknamed Girl Friday, because we had worked out they had an arrangement, whereby she – presumably also divorced with children – came to stay over every other Friday, the weekends when they were both child-free. And they always had sex, loudly, several times that Friday night or Saturday morning.

Rob and I probably knew their habits between the sheets better than they did.

'They were out until late last night,' Rob said. 'I vaguely recall having a chat with them in the corridor at about one a.m. I think I might have invited them in for some pasta and a nightcap.' He cringed. 'Thankfully they didn't take me up on it.'

This was typical Rob, he was definitely the friendliest drunk you could hope to bump into, on the rare Friday evenings when his alcohol intake was higher than mine.

'Excuse me!' I exclaimed. 'You actually *saw* Girl Friday? This is major!' Over the past six months that we had heard the shagging, we jokingly questioned whether she actually existed, because neither of us had witnessed her enter or leave the flat. All we had ever heard was the screaming noise she made at orgasm and the howl he returned shortly after. 'I don't think I could look her in the eye,' I continued, 'so . . .?'

'She seemed nice.'

'Oh, come on, Robert, you can do better than that,' I teased. 'Name, looks, hair colour, approximate age – do you remember *any* details?'

'Afraid not, I was drunk. Anyway, stop interrogating me, my eyeballs hurt. Tell me more about Mandy.'

'She was nice actually, and I met the rest of the team.' I talked Rob through my first impressions of Blair, Lola, Jimi, and Coco, my comrades for the next three months.

Nursing a mug of tea, I spent the afternoon carefully reading through the contract from Julie-Ann. In signing it I was also relinquishing my right to withhold any video or social media content that included me, my image, voice, or actions, if it was taken during the filming schedule at the house. And although I wasn't expected to play a major part in any filming, it clearly stipulated that I needed to sign the accompanying release to waive all of my rights.

It's standard, Julie-Ann had assured me in the covering note.

'They are suggesting you might be required to make appearances. How do you feel about that?' asked Rob.

'I'm there to do the styling job, and my life is infinitely less exciting than Mandy's so, let's face it, I don't think I have much to be worried about,' I replied.

There was also a clause about travel and the strong possibility I was required to accompany Mandy on a transatlantic trip during the coming months. It all sounded very exciting.

By mid-afternoon, I was glued to Instagram as paparazzi images of Mandy arriving and departing from the lunch emerged. There was a video of her walking up some steps to the venue – Annabel's private members club on Berkeley Square – shimmering in the flashbulbs like an aquatic goddess. Yes, she looked classy instead of brassy – less Florida and more Mayfair.

Mission one: accomplished.

I couldn't resist uploading a photo of her onto my own Instagram page with the caption: *Did some styling today. Meet mermaid Mandy. Thank you, Pronovias!*

And a blue heart and mermaid emoji.

Rob and I watched the film *Before Sunrise* that evening, after I was flabbergasted to discover he had never seen it. We curled up on the sofa together and I thought how much I would miss him during the weeks when I would be away.

'Does this mean I'll be your Girl Friday when I get back?' I teased, as we both put the date I would be returning home into our calendars. I nuzzled my nose into his neck and peppered it with kisses.

'You're my Girl *Every Day*,' he replied, pulling me in close for a proper kiss.

I felt content and thought about how some of the best moments between the two of us were the most simple; the inconsequential cuddles on the sofa, or when he came through the door after work, or the lazy Saturdays pottering around. His fry-ups. The slow snogs. Those were the things I was going to miss the most.

The next morning, an enormous box of flowers arrived at the front door from Pronovias. The publicity team had clearly seen the benefit of the gown being worn by Mandy, rather than my sister. They even said they were happy for Mandy to keep it if she wanted and would honour the cost so Lucy could come back and choose something else for her wedding day. I told them both the good news over WhatsApp. Mandy replied with a page of mermaid and fish emojis. And Lucy simply with the words, *Great. You're the best MOH. Will look online when I get a chance.*

I took this as a win from them both.

As the column inches on news websites and social media likes for Mandy's mermaid look stacked up, I witnessed first-hand the power that being a stylist to a superstar like Mandy could command. Some of my fashion contacts reconnected, commenting under the image that it was great to see me styling again; DMs from friends popped up on Instagram. Even my model-stroke-actress friend Poppy Dunn got back in touch, and I hadn't heard a thing from her since New York. *I'm so glad you're styling Mandy!!! Isn't she Ah-Mazing??? We must meet up when I'm next in London!!*

Vicky sent a voice note to tell me I was the bomb and that Mandy's look had made the Star Tracks spot on *People* magazine's home page in the US. I was buzzing.

Back on Planet Normal, Rob and I spent Sunday morning doing laundry, cleaning, and tidying our flat. With the Pronovias flowers arranged into three vases and dispersed around the rooms, it looked and smelt lovely. It restored a sense of calm to both of us and we were able to have a very adult conversation about how he would try to retain this sense of order at home going forward. Fortunately, this conversation was weighted in my favour, as I wouldn't be there for most of the time. Then I started to do some packing, but we didn't want to waste the whole of our last day together, so we decided to go for a walk around Portobello Road and have a beer at the Gold.

'Let's talk about our first impressions of each other,' I said when we were comfortably seated. 'You know, just like I asked you what your first impression of Girl Friday was, I'm wondering how you might have described me.'

He looked at me thoughtfully, his watchful green eyes scanning my face affectionately.

I took a sip from my bottle of Corona and waited a few seconds, as he considered what to say.

'You're taking too long!' I declared. 'Okay, I'll go first. I thought you really fancied yourself.'

Rob laughed so hard he spat out some of his beer.

'Fancied myself! *Really?*' He snorted in disbelief, still laughing as he mopped up the spillage from his chin with a napkin.

'Really.' I cast him a sideways look.

'Was that because you fancied me?'

'Of course not!' I giggled mischievously. 'But I do now. I mean the way you dribbled just then, it was *sooo* sexy.'

'Now you're being rude.' He laughed. 'You told me you gave me the nickname Handsome Rob – where did that come from then, hey?' He dug his index finger into my ribs. 'You fancied me straight away. Admit it.'

We both knew he was right. Rob's boyish good looks, dark denim and white T-shirt combos had caught my eye immediately, leading to the cheeky moniker I had given him when we first started working together.

'It wasn't just superficial though. I thought you were going places.' I smiled. 'I was impressed by your drive. You knew so clearly that you wanted to be a director, and you were going to achieve that. You had no doubts. It was attractive.' I paused. 'And I fancied your arms.'

He grinned. 'Just my arms?' A muscle on his forearm twitched beneath his jumper.

His eyes glistened, just like they had done when I first laid my eyes on him in Smith's boutique, where I honestly thought it was love at first sight for me. 'You do have great arms,' I said. 'And when I first saw you, I thought *I fancy him*. I still do.'

'But that ambition and drive,' he said, earnestly, 'do I still have that?' He bowed his head.

I cupped my hand around the side of his face and pulled him a little closer to me. 'What do you mean by that?'

'I mean that I'm not going places anymore, am I? And I'm not sure how to get that drive back.'

'If you're talking about your job at the moment,' I said, 'what's happened with the show really sucks. But it's not your fault, and nor does it define you, or your career, in any way.'

'But it's not very attractive,' he muttered.

'Rob, we're well past the first impressions stage now.'

'I know. I'm sorry, I just feel a bit shit about my life at the moment,' he said forlornly, moving a stray piece of hair away from my face.

'I know how it feels. Just last week I was feeling the same about Selfridges, but things can change so quickly. Try to keep positive.'

'I'm so pleased for you, baby. This opportunity, it's great for you.'

'Thank you,' I said, looking him square in the eyes. 'But remember, a job isn't your whole life. And one thing I have learnt is that nobody has it completely worked out all the time. Especially not me. How could I ask that of you? I never would.'

He smiled again. 'You're special Amber Green. I'm a lucky man.'

'I'm the lucky one,' I said, squeezing his arm. 'Now. It's time to maximise the remaining few hours we have left. So, let's do something that is guaranteed to make us feel really, *really* good.' I smiled at him.

'Go back to bed?' he asked wickedly.

'Buy two tubs of ice cream, eat them on the sofa, and get an early night.'

'Rock and roll,' he purred. We took the last sip of our beers. 'That sounds perfect.'

CHAPTER SEVEN

WEEK ONE

The next morning, we made a coffee each for the car, and Rob and I set off to drop me at Mandy's Surrey Hills mansion. Thirty miles down the A3 motorway from London, it took just over an hour, a journey little more than it could sometimes take to get across London on public transport. This made it easier to cope with, we thought, it wasn't too far.

It was a gloomy day and it rained non-stop as we drove slowly down a long lane, flanked by elegant old sycamore trees. The house stood back from the road, and a wooden sign stuck into the ground, which said 'Gables Manor', informed us that we were in the right place.

There were tall hedges all around the front façade, obscuring the building from immediate view. High wooden gates and fencing around the front gave it an unwelcoming impression – it seemed the kind of house that would keep people out rather than invite them in.

Rob pulled over in front of the gates to drop me off, as instructed.

'So, this is it,' he said, as he turned off the engine.

I swallowed a lump in my throat.

'You got this,' he added, sensing my nervousness about what I was walking into.

I opened the car door and battled to open my umbrella before it ruined my hair, which I had carefully straightened this morning. Rob popped the boot and dashed around the side of the car to lift out my heavy case, which he did in silence.

I turned to look at him and felt swamped with emotion.

'I love you,' I said, fighting back a few tears which had unexpectedly sprung into my eyes.

'I love you too.' He looked at me affectionately.

'Remind me – what am I doing here?' I asked.

'What you do best,' he said fondly.

'Don't forget to call me,' I muttered, as he walked around the car to get back in.

These words were to replay in my mind.

I pressed the entrance buzzer and, on instruction, said my name into a computer. The gates clicked into action, opening silently and smoothly to reveal a long gravel drive with manicured hedges in the shape of orbs on either side. It looked as though Edward Scissorhands had been at work. At the end of the driveway stood a magnificent Georgian manor house, the honey-coloured stone façade partially covered by creeping ivy yet failing to disguise a stately, symmetrical design, with at least ten windows on each floor. It was grand and impressive, just like its wealthy inhabitants. If it wasn't for the rain, we could easily be in the Hollywood Hills, rather than the Surrey Hills, and I guessed that could be the reason Mandy had chosen this piece of suburban real estate as her English home. Palatial, it most definitely was.

My case crunched over the gravel driveway, signalling my arrival at the central portico, which was supported by two stone columns. Above it, a pediment adorned with intricate carvings framed the entrance. I could just about make out a family crest – a lion and laurel wreath – etched into the stone lintel, having survived a pounding from the British weather over the decades it had proudly stood there. I wondered who the original family were.

The heavy wooden doors opened, and a tall older woman appeared in the doorway. She was wearing jodhpur-style trousers and a waxed jacket. Her greying hair was pulled back into a bun, her smile warm yet no-nonsense. A pair of spectacles hung from a gold chain around her neck.

'You must be Amber Green,' she said. 'We've been expecting you. Welcome to Gables Manor. I'm Philippa, the housekeeper.'

'Great to meet you.' I held out my hand, before retracting it when she wasn't forthcoming about taking it. 'I'm Mandy's stylist.'

'Hair, nails, clothes, topiary, interiors?' she asked wearily. 'We've had all kinds of stylists here.'

'Oh, definitely clothes – as far as I'm aware. I wouldn't dare go near those beautiful hedges.' I glanced over my shoulder. 'I'm taking care of Mandy's wardrobe.'

'Good for you.' Philippa had a way about her that made me think she probably knew her way around a gun. 'We all need clothes.'

Her unimpressed expression suggested that it was difficult for Philippa to comprehend why a celebrity needed all of these people just to exist. She struck me as the self-sufficient type.

'Is that everything?' She looked down at my case.

'Yes, most of the clothes for Mandy will be arriving over the coming days by courier.'

She tutted. 'Not very energy efficient.'

'Actually, sustainability is really important to me – we'll be borrowing vintage pieces wherever possible and sharing courier drops,' I said cheerily. Philippa wasn't going to break my spirit in the first five minutes.

She frowned. 'I'll take you to your quarters.'

Quarters sounded promising.

I was ushered inside the cavernous entrance hall, which smelt of beeswax polish and aged oak. There was wooden panelling on every wall and an impressive, sweeping central staircase in front of us, its balustrade intricately adorned with carvings. A crystal chandelier hung from the ceiling, above a large, faded red Persian rug on which stood a polished round Baroque-style mahogany table, with thick books arranged neatly in a pile on top. The glass facets from the chandelier caught the light, making the whole space look dappled and far prettier in real life than you would be able to capture in a photo. It was like stepping back in time into the kind of country home you'd expect a lord and lady to reside in – not an American reality star. Through a doorway to my left I caught a glimpse of an expansive lounge, with three wide cream sofas arranged around a large stone fireplace, where an open fire crackled gently behind an ornate fireguard, an array of shiny gold pokers on a stand

sat on the right-hand side of the hearth. There was a grand
piano in one corner and on the walls hung a blend of classic
and contemporary artworks depicting English country life
and portraits of stern-faced noble gentry who could well
have been previous inhabitants of this home.

In an alcove in the hallway, a pair of Ray-Bans and a
Prada baseball cap perched atop a white marble bust, the
modern touches at odds with the tradition of the home.
Philippa tutted loudly as we passed it, but I enjoyed this
cheeky detail, amongst the stiff order of a home clearly kept
in tight check, it showed someone around here had a sense
of humour. I wondered who put them there.

Instead of ascending the stairs, Philippa led me through
a thick wooden doorway at the end of the hallway, which
housed a boot room with a cool flagstone floor, olive green
tongue-and-groove panelling, and a long wooden bench
seat under which stood enough pairs of green Le Chameau
wellies to kit out the entire royal family. This room looked
to have been renovated more recently, and I admired a
newly upholstered bench seat in soft green velvet and how
it contrasted beautifully with antique embroidery on two
scatter cushions – a skilled layering of texture created by
someone with a fantastic eye for design.

We were then out of a backdoor and walking across a
small courtyard with a gravel path through the centre, to
the left of which was a stable building, and to the right, a
converted barn. Statues of nymphs peeked from behind a
hedgerow ahead of us, their weathered features adding to
the history of the house.

'The gym is in the old stable,' Philippa said, pointing it out. 'Staff quarters are in the barn. The family and two assistants are staying in the main house.'

I wondered what she meant by family. 'You mean Mandy and Jose?' I clarified.

'Mmm-hmm, plus her brother-in-law, Jimi, and executive assistant, Blair. I suppose you've met Jimi already?' she said, a note of disapproval in her tone.

I nodded in reply.

'As you can tell, the owners are meticulous about the details of this house.' She turned the handle on a freshly painted stable door. 'We try to keep it that way. Renters need to follow the rules in here.' She tapped on a lever-arch file on a wide windowsill inside the barn. 'The annexe is a more recent addition, and it's curated to perfection. Everything is itemised.'

She turned to me as she made that comment, to check I had taken note.

Is Philippa thinking I might steal something?

Philippa led the way into a tastefully decorated, light and airy, vaulted open-plan kitchen and living area with exposed oak beams. The style was more modern in the annexe compared with the main house, yet there was still an undeniable touch of chintz with a fleur-de-lis pattern on curtains and carried onto the heavy window pelmets, which hung boldly around the windows, at contrast with the modern, muted, earthy palette of the overall scheme.

'There are two bedrooms here, for you and Coco. She's already in the main kitchen preparing lunch. If you look out of that window, you'll see across to the gym – it looks out onto the formal gardens and hidden rose arbour – not that anything is in bloom at this time of year, it all looks rather sad. There's a games room in there too, if you get any time off.'

'It's beautiful,' I said in awe.

We both glanced up as the door handle turned.

'Welcome, Amber!' It was Blair, smiling warmly. 'I hope you like your digs. There are clothes rails and a full-length mirror arriving from Amazon later today, so you can set up a dressing area over here too. We're going to have a group meeting at two p.m. See you in the drawing room.'

'I'll be there,' I replied.

'I was just showing Amber her sleeping quarters,' Philippa interrupted, keen to get on with completing the tour. She opened one of two doors leading off the living area. Inside was a medium-sized bedroom with a queen bed, a fabric canopy above it, which carried through the fleur-de-lis theme. Four framed prints of botanical drawings hung in a row on the wall. And down one side, a decorative panel depicted a library with shelves stacked with books. 'Don't be deceived,' Philippa said, 'behind this is your bathroom.' And she pushed one of the shelves to reveal a tiny en suite.

Philippa peered out of the window. 'I'm sure the chickens will be your natural alarm clock.' Her eyes crinkled at the corners. 'They live at the back of the annexe. We never run out of eggs. Please don't be tempted to feed them, the gardener will take care of that. That's about everything. I'll leave you to get yourself sorted, lunch will be available in the kitchen from one p.m. – it's in the basement beneath the lounge – and see you at the two o'clock meeting.'

I'd effectively been handed the keys to a gilded life.

That afternoon, we all gathered in the drawing room of the main house. There was a flurry of comments about how beautiful our surroundings were, as we each took in the generous proportions of the room and marvelled at the embroidered lampshades atop polished side tables and traditional parquet flooring with soft rugs layered on top.

The atmosphere was full of excitement, with everyone talking over one another. All of us eager to please, to be heard, to feel valued by the superstar who had chosen us to be here. As I looked around me, I felt an uncomfortable stab of imposter syndrome; that there must have been some mistake in Mandy's hiring of me – perhaps she had got the impression I was better than I really was? I focused on my breath to ground myself.

You've got this, Amber Green. You can do it.

Wearing a loose-fitting cream linen shirt, cream track pants which looked like pure cashmere and her feet encased in cream Uggs, Mandy took control of the proceedings.

'To break the ice, I'd like to invite you all to take part in a little group ceremony,' she said. 'To commit to each other, so we set ourselves up for success as a group. Whilst we live in this house together, we are a family.' I looked around the room at my new 'family', and noticed that Jimi was now wearing the Prada baseball cap which had been on the bust in the hallway. 'We'll do our ceremony first, and then Jose will do some strength work.'

Jimi gave a little cough, thinking strength work was surely the personal trainer's area.

'Oh,' said Mandy with a chuckle, 'don't worry, Jimi – no weights needed, we're talking personality strengths. It's a fun way to get to know each other.'

Jimi was sitting on the floor, close to the fire, his legs were outstretched and when he leant back on his propped hands the bicep muscles twitched on his brown arms. It was hard not to acknowledge how good-looking he was every time he appeared.

I didn't turn my head, but I was always aware of him in my peripheral vision. When he lifted his baseball cap to scratch his curly hair beneath it, when he twisted the lid off a bottle of water and brought it to his lips, when he laughed at something someone said.

Philippa spoke from the corner of the room closest to the door. I hadn't immediately noticed her join us. 'This "ceremony",' she uttered, using her fingers to illustrate the inverted commas – she looked antsy, as though she would rather be anywhere but here – 'is that an invitation or—'

Jose interrupted her. 'It's not an invite you can turn down, if that's what you mean, it's mandatory for Mandy's team, and we consider you a part of it, Philippa.'

That told her. I got the impression Philippa was the kind of person who was comfortable with minimal conversation. The polar opposite of Mandy, who, by nature, was a fan of her own voice.

'It's painless,' Mandy added abruptly. 'We'll go around the room, and everyone has to say what they expect from the others. We will all say "I will" afterwards, and that's our binding contract to one another. It's a really beautiful thing.' At which point she and Jose exchanged an affectionate smile.

Jose added, 'Mandy and I expect commitment from everyone involved in our world. Would you like to go first, Philippa?'

Philippa pursed her lips. It was as though she'd been rudely ejected from her comfort zone with no way back. I'd bet internally she was cursing this LA-type who had invaded her British historic home with her crazy celebrity ceremonies.

'Right-o,' Philippa spoke reluctantly. 'I expect everyone to keep their quarters clean and tidy. And please try to keep noise to a minimum after ten p.m. That's it.'

'Fantastic!' Mandy replied warmly, before staring right into Philippa's steely, pale blue eyes, and stating firmly, 'I will.'

After a moment of silence, Blair then repeated 'I will', and one by one, we followed suit.

'Thank you, Philippa. Now, Coco?'

'I would like to request that we collectively agree to make healthy choices in this house, to remove temptation and commit to following my menus, which I will send around at the start of each week. Please let me know privately if you have any allergies, intolerances, or anything else I need to be aware of that might affect your ability to partake in my healthy-eating regimen. I can assure you it will be well-balanced and satisfying.'

'Easier said than done, when the nutritionist's name makes you think of chocolate!' guffawed Jimi. This time I turned to look at him, stifling a grin myself.

'Good point, well made,' Coco responded quickly, suggesting she had dealt with this comment before. 'Actually, cocoa itself isn't the bad guy. Unprocessed cocoa is rich in polyphenols, which have significant health benefits, including an ability to reduce inflammation and improve cholesterol levels. It can also be helpful for blood sugar and weight control. It's the processed stuff you have to watch, so, in my recipes, I always use a non-alkalised cocoa powder – I make a mean vegan chocolate mousse as it happens. And I do make an allowance for chocolate at times – it will be dark and a minimum seventy per cent cocoa. As with everything, it's all about balance and moderation. Does that answer your question?' Jimi gave her a thumbs-up and a wry smile.

Mandy looked impressed as Coco continued, 'I want you all to feel amazing from the inside-out, so whether or not you like my suggestions, I will keep your nutritional needs in check. So, can we all contract to eating healthily and removing temptation?'

'I will,' said Mandy and we all chorused after her. 'I will.'

Jimi went next, asking for our commitment to partaking in social media shoots with enthusiasm as required, and imbedding a solid fitness routine as part of our daily life, followed by some motivational words on enjoying exercise because it takes very little willpower to do something you enjoy.

Then it was my turn. I felt nervous as all eyes fell on me expectantly.

'Your clothes tell your story,' I began, 'they represent a powerful way to let the world know who you are and what you have to contribute. Fashion helps you to grow, to fall in love, to get through challenging times and, most importantly, find joy.' I paused, scanning the room to take in their reactions. Philippa looked confused, but, if I wasn't mistaken, Blair's eyes had moistened, and Mandy looked as if she was concentrating on what I was saying. 'All I ask for,' I continued, 'is your complete authenticity in working with me as the stylist. Fabulous clothes only do half the job you see – it's what's underneath that enables you to own them.'

This was directed at Mandy who, as far as I was aware, was my only client within the house.

'But what about glamour and grabbing attention – I thought that was the point of fashion?' asked Mandy.

I nodded gravely. 'That's valid,' I said, buying myself a small window to think. 'Fashion can be about fantasy, of course, but you and I need to work closely to decide how much of yourself you are ready to reveal. I don't mean literally, of course, I mean on a deeper level. The tide has turned, audiences connect when someone is truly themselves. Fashion is not just about wearing an amazing dress – it's about making the dress come alive because *you* are embodying it. So, the question is, are you ready to be the real you, Mandy?'

'Oh, I'm real, all right. Well, except for my boobs and filler, all the rest is a hundred per cent Mandy y'all,' she drawled. Sometimes she seemed to play up her southern Florida accent. 'I'm ready!' she squealed. 'And we can filter the shit out of anything afterwards, anyway!'

Philippa flashed me a crooked smile.

Mandy's last comment frustrated me – it also belittled my skills as a stylist. She seemed to read my mind. 'You okay, doll?'

'I'm afraid I'm not a fan of filters or manipulation,' I said, surprising myself by how forthright I was. 'I mean, there's influencing, and then there's being a bad influence. For what it's worth, I don't think you need any manipulation. You should be proud of the real you. And I think you have so much more to give, Mandy.'

Jimi made a slow clapping sound.

'Amber's nailed it,' he said, 'that's what the Brits want, Mands. Truth, authenticity, and realness all the way.' He put his hand on his heart as if swearing an allegiance to my proposal.

Is he ridiculing me or being supportive?

'So can we all commit to supporting Mandy in this process?' I asked.

'I will,' they each replied. All except for Mandy.

'Jury's out on this one,' she muttered, perhaps regretting her own ceremony. 'I thought I'd hired a stylist, not a therapist.'

I bowed my head. *Me and my big mouth. Maybe I should have kept quiet.*

Yet I knew I was right; I stood by my words. I wondered why Mandy was finding this hard. Or if she understood what it meant to be truly herself. I imagined this might be my greatest challenge in styling her. If she was to connect with a British audience, it was time to shed the filters and manipulation of images. That kind of gloss wouldn't wash on cynical Brits, and besides, that look was well past its sell-by date. It was time to unveil the real Mandy, the woman beneath the public persona, in a way that was honest and true.

'I'm sure we can find a way to work in your cowboy boots though,' I added, to soften the blow. She flicked me a cool half-smile in return.

Philippa muttered something about getting more wood for the fire and left the room. A cynic might say this whole exercise was a subtle way for the couple to communicate how Mandy wanted things to go in the house.

I looked at her, sat close to the roaring fire, her eyes reflecting its flicker. Things didn't seem to be going very well between us so far.

As if reading my mind, Mandy turned to me. 'Don't look so nervous, baby girl.' She tilted her head. 'It's only a bit of fun. I'm sure we're all going to get along fine.'

Alone in my bedroom a few evenings later, I watched raindrops slide down the window. I had been drenched each of the several times I dashed across the courtyard between the annexe and the main house. I would have to find a place to store Mandy's clothes nearer to her, as I couldn't be getting them wet, or risk dropping something in a muddy puddle each time I needed to prepare an outfit, if the weather continued like this. Outside the air smelt of damp earth and crushed herbs. I stopped for a moment to breathe it in.

The first few nights I missed Rob like crazy. Though we had a romantic phone call, it wasn't the same as falling asleep with his heavy arm across my middle. The arm that I felt sure would hold me in the night forever. I had really begun to imagine my whole life would have Rob in it. Yet despite the fact I was living in a house full of people, I felt alone when I finished work and a persistent feeling of not fitting in with the 'family' – a sentiment which had dogged me for most of my life thus far reared its head.

On the third evening, I distracted myself by taking a bath and sat on my bed scrolling through the camera roll on my phone. I found myself revisiting photos of Rob and me from the eighteen months we'd been dating. Aside from the ones of the two of us at the top of the Empire State Building, where he asked me to officially move in with him when we got back to London, the ones that made me pause the most were the insignificant moments, the candid snaps where one of us was caught looking tenderly at the other, just before we realised an image was being taken. The selfie outtakes and the shots I sometimes stole of him when he wasn't aware. The simple, everyday times that were not perfect enough to make it onto an Instagram square, but reflected who we were as two individuals who had joined together to make a couple.

I moved slowly through images of Christmas Day – December had marked the first Christmas we spent together, staying with my parents from Christmas Eve until Boxing Day. Rob's face lit up in one photo as he opened my gift to him – tickets to a music festival we planned to go to over the summer; me smiling as I opened his gift to me – a necklace with our initials on it; a selfie in front of the fire as we watched *The Holiday*. And then my gaze hovered on an image I hadn't paid any attention to before. It was of Rob looking intently at his phone. It must have been taken when Nora kidnapped my phone, because it was just before a string of close-up images of the back of my hair, which she had been plaiting on Boxing Day afternoon. I didn't remember seeing this photo at the time, but now it caught my attention because of the serious look on Rob's face. I zoomed in, curious to know what he was looking at on his phone that could have triggered such a reaction. It looked like Facebook Messenger was open, and I zoomed in as far as the phone would allow and could make out that the person he was messaging had a first name beginning with E and the surname an F. There was a lot of writing on the page, which indicated a number of messages back and forth. I felt a warming sensation in my face. A quick investigation revealed the slightly blurred image next to it wasn't any old E. F. It was Rob's ex-girlfriend, Emily Furlow. His ex-fiancée to be precise, the ex with whom he had a pregnancy scare when we were in LA, before the two of us got together.

I could vividly remember the sick feeling in the pit of my stomach when we were walking together at Runyon Canyon, when Rob told me the news that his then girlfriend might be pregnant. Every word he said cut me deeper as I realised the intensity of my feelings towards him. Rob had no idea how hard it was for me to hear about Emily at the time, because he just saw me as a mate. He learnt later, when it became impossible to hide my massive crush on him, but I could easily remember the moments back then when I physically ached for him to feel the same way about me as he did about her. It had been the biggest turnaround in events when it transpired that Emily wasn't pregnant, and Rob eventually called off their engagement. It turned out he had feelings for me too. It was a dream come true – our story could have been so different, and I was fully aware of the small miracle that had occurred when we fell in love with each other.

But the photo? Rob had told me recently that he had had no contact with Emily since the day they broke up. He said it was better that way as there was nothing more to say to each other. So why would there be so many words between them, right there, open on the screen? I suddenly felt so distant from him, thinking that he was messaging with her on Boxing Day. *Of all days, a day when you're meant to be with the ones you love.* I felt an uncomfortable insecurity about our whole relationship, knowing Rob was capable of lying to me. It was quite incredible how one person could make the entire world feel full one minute, and then completely empty the next.

CHAPTER EIGHT

Over the first week at work, my focus was on calling in a host of outfits for the various appointments Mandy had, plus an at-home photoshoot, organised by Jimi, to generate some content to introduce Mandy to her new British audience. With Jimi's input, I took my style inspiration from the Princess of Wales off-duty, calling in home-grown designer brands, and mixing-in high-street staples, to show Mandy adapting her wardrobe to suit the British countryside.

Deliveries arrived at the front door in a steady stream. There were Barbour jackets, Paul Smith suits, Penelope Chilvers boots, LK Bennett wedges, and soft cashmere turtlenecks to be worn with jeans, of which I had all the hottest brands. I mixed this in with silk shirts and pleated midi skirts for a look that was relaxed and timeless – less fuss, more function.

'Seriously?' Philippa tutted, as she arrived at the annexe, her arms straining under the weight of yet more dress carriers and a big bag containing three more pairs of shoes. 'Anyone would think you are dressing the entire cast of a West End show. How many outfits does one person need for one photoshoot?'

'I know.' I sighed. 'It seemed like madness to me too the first time I was on a celebrity photoshoot, but believe me – and as *everyone* else in this house will testify – you can't have enough choice.'

'But how much is *enough*?' she asked, disparagingly.

'Well.' I paused for a moment, considering how it was going to go down when I told Philippa that the rails were not even halfway full yet. 'I always have four options for each set-up, and we have at least five set-ups to get through tomorrow. The photographer and Julie-Ann will have the final say, along with Mandy. And you can bet she'll go for the one that I didn't have quite the right shoes for, or she'll need it in the next size, so I need to have all bases covered. So that's twenty looks. Minimum.'

'She's only got one pair of feet though,' Philippa quipped. 'It's another world, honestly. Hardy Amies used to visit this house, you know. He will be turning in his grave. He never went this overboard with the late Queen. And she was *The Queen*.'

'In some circles, Mandy's a Queen too,' I replied, feeling protective of my art. Philippa had already started scuttling off because the doorbell had gone again. 'At least you won't need to hit the gym tomorrow!' I called after her.

On the seventh morning, I woke early and FaceTimed Rob. 'You're up early,' he said woozily, his voice still gruff from sleep.

'Same to you,' I said. 'I thought we could wake up together.'

'Well, that's nice, I just wish you were actually beside me. Close enough for me to smell your bad morning breath.'

'Charming!' I giggled. 'You're one to talk.'

'Shall we start again?'

I took a deep breath and put on a sultry voice: 'Good morning, my handsome boyfriend. I thought we could wake up together.'

'Oh, hello, my beautiful, clever, sexy girlfriend, with breath like extra strong mints.' He smiled broadly, with a dimple appearing on his left cheek.

I loved the sleepy smile and sound of Rob's voice when he first woke up. But there was a tightness in my chest which was hard to shake ever since I had seen the photo on my phone. The thought of Emily also loving this smile – even worse, having *kissed* it – made me feel as though someone had just taken my favourite childhood toy and stamped on it.

'How did you sleep?' I asked.

'Terribly,' he croaked.

'What was up?'

'I've been worrying about work. Things are not picking up on the production side and I don't think I can stand the monotony of my current role anymore. I need to get out of Serious Global. It's making me seriously depressed.'

'Oh honey, I'm sorry,' I said tenderly. 'That's a rubbish night. I wish I was there to help make you feel better. Might any new opportunities come up?'

'Not at the moment, television is in crisis – networks are cutting back on new productions and there aren't enough jobs to go around.'

'What could you do to cheer yourself up?' I sighed.

'I don't know. I'll hit the gym later I guess,' he said.

'I wish I could bring you a cup of tea. What else are you going to do?'

He shrugged. This was unlike Rob, he was usually quick to find a positive in most situations.

'Could you call up an old friend?' I offered, thinking about what I would do in his situation. 'Make a plan to meet someone for a drink or dinner after work one evening this week?'

'Like who?' he asked. 'I've been rubbish at keeping the connection going with my uni friends. That's what shacking up with the love of your life and moving to another continent will do to your social life.'

I knew he meant it jokingly, but there was a strong element of truth in what he was saying. We had both been neglectful of our former friendship circles since getting serious about each other. Yet whilst I still had Vicky on speed dial and WhatsApp, the same couldn't be said of Rob. In fact, now that I thought about it, I struggled to remember the last time he had met up with someone other than a work colleague for an evening out.

As my mind ticked over, I couldn't shake a feeling pulling at my insides. I was itching for a confrontation, intentionally nudging the conversation in a certain direction.

'What about your brother?'

'Dan's away in the States with Florence at the moment.'

'What about *Emily Furlow*?' I said the words spontaneously, before thinking it through. They spilled out with more sarcasm than I intended.

There was a moment of deafening silence between us.

'Who?' he asked, after a pause.

I gulped down a large breath and stayed mute.

'Did you say Emily Furlow?' he asked. Rob was sitting upright now and his features had hardened. It made my heart race.

'I did. You know Emily, she's an old friend of yours?'

'She's my ex-girlfriend, Amber. You know that. Why would I want to get in touch with her?'

'Have you been in contact with her recently?' I asked, nervously, the momentousness of this question not lost on me.

A little crease appeared above his right eyebrow, as he tried to understand why I had brought up her name and what it meant. Neither of us were awake enough for this. I was half regretting it already.

Hopefully he'll prove me wrong. Come on, Rob. Prove me wrong.

'Why in the world would I want to message my ex-girlfriend?' he asked.

I swallowed hard. I hated any confrontation with him, even though I had asked for this.

'I was just wondering if you were still in touch,' I said, sticking to my guns.

If this was going to be *the* moment, I had to see it through. I felt my heart pound in my chest as I waited for Rob's response.

'I haven't spoken to her the whole time I've been with you, Amber,' he said defiantly. If I was a police officer questioning him, I would be convinced by this response.

But I know it's not true. I know they were messaging at Christmas because I saw them, clear as anything. Well, sort-of clear. As clear as a blurry zoomed-in phone image can be. Why won't he tell me?

'Anyway, why has this come up? Are you trying to suggest something?' His green eyes didn't look so warm now, as they searched my face for an explanation. I breathed deeply, trying to suppress the mild panic rising within.

'I just wondered,' I said calmly. I caught a glimpse of my alarm clock, and it was approaching eight. I needed to get out of bed and into my gym gear. I'd promised Jimi I'd meet him there at eight, to work out before Mandy did her nine a.m. session and I didn't want to be late. I bottled telling him about the photo. 'I'm sorry, I shouldn't have brought her up.'

I needed more time to think about my approach to what might be going on here. If Rob was lying to me – *which he is* – I needed to find out why, but now wasn't the moment.

'I'm confused about why you've asked me this,' he said.

'I'm really sorry,' I replied. 'I guess it's not seeing you every day, I got a bit jealous.'

'There's no need to be. There's only you, Amber. Shall we chat later?'

'I'll call you when I finish work,' I said.

I knew I had effectively thrown in a grenade and then retrieved it before it could explode, but it was still there, a ticking bomb in my pocket.

I texted Vicky: *I think Rob's having an affair.*

CHAPTER NINE

WEEK TWO

'Amber? Amber, can you hear me?' The voice was coming from above my head.

As Jimi leant in closer, I could feel his breath on my neck. I blinked.

'Are you okay?' he asked. 'Thank God. I thought you were completely out for a moment.'

I sat up onto my elbows and immediately felt a burning sensation on my upper lip. I moved my tongue to it and tasted blood. I put my hand to my face, to the source of the hot sensation, and when I moved it away there was fresh blood on my fingers, confirming my fear.

This feels bad. Really bad. 'What have I done?' I asked shakily, my eyes fixed on Jimi. 'It *really* hurts.'

'You slammed down a weighted ball and it bounced straight back up and whacked you in the mouth,' Jimi said, his concerned expression panicking me further. He even looked hot when panicked. 'You've got a fat lip.' He winced.

I moved my tongue upwards again. Things definitely felt bigger than normal up there. 'How bad does it look?' I asked, my eyes wide with fear. Jimi didn't say anything. 'Tell me, honestly – on a scale of one to ten?'

'Probably six?' he said in an airy tone that fooled neither of us. 'Make that nine. I'll grab you some ice.'

'It's stinging.' I cringed, my hand lifted to meet my lip again as a perfectly round drop of bright red blood landed on my leggings.

'I'm not surprised. You look like you've done a round with Anthony Joshua. You're lucky you didn't knock your front teeth out,' he called over his shoulder as he left the gym. 'I'll get a compress too. Philippa must have a first-aid kit in the house.'

I was still thinking about the call with Rob last week when I had reached for the medicine ball. I vaguely heard Jimi ask something about whether I had used this type of ball before, which I thought I had. I clearly didn't think about not slamming it down unless I was ready to catch it. The heavy ball had bounced straight back up and whacked me in the mouth at close range, throwing me backwards.

Amber, you clumsy fool.

I should have known better because I already knew that celebrity-style gyms didn't agree with me, following an unfortunate incident at Soul Cycle in New York last year. It involved me falling off a static bike and injuring myself midway through a class, because I was too busy trying to stalk the Victoria Beckham–lookalike on the station next to me, rather than listening to the litany of instructions and affirmations being shouted out by the instructor. Disappointingly, it turned out to be VB's doppelgänger, and I had the humiliation of being sent out of the class to sit in reception with a banging headache, a glass of water, and a badly bruised ego.

Today, I found myself in a similar predicament, having zoned out of listening to Jimi's commands, because the thought of Rob being in contact with Emily had filled me with a discombobulated feeling that no amount of weighted squats could shift. I hadn't felt this jealous since Vicky got the last pair of Chloé ankle boots in our size in the Outnet sale. And now my lip was throbbing too.

I had a visceral feeling that I wanted to cry, and I wanted Rob to comfort me.

A few minutes later Jimi returned with a champagne bucket filled with ice and a damp cloth.

'It's the best I can do.' He leant down and gently held the icy cloth against my lip. 'It's going to swell a bit and then I'm sure you'll have a nasty bruise. But you'll only look hideous for a day or so.'

'Thanks for letting me know,' I muttered.

'You're lucky it wasn't worse,' he said more sympathetically.

'What is Mandy going to say?' I winced, as the cold ice sent a shiver down my back. 'We're shooting today. This is a disaster. I'm such an idiot!'

'Idiot you might be, but your lip will heal. It won't look so bad once the swelling's gone down. Perhaps you can convince Mandy that purple's this season's lip colour?'

I smiled and then grimaced as my lips refused to do what they were supposed to.

'Wow – you really *are* Quasimodo.' Jimi pulled away from me jokingly.

'Stop it. I can't laugh, it hurts!'

'That's better. What was going on with you then? You seemed miles away.'

I slumped backwards to lean against the wall. I was feeling slightly lightheaded now too, I needed breakfast. Thinking about Rob again, the tightness returned, it felt as if something heavy was pressing down on me and I didn't have the energy to push it off.

'Oh, just boyfriend stuff,' I mumbled.

'Did he dump you?' Jimi asked. 'You really are having a bad morning.'

I wanted to laugh but didn't dare, for fear of ripping my lip open further.

'No, he didn't dump me,' I replied. 'Would you be a little more sympathetic if he had?' I was conscious of the fact that I was avoiding making eye contact, because he still looked like a model, and I was paranoid about the state of my face. 'We just had a misunderstanding about something on the phone this morning. We'll work it out.'

Then another face came into view behind Jimi.

'Oh my God, honey. Your face!' Coco didn't mince her words.

I pushed my hands against the floor and used the wall to steady myself as I stood up.

'I threw down a medicine ball and it bounced straight back up.' I winced, placing the ice back over my swollen top lip.

Coco gasped.

I gently dabbed the frosting of ice on my lip with a tissue. 'I mean, who's heard of a medicine ball that bounces?' I added, quietly pleased that there was something to blame, other than myself. 'It was the ten kg.'

'Ouch.' She made a face.

'Yes, ouch,' I repeated sarcastically. It was actually quite hard to speak.

Coco studied me. 'You look like you've had a lip job,' she said with concern, 'that went wrong.'

If I wasn't mistaken, her lip curled slightly with amusement. Instead of annoying me, it provided some reassurance that, if she was finding it funny, it couldn't be *that* bad. At least not in need of the hospital.

'Thanks. It feels like it too.' I pressed the pack onto my face again, to give myself some respite from the hot sensation of blood rushing to my lips. 'But how am I going to explain this to Mandy?'

Coco smiled. 'Tell her you went to Harley Street in the middle of the night to get your lips done, and it didn't agree with you?'

'Great idea, I'm sure she'll go for that,' I replied.

'Just tell her you got beaten up by a medicine ball?' Jimi offered. 'But not on my watch. I'm not sure my insurance would cover it.' He looked a little worried.

'Don't worry, I won't sue you,' I replied. 'I'm more concerned about the immediate future.'

'Come on,' said Coco, gesturing to the doorway. 'You'll survive, Amber, it's honestly not as bad as it probably feels right now. I came to tell you both that breakfast is ready. You'll feel better with something in you, and we can figure out a plan.'

'Morning, gang, what's on the breakfast menu?' Blair joined us in the large kitchen. 'Oh WOW. I didn't know Jocelyn Wildenstein was joining us for breakfast this morning,' they said, stunned. 'What happened, Amber?'

The bleeding had mercifully stopped now, but the fact my upper lip was twice the size of the lower wasn't something you could easily miss.

After we had eaten a breakfast of oats with turmeric, sultanas, psyllium husk, collagen, and hemp seeds – Coco blended mine so I could drink it through a straw – Blair nudged me. 'Come on, let's take a smoothie to Her Royal Highness. Lola will be here to do her make-up shortly, and Mandy needs something to wear to Harrods. The crew are coming to film.'

I followed them into the hallway and Blair noticed me stop in front of the large decorative mirror there, to peer at my lip.

'It honestly doesn't look *that* bad,' they said. 'I'm getting used to it. But if you're worried, why don't you accompany Mandy to her cryotherapy appointment? It will help bring down the swelling.'

I wondered what cryotherapy was. 'Does it actually make you cry?' I asked.

'No! It's basically a short stint in a giant freezer – for health benefits. Mandy uses it to "increase her metabolism", what she means is to lose weight. She *loves* going to it with someone new – and to be honest, I already feel like I'm walking on thin ice this morning because I've just had to tell her *HELLO!* magazine have passed on a photoshoot,' Blair said, looking down and quoting, '"We can see that Mandy has a big following in the US, but we're afraid she's not well-known enough over here to warrant a shoot at present. We would need a new 'hook' to consider it."

'*Not well-known enough*? That's four words Mandy hasn't heard in a very long time, and as for a *hook*, by that they mean personal news like a divorce or pregnancy. I daren't tell her that part,' Blair said.

'Did you try *OK!* magazine?' I asked.

'Are you joking?' Blair said, blanching. 'No global star would be in their pages. *HELLO!* will come crawling before long. We'll make sure of it. Anyway, she's been in a foul mood ever since. I call her Medusa when she's like this.' They waved their fingers above their head illustrating snakes.

'Don't make me laugh, it hurts.' I squirmed. 'Being in a freezer with Medusa doesn't sound like the most appealing way to spend an afternoon, but if you think it will help, at this point I'll try anything.' *How bad could it be?*

'Come on, let's get her ready for Harrods,' Blair said. 'I'll tip off a pap I know, so at least she'll get a column centimetre, if not an inch, going in.'

My dress code for Mandy about town was simple, effortless luxury – I had built her a staple collection of black, beige, and cream tank tops, matching cashmere, and white jeans, finished with fine gold jewellery. It was understated for a moment like this when she needed to look cool and chic when captured on camera as we entered Harrods. *Simple, huh?*

Except Mandy had other ideas, picking her most eye-catching bright yellow Prada handbag, and the silver Bottega Veneta mirrored knee-high boots currently trending on Vogue.com, to finish the look, commenting that she was looking for 'maximum eyeballs' during her visit to the upmarket shopping mecca.

It wasn't an outfit I would have put together myself, but I doubted anyone was sitting at home waiting to judge my styling today, so I decided it was best not to argue, and was thankful for the fact Mandy was so engrossed in prancing around the bedroom in the futuristic boots that she didn't notice I was sporting a pout to rival Victoria Beckham. This was one benefit of working with a star like Mandy – she didn't care about anyone else as much as herself.

With Mandy's outfit confirmed, I went back to my bedroom to quickly shower and get ready for the day. I opted for my staple uniform of black trousers, a grey Uniqlo roll neck and my trusty Veja pumps. On surveying my face in the mirror, thankfully I found that the ice had worked – my lip definitely wasn't getting any bigger, though it had started to turn purple. I rooted around in my make-up bag and found a deep-red Clarins lipstick which would help to blend it in. My skin felt tender as I applied it, but I nodded approvingly at my reflection. It was passable for a public outing.

I heard my phone buzz twice, the lip incident had at least taken my mind off Rob for two hours. I looked at the screen, hoping he might have messaged with some kind of explanation, but there was a WhatsApp from Vicky.

What makes you think he's having an affair?
　　Just heading out to Harrods with Mandy.
　　Chat later x
La-di-dar! I want your life.
　　You really don't. I've got a fat lip.

I sent her a quick selfie.

OMG! Have you had them done??
　　No! Accident with a medicine ball.
Sounds very Bridget Jones.
　　I feel very BJ.
Can't you orchestrate a trip to LA? I miss my best friend.
　　I'm on it. Got to dash – I'm doing Cryo.
I'm crying too! (laughing until crying emoji) Love ya xxx

After changing into swimming costumes, accessorised with a thermal headband to cover our ears, thick gloves, and some very unattractive socks, Mandy and I were ready to enter the Harrods cryo chamber. I hadn't anticipated Blair's phone would be trained on the two of us to record this moment and send to Jimi for Mandy's YouTube content, but there was nowhere to run. Mandy took my hand, turned to the phone, and screamed, 'It's time to freeze y'all! Let's do this!'

I tried to smile but my lip still ached when I did and I'm sure I looked more like a startled koi carp than a stylist about to enjoy a luxury wellbeing treatment. Mandy was in a really good mood having been snapped by two paparazzi photographers on the way in. As we weaved our way through the beauty counters, she instructed Blair to call the *Vogue* news desk and make them aware she was wearing limited edition Bottega Veneta boots.

We moved into a holding chamber first, which was cold enough, and then the door to the subzero room opened. It was like being instantly transported to the North Pole as the cold began to tingle and prickle my skin. When I breathed in, the air flowing into my lungs felt cool, but it was exhilarating and brought a clarity with it. *This might actually be okay.*

We could see the cryo therapist, Jody, through the glass panel across one side of the room. Then we heard her voice boom into the chamber, like the voice of God.

'Ground control to Major Tom!' she trilled. 'I'll be with you all the way, ladies. Mandy, I know you know what to expect, but Amber, it might feel a little strange at first as the low temperature stimulates nerve endings in your skin. Give me a thumbs-up if you know what I mean!'

With some uncertainty, feeling ridiculous, I raised both of my thumbs. Then I followed Mandy's lead, moving my body around through a mix of jogging on the spot, dancing, and waving our hands in the air to 'Don't Stop Me Now', which was being pumped out of the speakers loudly to try to distract us from the biting minus-ten degrees temperature.

'That's it, ladies – have a good dance, move your body, twist and shout – whatever it takes to pass the time!' Jody shrieked, seeming morbidly excited about watching us freeze to death. I felt like a deranged legs, bums, and tums teacher as I started to grapevine from side to side.

'She can't hear anything we say in here,' Mandy commented, now twisting on the spot, her hands moving in the opposite direction to her hips in short, sharp moves. She didn't seem to be experiencing the same numbness that was enveloping my body, as my blood tried desperately to protect its core temperature. I began rubbing my upper arms and the tops of my thighs in a pointless attempt to warm them up a bit. My flesh felt like bits of rubber.

Mandy took this moment to get something off her chest: 'Do you have a list, Amber?' she asked.

'A list?' I repeated. It was hard to focus on anything but my breath at this moment. Freddie Mercury sang, *'We're having such a good time, we're having a ball!'* but I could feel frost developing on my eyelashes.

'You know – a life list. Of things you want to achieve,' Mandy elaborated.

'A list? I don't think so,' I replied. 'But getting out of here would be top of it if I did. Do you?'

'Oh yes,' she replied, moving her arms and legs up and down in turn, like she was climbing an imaginary ladder. 'Why do you think I'm in here?'

'You're a sadist?' I shouted. It was becoming hard to speak as my face felt partially frozen.

'Can I trust you, Amber?' she asked.

'Of course.'

'I'm in here to kickstart my ovaries.' I looked at her puzzled. 'My list is simple,' she continued. 'One: get pregnant. Two: have a baby. I'm running out of time, biology is not on my side. I need a baby, Amber. My management wants one, Jose wants one, I want one, but it's the one thing I can't deliver.' She stopped and looked at me with a new intensity. I wondered for a moment if frostbite had set in. 'I need a baby to retain my fame,' she continued. 'No one wants a stagnant celebrity. I'm trying to shock my system into making one.' She paused to breathe in and out quickly. The cold was really uncomfortable now, and I feared that if I stopped moving for a second, I'd become a human ice sculpture. 'If I can't get pregnant, I'll settle for a baby any way I can. I'm desperate. Infertility is not fashionable, Amber.'

She shouted this statement even louder, over the sound of Freddie singing, '*Two hundred degrees, that's why they call me Mister Fahrenheit . . .*'

Is Jody having a laugh at our expense?

Outside the tank, on the warm side, Jody was jumping around too, in a show of solidarity. She waved her thumbs-up in the air, encouraging us to give her a sign back. As Blair held the phone up to the glass to capture us, I raised one thumb, indicating that I was still alive.

'Thirty seconds to go. You're doing amazing!' she informed us through the speaker.

The opening bars of 'Stayin' Alive' began to play. The temperature was biting now, and I had to focus hard on not letting my joints seize up. I kept my body and mind active by pointing my fingers and throwing some vigorous John Travolta–esque disco moves to the music, while I thought about what Mandy had told me. How could fertility be perceived as in or out of fashion? In my limited knowledge of fertility issues, I knew that having a baby generally wasn't related to keeping yourself in the news, as Blair had alluded to earlier. The desperation in Mandy's voice had been very clear, and I wondered about her motivation for telling me this personal information, in a place where she could be sure that no one else could hear. *What does she want me to do with this?*

I was midway through a jive routine when she spoke again. 'Tell no one about this, Amber,' she commanded. 'It's really important.'

'Of course,' I agreed. 'Promise.'

So now it wasn't just knowledge, but a secret – about one of the biggest stars in the world.

This was turning into the longest half a minute of my life.

Our eyes trained on Jody, and finally, we heard news we were waiting for. 'Ten seconds to go!' Jody announced, and both she and Blair held up both of their hands, plastic smiles spread across their faces, counting down the remaining time on their digits as Mandy and I found a reserve of energy and called out in unison, 'Eight, seven, six, five . . .'

Blair raised their phone again to capture our faces, barely able to smile back because our cheeks were so numb from the penetrating cold.

Jody was really enjoying this part. She was grinning broadly on the opposite side of the human freezer.

The second it was over, a siren sounded loudly and although I could barely feel them, my legs propelled me towards the exit at warp speed. Mandy flung open the first door into the adjoining chamber and then the second was opened by Jody. As we emerged, she handed us each a warm dressing gown, which we slung over our raw-cold bodies. I felt an adrenalin rush which I imagine is akin to what a marathon runner feels at the finish line. Relief swept over me, but I was still frozen to the bone, my teeth chattering.

'Wow, that was intense!' I said to Blair's phone, which they thrust in my face. They captured me pulling the thermal headband off my hair and uncovering my ears. My eyelashes felt crispy.

'Do you feel amazing?' asked Jody, beaming enthusiastically. 'The whites of your eyes look so clear, Amber. Take a look.' She encouraged me to survey myself in the mirror on one side of the dressing room, all the while Blair trailed me. 'Don't be surprised if you feel euphoric as the blood rushes back to your extremities.'

'My lip is still bruised,' I commented, checking myself in the mirror.

'The ice will have helped,' Jody informed me. 'Highly oxygenated blood will be flowing to that area right now, believe me, it will speed up your recovery.'

'What about you, Mandy?' Jody looked at my boss.

Mandy moved her arms through the sleeves of the warm dressing gown and pulled the belt tight at her waist. With her hair pulled back and minimal make-up she looked different – even more beautiful. I wondered whether the forty-five years she claimed to be her age on Wikipedia was correct.

I hadn't really thought about children in relation to Mandy until now. There had been rumoured pregnancies over the years and speculation in the media, but nothing ever confirmed. She seemed to be nailing superstardom, a permanent smile across her face, her success and achievements plastered almost everywhere you looked online, so I never imagined she might be struggling in any way. I felt a softening towards her after learning her intimate secret. As an observer, it would be easy to assume that Mandy had it all – the luxury lifestyle, wealthy husband, house, cars, and a wardrobe far beyond the wildest dreams of most normal people, but the one thing she really wanted – the top of her list – was to be a mother. I felt for her on that level, although it was the other part that intrigued me the most, the way Mandy spoke of a baby as if it was a commodity or the latest fashion trend. *Was it ethical to see a baby as something to give a celebrity currency – a spread in* HELLO! *magazine? What exactly did she mean by that?*

'I feel fantastic – energised.' She smiled. 'And lighter, even. Like I shed a tonne off my mind as well as my body in there.' She turned to look at me intensely. 'Do you, Amber?'

'I definitely feel invigorated,' I replied.

It felt as though Mandy was holding secrets and I wasn't quite sure whether I was being manipulated by her, or if she was just being honest.

After the session, when my fingertips had thawed, Blair and I accompanied Mandy to a nearby café. She was back to her usual chirpy self, chatting easily about the merits of oat milk over almond in hot coffee, but how she preferred soya in Frappuccinos. For a whole thirty minutes I experienced no double takes or unwanted comments from anyone about my top lip, which I took as a positive sign that it was returning to a normal size and colour.

'So, what have you got me for the shoot tomorrow?' Mandy quizzed as I sipped my coffee, grateful for the warmth in every sip. Before I could tell her about the natural hair and make-up and country pursuits theme I had in mind, Blair spoke. They had been reading a message on their phone:

'*Tatler* won't commit,' Blair said, reading it out. '"We are interested in following Mandy's career in the UK . . . blah blah . . . but . . . blah blah . . . Let's talk again in a few months."'

'Cruel,' sneered Mandy.

'It's not a total no,' offered Blair, replacing the handset face-down on the table. 'It's just not right now.'

'Which is basically a fuck-off,' clarified Mandy. 'Well, they can fuck off when they're desperate for me for the front page in a few months' time. They only sell a handful of copies a month anyway. And print is over, it's all about online. Where I have . . . what is it now, Blair?'

They seemed to know exactly what she was referring to and quickly overturned their phone again and opened the Instagram app.

'One million, eight hundred thousand and ninety-seven followers. Oh, and the new content is up on YouTube, where you have – wait – fifteen million subscribers worldwide!'

'Exactly. I think that tells us enough about where our efforts should be. Right, Amber?' She looked at me pointedly.

'Absolutely.' I smiled. 'The content is up already, is it?' I uttered.

'Sure is. Look how cute you look.' Blair held up their phone again, pausing the video on an image of me in my swimming costume in the chamber, looking like something that had just arrived in a morgue.

On cue, a young woman approached us cautiously. She was dressed fashionably in skin-tight leather-look leggings and big platform black boots. 'I'm so sorry to interrupt. But are you Mandy Sykes?' she asked, as I detected an American accent. 'I'm a huge fan. I subscribed to Bravo TV over here especially to get reruns of your shows. I love you! Are you making something in the UK? It would be so cool if you did. I'm so happy you've moved here. I can't wait to see how you enjoy living in the countryside!' she trilled, the verbal diarrhoea an attempt to mask her nervousness.

I looked at Mandy. It was as if all the lights in the house were turned on. The mega star came out to play, large, wide smile, twinkling eyes, and high energy. 'Aww you're so sweet! I love your boots. Would you like a selfie?' she replied loudly, as every head in the café turned to stare.

'Oh wow – yes, please,' said the girl, lifting her phone, and the two smiled cheesily for a photo. 'Thank you so much. This is amazing!' She turned to me. 'I hope your lip gets better. The cryotherapy must have helped. Aw, it looks so painful.'

I slunk back into my seat, muttering, 'Thanks.'

Mandy had barely registered her comment to me. 'Not well-known enough,' she said. 'Let's see about that.'

As the girl left the café, Mandy was visibly stoked. 'Who cares about the magazines. Doing our own photoshoot is the way forward,' she said cheerfully. 'This way we can have complete control and use it all for my social platforms and YouTube.'

'And don't forget the Mandy Sykes Homeware range we shipped will be arriving tomorrow, so we can get product placement in all the shots; fluff up the beds and sofas,' Blair added. 'Plus, we need to get your new loungewear collab with H&M in as many photos as possible, especially the track pants as they are new this season.' They were scrolling through a list on their phone. 'Oh and the collagen shakes and – fuck – the body chains! I don't think they've arrived yet.' Their face went pale momentarily. 'Did anyone tell you about the body chains, Amber?'

'Um, no.' I looked at Blair blankly. 'I'm not sure body chains and tweed are exactly—' They looked at me with narrowed eyes, suggesting this wasn't the right answer.

'Julie-Ann had this great idea about Mandy jumping on the trend for body adornment currently sweeping Hollywood and making it accessible over here. We're working on securing a collab with a jewellery brand – you know, a Swarovski, Pandora, Carat.'

'Bvlgari would do nicely,' Mandy interjected.

'We may have to lower our ask,' Blair muttered. 'We need to be realistic, Mands.'

'But not *too* real.' Mandy glanced at them. 'We have standards. Don't we, Amber?'

'Right, so to be clear, you're seeing this as loungewear

meets slinky chains?' I checked. 'I thought Julie-Ann was after something a little more . . . aristocratic.'

'Let's call it Sloane with sex appeal. It'll be fine, Amber,' Mandy replied. 'I'm sure you can tie it all together. That's what you stylists do – you can wave your magic wand over it all. There are a number of commercial partnerships to satisfy, that's all. My "bread and butter" – isn't that the phrase?'

'We can use different areas for different themes, there's plenty of space,' Blair added optimistically. 'There's no such thing as "no can do". Right, Amber?'

'Right. We'd better get back then.' I smiled nervously.

'Jose should have left by now.' She picked up her phone and glanced at it to check the time. 'He's about to take off to New York for a few days, to secure some more . . .' she paused, '. . . endorsements. I thought that next week, I could throw a little cocktail party – Julie-Ann's offered to invite a few of her UK clients over for some drinks: TV presenters, influencers, authors, life gurus, those types of people. Do you have a partner, Amber?' she asked, changing the subject.

'I do – he's called Rob, we've been together for a couple of years.'

'Charming!' she squealed. 'Shame we can't invite him too.'

'It's no problem,' I said shyly, doubting that Rob would actually want to come to the party after hearing about my experience so far. That's if he was still speaking to me. I thought about the weird phone call again, it was really playing on my mind.

'It'll be like a kind of housewarming, only hotter. If the chains don't make the daytime pics, they can come out for the evening. We'll get plenty of content. If *Tatler* thinks I'm unfit for their society pages, they can stick their . . .' Her voice trailed off because we were saved by Blair's phone buzzing. We glanced down instinctively, and I was relieved it was a call to tell us her chauffeur had arrived.

CHAPTER TEN

We spent much of the hourlong drive back to the Surrey Hills in near silence. I was busy working on my iPhone, doing some last-minute call-ins for the shoot by emailing accommodating fashion PRs. I was a little surprised by the number of British designer labels who didn't want to lend to Mandy, but I had a result from a lovely lady at new sustainable diamond brand Astrea London, who said they would be happy to loan some earrings. This ticked the high-society box at least.

Every time I mentioned a more high-street brand we could try, Mandy would respond with a mumbled 'maybe', signalling this meant 'no' and she had already moved on to thinking about more important things, like how to get one back on the editors of *HELLO!* and *Tatler*. Although I supposed Mandy probably had enough money in the bank to splash out on any of the designer items she really wanted in her wardrobe, like the Bottega Veneta boots, it was an indication that she had a lot of work to do to win over the elitist British style set. They were of the opinion that true class was something you were born into, rather than a position you can buy with Instagram followers, whether you have 1.8 million of them or not.

Back at the house, the rain was falling thick and hard, and it wasn't doing much to help Mandy's mood. She swore loudly, as Philippa came rushing out of the house with a large umbrella to ease her journey of a few steps from the car to the front door, but accidentally tipped it at the wrong angle, sending a small river of rainwater right onto her hair.

She pursed her lips. 'I don't know how you people cope with this horrible weather.'

Mandy seemed to hate the British climate with a vengeance. Her little digs at my motherland and our unpredictable weather were starting to grate. It wasn't as if the Crown had officially invited Mandy to set up a temporary home here, she had come of her own accord. And if she'd like to depart, well, I didn't think the Home Office would pull out all the stops to keep her here.

I took this as my cue to retire early for the evening. I had clothes to press, outfits to plan, chains to inspect, and jodhpurs to pack away. There was no doubt that this styling mission was going to be a test.

By the evening, both Philippa and I were on first-name terms with the UPS delivery man, and I could tell you the names of all four children of the Parcelforce guy. Deliveries had arrived thick and fast, and I worked late into the night getting everything ready for the shoot, so Mandy had at least four options for every look.

I had begun to see a more sensitive side to Philippa as she trotted back and forth with parcels and took pity on me, keeping me company as she correctly read the mix of fear and trepidation in my eyes, as I tried to fathom what might be on Mandy's imagined vision board for this shoot. Yet every time my voice rose and I started to panic, she artfully changed the conversation and brought me back down. At one point, when Philippa asked me if I had ever experienced such a high-maintenance boss as Mandy, I plunged into a mire of grievances about Mona Armstrong. She then regaled a brilliant story about the former lady of Gables Manor who had once asked Philippa to get into the car – in her pyjamas – to go to the end of the long driveway and collect her Deliveroo order *four times* because she couldn't use the app properly and kept ordering the wrong thing.

'As m'lady slurred that she hadn't been drinking *any sherry* and the "stupidsoddingfuckwit" app had kept changing things of its own accord, I just had to bite my tongue and do as instructed. But the great thing was that I ended up with three untouched delicious curry takeaways from the Bombay Bicycle Club, which kept me in free meals for the rest of the week. Lady Muck didn't make any reference to any of the orders in the morning, and I'm not entirely sure she could remember any of it, since I hid the evidence. Honestly, rich people do *crazy* things.'

As it neared midnight, Philippa announced she was going to bed, and before she did, returned with a mug of hot chocolate and a shortbread from her 'secret stash' to keep me going; a sight which made me genuinely happier than I had felt at any time since I arrived here.

I changed into my pyjamas and waited up for one final delivery, from a courier bringing a collection of blingy accessories I knew would be to Mandy's taste. I kept myself awake by scrolling through Instagram, chuckling at Vicky's latest Reel which showed her chihuahua standing in front of the screen on her Peloton, desperate for attention, and had the caption 'Wait ch-a minute!'

With Philippa in bed, I relocated to a kitchen stool near the intercom system for the front gate. I passed the time on my phone and idly wondering whether to resurrect my TikTok account. It had lain dormant for the past few months. Building my social media following had become an unhealthy obsession when we were in New York, it almost came between Rob and me, and I had been cautious of it ever since. Plus, Mandy and Jose had asked me to sign a lengthy and heavy-handed privacy agreement when I started, so it wasn't as though I could post anything of interest anyway.

When the buzzer rang, I could barely keep my eyes open and, on autopilot, mumbled, 'Come up to the main house – thank you.'

A few minutes later the doorbell rang, and like a robot, I had my arm outstretched to receive the bag. Only as the car turned and began heading back down the driveway, without anyone returning to it, did my brain register that the person on the doorstep was not a courier. It was Jimi.

'Sorry, Amber, did you stay up for me?' The soft Spanish twang to his voice was more noticeable sometimes.

'Only if you have a delivery,' I muttered sarcastically, holding the door open, but not wide enough for him to walk through it. I was slightly pissed off that he was teasing me like this.

He looked me up and down quizzically. 'Nice PJs,' he said, smirking. 'I forgot my keys.'

I checked him out. He was wearing jeans which were probably very expensive but looked as though a cheese-grater had been taken to them, partially covered by a large white puffer jacket and a white woolly hat with a few dark brown curls poking out. In his garish ski-resort-meets-dated-boy-band outfit, he would look more at home in Whistler than West Surrey.

'It's really cold out here,' he said, shifting his weight between his feet, to illustrate the point. 'Any chance you can let me in?'

'You're out late,' I replied, aware that I sounded like my mum.

A wind circled between us.

'Are you security now?' He asked the question with some disdain. 'Do you mind—'

He put his hand on the door to push it open. This riled me.

'I'm not the maid either,' I replied. *Seriously, I'm too tired for this.*

'I wasn't suggesting it!' he quipped.

I looked at him unamused.

'You seem annoyed at me. Or are we flirting?' he said.

After a beat, when I didn't respond, he said, 'Oh. You're angry.'

'I kind of am,' I muttered.

'Shall we start again?' he asked, looking up at me with very large brown eyes, the kind you might find on a chocolate labrador begging to be taken out for a run.

I nudged the door wider and let him in.

'Why are you up anyway?'

'It's lucky I was, isn't it?'

'Are you always this difficult to talk to?'

'I'm sorry, I'm tired. I'm still waiting for a delivery for the shoot tomorrow.' I looked at my phone. 'It's nearly half-past midnight on a Monday. Most people in this part of the world are asleep.'

Inside the hallway, Jimi pulled off his hat, turned towards the mirror, and gave his hair a ruffle. He was so attractive in such a classic, obvious way, it was momentarily paralysing. It didn't matter that he was also as vain as a peacock.

I immediately felt a rush of self-consciousness stood there in my pyjamas, which were covered in dachshunds wearing scarves. They were a Christmas gift from Lucy, in lieu of my not being able to get an actual dachshund until Rob and I had bought a house together. Which brought me neatly back to the reason I was right here, right now, wearing said pyjamas. *I am at work. I am being paid. Keep your eyes on the bonus and stop gawping, Amber.*

I pulled my pyjama top back a little over my shoulders, in an effort to lift up the front and hide my braless cleavage.

As he unzipped his puffer coat, I clocked the Moncler label on the arm. And then I noticed the very manly shape of his arms within his also white Moncler jumper. He looked at himself in the mirror again as he passed it. His beauty was hard to miss, even to himself.

Slowly and surreptitiously, while Jimi was hanging up his coat in the boot room, I released the scrunchy which was loosely tying my hair back and let my locks fall around my shoulders. This, at least, might make me look slightly better.

'You probably could do with a night cap then, while you wait,' he said, returning from the boot room, surprising me by this offer.

Within the next couple of minutes, we were sat in the drawing room with two tumblers of Disaronno over ice. After a short interrogation, I established some more information about Jimi. He was from Miami, and he was Jose's younger brother by fifteen years, as they shared a dad but had different mums.

He had been getting cabin fever so had taken it upon himself to walk to the local pub this evening where he had enjoyed a few pints and a lock-in with some locals.

At close quarters, in the dim light of the drawing room, it was easy to tell that Jimi was related to Jose. He had the same warm, olive complexion and expressive dark brown eyes, plus Jose's charisma when he spoke, in a way that made you stop and listen. *Jesus, he's so fit.*

'Anyway, you haven't introduced yourself properly yet – I don't even know your surname.' He spoke with a ripple of amusement on his lips, which made me feel like we were flirting.

'I'm Amber Green.'

'Like the British traffic lights.'

I sighed. 'I've never heard that one before.'

'You haven't?'

I yawned. He might be handsome, but he wasn't the sharpest tool in the box. 'To be completely honest, I'm a little tired for this. I was waiting up for the courier and I'm kind of hoping it will be here any second so I can go to bed. There's a big photoshoot here tomorrow, as you might remember.' I swallowed my last sip of Disaronno.

'Sure, sorry. I think I'm still on Miami time. Well, it's a pleasure to meet you properly, Amber Green. Why don't I wait up for the courier so you guys can get to bed?' He directed that question at the dachshunds. I very obviously blushed.

We both stood up at the same time, and as I smoothed my pyjamas, he moved back towards the door to the entrance hall. As he stepped through it, the flickering of the chandelier in the hallway reflected in his eyes.

We paused and I pondered whether, like Jose, Jimi was also one for kissing goodbye on both cheeks, and how I would handle that. I was saved by a buzz on the intercom.

'Parcel for Amber Green.'

Jimi let the courier in, and when he smiled, I noticed how straight his teeth were on the top and the bottom.

He took the parcel out of the courier's hands and read the label.

'The one and only Amber Green, lady of the manor, is right here,' he said grandly, turning to me with another butterfly-inducing smile.

'That's me,' I said to the courier, embarrassed. I took the parcel from Jimi and signed the docket in the same way I had done at least a dozen times throughout the day. Only this time, my hand was a little shaky and my pulse a little faster.

'I'll see you in the morning!' Jimi called, heading down the hallway towards the central staircase.

I felt a little flower of interest unfurl within me.

When I closed my eyes at around one a.m, I only reached a faint veil of sleep, because I'd forgotten to put my phone on silent. *That was me feeling hopeful Rob might message.*

At six a.m. on the dot, my phone pinged with a text.

It was Mum. *Lucy's got news!*

Swiftly followed by: *Don't tell her I've told you.*

And thirty seconds later, clearly as an afterthought: *Hope all is going well with the job? Call your sister. Love you, Mum x*

It was typical Mother – to the point and always first in line with the news. She would do well working at the *Daily Mail* if her legal career ever took a turn.

Now there was no way I was getting back to sleep for an extra hour. My finger hovered over calling Lucy, but it was going to have to wait, because my call time for the shoot was eight a.m. and I needed to do a final check to make sure everything was in place before Mandy was up.

It had been four days now since Rob and I had spoken. The longest we had ever gone without communication. In my mind, we were now in an unspoken stand-off. He could be stubborn at times, and so could I. I imagined he was annoyed with me for jumping to conclusions that he had been doing something behind my back, without any solid evidence. I was smarting because he had not done anything to convince me otherwise. *Or maybe he's just been busy? I'll call him the minute we're finished today.*

The exchange with Jimi last night had proved a welcome distraction, but although he was fit, I couldn't get the image of him wearing all-white Moncler out of my mind. He looked like a lost member of NSYNC. *Some people just cannot buy style.*

After I had showered and hurriedly dressed into my shoot day uniform of black cigarette pants, a skinny Gucci belt, and an untucked crisp white shirt, which I hurriedly steamed, I was greeted in the main house by Julie-Ann, who had arrived early to begin fluffing the living room. She had already made a start, plumping up cushions, moving things about on tabletops and checking that nothing unsightly was left on display. We were shooting in a number of rooms today, including the main lounge and Mandy's bedroom.

'Amber, sweetie, how are you finding Surrey life?' Julie-Ann asked absently, her head at an angle, as she peered sternly at a table and then nudged a vase slightly to the left, before moving it back to where it was. Her sharp blonde bob swished onto her cheek as she moved.

'Well, the house is amazing, obviously,' I began, 'and everything seems to be going well so far.' I bit my lip and winced, this was a lie, and my lip still hadn't quite healed.

'The photographer will be here in half an hour to set up the lights. He's on the clock, and he's more expensive than all the clothes you've called in, so we need to maximise the time. We can't get the bedroom ready until Mandy's out of there, but you could unpack all the items from the bed linen and beauty range and stack them outside the door ready,' she instructed. 'And then set up one of the spare rooms down the end of the corridor, we'll do a few pics on the bed in there too.'

Blair appeared as I was unpacking the bed linen.

'How's Julie-Ann this morning?' they asked, peering over their shoulder to check she wasn't listening. 'She can be a real witch on photoshoots. She's the only person Mandy is scared of though, so keep her onside and Mandy will be putty.'

'Thanks for the tip-off. Any sign of her yet?'

'Not yet,' they said, and then tapped my arm, indicating I should follow them. We wandered down to the end of the corridor and round the corner, out of sight. 'Between us,' they continued, whispering, 'Mandy's not in a great way at the moment. Jose's staying in New York longer than planned because something's happened. I'm not sure what exactly, but I heard them arguing on the phone yesterday. I think that's the real reason Jimi is over from Miami – he usually runs Mandy's social media from the States, but with Jose out of town, they think she might need more support.'

'And Jimi is reliable support?' I mumbled, thinking about how Jimi was out at the pub last night, rather than babysitting Mandy. I must have looked a little moony eyed at the mention of Jimi, because Blair shot me a look.

'Watch out for him,' they said. 'Playboy extraordinaire.'

I winced. 'Tell me more—'

'Breakfast is ready in the kitchen!' interrupted a voice from behind us. Coco materialised out of nowhere and grabbed my arm. 'No one's down yet – where are Mandy and Jimi?' She pushed me aside. 'There are freshly made

banana, cacao, and chia seed parfaits in the kitchen. And
plenty of coffee. As strong as you like. Come and get it!'
Coco skipped off. If there was an advert for good nutrition,
she was it.

Blair looked anxious. 'It's weird neither of them is up
yet.'

'Is everything okay?' I swallowed.

'You clearly don't read *Starz*,' Blair replied.

I made a mental note to google Mandy to find out the
latest gossip.

We began descending the staircase, Blair in the lead,
when Julie-Ann appeared with a sharpness to her voice.
'Blair. Hi. Can you do us all a favour and wake Mandy up?
The day has barely begun and we're already behind.' I took
this as my cue to slip off for breakfast.

After a few mouthfuls of parfait and two hurriedly
swallowed coffees, I was back in the annexe with BBC
Radio 6 Music playing, dutifully checking the rail of clothes
and line of shoes in the space we were using as Mandy's
dressing area for the shoot. Lola had arrived with boxes of
make-up and an array of brushes, tongs, straighteners, and
sprays, which she laid out in perfect symmetry, making the
tabletop resemble a display counter in Sephora. I played
around with styling the looks, pressed silk shirts, skirts, and
three dresses, and nearly an hour later, there was still no
sign of Mandy.

'It's not like her to be so late for her own shoot,' Lola
said worriedly. 'Let's go and find out.'

Lola and I went back to the main house to find a small

congregation gathered outside Mandy's bedroom door. Blair was attempting to look through the keyhole for a sign of life, but their heavy sigh filled us with little hope she was even awake.

'Maybe she's sick?' I offered.

Julie-Ann didn't seem to think so. She was now visibly *and* verbally stressed.

'This is ridiculous.' She huffed. 'I'm giving her five minutes before we bust the door.' She looked at Blair. 'Where's Jimi?'

'His bedroom door is open, he must have gone out. Maybe for a run.'

'Great. Brilliant,' Julie-Ann said. 'Really helpful.' Then she paced around the hallway in a fidgety manner, looking at her phone and fiddling with the top of her black, ribbed polo neck, which she wore under a grey suit, giving her a stressed exec vibe. Every now and again, she pulled the polo neck over her mouth and breathed deeply into it, like it might magically have the effect of an oxygen mask, and give her some extra strength. Then she would tut, swear a bit, and run her finger along a surface to check for dust and pace around again. I spotted Philippa hovering around the bottom of the stairs nervously, sucking in her cheeks every time Julie-Ann swore more loudly than was strictly necessary, like blasphemy within these hallowed halls pained her deeply.

The photographer had arrived – a hot-shot image maker who went by the mononym Mart. His name, Blair told me, was actually Martin Rambleswick, but that didn't sound very fashionable.

'This shoot *has* to work. We have all invested so much in this move,' I overheard Julie-Ann muttering to Mart, as I watched Blair hold a glass against the bedroom door. 'Jose's going to lose it if we can't monetise this trip. I don't understand why she's doing this to us. Blair, you're going to have to go in.'

Then a noise from downstairs made us all stop what we were doing. The front door opened and Mandy and Jimi appeared from behind it. Our six confused faces stared at them. Neither of them was wearing exercise gear, but they were giggling like naughty school children.

'Sorry I'm late, we had to see someone about something,' Mandy announced breezily. She looked as though she was trying not to laugh. 'Hadn't we better get started?'

Julie-Ann, wearing a pasted-on smile, responded on behalf of everyone. 'We sure had, darlings! We're just glad you're both okay. You had us a little worried there.'

Jimi looked sheepish and ran his fingers through his curls.

'Morning, Amber.' He smiled, catching my eye. 'Thanks again, for last night.'

Blair turned to me and mouthed, *Last night?*

'He was locked out!' I snapped.

'Sleep okay?' I asked Jimi, trying to look casual.

'Not enough hours, but I took two Ambien, slept like a branch. Anyone else need coffee?'

I sniggered. 'You mean a log.'

'Eh?'

'You slept like a log. Don't worry.' I shrugged, my heart beating hard and fast against my ribcage. Blair seemed to sense this and sideways-glanced at me.

'Jet lag is a killer this way. Nearly two weeks and I'm still not over it. I really need coffee. Do you want one, Mandy?'

'Yes, please, Blair will look after us,' she replied. 'Where do I go for glam?'

'Over to the annexe please,' Julie-Ann commanded. 'Lola, let's get her into hair and make-up. Amber, take Mandy through the clothes and then get the bedroom styled.'

Like clockwork, our glam squad sprang into action, treating Mandy like a real-life Barbie doll. Blair thrust a coffee into her hand, Lola linked her arm firmly – the equivalent of a headlock – and I led the way towards the annexe. Within seconds Lola had curlers in Mandy's hair and was starting on her make-up. She seemed in a peculiar mood this morning and continued to giggle as she asked Lola to pay particular attention to plucking her chin hairs, and then claimed the make-up brush Lola was using was 'too tickly'.

I popped back to the house and got to work in Mandy's bedroom, styling the items from her soon-to-launch homeware range, which included 800-thread-count Egyptian cotton bed linen, buttery smooth to the touch, and a plush cream bedspread with flecks of gold running through it.

It felt personal to be in Mandy and Jose's bedroom without anyone present, and it looked as though she had left in a hurry this morning because her dressing gown was strewn on the floor, and there were toiletries open on her dressing table. I carefully tidied it all up like a hotel chambermaid.

As I changed the pillowcases and artfully arranged a pile of scatter cushions at the top of the bed, I noticed something poking out from the top drawer of her bedside table. At first, I thought it was a pregnancy test. I couldn't help myself pull it out a little further and could see then that it was in fact an ovulation stick. I knew this because I remembered Lucy using them when she was trying to fall pregnant. There was a smiley face on it indicating a fertile day. I thought of the conversation Mandy and I had shared in the cryotherapy chamber, and how cryptic Jimi had been this morning. I wondered whether her fertility issues were what they had been discussing last night. To preserve Mandy's privacy, I pushed the stick out of sight, right inside the drawer. But, as ever, I wondered if I'd ever really know what was going on in Mandy's life?

CHAPTER ELEVEN

To say the shoot went badly would be an understatement. As the day progressed, rails of my carefully chosen pieces from top British brands ranging from Burberry to Rixo remained untouched, as it became clear that Mandy was much more Florida than London Fashion Week. It was challenging to ask her to wear anything with a high neck, below the knee, or made of silk. Julie-Ann's brief to make her style more English rose than *the* Kate Middleton was frankly a joke. At any given opportunity she'd insist on a last-minute change into a Bardot-style off-the-shoulder neckline, or on adding big gold hoops, or aviators. At Mandy's request, music blared from the Sonos system, and a stream of explicit rap rang out in all rooms of the house. Mandy would get lost in the vibe of the music, throwing herself around. Jimi wasn't being much help, goading her on, encouraging her to pose seductively on the bed. The neutral bed linen and William Morris vibe of the house jarred with the unashamedly garish celebrity before us. Even Mart – the so-called creator of dreams, who had worked for the coolest stars and fashion magazines – was struggling to find a workable theme here.

I was thinking on my feet, making suggestions like adding a faux fur jacket to some of the looks to introduce more softness. This proved a mistake because Mandy became obsessed with the texture, burying her head in it like a kitten on heat.

'It's so soft! Feel it,' she purred, her pupils large as her eyes glowed with excitement. 'Oh, I could lose myself in this jacket, I'd like to live in it. Can I keep it, Amber? Do you think you could ask them if I can?'

I feigned excitement, it was all I could do. 'Isn't it amazing, Mandy? Sure, I'll ask the PR.'

Her behaviour was bizarre on every level.

I had one ear trained on Julie-Ann, and could hear every word she was saying as she peered over Mart's shoulder to see thumbnails from the shoot as they appeared on a laptop in real time.

'The styling is a *disaster*,' she quipped. 'Britain is not going to bond with this brash American, who has not won the right to hole up in one of our most historic homes. This is a mess.' It made my insides tighten and a prickly heat rose through my body.

The styling is a disaster. Five words no stylist ever wants to hear. Five words that could end a photoshoot. A job. A career. A bonus.

I was standing to the side of the bedroom, a soft brown cashmere rollneck dress laid carefully over my left arm, as I cautiously suggested a compromise – keeping the snake-print boots, but teaming them with the cashmere dress, rather than the skin-tight, scoop-neck, python-print mini dress from her own wardrobe that she was currently sporting.

'Where are the body chains?' Mandy snapped at me, her scowl broadcasting her disdain at my choice of clothing once again. 'Fashion is all about putting on an act, grabbing attention, creating moments that will stop the scrollers in their tracks. You've got to fake it 'til you make it. C'mon, girl! Where's the glamour?'

I felt humiliated and looked across the room in desperation, trying to get Blair's attention with my eyes, then scanning right to Lola, who was standing a couple of feet away, to Jimi in the wings, and then across to Julie-Ann and Mart by the laptop station. They all looked away, suddenly busy with something. *Why was no one backing me up?*

Surely, they knew what Mandy was like, and could see what was going on. She was manipulating me – going against everything I had been briefed and that we had previously discussed. It wasn't that I didn't have the right clothes for Mandy, it was that she didn't want to wear them. I felt hopelessly alone as they all avoided eye contact. *No one knows how to handle her.*

'OK.' I smiled, taking a deep breath.

I can either give up or stand up for myself.

There was nothing for it, but to be relentlessly positive.

I took a breath. 'What about looking at this another way?' I began. 'What if we stop letting the clothes do the talking, and *you* become the star of the photos? I'd like to see you steal the scene here, Mandy – and I'm pretty sure

I'm talking on behalf of not just everyone in this room – but all of your British fans. I'd like to see the *real* you.'

Mandy was quiet for a moment, like she was at least listening. I held my breath as I waited for her response. The silence seemed to grip the whole room. Half of me wanted to crumble like a dry sandcastle, but deep down I was proud I had stood up to her. My stomach was in a knot.

Slowly and silently, Mandy sat up on the bed on which she had been posing seductively just a few seconds ago. She shimmied until her legs were hanging over the edge, then she leant forward, reached for the heel of one of the boots which she firmly tugged and pulled off, throwing it onto the floor. The second one quickly followed. Then the corners of her mouth rose upwards, and she threw her head back. 'The *real* me?' she roared. Then she began laughing.

The tiny dress rode up her legs, revealing a large expanse of puckered skin on her ample thigh. It was pale in comparison with the lower section of her leg which had seen a hefty amount of instant tanning lotion applied to it by Lola.

'Cellulite, muffin top, belly fat? Oh, I've got plenty of that!' she exclaimed, prodding her side. 'You think people really want to see this?'

'You look fantastic,' I replied. 'Don't be ashamed of who you are.'

I looked around me and noticed that Julie-Ann had a sceptical look on her face.

'Don't you think this will lose me followers rather than gain them?' she continued. 'This is absurd.'

'Not at all,' I replied. 'Fashion is changing. I mean it's always been about making someone look their best but, for maximum appeal, that best must now be real – it should be raw, unfiltered, authentic. Show them you're as vulnerable as the rest of us.'

Her eyes laser-focused on me, like I was a strange specimen she hadn't seen before, and she couldn't work out whether I was friend or enemy. But she seemed to be listening at least.

'But what is *real*?' she asked.

'Well, who are you, Mandy?' I continued. 'And I don't mean your profession, your wealth, or your personal status as a wife and celebrity. Who *are* you?'

The question seemed to flick a switch inside her.

Mandy turned her head and looked out of the window. It was a simple question, but it demanded deep consideration.

After a pause which felt like an eternity, she whispered, 'I don't know.'

She hung her head. This felt like a private moment, except the room was full of people.

'Think back to the past, if it's easier,' I probed, gently. 'What comes to mind?'

Mandy looked upwards, I could almost hear her brain ticking.

'I guess if I think of myself as a little girl,' she began, 'I remember the self-confidence I had. I used to disco dance and I would wear this kind of all-in-one leotard. I loved the whole performance aspect of it. I was so blissfully unaware of how I looked and what people might think of me. It was so freeing.'

'What happened?' I asked.

'That little girl grew up.' She shrugged. 'She realised that everyone has an opinion. Young women are expected to be a certain way, and society has a beauty standard – it judges you harshly against it. She gave up dancing because she felt fat in those leotards.'

'What would you tell that little girl now?' I asked.

'I'd tell her not to give up. That she shouldn't listen to what other people think, but enjoy how dancing makes her feel.' She smiled wistfully to herself.

I took a step back to give Mandy the space this moment deserved. You could have heard a pin drop in the room as thirty seconds passed.

'So, who *are you*, Mandy?' I asked again, softly.

Her whole demeanour seemed calmer now.

'I am enough,' she said.

'Hold it. Right there,' Mart announced, camera in hand and springing into action. He waved his free hand, to signal for his assistant to move the softbox closer, quickly. Mandy lay there gazing out of the window as he began clicking his lens, a gentle tap as flashes of light from the softbox caught her small movements on the bed. Occasionally she would gently shift her position to be more comfortable. 'This is *beautiful*,' Mart purred.

We continued like this for a few moments, with Mandy tweaking her position very slightly, chin raised and turned a fraction, then back again. Her hair undone, dress twisted, flesh exposed. The music had stopped, and Mandy didn't notice, she seemed fully in the moment. While Mart photographed her, all of us watched in awe. It felt as though a bit of magic was happening before our eyes.

'I think we've got it,' Mart declared just a couple of minutes later.

He was then joined by Julie-Ann, Lola, and Blair in a huddle around the laptop. The blood coursing through my veins picked up speed. *Were they happy? What did Julie-Ann think? Would Mandy push to have me fired?*

'Let's all take five,' Julie-Ann announced, sensing correctly that we needed to come up for air.

I let out a huge sigh and took the opportunity to call Lucy.

'How's it going?' Lucy's voice on the other end of the line was a comfort.

'I'm on a shoot so I can't be long,' I whispered, as I left the room and went into the hallway, away from the rest of the team. 'I just thought I'd check in; see if you're all okay.'

'How's the shoot going?' she asked.

'Other than Mandy refusing to wear anything I've prepared, and fearing that I will be sacked at any moment, it's going brilliantly.'

'That sounds tough,' she replied, 'but what is it you'd say to me – you can do tough things? It's not as if you're not used to working with difficult people. Remember?'

'I remember all too well,' I said. 'In fact, I still have PTSD. Why do I always attract the strong personality types?'

'Well, what did you expect from a Leo?'

'How do you know that?'

'Checking her star sign was the first thing I did when you told me you were working with Mandy. This is me, sister.'

'Care to share any tips on how to handle the leader of the animal kingdom?'

'Always be honest and make her feel special,' she replied. 'Fiery she may be, she'll be loyal once you win her trust. Show her you can listen.'

'I feel like I've had a little breakthrough with her just now,' I replied. 'Anyway, I didn't mean to call the Mystic Meg hotline. I wondered how you're doing?'

'I've actually got a bit of news to share with you,' she said.

My heart rate sped up.

'I caved, and we found out the sex of the baby yesterday. We're having a boy!'

'Oh, Lucy!' I exclaimed, my heart swelling. 'This is amazing news! I'm so happy for you all. How are you feeling?' My voice trailed off into nothing, as I noticed out of the corner of my eye Mandy standing in the doorway.

Got a minute? she mouthed coolly.

'Luce, I want to talk more, but I think I'm needed. I'll call you again later.'

'Okay, good luck.'

I walked slowly towards Mandy.

'Is everything okay?' I asked.

'Have you got a new job already?' she quipped, as I joined her by the entrance to the bedroom. The rest of the team had disappeared to the kitchen for refreshments.

'Er, no,' I replied, biting my lip. 'Should I?'

'Julie-Ann's read me the riot act. I come in peace.' Her eyes looked warmer, and she held out her hand to meet mine, giving it a gentle squeeze and then letting me go.

'It's okay.' I gave her a wary smile.

'What's the news then?'

'My sister – she's having a baby boy,' I said. 'It's her second.'

'How lovely for her,' she said unconvincingly. A moment passed between us. She looked as though she was going to say something else and then thought better of it.

'Yes, it's great news. We thought she'd stop at one.' I smiled.

'She's lucky,' Mandy murmured and turned back to join the crew, signalling the conversation was closed.

The shoot went much more smoothly after that. We ripped up the tear sheet for aristocratic styling and put Mandy at the centre of every photo. The conversation we had shared earlier seemed to have had an impact and she appeared much more thoughtful. Although she'd still be giggling for no reason one minute, the next she appeared spaced out, or she'd get obsessed with a little detail on an outfit. I felt equally perplexed by Mandy's push-me, pull-me attitude. One minute telling me her secrets, the next making me feel like I was for the chop.

As I watched her, I couldn't get the ovulation stick I found this morning out of my mind and had a pang of regret for telling my sister's baby news to her so flippantly. Mandy may have thought I was being insensitive. It may be a fertile window for her, but with Jose away, it was unlikely to yield the result she was looking for. There were so many things about her that I couldn't get a handle on.

CHAPTER TWELVE

Mandy arrived at dinner that evening wearing the cashmere rollneck dress she'd refused to wear on the shoot, and some incredible lab-grown diamond drop earrings from Astrea London, which were worth north of ten thousand pounds. The same ones she had declined to wear all day, claiming they were 'fake', despite me informing her that not only were they a sustainable choice but almost entirely devoid of impurities, graded to a more superior quality than mined diamonds. Finally, the news seemed to have sunk in and they appealed to her, just hours before the security guard would be arriving to collect them. *Typical.* Yet, I wondered if this was her way of making a peace offering to me, by acknowledging that I did know what I was doing after all.

Blair, Coco, Jimi, and I sat around the dining table watching Mandy poke her tofu, raw radish, and artichoke salad. I scrutinised her every mouthful, praying she wouldn't spill anything on the cashmere, because I'd have to use my expenses for dry cleaning before it could be returned.

After a few forkfuls, she laid down her cutlery and moaned to Coco, 'I'm sorry, but I don't think I can do any more of this food. I feel bloated and disgusting. What's the point of having a nutritionist if I'm not getting thinner?' She looked at Coco so disdainfully, it made the slight woman recoil into an even smaller space than the one she naturally occupied.

'Mands, the idea was never about weight loss.' Blair leapt to Coco's defence. 'It was about health – you know, less saturated fat, more vegetables, enough protein, complex carbohydrates. A *fertility*-inducing diet.'

'Complex carbohydrates?' Mandy spat the words out feebly. 'As if my life doesn't have enough complexity already. I'm getting older by the second, and coupled with this strange "lady of the manor" persona everyone seems to want me to adopt, it's just not working. Today I lost twenty thousand followers. Twenty K. Why is it only me who can see this is a problem?'

I looked at my plate and prodded a piece of rubbery tofu. I thought it best not to point out that we're all getting older by the second. *Though, to be fair, she has a point about the salad.*

'Plus, someone commented on Instagram today that I have no right to be in the UK, because I'm fat trailer trash,' she continued, with a howl. 'And that post had thousands of likes and its own Thread. It's not working. Do you all hear me? We need to go back to what I know – make me look thin and young, dial up the filters, get some serious face and body tune on every image before it leaves this building. Up the sex appeal. And ditch the shit food!'

To emphasise the point, she pushed her salad bowl across the table with such force that Coco leapt up and dashed around to stop it shooting off the end. Her face collapsed in misery.

'I actually think the tofu is good,' Jimi said absently.

I sank into my seat and sighed. Mandy seemed to have completely forgotten everything we talked about on the shoot. The atmosphere felt thick and awkward as we all avoided eye contact, especially with Mandy.

It was depressing. I really thought I'd had a small breakthrough earlier – something seemed to have got through to her, and in my mind, I could see so clearly how we could turn this around for Mandy. The question was how to get her to see it too.

I can't style someone who is afraid of who they really are; someone so unhappy in her own skin.

Then a thought came into my mind. I took a deep breath. 'Can I make a comment?' I asked bravely.

'Another one?' she snarled, glancing sideways at me. This time I didn't look away. 'Okay, go ahead' – she sighed – 'but it will make no difference.' Mandy's voice had an edge, but she was looking at me, suggesting she wasn't completely against engaging.

'All I ask is that you hear me out.' I examined her face. I cleared my throat, took another deep breath, and crossed my index and middle fingers for extra luck. 'Shouldn't worrying about what your body looks like be the least important thing about your life right now? Imagine how much time and space that would free up to conquer all the things you have on that list you told me about in the freezer?' Mandy's ears pricked up when I mentioned the list. She didn't need to worry, I wasn't about to reveal the big thing on it, although judging by the comments from Blair, maybe it wasn't such a secret to anyone else.

'All the time, effort, energy, and passion you are wasting on not being able to accept your own body – it's exhausting,' I continued. 'Mandy, you are so much more than what you weigh, or how close your body is to the current standard of beauty – a barometer that isn't even real because we have become so used to an image of "perfection" that is completely fake. Most of what we see on social media is manipulated, it's like we're being conditioned to avoid our own reflections. It's time to get real – to be proud, to relax, to be your beautiful self, and to love your body for what it is. One that moves, breathes, pumps blood, wriggles, and dances around happily. Complete with wrinkles, cellulite, and wobbly bits which jiggle when we laugh – bits that are totally, gloriously, amazingly functioning and normal – not to mention unique to each one of us! Your body is the only home you will truly have for your entire life. I mean, the thought of that blows my mind. So, isn't it time to appreciate it a little more – just like you wish your younger self had done?'

'Here we go again,' she said with sarcasm. 'The problem is, Amber, I grew up, I changed. The world moved on. I can't do anything about the situation we find ourselves in today. It's pointless and, frankly, naive to think otherwise.'

I took a breath. 'That's not true. No one, Mandy, is in a more powerful position to do this on a public stage than you. You can set a new fashion trend – the biggest one of all – because this one is timeless.'

'Timeless? How?' she asked curiously.

'Because it represents self-love. You only get one chance at life – and your body is so much more precious than any passing trend. And this is from someone who worships trends! Look, it might sound overwhelming, but there is a huge opportunity here – and it's easy, because all you have to do is be *you*! And you are enough. Remember?'

She looked sceptical. 'But what about the "Princess of Surrey" thing? "More royal than Kate Middleton", you all said gleefully – isn't that what we're supposed to be doing here?'

'I'm sorry if I was trying to turn you into someone else, but I was following orders.' I was glad Julie-Ann wasn't around to hear this. 'But now I'm ready to tear up that brief and help you to be you.'

I paused and scanned the room, passion mixed with desperation in my eyes. 'We're *all* ready, aren't we?' I put myself out on a limb here and I was hungry for support from the others. My throat felt incredibly dry all of a sudden. I took a sip of water.

The room remained quiet. No one leapt to my defence.

One by one, we realised Mandy's face looked like a thundercloud, seconds away from exploding.

Her eyes narrowed. 'Great speech, Amber, Oscar-worthy in fact,' she muttered. 'But, have you asked yourself whether *I'm* ready for this? This "self-love utopia" you talk of? This is not a simple ask. You really have no idea, do you?' She looked around the room at the others, who stood there like stone statues. Then she pushed her chair away from the table and started to march out of the room, spitting out a cursory, 'Just leave me alone.'

Blair stood up too, about to go after her, their chair making a scraping sound on the floor.

Mandy turned to them. '*All* of you.'

The colour drained out of my face. I looked around and noticed Philippa hovering by the door, undecided about whether to come in or not, but nosy enough to overhear everything. When I caught her eye, she slowly shook her head.

What have I done?

Coco cleared her throat. 'Flourless cookie, anyone?'

Half an hour later, with no sign of Mandy re-emerging of her own accord, Blair and I found ourselves sitting on the landing outside her and Jose's bedroom, the sound of a nose being blown and then a bath running audible through the door. I hadn't been able to wipe the panic off my face since Mandy stormed upstairs.

'It's okay, she needs to let it out,' Blair whispered. 'She's growing as a person right now, and it hurts. It's a pain she's not used to, Amber. I don't think anyone has ever spoken to her like that before. Not even Julie-Ann.'

This horrified me further.

'Do you think I'm going to get the sack?' I asked, reeling from what I had done. 'I'm pretty sure she's in there plotting to ensure I never work again.'

Blair leant in until they were very close to me. 'To be fair, I've never heard of a stylist talking themselves out of a job this early on – you basically told her she doesn't need fashion.'

I sank down lower towards the floor, arching my back and pulling the sleeves of my black jumper over my hands, as if it might comfort me somehow.

'Babes, she won't sack you. Mandy can be flighty, but she's not stupid. You basically held up a mirror, and she didn't like what she saw. Her mood has been really weird today. She's been up, down, all over the place. But she'll be thinking things over in there. Believe me. Just give her time to calm down.'

'I hope you're right. I should have held back, but I just felt so incensed that she could feel that way. It's so wrong. Perhaps I should have shut up and carried on treading that delicate and deeply unfulfilling line between what Julie-Ann wants and what Mandy wants, and ended up with Princess Kate on steroids. Perhaps I should have just shut my big trap.'

'Oh babe, you said what you felt. I mean that speech seriously *was* awards season worthy. Let's face it, she won't be able to hide for long.'

We sat watching the door in silence until the sounds from the room began to abate. Even though it was plain she wasn't going to come out again this evening, we decided to wait a while longer, just in case.

'It's interesting,' I whispered as the sky became pitch black outside the window. 'I thought I knew Mandy after following her for so many years. She's got this presence almost everywhere you look. She puts it all out there and seems so robust at handling whatever comes her way. But she's just a normal human being at the end of the day. And I don't know her at all.'

'You're right about that. She surprised me today,' Blair replied, picking at the blue gel paint on one of their nails. 'And maybe she surprised herself too. I thought she was going to get onboard with you at one point, and then she went totally the other way.'

'I got caught in the crossfire all right,' I added, beginning to see a little humour in the situation now.

'You did.' Blair smiled. 'I mean she offered you a one-way ticket to Self-Love Utopia – wherever that is. You better go pack your case, honey.'

'I wonder if BA fly there?' I added, and we both stifled a giggle. 'What is it that Winston Churchill once said? "If you're going through hell, keep going."' I smirked.

'You were bang on,' they continued. 'Especially that point about getting to know yourself being the most difficult process.'

They paused thoughtfully.

'Are you speaking from experience?' I asked tentatively.

It wasn't as if either of us had anywhere to go right now, so it felt like a good time to get to know Blair a little better.

They sighed. 'Oh, I related.'

'I'd love to hear your story, if you're comfortable telling me.' I hoped I hadn't overstepped the mark.

'It might take a while, get cosy,' they said. 'My story started a long time ago. I was probably around the age of three or four.' I nodded at Blair, encouraging them to go on.

'I guess I grew up feeling different. I was the little boy who wore dresses for "fun" and never wanted to take them off. I preferred to hang out with the girls, yet I was the best at football, and the school tug-of-war champion. You should have seen me at clip 'n' climb – like a mini-Spiderman! – I was so fast and strong. I always fancied girls and my first kiss was at aged ten with one of the prettiest girls in my class. She was called Amelia and it happened in the park on the way home from school. We were the talk of the year, we'd walk around the playground together holding hands at break. For a long while I enjoyed playing up to my image as a stud. I used to get through a tonne of gel styling my hair every morning and I got one ear pierced the moment I was allowed to. But the thing I loved most about it all was the preparation, the whole process of putting on an act. Then, when I was about fourteen, one night on a Scouts trip, I ended up sleeping in the same creaky single bed as one of my male friends. I remember our hands touching and lacing together for the briefest moment in the night, and it was like an electric charge. It was as though I had stoked a red-hot furnace, and the sparks wouldn't go out.' They hesitated. 'In the morning, we barely said a word to each other, we were so embarrassed. We both knew what had happened, that was plain. I played it over so many times in my mind, hoping that I might get to feel that again.'

My mind turned back to my first kiss with Rob, how the reaction in my body had been like fireworks going off. 'What happened next?'

'My family were religious. I grew up in this tiny village

in Derbyshire and there were literally no gay or bisexual people we knew. I was terrified about what would happen if anyone – my family or friends – found out about it. I thought I could be kicked out of home for having feelings about other boys. It was lonely. I would stay in my room a lot, googling "Am I gay?" quizzes online. I got bullied badly at secondary school, after the kid from Scouts decided to turn against me and told everyone I had tried to hold his hand that night. They called me names and excluded me. I was lucky he didn't tell his parents, because I have no idea what would have happened then.' Instinctively I reached out and squeezed their arm.

'I found solace in an online community,' Blair continued, 'chatting to others on DM and via dating apps, but being too scared to ever take it further. Everything and anything to do with exploring the real me, and the feelings I was having, had to be done in secret. It was hard to make sense of who I was. The only way to describe it is, I felt like a treasure trove of disconnected items, like I wasn't going to have the straight trajectory most kids have.'

'Really? Do you think most people are straight forward?' I asked. 'The older I get, the more I realise that no one knows what they're doing, least of all the adults. It must have been hard,' I sympathised. 'But look at you now. How did you find a way to express yourself?'

'Fashion had a huge role in helping me to feel comfortable in my skin,' they continued. 'There was a show on TV called *You, Me and They* with a queer storyline at its centre, and a character who embraced gender-neutral fashion. It made me feel seen and inspired me to create my own identity rather than chase the one imposed by society. When you forget about there being clothes for men and clothes for women, once you remove those barriers, then you open up this kaleidoscopic world in which you can have fun and truly be yourself. I go into shops and sometimes I'm drawn to women's clothes, thinking they're amazing, and other times I gravitate to the traditional men's section. I love mixing the two together.' They looked at me. 'Why do we need to limit ourselves? I try not to think too much about what it means – I'm just doing me.'

'You do you so well,' I acknowledged. 'I love how you put your looks together. It's so creative. It's cool. I'm learning a lot from you.' I smiled, and then asked, 'Did you come out to your parents in the end?'

'I waited until my eighteenth birthday,' they said. 'I'd been watching the second season of *You, Me and They* religiously. Mum had seen some of it too, and she hadn't yet banned it or run out of the room in disgust, so I figured she was at least aware that not everyone fits a heterosexual mould. By this time, I was quite clearly dressing differently to other lads my age. I'd even had a few dates with a guy I met through my Saturday job, working in a bar in Derby. The whole family was gathered around in the garden, and we popped some champagne, and I did it – I told them I was bisexual and gender fluid.'

'How did they take it?' I asked them.

'Mum said she'd guessed as much, and Dad gave me a hug. My sister's exact words were "No shit, Sherlock! But you're not borrowing any of my Vivienne Westwood." It was such a relief. I even felt silly for not talking to them about it sooner. After that, the floodgates opened, and I felt like I had stepped across a border onto the yellow brick road. Like someone had turned the lights on in a dark attic – and they were multicoloured mobile disco lights at that.' We both giggled.

'How old are you now?' I asked.

'Twenty-two. I went to fashion college straight after my A-levels and did some work experience at *Wonderland* magazine. That's where I met Mandy on a cover shoot. They photographed her suspended from the ceiling of a church in a white fluffy bikini, garter, and these incredible custom-made fluffy angel wings attached to her back. There were lit-up crucifixes everywhere. It was epic.'

'I remember that cover! It was off the scale,' I raved. 'I loved it.'

'She did too. I went fully camp for the shoot and wore a pink fluffy cropped jacket and skin-tight pants with Doc Martens, expressing my individuality in all its glory for the first time at work. I figured this was the place to do it.'

'I bet you rocked it.'

'Mandy said she loved my outfit,' they said, blushing. 'I looked after all her needs on that shoot, from angling the wind machine to cutting up her chicken breast into bite-sized pieces so it didn't displace her lip gloss when she ate. I even went to Boots to pick up a treatment for her recurrent vaginal yeast infection – and that news *did not* find its way onto Popbitch.'

I put my hand over my mouth as I laughed. 'Seriously? Tell me she didn't *really s*end you out for that?'

'She seriously did.' Blair put their ear to the door. 'Shit, I *really* hope she can't hear any of this.'

I did the same. 'It's completely quiet, she must have fallen asleep.'

'I basically did whatever Mandy wanted,' they continued. 'I was her fluffy camp lap dog. Maybe it was a test, because, at the end of the shoot day, she asked when my work experience was ending. It turned out that Mandy needed a personal assistant, so she and Jose took me on. I guess they judged correctly, by my painted nails and pussy bow shirt, that I wasn't going to threaten Jose's position as the manly man of the house.'

'Well, you were unlikely to try it on, now you knew about her issues down below!' I giggled.

'I'm pretty sure it was all fabricated to see if I had what it took,' they said. It reminded me of the made-up scenarios Mandy had used in my interview process as well. 'And Jose judged correctly that I was more interested in the hot male photographer's assistant, than the superstar striking the poses,' they said wistfully. 'He was right, because I also gained a boyfriend in Patrick that day.'

'Result!' I held out my clenched fist and we bumped.

'But test or not, more accurately, you got it because you're brilliant at what you do,' I said. 'Trust me, I know first-hand how hard it is to have a diva for a boss, I used to assist Mona Armstrong. She, who would only drink caffè macchiato from one particular London coffee shop, and had a penchant for never answering her phone, or being polite to people. It's the hardest job in the world – you have to develop the patience of a sloth and be skilled in literally everything.'

'Bump back to you for sticking it out with Mona Armstrong,' they said, as we tapped knuckles again. 'I've heard her reputation precedes her. They ended up putting a ban on working with her at *Wonderland*. She was more high maintenance than the A-list stars.'

'Perhaps your wonky trajectory stood you in good stead,' I offered.

They smiled. 'Yeah, you're probably right. I was definitely resilient – you have to be, when bullies are on your back. The same skills come in handy when navigating life with a celebrity.'

'It sounds to me like you understood who you were from a young age. It just took other people longer to catch up. I really believe we're all at different points on one big scale – labelling people is where the problems lie. I wish we didn't have to use labels at all. But now the world is becoming more open, it might not be so hard for future generations. Are we full circle with my "Self-Love Utopia"?' I smiled.

Blair looked me straight in the eyes. 'I love your positivity, babe, but the world isn't nearly there. I think there is more polarisation than ever. It's up to people like us to make a difference – I'm looking to you to keep doing what you're doing and encouraging authenticity. There's no way we can break down barriers if we keep pretending to be somebody else. We can all have influence, in big or small ways. When

I think about that show I watched and how it enabled me to come out to my family, it literally liberated me from a prison. It has stuck with me. We have a really important job to do here, Amber, we have the possibility to make change.'

'Wow.' I bowed down before them. 'Can you run for Prime Minister now, please?'

'Ha.' They grinned. 'That's your job. I guess this is what I wanted to say to everyone on the first evening, but I felt too embarrassed. Plus it was a little premature,' they said.

'I think we've crossed that line now.' I cringed. 'The question is whether we have to go back the way we came, or move forward. We're still not even through the first fortnight.'

'We have to try to convince her,' they said. 'If a star like Mandy decides to let down her guard, this could be huge.'

'I'm with you.' I smiled. 'And Blair – thank you for telling me all this. We owe it to you and all the other Blairs out there, to continue encouraging individuality. I think we all have a role to play in this.'

They held out their pinky towards me and instinctively I linked it with mine. 'BFFs in here?' they said.

'Yes, baby, to Beautiful Furry Friends living in a Self-Love Utopia!' And we laughed together, until we remembered we were meant to be quiet.

After another quick door check, through which we both thought we could hear a soft snore, I unfurled my legs from underneath me and slowly stood up. My knees cracked as I rose. 'I definitely shouldn't be this stiff at twenty-six,'

I muttered. 'If she's sleeping, I'm going to steal from the bread bin. I'm starving.'

'I'll join you down there in a bit. I've got to do something first,' they said, taking my outstretched hand to help pull them up. 'I just want to call my mum to tell her I love her.'

CHAPTER THIRTEEN

Blair's last comment stayed with me. I needed to call Lucy back, and I really wanted to speak to Rob. I headed back to my room to change into my comfy onesie and check my phone. I found a missed call from Rob. Typical. He called in the one hour I wasn't incessantly checking it. The fact he had made the first move was quietly pleasing.

I FaceTimed him back.

'Hey,' he said, his voice lacking energy.

'Hey, I can barely see you.' It was very dark where Rob was, I could only just make out his features. 'Are you in bed already?'

I glanced at the time at the top of my phone, it was only eight p.m.

'Yeah, I felt tired, so I thought I may as well hit the sack,' he said half-heartedly.

'Doesn't sound like you. Nothing to even watch on TV?'

'Nothing I fancied.' This was unlike Rob. Working in television, he was always keen to see anything to keep up with trends, and talk me through the technical details of how they would have been filmed. I don't think I had ever known him at a loss for something to watch. 'Anyway, how are you doing?'

I explained the weirdness on the shoot today and this evening, and Rob listened. I was always interested in his verdict on celebrity goings-on. He was a voice of reason and had seen plenty of it before, having produced a number of series with stars including the crazy Angel Wear show we did together in New York.

'Hopefully she'll come round,' was all he could muster at the end.

'You sound pissed off. Is everything okay?'

'Yeah, I'm fine.'

'You don't sound it.'

'Have you decided to trust me again?' he asked. I was jolted into remembering why we hadn't spoken for a few days.

'Should I?' I bit back.

'Amber, there was no reason for you to ever not trust me,' he said. 'I'm not in touch with my ex, and I don't intend to be. Where did you get that thought from?' He paused. 'Be honest.'

'Okay, truth is, I zoomed into a photo on my phone, of you at Christmas.'

'A photo?'

'Exactly what I said, Rob. I zoomed into a photo I found on my phone of us on Boxing Day, and it showed your Facebook Messenger open, and an image that looked very much like Emily's profile picture next to the chat. So, *naturally,* I assumed that you were in touch with her and—'

'And you assumed I was having an affair,' he said, finishing my sentence. 'Without even being sure that it was her profile picture, or that there were any new messages, or *asking* me about it. Or being a little more rational about it before accusing me of infidelity? Never mind the fact that you were spying on my phone.'

'Indirectly. I was actually spying on my *own* photo, on my *own* phone.'

'Amber, I wasn't texting Emily. I haven't been in touch with her for a really long time. Send me the photo and I'll help you verify what you believe you've seen, if you like.' He gave an even bigger weary sigh. 'It really upset me that you'd think I'd do something like that.' Now that he put it like that, it did sound as though I had accused him of something big without any hard evidence. 'Seriously, send me the photo if you want. We can get it forensically analysed.'

I listened for any indication of guilt in his tone, and there seemed to be none. Rob's brow was furrowed as he waited for me to respond. A bit of me did want to examine the photo again – *I'll do that in bed later* – but, for now, it seemed pointless belabouring the argument. I wanted to believe him, and if I wanted to make things good between us, I had to.

'I'm sorry,' I murmured. 'I made an assumption, and I shouldn't have.'

'I'm glad that's sorted then.' He let out a sigh.

'Are you okay, Rob?' I asked again. 'You don't seem yourself – you sound really down.' Granted the room was pretty dark, but even the whites of his eyes seemed grey and lifeless. There was none of the usual Rob spark when he looked at me. 'Look, I really am sorry,' I continued. 'I didn't mean to make you feel this bad. I shouldn't have been so accusatory. Am I forgiven?'

'You're forgiven,' he replied. 'I'm sorry I haven't called sooner. It's been a shit week to be honest.'

'Oh no, work again?'

'Yep, same old story, it's rubbish. There are no new productions. I'm pretty sure I'm going to be let go. I feel like I'm waiting to be called in for a "chat" with Mike and that will be that. It's doing nothing for my confidence. But the worst thing about it? I don't even care anymore, Am. I'm over working in TV. But I have absolutely no clue what I want to do. Or what I'd be *able* to do.' He looked down, unable to make eye contact.

My eyes searched his face. 'Well, maybe you won't be let go. Is it worth having a chat with Mike to tell him how you're feeling? Maybe there are other roles that you could go for?' I felt helpless that I was here and he was all alone worrying about this. 'And if it's not TV, of course there are plenty of things you could do. You're so talented! Why do you think I'm dating you?'

Silence. He didn't even crack a smile at my attempt at a joke. *This is really bad.*

'I can't tell my boss the truth,' he snapped. 'If I did, I'd be let go for sure. And how will that help us, with rent to pay and a mortgage to try for? I need to keep my job, Amber. I just hate it.'

'Look, I'm doing this job with Mandy to help us save,' I said, trying a change of tack. 'You're such a brilliant director. You've nailed every project you've worked on. What is it about TV you hate?'

'Babe, they've all been low-budget celebrity crap. I'm hardly winning Emmys. I just find that world so one-dimensional now – besides, it's old, none of that stuff is winning ratings wars anymore. The main channels want eyeballs, hard-hitting documentaries, true crime, or slick Oscar-worthy dramas created in virtual worlds.' He sighed heavily. 'Maybe I should become a pilot.'

'I don't think your eyesight is good enough.' It was a bad attempt to be funny.

He didn't react. 'So, what else has been happening?' he asked.

'I've had all kinds of shenanigans from Mandy since I've been here,' I muttered, hoping to show him that work is rarely a ball all the time for anyone. 'But this will make you laugh . . . I bruised my lip in the gym the other morning and Mandy took me to a cryotherapy chamber to try to stop the swelling.'

'Cryotherapy?' He winced.

'It's basically a giant freezer.'

He feigned interest. 'Sounds painful.'

'What are you doing at the weekend?' I asked.

He shrugged. 'No plans yet. Will you be working all of it?'

'Mandy's having drinks at the house tomorrow evening. I wish you could come. I could ask, she might be willing to make an exception?'

'It was fairly explicit in your contract that guests aren't allowed,' he replied. 'Anyway, I'm not really up for it,' he said resignedly. 'I feel like a total party pooper at the moment.'

'I'll call you instead, it'll be nice to commiserate with you when they cut short my contract.'

'Oh baby, you never know – be positive, okay?'

'I'll try.'

After we said goodbye, I stared into space for a few moments, thinking about the call. Something didn't feel right. I'd rarely heard Rob so lacklustre. He felt so far away. I couldn't think about it for too long because I needed to get back downstairs in the annexe to start packing up the clothes from the shoot.

As I began carefully folding up items and putting them back into the bags in which they arrived, I remembered with alarm that Mandy had been wearing the diamond earrings earlier in the kitchen. They were on a strict twenty-four-hour loan and would be collected by a security guard later this evening. With a price tag of over ten thousand pounds, I could *not* afford for them to go AWOL.

I WhatsApped Blair to see what they thought I should do but got no reply.

So that was how I found myself on all fours outside Mandy's bedroom door half an hour later, trying to look through the keyhole. The house was really quiet. Everyone involved with the photoshoot had long gone, and I hadn't seen Jimi for the rest of the day, after he disappeared from the kitchen when Mandy did. Coco and Philippa were pottering around in the kitchen.

There was no response from Mandy's room when I knocked softly, although there was every possibility she couldn't hear me. Either that, or she was sleeping soundly. There was no option other than to creep into Mandy's room to retrieve the earrings; hopefully she had left them somewhere obvious – on the dressing table, a bedside table, or perhaps in the bathroom. If I couldn't find them, I'd just have to come clean and find a way to delay the collection.

I pushed the door open slowly and poked my head around it. The room was in complete darkness. Shadows hid the corners, making the space feel larger than I knew it was. I edged forwards, my eyes slowly acclimatising to the darkness. I could make out a light around the closed door to the en suite, and then the edges of pieces of furniture. At the far side, the end of the bed was becoming visible, and to my left, Mandy's dressing table. It was there I decided to look first.

I crouched down, figuring it was better to crawl to keep out of sight, just in case Mandy woke up. The contour of a body in the middle of the bed told me she was in it. I was about halfway across the floor when I heard a floorboard creak on the other side of the room.

I looked towards the door to her en suite, an orangey glow under it suggested a light had been left on in there. I scuttled forwards towards the end of her bed, and a less vulnerable vantage point. A shadow moved across the spool of light under the door, and the floor creaked again. The Mandy-shaped mass in the bed stirred and rolled over. I froze, holding my breath. I could hear my heart thudding in my chest, it was beating heavily and more quickly with each second. Someone was in the bathroom.

A moment later, the door opened a little, and I glimpsed a shadowy shape. It was tall, muscular, definitely human. And definitely not Mandy. Could it be Jose? But I thought he was away. *Who could be in Mandy's bathroom?*

My next thought was of an intruder. I'd heard of this happening in celebrity houses – a criminal climbs in through an open bathroom window, grabs whatever valuables are on show, and gets out again.

My heart continued to pound as I slunk back, crouching close to the floor at the end of her bed, my body tight. I bowed my head, eyes fixed to the floor, desperate to keep myself hidden so whoever was there wouldn't see me.

The intruder kept moving very slowly. The bathroom door opened a little wider, and a quick glance up revealed the figure was wearing nothing but tight black Calvin Klein boxer shorts. I could see now they were holding an iPhone and using the torch for light. They were illuminated for a split second, before the light was extinguished. My gaze wandered up, it was impossible not to notice their perfectly defined body, tanned skin, and a large bulge in the tight underpants. The darkness moulded them into a rough form again. But in that split second of light, there was no mistaking it. There weren't many people on the planet with a physique as perfect as his. It was Jimi.

What is Jimi doing in Mandy's bedroom, half naked, while she is asleep in bed?

A moan came from the bed, Mandy was stirring. She

turned over in her sleep and called out, 'Baby, are you back?' Her voice was muffled, sleepy.

Jimi didn't reply.

She rolled over again, nestling into her duvet, and purred something indistinguishable in the other direction.

I froze again, afraid to move a muscle, too scared to breathe.

Did Mandy just call Jimi 'baby'? This wasn't the way she normally referred to him. A panic set in. I knew I had to get out of here. Fast.

If I have just uncovered what I think I've uncovered, there is no question that I am done for.

But getting out was not so easy. In one direction was the bathroom, in the other was a sleeping Mandy, and I was metres away from the safety of the bedroom door through which I had entered. Any chance of finding the earrings in the darkness, with two people to avoid, was feeling more and more hopeless. I was berating myself for thinking this was a good idea in the first place.

Jimi hadn't moved since Mandy called out. He definitely wasn't hurrying to get back into bed with her. When the room fell quiet for a few seconds, he began moving again, very slowly. I watched from my position on the floor as he carefully closed the en suite door and padded across the carpet. A floorboard creaked again, more loudly. The hairs on my arms stood on end. Jimi froze like a statue. The sound made Mandy jerk awake, she appeared to sit up briefly.

'Is it the morning?' she muttered drowsily.

Jimi stealthily, silently, dropped down to the floor, like a ninja. Now he was just a few feet away from me, around the other side of the bed. It seemed that Jimi didn't want Mandy to know he was in her room either. I could hear him breathing, he was so close. *Shit. Now what am I going to do?*

We both waited. As I listened to his every breath, I tried to hold the air within my lungs so he wouldn't notice me. He began moving again. I stayed still, aware that I didn't want to give Jimi the shock of his life, only to have him scream and wake Mandy for sure. How would we explain *that*?

I tucked myself in close to the bed, just as Jimi's face appeared around the corner. Suddenly we were nose to nose. His eyes widened as he took me in. 'Fuck! Amber!' he whispered.

'Shhh!' I raised my finger to my lips.

'What are you doing in here?' he breathed.

'What are *you* doing here?' I spoke, no louder than a whisper.

Both of us were equally stunned, yet united in our determination not to wake up Mandy.

'Are you having an affair?' I whispered, accusatorily, aghast at the words coming out of my mouth.

'Of course not!' he said, as if I had asked the most ridiculous question in the world. He glanced over his shoulder, as we both heard Mandy sigh. 'Let's talk about this outside!'

In a kind of haphazard bear crawl race, we both made it back to the door and into the hallway in seconds. I very quietly closed the bedroom door behind us. Hearts beating fast, all we could do was pray she hadn't heard anything.

'Amber, what the actual fuck?' Jimi was looking at me as if *I* had done something wrong, when *he* was the one in his underpants in Mandy's bathroom.

How is he going to explain himself? I felt incredulous that he could be looking so accusingly at me.

'I was getting something!' I said, trying to get my breath back. 'Some earrings as it happens. Expensive diamond ones which need returning. And which I didn't manage to get – thanks to you. Anyway, I'm not the one who was practically naked in her bathroom!'

Jimi paused for a moment. He looked around to check we weren't being overheard. We both knew by now that Philippa had a way of covertly appearing whenever an important conversation was taking place.

'Come with me.'

We went into his bedroom, which was at the end of the same corridor as Mandy's. It was a lot smaller though, just a double bed, with a wardrobe and a chest of drawers. A rack of dumbbells stood in a corner and an exercise mat was laid out on the floor. It smelt vaguely of ripe exercise clothes and his zesty aftershave.

'I know how this looks,' Jimi continued. 'But I was just going to bed when I had a horrible realisation. I didn't even have a chance to get dressed – I guessed I'd be in and out of there quickly, so I took my chance.' He stopped.

'Took your chance to do what?' I asked.

'Drugs,' he said. My eyes widened. 'Magic mushrooms, to be precise. Not a huge amount, but enough.'

'What do you mean enough?' I asked fearfully.

'I gave Mandy some mushroom powder to make into a tea, to keep her anxiety at bay; help with focus. She needed that ahead of the shoot. I've been using it for years – you simply drink it – sometimes I pimp it up with a load of nutrients, it's legal and really helpful. But—'

'But?'

'But I gave her the wrong kind – a friend had sent me some of the illegal stuff from California, pure powder. You can get it on the black market and it's legal in some states of America. I use it occasionally for a bit of fun when I'm going out. Anyway, I accidentally gave Mandy the wrong stuff this morning and I needed to get it out of her bathroom before she took anymore.'

My jaw fell open as Jimi was telling me this. 'So Mandy was basically microdosing magic mushrooms on the shoot today?' I asked.

Jimi nodded remorsefully.

I shook my head. 'Shit, that's bad.'

'I know it's fucking bad! Why do you think I was trying to remove all the evidence? Anyway, it's fine, she's breathing, she was already back to her old snappy self at dinner, and she will have slept if off by now anyway, she's been out since seven o'clock. I got the rest from the bathroom, and judging by what's left, she didn't take too much.'

'What effect will it have had on her?' I asked gravely, having never taken magic mushrooms before.

'Nothing major, just the giggling earlier, the sensory reaction to her environment, like colours becoming much more vibrant, surfaces pleasing to touch, a greater appreciation of words and music. Psilocybin can help rewire the mind – opening it up to allow new thoughts and creativity. The trip only lasts a matter of hours.'

'Oh great, so you're telling me she was tripping when she decided to go along with my suggestions for the photoshoot?' I said bashfully. 'I thought she actually seemed to be listening.'

'Hopefully it made her more willing to try something new,' he offered. 'It gave me a heart attack when I realised though. I didn't want to risk her enjoying that feeling so much she'd reach for the rest. So now you can understand why I leapt out of bed and went to get it back. You'd have done the same.'

I believed Jimi. He looked panicked, and it seemed far too elaborate a story to have made up on the spot if he was covering up for having an affair with Mandy. Although the fact they had been out together early in the morning now occurred to me as slightly suspicious too.

'You spend a lot of time together though – she confides in you, doesn't she?' I asked.

'Listen, Mandy and Jose have got all sorts going on at the moment, as you may have realised.'

'I know she's wanting to get pregnant,' I admitted.

'It's more than that – she's *obsessed* with it. She even asked me if I would consider being a sperm donor for a baby. That's where we were this morning, she had me meet a doctor friend she's been talking to.'

He exhaled quietly through his mouth. 'She doesn't want Jose to know, it's kind of . . . personal for him.'

'Oh.' I sighed.

'There's no way he can father a child naturally,' he whispered sadly. 'They've tried everything. And with her endometriosis, it's been a difficult time.'

'That's really sad news,' I said. 'It must be hard for them to figure out what to do. She opened up to me a bit about this in the cryotherapy chamber yesterday.'

'You too?' He smirked. 'That's her favourite place to corner people. Mands first asked me about being a sperm donor in there. She knows it's hard to say no when you're trying to stop your blood from turning into a slushy.'

'So, are you going to do it?' I asked.

'No,' he replied firmly. 'I couldn't do that without wanting to be the legal father. She was requesting I would hand over all my rights. My name wouldn't be on the birth certificates, no say in how the baby is brought up. Seeing a baby every day and knowing you're the dad but not being able to act it?' Tears glistened in his eyes. 'I couldn't do it. Even for my brother.'

I pondered this thought. 'It's a massive thing to ask of someone. I'm sure she understood.'

'I think she has a few, how should I put it, irons in the fire when it comes to that. Anyway,' he continued, 'she took it well enough, and I gave her the mushroom powder soon after, to help take the edge off. Only it was the wrong one.'

I shook my head, realising that my mouth had dropped

open in a very obvious way somewhere in the middle of this conversation.

'It's no wonder she was so open yesterday,' Jimi continued. 'The drugs helped. Are you okay, Amber?' He turned to me.

I nodded, taking in what he had told me. As someone who had never touched drugs, it was a lot.

'Don't be freaked out, everyone's doing them,' Jimi reassured me. 'From bored housewives, to high-flying founders of multimillion-dollar companies, to Silicon Valley executives – it's the new alcohol or cocaine. But needless to say, this is all *top* secret.'

'Does Blair know?'

'I don't think so.'

'Just call me Fort Knox,' I said, drawing an imaginary zipper across my lips.

'Hopefully she'll be sleeping it all off in there anyway,' he added.

'I kind of liked the relaxed version of Mandy – more than the one who lost it at dinner,' I responded.

Jimi smiled. 'Thank God it only made her more relaxed.'

'Isn't Mandy fiercely anti-drugs?' I asked.

He nodded slowly. 'And if Jose had been here, or if Julie-Ann had noticed anything, it could have been horrible. But it's done, she doesn't need to know about it. No one does. Okay?'

'Okay,' I said solemnly.

'I only told you because you were about to jump to an even worse assumption.'

'In return for keeping this secret, can you help me get the

earrings back?' I asked, remembering that it was now about twenty minutes until the security guard would be here. 'If I don't have them packaged up and ready to go, then I will be in big, *big* trouble.'

'Fine,' he said, 'you go in, and I'll put some clothes on and keep guard by the door. If she wakes, I'll think of something. But after the day she's had, I'm pretty sure we're safe.'

We walked back towards Mandy's bedroom door, and like trained marksmen, I opened it slightly and Jimi covered my back. There was still a Mandy-shaped lump in the middle of the bed, so I skirted around the edge of the room, keeping within the shadows, with more certainty about where I was headed this time. I used the torch on my iPhone to briefly light up the surface of her dressing table, and to my relief the earrings were right there, along with several other pieces of jewellery we had used on the shoot. I scooped it all up carefully and placed the expensive, twinkling bundle of jewels into the roomy central pocket of my onesie, as Mandy continued to sleep like a baby.

Before leaving the room, I stole a look at her fast asleep. Her big, glossy hair, still perfectly curled from the shoot, was splayed out on the pillow. She looked so peaceful and beautiful, like a sleeping Grecian goddess. I felt a sort-of fondness for her and everything she was going through. I could forgive her mood swings earlier, now I knew the full backstory.

I hope your wish comes true, Mandy, I whispered internally.

CHAPTER FOURTEEN

The following day I lay low, tending to the returns from the shoot and calling in new pieces for engagements in the week ahead. I didn't see much of Mandy. She was a figure fleetingly leaving the kitchen as I entered, or dashing out of the front door and into a waiting car.

The next morning, as the final moments of sleep drained from my body, I lay in bed and a sick feeling went from my throat to settle like concrete in my stomach. I expected that today, Mandy would speak to me about the dining room incident. I picked up my phone and scrolled between WhatsApp, email, and Instagram. Blair had gone quiet, which potentially meant they were trying to stay out of it and would accept no blame when I was fired.

I opened the Mindful Moments app and tried to do some breathwork.

'Inhalation . . . exhalation . . .' said the woo-woo person in the video. I couldn't get past two breaths before I gave up and put down my phone, only to pick it up a second later when it buzzed with a WhatsApp from Jimi.

Morning! Just a reminder that everything we discussed must not go anywhere.
  Don't worry, it won't.
Fancy a Pilates session? Mandy's just cancelled so I'm free.
  Sure, I'll meet you in the gym.

I had harboured an irrational fear of these machines until the session with Jimi, who took me through a series of exercises and made it seem like fun, although my abs were already sore. Being in the gym with Jimi had offered a distraction from worrying about whether my time here was about to be cut short. He was so busy delivering instructions, and I was so busy trying not to injure myself again, or accidentally fart whilst doing roll-ups, that an hour passed in a flash, and we didn't get a chance to talk about anything else.

When I looked at my phone for the first time after the session, I read a WhatsApp message from Mandy. *Your attendance is required at a team meeting this morning. 10am sharp in the drawing room. It's mandatory.*

Jimi picked up his phone and read the message at the same time as I did.

'Jose's back,' he said.

'Do you think he's come especially to sack me?' I asked, a tightness emerging in my throat.

'I doubt it, but I think we'll find out what Mandy thinks of the photos.'

I sighed.

'But if she hates them, you do know it's not your fault, don't you? Everyone was a part of the shoot. You saved it, if anything. I'm going to change my T-shirt quickly, I'll follow you down.'

I looked at the side of Jimi's perfectly formed face. He had said exactly what I needed to hear.

I hurried into the drawing room to discover Jose sat on the sofa next to Mandy. Blair, Coco, and Lola were already there, stealing the best seats – the ones furthest away from Mandy and Jose.

Jose must have got in from New York late last night or early this morning. His hair was still damp as though he had not long showered, and the familiar whiff of fresh aftershave created a warm bubble of fragrance around him, just as it had done on the day I first met him.

'Julie-Ann will be joining us shortly,' Mandy informed us, setting herself up as chairperson for the meeting. 'She's running a bit late, but she's bringing the photos with her – so we can all look at them on the big screen.'

'Morning!' Jimi said on cue, strolling through the door. He came and sat next to me. It felt nice to be close to him again.

I focused my gaze on the tightly clasped hands in my lap. So far, Mandy had avoided direct eye contact with me, which wasn't a good sign.

Philippa entered the room, making us all look up. She was a welcome vision, holding a silver tray containing a cafetiere of fresh coffee and mugs. 'Stimulants are served,'

Philippa exclaimed in her deadpan manner, as she deposited the tray on a large, low coffee table in the middle of the sofas.

I nudged Jimi's side subtly with my elbow.

He knew exactly what I meant and surreptitiously dug a firm finger into my ribs. It got me in exactly one of my most ticklish places. When I looked at him, his eyes widened. This led me to have a sudden, uncontrollable urge to laugh. Instead, I let out an ungainly loud snort through my nose which I immediately had to pretend was a coughing fit.

Everyone looked at me.

'Are you okay?' Blair said.

'I'm fine,' I spluttered.

Blair was on their feet, arm outstretched, offering me a glass of water. 'Here!'

'Oh God, I'm honestly fine, just a little dry.' I cleared my throat to emphasise the point.

Jimi seemed to find this amusing and was giggling behind his hand.

'Thank you.' I took the glass from Blair and sipped. There was no way I could make eye contact with Jimi again, he would definitely set me off. I managed to steady my breathing and swallow without spitting the water out or collapsing into giggles.

'So, coffee?' asked Coco, mercifully taking the attention off me, and pouring from the cafetiere. Philippa had melted into the atmosphere.

Normally we would help ourselves to coffee from the kitchen mid-morning, so this indicated a formality, which put me on edge. The air in the room settled back into silence as we all watched Coco, like pouring coffee was the most fascinating thing we had ever seen.

Blair broke the ice. 'How was your trip, Jose?'

Jose sucked air into his cheeks. He looked more clean-shaven than normal today, and with his pronounced jawline, tanned, blemish-free skin, and bright, clear, brown eyes, he was a good-looking guy – it was obvious he and Jimi were related.

'All good,' he replied. 'Busy. I came back early in the end. The snow was coming in as I left.' He seemed reluctant to give away many details.

'I love snow in New York!' Blair and Coco said practically in unison.

All the while Mandy had her arm tightly linked with Jose's, as if she were clinging on to him for her life.

We were saved from more excruciating small talk by the bell ringing and a clattering sound from the front door. A minute later, Julie-Ann hurried into the room along with mutterings about the M25, weather, and bad drivers. She was visibly flustered and seemed embarrassed to have kept her biggest client waiting. She hastily set up her laptop on a mahogany table, moving it closer to us all. Everyone shuffled forwards to get a good view as the thumbnails from the shoot began to appear on the screen.

I held my breath. Julie-Ann seemed to know what she was looking for and scrolled through the thumbnails briskly, not stopping to pause on an image long enough for us to take a detailed look: The lounge set-up, the spare room, some product shots . . . she skipped along quickly, suggesting that she wasn't open to opinions on these. At last, she seemed to find what she had been searching for. Julie-Ann double-clicked on an image from the master bedroom set-up, and a photo of Mandy appeared, filling the whole of the screen.

It was the portrait of her lying on the bed. I recognised it instantly as the candid moment just after our exchange, when she had pulled off her boots in a huff and stared out of the window. It was more 'undone' than 'done up', thoughtful, more body on show than many of the others. I would even call it raw. Yet there was something so beautiful about it too, almost otherworldly. The sun had been shining in that moment and it caught her eyes, making them sparkle intensely green. The blue of the winter sky outside, the sharp, spiky foliage creeping around the window, at a juxtaposition with the soft, womanly shape of her body splayed across the bed. Her skirt was riding up a little, her thigh skin was visibly puckered, cellulite and stretch marks on show; there were indentations on her legs where the boots had been. Her hair hung loose around her shoulders and her lip gloss was barely visible. Nothing about it was provocative, it was just real, feminine, human.

'*This*,' Julie-Ann said. 'I think this is really special.'

'Are you serious.' Mandy spat out the words more as a laugh than a question. She looked among our stunned faces, all of us gawping at the photo. I felt her eyes glance over me, then fix on Jimi, she was desperate to garner support from one of us. *Surely family will fall into line?* Jimi looked away.

'Seriously, this cannot be The One,' she continued

desperately. 'At least not without a ton of Photoshopping, surely?'

I realised I was still holding my breath. I gulped it down as she spoke again: 'Someone, for God's sake, speak some sense . . .' She looked around the room in a panic. 'Right about now, would be good?'

I fiddled with my bracelet, twiddled a piece of hair, and did what I could to avoid Mandy's gaze, feeling responsible for the image in question. All the while, a hundred reasons why this *was* the perfect photo – just as Julie-Ann had said – whirled around my mind.

The love handles, the crow's feet, laughter lines, it was such a brilliant photo. I wished Mart was here to give his take on this candid portrait.

Finally, Jimi spoke. 'This is you.'

Mandy let out a pained wailing sound. One that you might expect a cat to make if you accidentally stood on its tail. We all looked in trepidation as she turned her face away from the screen. And then her eyes filled with tears. Jose held her close, and no one said anything.

I could understand it must be intense to see yourself looking so vulnerable in front of an audience, but it wasn't as though Mandy wasn't used to being the centre of attention. She had lived in the spotlight for most of her adult life. Yet the UK instalment of Mandy's life had a lot of pressure resting on it, if her fame and fortune were to soar higher over here too. And there lay the problem, times had changed. Audiences were becoming less engaged with high-octane glamour and impenetrable perfection.

I could see Julie-Ann on my right, looking fidgety.

'Personally, I think it's beautiful,' she said softly.

I wanted to agree with Julie-Ann, but I felt too nervous to stick my neck out again. I couldn't afford to lose this job, my future home depended on it.

Mandy pursed her lips and turned towards the screen again. She cocked her head to one side as she studied the image.

'What do you think?' She turned to Jose and asked pointedly, 'Do you think it's beautiful?' I felt a familiar pull in my stomach.

'I think Julie-Ann is right,' Jose replied, looking at her directly, telling her with his eyes that he meant it. 'I think you're beautiful, vulnerable, and sexy in this image – this is the you that I see.' He put a hand on her knee.

'Oh Christ, Jose. This is how you *see* me? Seriously? I don't know whether to hug you or leave you!' she exclaimed, but her appearance had softened. 'Does anyone else agree?' She looked around the room at Blair, Coco, Jimi, and me, and we all nodded slowly in agreement.

Blair smiled at Julie-Ann, cautiously. They knew what this meant too, Jose championing the team over Mandy. This was big.

Jimi pushed his leg into mine, making me want to sigh.

'I honestly think we're all agreed: this is a stunning image. *The* image,' Julie-Ann continued.

Mandy was obviously taken aback being overruled like this, but she couldn't think of an immediate rhetorical slur to hurl at all of us. I pretended to focus on an abstract picture on the wall.

'It seems to me that fashion is no longer just about clothes,' Jose said profoundly. 'Look how much talking this image does. Your audience will love it.'

'But baby, I'm an influencer!' Mandy exclaimed. 'I kickstart trends. The whole point is that I wear clothes – and make-up, accessories, bunion corrector socks or whatever the hell it is that needs some influencing. When did that change? I mean I love clothes!'

'So do I!' I said, finding my voice and giving Mandy some support. *I'm not having Jose talk me out of a job here.* 'And you *will* be wearing clothes, don't worry about that. I worship at the altar of the best design talents in the world. But I think Jose makes a good point. Don't let the clothes wear *you* – you wear *them*.' I paused, and then said calmly, 'That's the difference between being an influencer and a bad influence.'

I turned my attention back to the image of Mandy on the screen. The more I looked at it, the more I loved it. Mart had captured such a perfect moment. It was ethereal and unguarded, yet there was something so strong and defiant about the shot too.

Jose said, 'When your fans see this, they will love you for it, Mands. Just like I do. You'll be more influential than ever.'

'For what it's worth, I love it too,' said Jimi, contributing to the conversation. '"Don't let the clothes wear you" is a killer concept. It's going to fly online.'

I was chuffed he had quoted me, and felt my cheeks redden.

'Yes,' added Julie-Ann. '*This* is what will endear you to the British public. Not Mandy Sykes trying to look like an English toff, but being yourself. The Brits like *realness*.' She glanced at me to accentuate her point. I knew I was looking very 'real' this morning, slightly sweaty and in my gym gear. 'The tide has turned. We need much more of this to build a social campaign. We need another shoot.'

The tide has turned. That's just given me a brilliant idea.

'West Wittering!' I announced. The room turned to look at me. 'It's on the Sussex coast, not far from here. There's a long sandy beach and dunes.'

'Sounds delightful. But what about it?' asked Julie-Ann.

'We could do another shoot there, get away from the stuffy stately home vibe and keep it as natural as possible. If we want realness, it's the perfect backdrop drawing together the wholesomeness of nature with the imperfect beauty of the human form – it will be wild, windy, provocative. With any luck, it will rain, to complete the picture.'

'This is so far outside my comfort zone, I think I'll need my passport,' Mandy muttered, a glacial expression on her face.

CHAPTER FIFTEEN

WEEK THREE

I managed to spend the next few days quietly getting on with the styling assignments asked of me, without drawing any unnecessary attention to myself. Using the gym with Jimi had become one of the highlights of my days here. Between putting me through my paces on the Pilates machine, we would talk about all kinds of things – from how guacamole is one of the best inventions known to mankind, to Mandy's volatile moods, and how much he was missing the Miami sunshine. Sometimes I would feel a frisson of attraction between us. We had neglected to discuss our love lives with each other, so I wondered whether he was attached. Although sometimes I questioned whether he was even straight, because he seemed a bit too good to be true. From time to time, I'd notice his cap and sunglasses perched on another statue in an ornate corner or stone alcove in the house, and it became our running private joke to guess how long it would take Philippa to notice and remove them, replacing them quietly and neatly back in Jimi's room and mentioning nothing of it.

Jimi was enough of a distraction to ensure that even when Mandy turned down my polite request to wear the floral silk chiffon gown to an afternoon event, or the tuxedo to a premiere, it didn't have the power to get me down for long. No one had mentioned emailing me my P45 yet, so I considered this a win.

As the days went on, I noticed I was spending less time checking my phone for messages from Rob. And it was only towards the end of the week that I realised I hadn't heard from him for a few days.

It was the day of the cocktail party, and Mandy had announced via WhatsApp that she was giving us the afternoon off to get ready.

Fancy a chat? I messaged Rob on WhatsApp. *There's a party here tonight, but I can speak first?*

To which he replied, *I'm sorry I've not been in touch, I've been in a weird frame of mind. I'll drop you a line when I've cheered up. Have fun.*

This wasn't like Rob. I immediately pressed the little green phone icon. Perhaps if he heard my voice, he'd feel better.

He didn't pick up, although he was online according to WhatsApp.

Then another message arrived. *I'm not up for chatting right now. Have a great time. Love you x*

Outside the window I noticed a lone magpie on a low branch of a tree, the branch still bare from winter. It was cold, crisp, and sharp outside today. Even sharper now that I had a tight, spiky feeling in my chest. I had been so looking forward to telling Rob I planned to wear a jumpsuit this evening, and the silver boots he gave me for Christmas – he always said my bum looked sexy in that jumpsuit. Tears sprung in my eyes. I realised I felt homesick for Rob. I fought back tears by anchoring my eyes on the magpie.

Where's your wife and your children?

I scanned the area around the bird in a bid to spot another magpie. I've always been superstitious about them. In fact, I still blame the E I got for A-level Economics to the fact I saw a lone magpie on my way to school that morning.

The magpie in my view was twitching its head. It turned almost 360 degrees, searching wildly for its family too.

Where are they? Where are you, Rob?

I watched the magpie fail to find his mates and eventually give up and fly off.

I lay down on my bed, my hands behind my head. My thoughts turned to Rob's feather tattoo, an intricate design on his upper arm. It symbolised the freedom of flight. He'd had it done before we got together, when he'd returned to London after a few months travelling in Australia. He told me it was a marker in the sand, or rather the skin, that he was his own person, symbolising the fact that he was free to fly wherever and whenever he wanted – an untamed spirit. It was partly what attracted me to him in the first place. I hung on to every word, captivated by the spiritual side of him. But now he was my boyfriend, it was also a concept that scared me about Rob on a deeper level.

From the day we got together, I'd had this unshakeable sense that he was too good to be true or, more precisely, too good for me. I'd become quite used to deep-rooted fear that one day Rob might decide he needed to fly, and he would leave me. I reasoned with myself that the feather could symbolise us flying off together – travel had always been high on our list, and I fell in love with him in LA after all. So, the fear was probably more about me and my opinion of myself – that I wasn't the kind of person any sane, gorgeous, and successful bloke might like to settle down with.

I once messaged Dear Destiny, a world renowned 'spiritual guide' with 2.5 million followers on Instagram, about this conundrum and actually got a reply. I keep the screenshot on my phone.

Dear AG

If you are in a relationship and concerned whether the other person is as committed to you as you are to them, or you are questioning your own commitment to a long-term relationship, firstly, may I strongly suggest that you do some work on yourself. This kind of question reveals a deep insecurity and a lack of trust that is likely to make any suitor catch the first bus out of your area. Secondly, you need to get out there and enjoy having a full relationship without fear. Thirdly, remember that no one can actually climb inside anyone's brain, so it's impossible to know if they are truly yours, all you can do is trust them – until they show you otherwise, which might be never or might be tomorrow. Work with factual information, AG, because guessing about a person is the road to ruin. And be thankful they can't climb into your mind either – that really would be the death of nearly all relationships, wouldn't it? AG, you must believe in your ability to love and be loved in return.

Best of luck,
Dear Destiny

I had discussed this with Vicky too, and she confirmed Dear Destiny's sentiment. 'You can never actually own someone, that would be slavery – and it was abolished in the nineteenth century, as you might recall.'

'Well, I'm yours,' I said. 'You're my ride or die.'

'Ditto,' Vicky replied. 'But we're different. We're best friends.'

It left me thinking how unfair it was that a boyfriend couldn't also be your best friend. *Why does there have to be a different set of rules?*

'Because mixing bodily fluids changes stuff,' was Vicky's analysis. 'Some people like to call their partner their best friend, but, personally, I think that's weird, and I'm greedy enough to want both a lover *and* a bestie. Anyway, that's why marriage was invented, so it's harder to leave when the going gets tough. You don't get that with a friendship.'

'Does marriage really give you that security?'

'It's meant to. That's why I'm going to propose to Trey the next leap year. I'll be waiting forever if I don't. And I want half his bank balance – that will give me security.' She giggled loudly.

'You blatant gold digger!' I laughed back.

'I love him too!' she assured me, as an afterthought.

Married or not, I still wondered whether there was a bit of you that would ever feel completely certain that something would last forever. *Maybe this is exactly the point of love? You never know how the story will end.*

I thought of Rob's tattoo again. This time instead of seeing it as a symbol of what might *not* be between us, maybe now was the time to believe that it could symbolise moving into a new chapter *together,* and being at ease with living in the moment.

I had an urge to phone him again to tell him this, so I did, and still he didn't answer.

I sank back into my pillows.

There are certain moments in life when you get a strong feeling that something is at a turning point. Some people call it a sixth sense, others intuition, although we have no scientifically proven way to see into the future, sometimes you *just know.* Rob not calling me back was a turning point in my life. I knew it meant that something more was wrong, because it wasn't like him to be this distant. I had a feeling something was up.

CHAPTER SIXTEEN

By seven o'clock I had gone to Mandy's room to drop off her outfit – an incredible Studio 54-inspired, gold metallic floor-length gown with bat wings, borrowed from a vintage rental platform. I then spent hours getting glammed up whilst listening to *1989 (Taylor's Version)*, twice, and then a medley of some of my favourite pre-party songs, thanks to the Echo in the annexe. I was wearing the silky emerald-green jumpsuit I had bought from a pre-loved website, accessorised with a vintage Gucci belt and the silver ankle boots, which were my (self-chosen) Christmas present from Rob. Some might say the look was more 'bogey' than Balenciaga, but I didn't care, because I thought I looked cool. If fashion was about celebrating individuality – the theme I was pushing for Mandy – I had to be true to myself too. Wearing green was also my way of conveying a need to feel grounded, and to instil a sense of calm. I hoped it would have the desired effect this evening.

I spent a pleasurable amount of time washing, blow-drying, curling, and re-curling my hair into tousled waves, dousing it in hairspray to hold all night.

I put on extra mascara, went for it with a shimmery

cream blush, applied ample powder, and finished off with a glossy lip. Then I spritzed my Le Labo fragrance into the air and walked through its wet cloud twice, a trick a make-up artist once taught me for ensuring your perfume lasts all evening because it clings to your hair and clothes more evenly. I have no idea if it really works, but I enjoy the ceremonial aspect of getting ready for a big night out, or in this case a big night in.

It felt good to put so much effort into my look this evening. Although, feeling rebuffed by my own boyfriend, I couldn't help but acknowledge that a little part of me knew I was doing it in the hope that Jimi might notice.

'Babes! *Love* your outfit. What a colour!' Blair squealed as I entered the lounge.

'And look at you! So chic.' I grabbed the end of the mustard-yellow feather boa flung casually around their neck, and admired the brown houndstooth suit Blair was wearing with nothing underneath. On their feet were a pair of iconic Gucci fur loafers.

'I'm calling this look "country house meets Harry Styles with a touch of Dame Edna Everage".' I smiled.

'Who?' they said.

'Never mind.'

'Don't let the clothes wear you, remember, babes!' they replied, smiling.

I went to give them a hug, but on lifting my arms I noticed how tight and achy they felt.

'You okay?'

'Jimi had me on his Pilates torture machine earlier and it

seems to have done something to arm muscles I didn't know I had.' I rubbed my right upper arm with my left palm.

'Where is your handsome date?'

'What?' I felt my cheeks flush, assuming Blair was suggesting Jimi.

'Rob. Your boyfriend?' they clarified. 'I was half-thinking you might sneak him in tonight. I want to see if he's as hot as he looks on Instagram.'

'Oh.' My shoulders relaxed. 'Partners are strictly NFI, remember? Anyway, who's here?'

I scanned the room. Lights had been dimmed and there was a smattering of people I didn't recognise in small groups. Some background electronic music was playing. Then I noticed Jimi was behind the decks. Well, when I say decks, I mean he was standing behind a small table in the corner of the room on which there was an open laptop, and the distinguishing DJ feature was some large headphones around his neck. He looked up for a second and smiled. I felt something leap in my stomach.

'They're all Julie-Ann's clients,' Blair continued. 'Mandy is easily the most famous, so this was a hot ticket for most of them. See her over there?'

They nodded subtly to our right, towards a woman deep in conversation with Mandy, who looked incredible in the gold dress.

'The one wearing the gloves?' I asked.

'Why do you think she's wearing them?'

'She's cold?'

'Wrong. She's got the most expensive hands in Britain,

probably the world. She's called Kate Santini, she's a hand model – doesn't take her gloves off for less than twenty grand an hour. Seriously. She was the hand in the new Ryan Gosling coffee commercials. She told me she had him in the palm of her hand.' They laughed. 'Short life span, that career though.' They elbowed me in the ribs.

'You're on fire this evening, Blair,' I said sardonically. 'I've got to hand it to you.'

And we both giggled at our crap jokes.

'Mandy looks good, doesn't she,' I commented, looking across at her holding court with the hand model. Julie-Ann had now joined them, with two striking young women who looked like identical twins. Mandy shone like a real-life, polished Oscar statuette, the dress hugging her curves. Her hair was tonged, glossy and perfect, her skin glowing. She looked like the superstar she was.

'She's radiant!' Blair commented.

'Everyone is so beautiful,' I gasped. 'I think I need a drink to cope. Any idea where the cocktails are?'

We were just about to leave the room to find out, when I felt a gentle yet firm arm around my back. It was Julie-Ann guiding me over to the opposite side of the room.

'Come and mingle,' she said. 'Everyone loves meeting the stylist.'

'They do?'

She led me over to where Jose was talking to a woman with blond hair scraped back into a high ponytail, her lips pink and pillowy. She was introduced as Aneka, by way of Julie whispering loudly into the back of my neck. 'Ageing model. Used to be massive, on the cover of all the foreign *Vogues* – except US and UK, *obviously* – reinventing herself as a life coach.'

'Oh darling, I've been supporting a friend who has been crying for the past week,' said the woman to Julie-Ann, as Jose took his cue to quietly disappear.

'What about?'

'The cruelty of life.' She looked wistfully out of the window.

'Have you met Amber, Ane? Ane meet Amber.'

The model ignored her.

'Of course, there was a trigger for this. She could remember the moment so clearly. She saw herself in the *Vogue* social pages at the Annabel's anniversary party, and it had happened.' She stopped, clocking my presence by looking me up and down. I wasn't sure if my green jumpsuit had prompted the look of disdain, or whether it was related to what she was about to tell us. 'Sorry, I didn't catch your name?'

'It's Amber.'

'It had happened, Amber,' she repeated dramatically.

'What had happened?' I asked, noticing Julie-Ann had conveniently sidled off too, leaving me alone with Aneka.

'She looked different,' she said, earnestly.

I was confused about what she meant by this – had her friend's aesthetic doctor messed up her latest round of fillers?

'She had aged,' she continued morosely. 'She had tipped off the precipice of youth and into the cavernous realm of the "older" woman. That is what she meant by the cruelty of life.'

'It's going to happen to all of us,' I offered, helpfully.

She looked at me intensely. 'How old are you?'

'Twenty-six.'

'You wait until *no one* gives you a second glance anymore. It literally happens overnight. No amount of "good light", filtering, or make-up will help you in day-to-day life. Your whole reality changes. It's a kind of trauma.'

'Sounds intense,' I muttered.

'Oh, it is. That's precisely why I am retraining. I want to help people like my friend come to terms with the ageing process. Many of them are in mourning.' She sighed.

'Mourning?'

'For their old face.'

I offered a pained expression.

'Can't age be an asset?' I asked after a pause.

'Every age is an asset, of course,' she replied. 'The trick is being at ease with it. That's the hard part. No one teaches you about that.' She shook her head.

'I'm sorry for your friend,' I said.

As we looked at each other awkwardly I was saved by Jimi approaching.

'Ane, have you met Jimi yet? He's Mandy's personal trainer. He helps her stay young.'

'Pull up a pew,' she said, squeezing his bicep without invitation.

Then, as if we were playing the human equivalent of pass the parcel, I kindly smiled and muttered, 'It was lovely to meet you, Ane. Excuse me, I need to find the alcohol . . .'

As the evening progressed, I proceeded to get pleasantly

drunk on strong martini-based cocktails. I had a chat about
the benefits of adding apple cider vinegar to absolutely
everything you eat with Ro and Matty, two guys from the
'Somerset Set', who were dressed like Björn and Benny from
ABBA; a deep conversation with a lady called Star who was
over from California to promote her work as a self-made
'orgasmic meditation guru'.

'Julie-Ann has been the most incredible guide and
mentor,' she told me, with so many pregnant pauses
between words I wondered if she was in a state of orgasm
at that exact moment. 'She's got me on *This Morning* on
Monday, and then we're meeting with an events producer
to see about bringing my one-woman show to London. Can
you imagine, *Orgasmic Manifestation Live at the O2*?'

'No, I mean, yes,' I replied, unsure where to look.

'Have you ever created an orgasm with your mind,
Amber?' she asked, looking right between my eyes. 'It's
called "Thinking Off". Unbeknownst to many, the brain
is the largest erogenous zone in the human body. You can
bring yourself to orgasm by stimulating your mind with
your biggest fantasies. You should try it some time.'

'Yeah, I definitely will,' I said unconvincingly.

'I can show you now, if you like?' Star offered.

I made an excuse to swiftly move on.

The party was well underway, and I was feeling a bit
tipsy when I wandered outside into the garden to try and
ring Rob again. He hadn't been far from my thoughts all
evening, and I wanted to share some anecdotes with him
about the strange array of guests Julie-Ann had brought, and

whether the Somerset Set would fly back to their apple farm in one piece. I couldn't wait to tell him about the orgasmic guru – he would find that hilarious. I paused on the thought of orgasms. The idea of being romantically close with Rob already felt a distant memory. I missed pressing my body into his and waking up with his arm flung across me.

He didn't pick up. Again.

Maybe he is expecting me to be busy.

Maybe he's busy.

Maybe he's asleep already.

Maybe he doesn't want to speak to me.

Maybe it's over.

I also needed some air because Mandy was holding court in there, being vivacious in such a loud, brash way, clinking glasses and saying 'Cheers!' in a phoney British accent at every opportunity, and it was starting to grate. Coco and Philippa seemed to feel the same way, because I found them sitting in a dimly lit corner of the kitchen drinking wine as I wandered past, swiping three trout cocktail boats on my way.

Outside, the air was fresh and damp. It smelt of recent rainfall on soil mixed with the nostalgic scent of burning wood from the multiple crackling log fires inside the house. It was reassuring and reminded me of home and my parents' garden, albeit theirs was one hundredth of the size of this one.

I wandered down beyond the patio area, across the grass and onto a little gravel pathway that led into a small, classic walled cottage garden. We had been so busy over the last few weeks, I hadn't yet had a chance to properly explore and appreciate the grounds, only glimpsing the garden from various windows and doorways rather than walking in it.

Although not as lush and colourful as it would look during summer, it was a really pretty, quintessentially English garden, with blossoms starting to appear on sculpted bushes in the shape of orbs, carefully pruned rose bushes, and snow-white blossoms on fruit trees heralding the start of spring. Along the side were two covered raised beds showing signs of heads of lettuce growing under a poly tunnel. It looked like someone was taking loving care of this part of the garden, and I wondered if that responsibility fell to Philippa as well.

I kept walking and even though it was dark I could see enough, thanks to a single row of dimly lit festoon lights hanging overhead, swaying gently in the breeze, and a pretty line of snowdrops on the edge of the central path. I thought about how I should have grabbed a coat or scarf as I left the house and rubbed the top of my arms.

I paused and let nature envelop me, a quiet welcome break from the constant chatter inside. In the distance I could still hear the muffled sound of music and laughter, but it was peaceful out here. At the far end of the walled garden was a small pond, where I spotted a gnome who had seen better days, and two stone toadstool-shaped stools by the side of him. I perched on one, the cold sensation on my bottom making me sit up straight.

I turned to the gnome. 'Hiya, mate, how's it going? Needed a bit of space too?' I gently brushed some moss from his face to reveal two rosy, red cheeks. 'Yep, it's a madhouse in there.'

The gnome in his bottle-green painted-on hat, decorated face, and moony perma-smile, despite being a little chipped and faded, seemed to agree with me. It reminded me of a gnome couple my grannie had in her front garden for years – the welcoming committee, she used to call them.

'You're wondering what you're doing here too? Shall we make a break for it?' I asked the gnome.

Then I lifted my face to the sky, noticing for the first time that the moon was large and full.

From a little way down the path, in the direction I had just come, I heard leaves crackling. I looked up sharply and could make out the dark shape of a person walking towards me.

I heard a squelchy sound followed by some words in Spanish. '*Mierda! Este lugar se va a la mierda!*' Some heavy breathing followed, and then, '*Hola, guapa.*'

I knew who it was because I could see his white jacket – you couldn't miss it – bobbing along the pathway like the gaudy cousin of the Michelin Man, at odds with the muted beauty of the garden.

When Jimi came into the lit area near me, for a moment we both took each other in. He seemed more startled. '*¿Que tal estás guapa?*'

I looked at him confused. 'I'm sorry, I don't speak Spanish. Unless you count *hola* and *jamon*.'

'Both useful words. Sorry. After a few drinks, I'm back in Miami in my head. I thought you were with someone?'

'Me? No, I came out to make a call.' I held out my phone as proof.

'It's cold.'

'It's freezing. I thought you were DJing?'

I was a bit annoyed he was spoiling this moment of solitude for me. I'd come out here for some peace.

'It's hardly DJing when you have a playlist. Anyway, Mandy's taken over – she loves a celebració. I needed a vape. Would you like some?'

'I haven't vaped since I was at uni,' I said, kicking a little stone with my foot and watching it plop into the pond. 'It's still bad for your lungs.'

I stole a glance at the side of his face as he lifted the vape to his lips. He really did have the most symmetrical face, the kind that probably wouldn't get chosen to front an ad campaign in 2025, because a casting director would say he was *too* classically perfect.

The walls gave us privacy from the main house, and also a bit of shelter from the cold whip of the wind. It felt intimate sharing this space together.

'If you heard me talking, I was chatting to the gnome,' I said, trying to make him feel comfortable. 'I promise I'm not actually mad.'

'Gnome?'

'Him over there.' I nodded towards the stone ornament.

'Oh right – that's a gnome. Was he getting told off by you too?'

'Fortunately, gnomes can't answer back, sorry to break it to you. Did you think I was telling you off?'

'The vaping. I think I'm old enough to make my own decisions, Mom.'

I sound like his mum, this is not good.

'Sorry. I'm just a bit fed up, I guess.'

'Fed up, why?'

'I constantly think I'm going to get fired,' I replied.

'Mandy isn't the easiest client, we all know that. I tune out the nonsense now.'

'I can't lose this job.'

He made a sympathetic sound. 'You won't lose this job, trust me.'

'You don't know that.'

I watched smoke leave his lips and dissipate in the air. His lips looked like soft pillows.

I bet he's a really good kisser. I bet he's slept with so many beautiful women.

He offered the vape to me and this time I decided to take it. The soft fruity taste hit the back of my throat giving me an enjoyable buzz.

'Do you know what's just across that field?'

I shook my head. 'Some sheep?'

'There's a gin distillery. I saw it on Google Maps. It's walkable and they have a bar.' He leant closer to me, close enough for me to feel his breath on my face. 'It's quick if you go cross-country.' His eyes were shining.

My gaze drifted down to his coat.

I wish I wasn't such a snob when it comes to clothes, but I can't go into a local gin distillery with someone wearing a white puffa. Can I?

Then I looked at my feet. 'I'm not sure these boots were made for fields.'

'You're right. It's a stupid idea to go across a field in this weather.' His face collapsed, and I felt bad for quashing his enthusiasm. I shivered.

'Here, take my coat. You're cold.' He stood up and began peeling it off.

'No honestly, it's fine.' It did look warm, but I had standards. 'You kind of get used to it when you live here.'

Vicky would be cringing so hard she'd probably fall off the toadstool and pull me into the pond with her if she could see any of this.

'Amber, please put it on,' he said firmly. 'You're shivering.'

He draped the coat around my shoulders, it was warm from his body, and it felt nice. He was sitting palpably close to me. Even his vape-y breath smelt good, and there was a whiff of aftershave on the coat. I was distinctly aware of every small movement his body made. I looked sideways at him, wondering what to say next.

'That's better. Thank you.'

He shrugged.

'Do you meditate, Amber?' Jimi asked, changing the subject.

'Not really, I mean I have a few meditation apps on my phone. I just can't seem to sit still for long enough,' I answered. 'Why, do you think I need to?'

'You have an amazing, calming aura,' he said. 'I can feel it when I'm around you.'

Seriously, Vicky would now be in full-scale hysteria.

'I don't feel very calm at the moment,' I replied. 'In general.'

It was quite a shock that I could feel myself blushing.

'Mandy looks amazing this evening, that dress is a winner. You handle her so well. You are the first to lead the charge and the last in the retreat.'

I looked at the side of his face. Jimi could say things in such a way that it was hard to know whether it was the profound statement of a genius, or just an unbelievably cheesy line he'd heard in a film. I couldn't work him out. But I erred towards the last option. It was confusing, because there was also something endearing about his cheesiness.

'Mandy's not the easiest client,' I said, deflecting the conversation. 'But I'm enjoying it most of the time.' I felt cautious about telling tales about my boss, especially as Jimi was related to her.

'The moon's big tonight,' I commented, seizing the opportunity to change the conversation again.

We both looked upwards.

'You're brave, but also kind.' He was looking at the side of my face.

To the right of the moon there was a cluster of stars, one was particularly bright.

'And funny.'

I felt embarrassed he was complimenting me. I thought about Rob then, feeling guilty that it wasn't him saying these words.

'Anyway, much as I would love to drink some gin in the distillery, I'll probably get paralytic if I do,' I announced, thinking I'd better get back before anyone noticed we were both missing. 'Which probably isn't the best idea.'

'Paralytic?' He looked at me quizzically. 'Are you stiff from the Pilates this morning?'

I chuckled. 'It's okay, I can move. It means very drunk.'

'I'll come with you,' Jimi said, and we started walking back down the path, me feeling a little unsure about how it would look if we were seen coming out of this part of the garden together. I didn't want to give anyone a reason to gossip.

Out of nowhere, I lost my footing on a raised tree root and fell to the ground. Quick as lightning, Jimi was there, putting his arm under mine and holding me up. *What an idiot, Amber!*

'Are you okay?' he asked gently, his expression concerned.

'I'm fine.' I shook my head. My palms had mud on them, so did my silver boots.

Jimi's gaze dropped and I noticed the white puffa now had mud on it too. 'I'm really sorry, I'll get it drycleaned.' I felt defeated.

'Don't worry about it – this is what happens in the British countryside. Anyway, I hate this jacket, I only wore it because it was a present from my brother. I didn't want to offend him.'

'You hate it?' I let out a surprised laugh. 'It is very . . . white.'

Then I saw something blossom in Jimi's face. Genuine affection. I felt it too.

'You're the stylist. What do you think of it? Wait a minute—'

He gently brushed a piece of dirt I didn't know was there off my lip.

There was a moment when we were standing there, looking at each other.

'Honestly? I hate it.'

We both giggled.

'I could tell. You can't hide anything, you know, Amber.'

'What do you mean?'

He shook his head and chuckled to himself. 'I mean I could tell you hated it from the minute you saw it. I think you were unsure about me too.'

'Really? Not at all!' I said, embarrassed.

'You think I've got something to prove. What's that phrase – don't judge a book by its cover?'

'Or a man by his puffa?'

We both cracked up. When he laughed, his whole face lit up, turning into even more perfection than before.

I sensed Jimi had something else to say, but whatever it was, he resisted.

A part of me wanted his hand to stay there, on my lip. The human contact felt nice.

'You're cheeky too,' he said.

'Takes one . . .'

'What?'

'Nothing.'

'You go in first. I'll wait a bit.' He looked at me with smiling eyes.

It did feel as though being out here together, we had something to hide.

I looked at him, weighing him up. Thinking about what Blair had said, about him being a playboy. As I turned and pushed open the back door to the house, I squeezed my eyes shut.

This is fine. Absolutely fine.

Shit, I fancy him.

An hour later, disappointed to find none of the usual bowls of salted peanuts, tortilla chips, or hummus found at the house parties I usually frequented, I wandered into the kitchen on the hunt for sustenance. I was beginning to miss hummus almost as much as Rob by this point, and I probably would have done something regrettable with Jimi in exchange for some Popchips.

On the kitchen island was a tray of individual gem lettuce leaves, like perfectly formed open shells, each filled with small cubes of watermelon and feta. A chopping board with some half-chopped chives sat next to it, indicating Coco couldn't be far away. I looked over my shoulder before swiping one of the canapés.

'Saw that,' snapped a voice, coming from the other side of the island. I peered around the corner and saw Coco sitting cross-legged on the floor, her back to the wall.

'Blatant daylight robbery,' she said, looking up at me glumly.

'Nighttime actually,' I replied, noticing that she was making no effort to stand up and join me. I noticed a wrapper beside her and something in her hand.

'Are you okay?'

'You know it's bad when you hit the cooking chocolate.' She sighed. 'And it's ninety-eight per cent raw cacao – it's so bitter it barely passes for chocolate. It tastes like shit.' She threw the chocolate down.

'Why are you eating it then?' I knelt down and joined her on the floor.

'Because there's nothing really, *really* calorific in these cupboards. I've considered mainlining the Manuka honey.'

'Hmm and who is to blame for that . . .?' I muttered, enjoying the opportunity for a sarcastic side-eye glance. This would make a funny reel if I'd had my phone handy: *Celebrity nutritionist gets high on cooking chocolate.*

'Are you prepared to share any of it, so I can check?' I joined her on the floor.

Coco shifted her tiny bum a few centimetres so I could slot in next to her.

'Shall I finish the canapés?'

'If you like, but I doubt anyone will notice. They're all high on some mushroom stuff Jimi's been handing around.'

I nodded.

'Even Mandy.'

'Thank God there's no press here.'

'We think. Do you take drugs?' she asked.

'No, it's never been my thing. You?'

'Not really. My ex-girlfriend used to smoke a lot of weed and I saw what it did to her. She became paranoid.'

'Paranoid?'

'She hadn't come out to many of her friends or family, and much as we had some great times when we were together, I got fed up of feeling like a big dirty secret. And there was also the thinking I was being unfaithful, accusing me of things I hadn't done, fearing the world was against her. It was a lot to hold.'

'Are you still together?'

Her bottom lip began to quiver. 'Not anymore.'

'It's fresh?'

'Very. We ended on the phone yesterday.'

'I'm so sorry, Coco. Do you want to talk about it?' I put an arm around her shoulder.

'It was something you said, Amber. About authenticity. It really hit home – I don't want to have to hide my relationship anymore. I need to be with someone who can be proud of me. I need a fresh start.' There were tears in her eyes. She sighed heavily. 'Anyway, it's over. I'm over it. Tell me about you – boyfriend, girlfriend, both, neither?'

'I'm in no hurry – let it out.' I pulled her close.

'You know, I haven't asked anyone that question for so long,' she said, 'because I was always afraid of the reciprocal question. I now see how ridiculous that is.' We both paused. 'I've got you to thank for this.'

'Me? I don't seem to have made you feel very happy. I'm just muddling along trying to make Mandy wear less offensive clothing.'

'But it's so much more than that.' She wiped away some moisture from under her nose with the back of her hand. 'You're making a difference to people.'

'Clothes can only do so much,' I said. 'You've got to believe in yourself first.'

'Tell me about you,' Coco said.

'Boyfriend. Although it doesn't feel like it at the moment,' I replied.

'Oh, I'm sorry. Is everything okay?'

'I don't know, because I can't reach him.' I stopped for a second. 'Did you say there's proper chocolate *anywhere* in this house?'

'I wish. I could murder some Dairy Milk. I might be a nutritionist by profession, but chocolate has always been my weakness. I love it too much.'

'Have you tried imagining you don't like it, when you eat it?'

'Name something you don't like then?'

'My boyfriend's breath after he's eaten cheese.'

Coco snorted.

'She laughs!' I smiled.

'There's nothing worse than cheese breath.' Coco giggled. 'I'll give that a try next time.'

'Did someone say cheese?' It was Jimi coming back into the room. My heart did a little flutter when I heard his voice.

'I was hoping to find some food – *proper* food – in here. Until I remembered this place is a health retreat.' He took us both in as we sat on the floor together, Coco's eyes a little red. 'What's up?'

'Health-retreat-meets-rehab would be more accurate.' Coco sighed.

Jimi snorted. 'Is Amber bringing you down?'

'Hey!' I exclaimed.

He ignored me. 'Are there *any* salty snacks *anywhere*?'

'I'm only doing what I'm told.' Coco held her hands up.

'I'd settle for some more alcohol,' I said.

'Philippa was meant to go on a mission to find some, but she hasn't come back,' added Coco.

'She's upstairs with a bunch of influencers,' Jimi told us. 'Running tours of the house and giving away all of its dirty secrets. Gables is going to be trending on Instagram soon, believe me. Anyway, I have this.' With a cheeky grin he produced an unopened bottle of champagne from behind his back. 'As long as it doesn't paralyse you, Amber.' He winked at me.

'Aren't you meant to be doing some influencing for Mandy right about now?' I asked, keen to avoid looking flustered.

'Hand it over then.' Coco took the bottle from him.

'Enjoy, ladies, enjoy. I'd better do some influencing and get back on the decks,' Jimi said. I felt disappointed he was going again.

'If I was straight, I totally would,' Coco whispered as we both watched him leave the room. He even looked good from behind. 'He is *so* hot.'

'A bad influence. And cheesy,' I added.

'I bet he doesn't have cheesy breath though,' Coco quipped. 'I bet it's really minty and fresh.'

'I bet he uses whitening stripes,' I added with a giggle. The thought of the inside of Jimi's mouth made me feel funny inside.

Coco looked at the side of my face. 'You fancy him.'

'I don't!' My voice sounded trill.

'You so do,' she teased. 'And I bet he has full veneers.'

We both cracked up.

A couple of glasses of champagne later Coco and I went back into the lounge, where the music had been turned up, and sofas pushed back to create a makeshift dance floor in the centre. Bodies writhed, a jungle of limbs and hands in the air, phones lifted, a lot of laughter. Mandy and her guests looked like performers from a contemporary circus troupe. She was holding court, of course, standing on top of a round, upholstered ottoman coffee table and waving her arms in the air, while Aneka whooped in appreciation. House music was playing.

'Please don't break a leg!' Blair shouted at Mandy. She ignored them and continued gyrating. 'I can't believe I've turned into the responsible one.'

'She's doing better than most of us,' I replied. 'Good on her!'

Mandy flicked her head at Blair before kicking off her vertiginous platform sandals, opting to go barefoot. One flew across the room, narrowly missing an influencer.

She began waving her arms in exaggerated movements and dropping into sexy squats in time with the beat. The ottoman became her stage, as if she was performing in front of legions of adoring fans, which wasn't far from the truth. Jose goaded her on, looking at her adoringly and videoing her moves on his phone.

The music segued into a mash-up of 'Independent Women'. I glanced across and gave Jimi an approving look. The heavy beat made my throat pulsate.

'Come on then.' Blair grabbed my hand and led me onto the dance floor with them. Self-consciously I began to move. I was definitely a level above tipsy by now, my head a bit spinny as I swayed, but the music was brilliant, and I was a happy drunk. It felt great to let myself go.

Jimi and Coco joined us dancing and even Julie-Ann was throwing shapes, swaying her head from side to side, her blonde hair lashing her cheeks, a wide smile across her face.

I kept looking across to Jimi and noticed his eyes kept coming back to me. Even between all the bodies, he found me. Sometimes he would smile at me, as if he was checking whether I was still there and was pleased that I was. It was nice. I felt special. I started to play a little game with him, vacillating between smiling back and pretending I hadn't noticed he was looking at me, although I kept him in my peripheral vision, aware of his movements.

When the numbers started dwindling, Mandy and Jose excused themselves. Coco had disappeared off to bed, and it dawned on me that I really should get some sleep too. I'd been chatting to a woman about her business making real-hair extensions for celebrities, and my eyes were starting to glaze over, as I struggled to keep up with her detailed recounting of trips to India to source the finest quality human hair to make clip-on ponytails for Ariana Grande. Plus, my boots were starting to rub, and my head was aching – an early sign of the hangover to come.

As I crossed the small courtyard to reach the entrance to the annexe, I felt a hand on my shoulder.

'Are you really going to bed?' Jimi asked gently.

'I really am,' I replied snoozily.

'I thought we could have a nightcap.' It could have been a question, but he said it as a statement.

'Does nighttime tea count?'

'Does it contain mushrooms?' he asked, innocently. 'They're all high in there.'

'Don't go there,' I replied, rolling my eyes. 'No, it's herbal. And definitely not illegal. There's a kettle in the annexe if you fancy it?'

'There's a kettle in the annexe,' he replied jokily, mimicking my British accent. 'You are so English.'

I shrugged. 'I can't do much about that.'

'Well, I don't mind if I do.' His eyes sparkled.

I secretly loved that Jimi felt familiar enough to rib me.

When we got to the small kitchenette in the annexe, I filled the kettle – which was one of those silly mini kettles which barely make enough boiling water for two mugs – and flicked on the lamp on a small side table, next to an antique-looking red velvet two-seater sofa, with gold trimming peeling off in places. It looked like something you might find in a neglected corner of Buckingham Palace. Clearly all the furniture no longer deemed smart enough for the main house had been moved across to the annexe, because it was a menagerie of mismatched items that wouldn't look out of place on a Portobello Road stall. We both sat down at the same time and shuffled apart awkwardly.

'Have you always been a DJ?' I asked, thinking what a terrible opener this was. But I couldn't think of anything else at that moment.

'God no. I worked for an advertising agency for a few years.'

'Oh, interesting. Did you work on any campaigns I might have seen?'

'It's unlikely. I wasn't on the fun stuff. I did the website development, social media, and SEO optimisation; until I realised that it was slowly eroding my brain of any fun. I got so bored of going to work. Like a hamster on a wheel, round and round, days and weeks go by, turning into months and years, and before you know it, you're not really living, you're surviving. I didn't want that from my life.'

'Hard relate.'

'You worked in tech?'

'No. But I once worked in a call centre for an insurance company, and it was honestly the most soul-destroying way to earn money I've ever had. It was even worse than giving out free yoghurt pots for one whole summer at railway stations.'

'Did you learn anything about insurance?'

'Nothing. Let's just say I left that entire industry – my brain isn't wired that way. At school, for a long time, I seriously thought that working in STEM meant a career in floristry.' He didn't seem to get that joke. 'So, you got out of tech?'

'I followed my love of fitness and became a personal trainer. My tech skills also meant I had learnt enough to help Mandy with the social media side of things. She wanted someone she could trust with her accounts.'

'What about DJing?'

'I've always loved music, so I thought I'd give it a try. Jose opened a few doors for me in the top clubs and it wasn't too hard to get gigs, especially if you're happy to take the warm-up shift. Mandy had me play at her launch events which really helped too; and then I ended up doing some support for Jose on their business projects as well. He's been a good brother to me.' He paused. 'What music are you into? Put something on.'

I thought for a moment, not about what my favourite music actually was (anything by Taylor Swift), but what was the coolest thing to say right now.

'I'll put something on. Do you like British radio?' I asked.

He shook his head.

Then an excruciating moment happened when I commanded, 'Alexa, play Six Music.'

And Alexa said, 'Now playing music to have sex to.'

I sprung out of my seat, towards the speaker, shouting urgently, 'Alexa, stop! I said, play Six Music!'

Jimi burst into hysterical laughter as Alexa simply repeated, 'Playing sex music.'

And I had to scream, 'Alexa! Stop!'

I knew Alexa could play BBC Radio 6 Music, because she'd been doing it perfectly fine yesterday while I was working.

By now, tears were streaming down Jimi's cheeks. 'You're so forward!' he teased.

I died on my feet with embarrassment.

'Alexa, stop! Please play "Everywhere" by Fleetwood—' I kept getting the giggles and couldn't finish the request properly and then got annoyed with Alexa again, as she said, 'I'm sorry, but I can't find "Everywhere"' – all the while feeling horribly self-conscious about how my voice sounded as I veered between idiot and shouty person.

Finally, the intro to 'Everywhere' began and I breathed a sigh of relief, but it had missed the moment. I turned and realised Jimi was still laughing.

'You should have left it on sex music,' he spluttered. 'I wanted to know what she was going to play!'

'I told you I would never get a job in tech,' I said. 'Even Alexa hates me.'

Jimi stopped laughing now, stood up, and crossed the room to take one of my hands in both of his. But instead of making me feel embarrassed, it was a sweet, genuine gesture.

'Oh Amber, how could anyone hate you?' he asked. I felt an electric current run through me. 'Come and sit back down. Tell me about your boyfriend. How did you meet?'

'How do you know I have a boyfriend?'

'I overheard you talking to Coco earlier.'

'Really?'

'I wasn't spying on you, don't worry. I just heard you mention it, that's all. Is he a secret?'

'Of course not.'

'Well then – how did you meet?'

'We met through work, when he was a producer of a documentary being made about this crazy stylist I was assisting for a while. We worked together for a bit, and then we got together. We lived in New York for three months, and now we're back home.'

'Is everything okay?' He looked at me quizzically.

'What else did you accidentally overhear?'

'Nothing. Why?'

'Things have been a bit . . .' I thought for a moment about my choice of words and settled on, 'weird, recently. We haven't spoken much since I came here. I also thought he'd been in touch with his ex, and it spun me out.'

I had conflicting feelings about continuing this conversation. It felt disloyal to Rob to be talking about him to Jimi. But on the other hand, I was slightly drunk, and it felt good to have someone listen to me so attentively. Perhaps Jimi would be able to advise me from a male perspective.

'Why would he do that?' he asked, concerned.

'I don't know.'

'Do you have any evidence?'

'A photo.'

'Let's see it.'

I pulled out my phone. I scrolled to find the photo and we looked at it together.

Jimi took my phone and studied the image. He zoomed in on the central piece of evidence around which I had based my assumption of Rob's infidelity. I hadn't imagined this would be happening, not with a guy I half-fancied.

'This photo doesn't prove anything,' Jimi announced.

'You think so?'

He nodded.

'Now I feel really bad.'

'Maybe you should. So, what are you going to do about it?'

'Well, if he would phone me back, that would be a great start.'

'Just give him a minute. Relax.'

We paused. I became aware that he was looking at the side of my face.

'You're beautiful,' Jimi murmured.

'What?' I turned to face him. *Now I'm imagining things.*

'I said, you're beautiful.' He stopped me in my tracks. 'Your boyfriend is a lucky guy.'

Jimi looked at me straight between the eyes. Then I swear his gaze lowered to meet my lips. He broke the spell with a smile. An instant red blush rose from my neck to my cheeks. 'Especially when you blush.'

'That is literally the worst thing you can say to someone who blushes easily,' I replied, my face firing up again.

He laughed. 'I'm sorry.'

'Yeah, thanks.'

'I won't mention your rosy-red cheeks again.'

We lingered for a few seconds as the words hung in the air. Then he slid his phone from his pocket and looked at it. It had to be around two a.m. by now.

He didn't tell me the time, but said, 'I suppose I'd better go to bed.' Then he leant forward and pecked me on my very hot right cheek. I noticed he looked amused.

'Night night, then,' I said, self-conscious that my face was so obviously aglow with a mixture of embarrassment, tiredness, and alcohol.

'See you in the morning,' he added, straining to sound casual, perhaps wondering if he had overstepped the mark.

As Jimi turned and left the room, I let out an involuntary sigh.

In the deepest crevice of my brain, and somewhere closer to my groin, there was a stirring of an emotion I hadn't felt for a long time. Lust.

CHAPTER SEVENTEEN

The next morning, as my eyes opened, the memory of last night began to fill the room. Jimi was lodged in my consciousness.

I tried to bat away the thought of him, trying to turn my mind instead to thinking about Rob waking up in our flat. the familiar shaft of morning light above the curtains no doubt bothering him as usual.

Rob and I were really good at Saturdays. We would rise late, often after sex. One of us would bring mugs of tea back to bed, we'd bake frozen croissants, get dressed, ignore all the washing-up in the sink and go for a walk around Portobello Road, perusing market stalls crammed with oddities, and pick things out for our fantasy future home. His mum still lived in Holland Park, and Rob grew up in the heart of wealthy West London, so he knew the streets really well. It was so attractive when I first met him, because his family were part of the original Notting Hill Set. He could always get a table at Osteria Basilico, knew the Oxfam shop where you could bag an authentic designer bag if you were lucky, and exactly what time was best to beat the queue at the small Portuguese bakery selling pastel de natas that melted on your tongue. Sometimes we would buy a second-hand book each from the quaint back-room bookstore near Ladbroke Grove and take them to the Windsor Castle pub, ideally finding a table by the fire to settle in for a couple of hours. I didn't question whether I was a twenty-something living a fifty-something life, because we were so comfortable with each other, and I was content with that.

At least I thought I was – until I met Jimi. There was something so intriguing about him, perhaps it was the contrast to the life I knew. Yet when I tried to piece together the details of last night, my memory was sketchy. *Had he called me beautiful in a way that meant something?* Blair had given me the impression he was a lothario, *so why did this feel so good? Am I imagining the connection between us?*

I gulped down the glass of water next to my bed and popped two pills, but it didn't feel as though they would make much of a difference. Short of injecting paracetamol into my eyeballs, I knew this hangover was going nowhere today.

I went to lift my phone, but my arms didn't seem to want to respond. A few twinges from the Pilates reformer had turned into full-scale delayed onset muscle soreness. Keeping my arms close to my sides, I slid my finger from WhatsApp, where there was still nothing from Rob – although, I was almost past expecting him to call – to the phone icon, where I saw a missed call from Vicky. Then I scrolled on to Instagram, noticing a high number of new followers to my profile, which had admittedly lain dormant since I'd moved in with Mandy, because I was so heavily restricted from posting anything by the NDA I signed.

Sitting up straighter, I noticed I was tagged in a reel which had been reposted hundreds of times. It was from last night, and I was dancing in the foreground, with Mandy behind me, dancing on the coffee table barefoot, carefree. A number of the images had a red ring scrawled around Mandy's middle. The same question was circulating widely.

Baby news for Mandy???
Is our Queen expecting?
That looks like a bump to me!
Baby Baby Baby!

I hadn't noticed last night, or even during the photoshoot, but it did look as though there was, perhaps, a slight roundness to her middle. But it was negligible at most and could easily be the angle.

My immediate thought was how horrible it must be to have this kind of scrutiny over your body. In the online world it seemed even your own body was public property. It wasn't right, especially if all you wanted was to become pregnant.

Poor Mandy. I wondered whether she had looked at Instagram yet this morning.

I was still pondering this thought when my phone rang.

'Finally! I've been trying you all night!' Vicky said.

'Babe, you do realise it's only seven a.m. here. I've not even had five hours' sleep.'

'It's gone midnight here. I've been match-sticking my

eyes open, I was so keen to speak to you. After that text you sent, I've been desperate for an update.'

'What text?' A foreboding feeling melted over my delicate, hungover body.

'The one saying that you were about to do something you might regret with a hot guy from Miami? Did you really think I could just switch off my phone and go to sleep on that kind of cliffhanger?'

'Oh. Sorry. I don't remember sending that.'

'Spill then – did you or didn't you do something you might regret?'

'I didn't.'

'Oh, how disappointing. Who is this Miami hottie then?'

'He's called Jimi, he's Jose's brother. He's ridiculously fit. We hung out a bit last night, but now I'm feeling stupid for fancying him and I can't really remember what happened.'

'Why stupid?'

'Because he's from Miami, a DJ, and a PT, he wears a white puffa jacket and he's got "I'm not the kind of guy you should fancy" written all over his face. Plus – and you know this – I'm in a relationship!'

'Listen, babe, I know you. I know you would never intentionally hurt a fly. But you haven't said much about Rob recently – how is he?'

'I wish I knew. We've barely spoken since I've been in here. He doesn't call me back. So, things have been a bit crap since I moved into this house.'

'Excuse me while I fall asleep,' she said, yawning, 'I can see why you're looking for some excitement.'

'Jimi has been a welcome distraction to be honest. In fact, I can't stop thinking about him.'

'It sounds like you fancy the boxers off him.'

'What am I going to do about it?'

'Life is short, Amber Green.'

'But he's probably a massive player.'

'Or maybe he's not? Having a spark with someone is special.'

'Is it? Aren't there lots of people you could spark with? The real test is whether you act on it or not.'

'So do you want to act on it?'

'Hmm.'

'Well, that tells me everything I need to know. If you were technically available, would you?' Vicky asked pointedly.

'I guess so. But I'm not.'

'Well, all you've done is moan about Rob and gush about Jimi. Maybe you and Rob need a break?'

'A *break*?'

It sounded so big. Massive. Crushing. I mean, it's not as if it hadn't crossed my mind until now. But a break?

'That's what I said. You're not married, are you?'

'I think you'd know if we were.'

'And it's not as if you have children,' Vicky added.

'Sometimes it feels as though we've been married for twenty years,' I said morosely.

'You could have couples' counselling,' she replied.

'To be honest it feels premature to be thinking about relationship counselling when we're only two years in.'

'I think you know the answer, babe,' Vicky said.

'Remember, it's not really a biggie, people have breaks and get back together all the time. Or they don't.'

'But we live together.'

'You *rent* together.'

'But we're thinking about buying together. That's half the reason I took this contract, to help save for our deposit.'

'Circumstances change. Maybe this is the test you need.'

'You can be so callous. What about supporting Rob when he's going through a low patch?'

'If he'd let you! But anyway, ask yourself not what Rob's going to do, but what *you* want to do. What do you *need*, Amber?'

'I need an orgasm.' We both giggled.

'You can get that without a man!' Vicky replied.

'Do you think Jimi's been put into this house to test me?' I asked.

'Perhaps. I know what I'd do.'

'So do I.'

'And that's precisely why you drunk-texted me last night. You wanted permission.'

'I didn't!'

'You so did!'

'I'm just going to avoid him today. He's a bad influence.'

'Yeah, good luck with that. I need to go to bed now. Text me if there are any juicy updates. Love you, babe.'

'Love you too.'

Vicky had got me thinking, I wasn't imagining a distance between Rob and me, there really was a gulf. We still hadn't ironed out why he was messaging his ex either. *Irrespective*

of Jimi, maybe we do need a break? I tried to think about
how I would feel about not having Rob to go home to when I
finished the contract with Mandy, and it didn't fill me with the
same kind of fear it once would have done. Maybe it wasn't
just in my head, maybe Rob and I really were drifting apart.

After breakfast, Jose called us all together in the lounge,
which had been magically cleared up from last night,
presumably by Philippa and her cleaning elves. When we
assembled, in varying states of hangover, he cleared his
throat and delivered the news.

'West Wittering,' he said, 'is going to have to wait.
Amber, Jimi, you need to pack – we've swapped that idea
for a flying visit to West Hollywood. Just the four of us. The
car leaves at five a.m. tomorrow. Amber, you and Jimi will
ride together, and we'll meet you in the lounge at T5. The
flight details should be in your email already.'

Registering the fact that my face looked like I'd just seen
Jimi walk into the room naked, Jose looked up and caught
my eye. 'All okay, Amber? You have your passport, right?'

'Um, yes.' I stole a look at Jimi, and he smiled back at me.

I was so startled I hadn't even properly registered that
Jose's reference to 'the lounge' meant we weren't flying
economy, which ordinarily would have been reason to
instigate a conga around the room. Instead, the thought of
being in close proximity to Jimi in a car *and* on a plane *and*
in LA made me feel a mix of panic and exhilaration.

'What's the plan over there?' I tried to act cool, looking
towards Julie-Ann for an answer. But she looked worse for

wear, her normally poker-straight hair was flicking out and if I wasn't mistaken, she was in the same sequinned skirt she'd been wearing last night, with a hoodie on top which I was sure I'd seen on Coco before.

'Mandy has a new launch. It's all happening fast and, contractually, she needs to get out there to work on some content to promote it,' Julie-Ann said, her voice sounding hoarse.

'Exciting – what's the launch?' I asked.

'Baby Mom by Mandy,' Jose announced. 'An eponymous new fragrance to add to her collection, this one is for mums-to-be. We'll be undertaking the final product checks, hopefully see the first bottles come off the production line and shoot some content ready for launch.'

Coco and I caught each other's gaze. *Baby Mom?* She mouthed the words back at me.

'We weren't planning to launch so early, but it seems our hand has been forced,' Jose continued. I noticed him squeeze Mandy's arm.

'I'm not sure if you've seen social media yet this morning, but—'

'I don't think I can hold it in any longer. Literally!' Mandy blurted out.

Jose wrapped an arm around her shoulders protectively and pulled her in close.

We all looked at them in anticipation, guessing what was coming. They looked like love-struck teenagers.

Mandy stood up to further enhance the moment and squealed: 'The rumours are true – we're pregnant!'

Julie-Ann was the first to shriek. She rushed forwards and launched herself at Mandy with open arms. She was quickly followed by Blair and Coco. I stood gawping at Mandy for a moment longer before joining the queue to embrace the couple. When I say embrace, I actually mean a small, rigid hug, on account of the stiffness in my muscles. Finally, Jimi sauntered up to Jose and gave him a handshake, which turned into a brotherly bear hug and a number of firm back slaps, before kissing Mandy fondly on each cheek.

Right on cue, Philippa appeared with a rattle of champagne flutes on a tray and a bottle of Dom Pérignon on ice, to toast the happy, expectant couple.

I looked around me in disbelief. *Am I the only person in this room who is genuinely floored by this news?* I mentally pieced the evidence together. The chat in the cryo chamber, the fact we were even *in* a cryo chamber, the ovulation stick, Jimi's story about the sperm donor, the fertility-inducing diet, magic mushrooms, knocking back champagne last night – although I couldn't be sure Mandy wasn't drinking mocktails. I understood many people kept things quiet in the early days of pregnancy, but she had certainly fooled me.

'May I ask how far along you both are?' Julie-Ann enquired, while our glasses were being charged by Philippa.

Mandy looked at Jose. 'Nearly four months.' She smiled. 'The baby will be due this summer.'

'Wow, you kept that secret!' Coco gushed.

'We wanted to get a couple of scans done first, to know everything is okay. And thankfully, it is,' Mandy revealed, beaming.

'How do you feel?' Jimi asked. 'I wish you had told me before I gave you that workout on the Pilates machine last week!' He said it jokingly, but he must have meant it. *And what about the mushrooms? I bet Jimi wished he'd known about the pregnancy before he fed her recreational drugs.*

'We appreciate your good wishes and would like to impress upon you that this is strictly confidential information,' Jose added. 'We consider you our work familia now, hence we wanted to let you know the good news first. Rumours are rife, but that's all they are at the moment, so it needs to stay within this group for now. It's really important we can rely on you for complete confidentiality. We'll let the rumours swirl while we're in the air and hit fans with the official public confirmation on Mandy's socials when we're back on home soil in Los Angeles. Mandy's US fans will appreciate that. And then we can press ahead with the Baby Mom campaign activity, and it will be all the more poignant. The fragrance is going to fly when the world knows about this. We'll do a full pregnancy shoot when we get back from LA – maybe at the beach location you mentioned, Amber. Blair, Julie-Ann, while we're away, can you pull together a call sheet for that please?'

'Of course, boss,' Julie-Ann said, giving him a salute.

'On it,' chirped Blair, springing up from their seat like a foot soldier.

'I still can't believe it's really happening – that I'm going to be an actual Baby Mom. It feels so good to share our news, it's a dream come true!' trilled Mandy, her excitement palpable.

'Well, congratulations! Or cheers! As you say in England,' Jose said, leading the toast. 'To Mandy and our baby!'

We all called out, 'To Mandy and your baby!'

Jose and Mandy gave me instructions to get her wardrobe sorted for the trip and to pack. I went back to my room and onto Instagram, replaying the video from last night. The rumours were escalating across TikTok, Snapchat, and X, and it was now a trending story on *E! News* and *MailOnline*. I scrutinised the video, wishing I hadn't been captured doing what looked like a bad rendition of 'Gangnam Style' in the foreground.

I pulled my empty suitcase down from the top of the wardrobe and opened it on my bed, then I fidgeted with my phone a bit more. I was struggling with being in possession of some Really Big Celebrity News and having no one to discuss it with. I knew I should be focusing on Mandy's looks for LA, but this news was big and *very* distracting. I knew I had signed an NDA, but with rumours swirling faster than a sugar-high child on a roundabout, there was sometimes only one thing you could do: call a trusted confidante and swear them to secrecy too. Normally I would ring Vicky, but she would definitely be asleep now, and Rob wasn't picking up, so I called Lucy instead.

'Hey sis!' I whispered. 'You'll never guess what.'

'What? Are you okay?'

I didn't even get through the pleasantries before spewing it out. 'Mandy's pregnant!'

'Oh, that's so lovely for her. I thought so, after seeing that

video. Great dance moves by the way.' She snorted. 'How
are you – hungover by any chance?'

Lucy seemed frustratingly nonchalant.

'It's top secret. I'm actually not meant to be telling
anyone, but I can trust you with my life, right?'

'There's no need to fear for your life. It's all over the internet
and I don't know who I'd tell. Anyway, how are you?'

*You can always rely on family to bring you back down
to earth.*

'Can I ask you something? At four months pregnant did
your bump show?'

'Absolutely. I'm bang on four months now and I look
like I've swallowed a bowling ball. But it's not like that for
everyone. Some people don't show until later. Why, how far
along is Mandy?'

'Four months too.'

'How old is she – must be early forties?'

'Forty-five. I don't think it was easy for them to fall
pregnant. I'm really happy for her.'

'Adds a new element to styling her, I guess?'

'Yup, I've got to get my head around designer maternity
wear now. I'm not sure if Lanvin does stretchy leggings.'

'Has Mandy been sick?'

'Not that I've noticed.'

'Lucky thing. I'm praying this is the month I stop puking
every day.'

'So, wedding plans – what's the latest?'

'We've made the drink selections and I'm royally pissed
that I won't be able to glug all the free champagne at my

own wedding, obviously. *And* we've had to ditch the baked camembert starters. But Rory and I are of the feeling that we've waited so long to get hitched, and we'll never do it unless we do it this year. And can you imagine telling Nora she won't be a bridesmaid?'

'I hear you.' I shuddered. 'There are benefits to being a sober bride, sis – you'll remember everything about the day and will be the only person not hungover at breakfast. You'll be so smug.'

'Eurgh, yes, drinking anything acidic like champagne gives me chronic heartburn, and the Gaviscon chaser I need straight after kills the enjoyment. Bubbles and babies are a terrible combo in my opinion.'

I giggled. 'You're really selling pregnancy to me. Anyway, no one wants to eat camembert at a wedding anyway, because it makes your breath stink. Rob's especially.'

'How is he doing without you?'

'I've got no idea.'

'How come? I thought you'd be talking every day?'

'Far from it. He barely calls. And tomorrow I go to LA for work, so with the time difference it will be even harder.'

'Want me to send Rory over to check on him?'

'Oh, would you? That would be so kind, sis, thank you. I'm sure he's fine, he's probably busy with work, which is good if things have picked up. Also, we need to finalise numbers for your hen do.'

Lucy sighed. 'I wanted to talk to you about this. With how I'm feeling right now, I can't imagine trying to have a night out, let alone one where all my friends are drunk and

I'm high on lemonade. I've been thinking, let's cancel Paris. I'll enjoy it so much more when I can eat all the cheese and drink red wine.'

'But it's your hen do,' I replied carefully, unsure whether some gentle persuasion might help. My sister could be hard to read sometimes.

'I know, but given this pregnancy, what I'd love the most is a spa day with you and Mum.'

'Are you sure?'

'I'm absolutely positive. I think it would be really special to spend some girlie time together, and I can make up for the hen with a blowout with my friends on the other side of the baby and wedding. It makes so much more sense.'

'Sounds good to me, if you're sure. I'll get it organised.'

'Thank you, sister.'

'Love you.'

'I love you too and safe travels.'

Fuelled by nervous energy at spending more time with Jimi, I set about emailing and calling PRs to source outfits for Mandy's LA trip. As it was so last minute, I tried to use global brands and LA-based rental agencies, so most of the items could be sent directly to her and Jose's home in the Hollywood Hills. It made the rest of the day pass quickly and I almost forgot I was hungover.

I was about to start packing my own things for the trip when there was a knock at my bedroom door.

'Come in!' I yelled, expecting it to be Blair to run through the plan for West Wittering with me before I left, but Jimi's face appeared around the corner.

'Ciao, bella. Are you decent?' he asked.

'Hi, Jimi. Come in – I'm clothed!' My cheeks reddened as I immediately imagined what might happen if I wasn't fully dressed in front of him. And having glimpsed parts of Jimi's body in our gym sessions, the thought of seeing more of him was an enticing prospect.

'How's it going?' he asked, smiling at the clothes strewn around my room.

'Slowly,' I replied, thinking I wanted to say something which would acknowledge last night, whilst making it clear that we were just friends. Something natural. But all I could think of at that moment was, 'I can't move my arms properly.'

'What do you mean? Are you okay?' He looked at me concerned.

I took a breath, I hadn't meant to panic him. 'I mean, they just ache a bit. From the torture table.'

'The reformer?'

'That's the one. Brutal.' I went to lift up my right arm, to illustrate, and winced.

Jimi laughed.

'Oi!'

'I'm sorry. You've not having much luck in the gym at the moment, are you? First your lip. Now this.'

I smiled, in spite of myself.

My phone rang. I slid it from the back pocket of my jeans and saw it was Rob calling. *Typical timing*. A reaction must have shown on my face, as Jimi looked at me quizzically.

'It's no one important,' I said, telling my first lie to him.

'Are you packed?' he asked. 'I was sent to check, and to remind you that we leave at five a.m. I can come and help you with your case if you like?'

'It's okay, I'll manage.'

'See you in the morning then.'

'See you.'

CHAPTER EIGHTEEN

WEEK FOUR

I had just taken half a sleeping tablet when Mandy appeared in the premium economy cabin on the plane. She was wearing the plush first-class loungewear and looked worried.

'I wondered if we could have a little chat?' she asked pensively, as the guy I was sitting next to involuntarily snorted in his sleep. 'Shall we go somewhere private?'

'Like where?' I asked, looking around me. The baby in the bassinet on the row to my right hadn't stopped wailing for the last forty minutes, and most of the passengers who were awake, which was most of us, were now gawping at Mandy.

'No way. That's Mandy Sykes!' I heard a woman in the row behind whisper loudly.

'Who?' replied the man sitting next to her.

'This is hell,' Mandy muttered.

I wonder if she's referring to not being recognised or being this far back on a plane?

'Come to the front. They won't mind if we have five minutes, they're looking after us so well.' She smiled broadly, so as many people as possible could hear.

I felt a little disgruntled that I didn't even make it to

business with Jimi for this flight, although I knew it wasn't justified – I was just staff, and premium economy was at least one step up from the economy cabin where Mona always sat me.

We moved through the plane, passing Jimi in business. I tried not to obviously stare, but noticed he was lying flat on his bed, arms folded casually across his broad chest, eyes closed, his lush, dark curled eyelashes long enough to windsurf on. *Dreamy.*

'So, Amber, how are we going to handle the styling?' Mandy asked when we reached her mini suite in row one of the plane. She moved the four-hundred-thread-count bedding out of the way and indicated for me to join her and sit. An attendant approached and offered me a drink.

'Champagne?' Mandy asked.

I politely declined. Although I generally enjoyed working with Mandy, there was often a sense that she was playing with me; that she might dangle something tantalising and then disapprove if I took her up on it.

'This pregnancy,' she confided, 'it's new territory for me and I'm nervous.'

'That's natural,' I reassured her. 'I've not been pregnant myself, but I imagine every mum-to-be must feel the same.'

'So how do you suggest we work it, style-wise?'

I'd been thinking about this a lot, so I was prepped. 'I think we should approach it with complete authenticity,' I said assertively. 'We can embrace maternity brands, but also let your audience in on the insecurity you feel about your changing body and worries about dressing for your evolving shape. Let them come on the journey with you as we figure out your identity as an expectant mum.'

'But stretch marks, cellulite, swollen ankles, the bigness . . . there's nothing sexy about it,' she muttered.

'Some people find pregnancy sexy as hell,' I replied. 'It's the most beautiful gift and there's nothing more stunning than a woman's body in pregnancy, I think. Anyway, if you've managed to avoid morning sickness – as far as I know – maybe you'll be lucky with the rest of your pregnancy?'

She bit her bottom lip. I got the impression Mandy was toying with saying something, but didn't, so I continued. 'I think we can show pregnancy can be an empowering time when it comes to dressing. Plus, I think we need to up the sustainability angle too – look for ways to break into the fashion press, for all the right reasons.'

'What do you mean?' Mandy asked. 'The most sustainable thing I'll ever do for the human race is bring a new life into the world. Do I really need to wear compostable dresses while I do it?'

'I'm not suggesting that.' I giggled. 'I'm just thinking we have a great opportunity to create a fashion moment here, something that will go viral for all the right reasons.'

The word *viral* made her nose twitch, a habit I noticed Mandy had when something caught her attention.

'Remember that image of Demi Moore, naked, on the cover of *Vanity Fair*? Or when Kim Kardashian wore Marilyn Monroe's dress to the Met Gala?'

She nodded.

'Both sustainable fashion choices that set the internet on fire. I know an incredible vintage shop in Beverly Hills called Decades, I'm sure they will have something to fit the bill. And if you fancy doing a Demi, well, that would grab attention.'

'Are you suggesting I go naked?'

'Would you consider it? Demi showing her bump in all its glory was the most powerfully dramatic symbol of femininity. People were talking about it all over the world. It was also a stunning work of art that conveyed a potent message about female liberation. I think that image could do with a 2025 reboot. What do you think?'

Mandy thought for a moment. 'I'll consider it. When the bump is big enough. For now, go to this Decades store when we land and find something sustainable. Something that isn't a fig leaf.'

'You got it, boss.' I yawned, my eyes started to feel heavy.

'I think you'd better get some sleep,' she advised. 'It's going to be a busy few days.'

Touching down in Los Angeles instantly filled me with nostalgia for the balmy awards season I spent out here two years ago. The weather was a warm twenty-seven degrees and the smell of dry concrete and exhaust fumes outside LAX instantly transported me back.

Jimi and I rode together in a car from the airport. I was glad of the opportunity to indulge myself in the scenes around me – him included. Once we hit the highway, I took in the wide roads backed up with traffic at every time of day, the blue skies, palm trees, and actual Americans at the wheel of large SUVs and Teslas. It was all so different to the UK. So *big*. I lowered my window and the heat from outside hit me like a wave rolling in from the sea at Santa Monica. April was as hot as a day in August back home. As we neared Sunset Boulevard, I appreciated the iconic Hollywood Hills in the distance above us. It was as intoxicating and exciting as the very first time I came here.

'You look like a kid in a candy store,' Jimi commented, looking across at me amused.

'I feel like it,' I replied. 'I love this place. Do you?'

'Not so much.' He sighed.

'Why's that?'

He frowned. 'We lived here when I was young, until about the age of ten, when we moved to Miami. It was a turbulent time.'

'Why?'

'That's for another day. You just enjoy the view – and the fumes.' He leant against the side of the car and closed his eyes, signalling the conversation was closed.

The winding road leading to Mandy and Jose's mansion high up in the Hills was decorated with ancient eucalyptus trees, their leaves gently rustling in the breeze like they were whispering the secrets of old Hollywood as we wound our way around them, climbing up so high my ears popped. Our chauffeur navigated the curves with practised ease as we reached a cul-de-sac and the Sykes' mansion materialised before us, a sleek futuristic building protected from view by large, high black gates. If the Surrey home was palatial, this was a modernist's dream, straight from the pages of *Architectural Digest*.

'It's a ground-up,' Jimi announced as the gates opened automatically using state-of-the-art iris recognition triggered by the chauffeur. I looked at him confused. 'That means it was dust when they bought the plot. You'll understand why Surrey's such a struggle when you see inside.'

The gates silently glided open to reveal a glass façade shimmering in the afternoon sun. I watched Mandy step out of the car in front of us, her heels sinking into the polished gravel driveway. The air smelt of jasmine.

A further iris scanner opened the front door, and we were greeted by an expansive hallway with black-and-white floor tiles and bone-white walls. A large, modern clear-crystal-and-gold chandelier, which could have been plucked from a high-end hotel foyer, hung like a frozen waterfall in the middle of the room. Beyond the hallway, floor-to-ceiling windows framed a circular central atrium full of lush tropical foliage, and a curved infinity edge pool highlighted the emphasis on indoor–outdoor living, perfectly suited to the Southern Californian climate.

'God, I have missed this pool!' Mandy declared, kicking off her heels. 'This house was two years of hell in the making, Amber, but worth it.'

I struggled to contain a gobsmacked expression on my face as I took it all in.

'And you moved to Surrey, from *this*?' I remarked.

'Madness, as it turns out.' Mandy laughed. 'It's good to be home. Hola, Louis!' She turned to warmly embrace an immaculately groomed older man, who had silently appeared with cold towels on a tray. The Hollywood equivalent of Philippa.

'Hola, Mandy, Jose, Jimi,' he said, and they all greeted him jovially.

'This is Amber' – Mandy turned to me – 'my stylist. She's staying here too and can take the second guest suite.'

'Very well, it's ready,' Louis replied, bowing his head compliantly, then turning to offer me a towel too.

I don't mind if I do.

My room was far better than any hotel room I'd ever stayed in. It had a small terrace overlooking the twinkling lights of Beverly Hills beneath. Later on, as the sun nearly dipped below the horizon, I took a photo of the view.

I wish you were here, I typed into WhatsApp and sent to Vicky. Then I copied and pasted the same message, sending it to Rob. He hadn't called me back after I missed his call before we left, and though it would be the middle of the night back home, I wanted him to know I was thinking of him.

After she had shared her news with us, Mandy's pregnancy bump seemed to pop out overnight. When I met her as instructed in her spacious dressing room early the next morning, she was already in a flap about the day ahead. I began familiarising myself with the cacophony of open shelving displaying designer handbags, and shoe carousels crammed with strappy sandals in all colours. It was barely conceivable that none of the items in here had made it to Surrey.

The pregnancy announcement had been moved forward to this morning, so as to attract maximum traffic from all corners of the globe, which meant we didn't have time to go to Decades.

'It's no problem. We'll go shopping in your wardrobe!' I smiled brightly, trying to sound a lot less nervous than I felt.

Mandy's LA-based glam squad, a make-up artist called Sandy and hair stylist Ace, was working on her makeover in the bedroom while I prepped the clothes. Jimi popped in to offer me a coffee, which I gladly accepted. I had felt a little shy around him since the night of the party, though he didn't seem to act any differently, which made me question whether I had imagined the connection between us. But there was little time to dwell on it right now.

Mandy had the dream closet, and I went through her wardrobe, getting acquainted with the designer goods in there, considering items, pulling out possibilities, and curating my choices into 'maybes' and 'definitelys'. Once complete, I hung up the 'definitelys' carefully at one end of the wardrobe to be reviewed by Mandy, as we made the final selection for her baby reveal look.

With her caramel waves tousled to perfection, Mandy came and surveyed my selection. She tried a figure-hugging Hervé Léger peach dress and a striking Saint Laurent silver slip, and we even pondered a stunning cropped, tuxedo-style dinner-jacket and trousers combo by Dolce & Gabbana. But nothing felt right to Mandy. I shuttled to and from the wardrobe adding more to the 'maybe' pile, but still she wasn't convinced by any of my choices, and to be honest, neither was I. Her bump was now clearly there, and she was feeling self-conscious, getting changed in the en-suite bathroom each time, instead of in front of me, as she had been happy to do previously.

'We can at least save the Hervé Léger for the Baby Mom launch,' I suggested optimistically, when she emerged for the fifth time complaining that the stretchy, body-hugging design was too dressed up for the purposes of this announcement. Yet, the empire-line creation I had dressed her in before was too relaxed.

Finally, with time ticking, I suggested we take a break and regroup in ten minutes, by which time I would have pulled out even more options. As Mandy cautiously left the bathroom, I held up a white bathrobe for her to thread her arms into, feeling like a waiter in a posh restaurant.

She slipped out of the towel underneath and moved across to the huge, full-length mirror at one end of the dressing suite. She stood there quietly surveying herself as, right on cue, Jose came and stood behind her, taking in his wife's beauty. He put his arms around her waist and spontaneously created a heart shape with his fingers over her bump.

'You look beautiful, my babies,' he swooned. Mandy lifted her face and twisted to kiss him on the lips, before placing her hands on top of his.

'That's it!' I called, in a flash of inspiration. 'Stay there!' It didn't matter that the scene around them was full of discarded clothes, including a couple of bras, in fact it added to the ambience.

'The robe is perfect! Quick, Jimi, bring the phone!' I called out. 'Sandy, flick out her hair just slightly. Ace, a touch more powder on both.' I moved around the couple, both of them barefoot, Jose wearing white joggers and his trademark white T-shirt, a chunky silver chain bracelet around his wrist. I darted around the front and loosened the dressing gown belt around Mandy's waist to accentuate her middle even further.

Mandy cupped my face with her hands. 'You're a genius, Amber!' She smiled contentedly.

Jimi crashed into the room, iPhone in hand. 'Are you ready?'

'Yes, shoot some video too!' Mandy commanded.

In just thirty seconds, the perfect social media content was created: an intimate moment between a pregnant couple marvelling at the miracle they had created.

It did not require an expensive fashion photographer, assistants, lighting rigs, or management barking orders, it felt completely natural.

The resulting video and stills were relaxed, romantic, and real. Within minutes, Jimi had edited it into a ten-second video, set it to a song Mandy had recorded several years ago, aptly entitled 'Ooh Baby', and uploaded it to YouTube, TikTok, Instagram, X, and Snapchat simultaneously.

We busied ourselves tidying the room and waited.

CHAPTER NINETEEN

Watching a moment go viral is a bizarre experience. It's like being in Wembley Stadium with ninety thousand adoring Taylor Swift fans all screaming for their heroine, only the volume is on mute.

Like a commentator reporting on a World Cup final, Jimi kept us constantly updated. 'We're at 100k likes, comments are in the thousands,' he said excitedly, sitting on the chaise longue in Mandy's bedroom, as she and Jose reclined on the bed. 'We'll hit a quarter of a mill in a second. It's flying.'

'Oh my God!' Mandy squealed like a child on Christmas morning. 'Is this faster than the bunion pics?'

'*Way* faster,' Jimi informed us. 'Like a hundred times more already.'

'And the comments?' Mandy asked, buzzing.

'All great. "Congratulations, I'm so happy for you. Ooh baby. Hot mama. Yes, mama! Blah, blah, blah . . ." Have a read if you like.' He handed the phone to her.

We watched as Mandy began scrolling. If I wasn't mistaken, there were tears in her eyes.

'Wow,' she whimpered. 'There's so much love out there.'

An hour later, the likes had topped three million, views

of the Reel were over ten million, and the news had hit all major gossip sites globally. Julie-Ann had apparently texted to say that both *HELLO!* and *Tatler*, as well as *People* magazine, had been in touch about photoshoots. 'So *now* they want to know me,' Mandy cooed smugly.

We spent the rest of the day with Mandy at a showroom in Beverly Hills, as she approved the final packaging and tested the Baby Mom fragrance which had arrived by the crate-load. It was clear that falling pregnant was lucrative, as well as good for Mandy on a personal level, and the comment she had made to that effect in the cryotherapy chamber made sense. Mandy and Jose must have had all these business ventures lined up and ready to go the second they got the green light.

That evening, Jimi and I finally had a chance to chat. 'So, what is it about this city that doesn't work for you?' I asked, as he poured us each a glass of wine on the terrace outside my room. The sun was about to disappear behind the hills again and the sprawling city twinkled against the inky sky.

'It's not that it doesn't work for me, I'm sure it could again,' he said. 'It's just full of memories, some of which are difficult.'

'Do you want to talk about it?'

'Not right now. More wine?' He had already downed his first glass and began recharging it. I took a large sip and offered mine for a refill too. 'Tell me more about you. Family?'

'There's Mum, Dad, and my older sister, Lucy, she's

expecting her second baby around the same time as Mandy. I love being an auntie to my niece, Nora.'

'What kind of aunt are you?' His eyes twinkled mischievously.

'Oh, you know, hilarious, fun, feeder of chocolate and crisps, and creator of an epic dressing-up box – the best kind. How do you feel about becoming an uncle?'

'I can't wait.' He smiled gently.

'It's the best role. You can do the odd babysitting, spoil them, let them stay up too late, feed them sweets so they'll love you forever – and then give them back. It's ideal.'

'I'm like you, I don't want to actually keep them.'

'I didn't say I don't want to keep one.' I instantly felt a little sweaty palmed to be talking this personally with Jimi. 'I mean, I definitely don't want one now, but I'd like to be a mum one day. Would you feel differently if it was your own?'

'Marriage, kids, it's not a life I would choose,' he replied.

'Really?' I don't know why this caused my stomach to sink. I reached for the bottle to fill us up again. The wine was slipping down really well this evening.

'Not after seeing what happened to my parents,' Jimi said, his eye-line fixed on the horizon. 'They had a dramatic split.'

I looked at him carefully. 'What happened?'

'Do you really want to know?'

'If you want to tell me.'

'Mum's infidelities caught up with her. One night, when I must have been no more than six, it all came to a head. Mum and Dad had a huge row. He grabbed a bottle of wine from the cellar, and I came into the cinema room to find him watching their wedding video in bits, while she was upstairs stuffing her suitcase. After another explosive exchange with Dad on the patio, she tossed her wedding ring into the swimming pool and left. We never saw her again.'

'You never saw her again?'

'Not until many years later,' he muttered. 'No one expects the mum to leave in this way, but it happens. She went on to have another family with the other guy, and before you ask, yes, I do have abandonment issues. Yes, I struggle to hold down relationships because of this. Yes, I love women, yet shy away from commitment. Yes, I have a therapist and, no, I'm not quite there yet but I hope to be one day. Does that answer all your questions?'

I listened intently to what Jimi was telling me and then paused as I took it all in. I nodded sympathetically. 'I'm sorry if I overstepped the mark by asking,' I said. 'I didn't mean to pry; I was just trying to be a friend. It sounds like you went through a lot as a child and I'm glad you got the help you needed.'

'It takes continual work, every day.' He sighed. 'It's like I'd sabotage my own life if I had a chance.'

'In what sort of way?'

'Do you ever stop asking questions, Amber?' He smiled. I stared at him in fascination, searching his face for a fault. The messiness of his past only made him more attractive in this moment. *He does have quite a big nose. But it's a handsome big nose.*

'Sorry. I'll change the subject,' I replied. 'Isn't this

view incredible?' I looked out at the twinkling lights of Tinseltown beneath us.

'More questions. Yes, it is.'

'Look at the tiny cars, like beetles crawling along streets.'

'What are you *talking* about?' Now it was his turn to search my face with bemusement.

Is he laughing at me?

I opened my mouth to say something, but Jimi gently put a finger to my lips. He fixed his eyes on me. I swallowed. His touching my lips felt intimate. It was presumptuous, perhaps, but he judged correctly that I didn't mind the closeness. Something stirred in me. Reading the unspoken signs, Jimi moved his finger and took this moment to lean forwards and hold my face in his hands. I didn't move away or do anything about it, because it felt as though time was frozen. I stared at him, weighing him up, thinking that there really was no way of looking at Jimi and not liking what you saw. *Even the slightly big nose.* He had this power to make me feel like the most fascinating person on the planet.

A heartbeat later, his lips were on mine. My eyes were wide open, I felt surprised and excited at the same time about the novelty of someone new. It felt nice.

My body must have tensed.

'Relax,' he whispered, his hands moved around my head, his fingers were in my hair. And then our lips joined again. He felt soft and tender, and although there was no suggestion of a probing tongue finding its way in, to be completely honest, I would not have complained if it had. A few seconds later, he pulled away. It had been a lovely, impulsive, longer-than-was-strictly-necessary kiss on the lips. One that left me longing for more.

'Mierda, you're a good kisser,' he said when we were detached from one another.

'Thank you,' I whispered back. Then I felt silly for thanking him.

What for? We hadn't actually properly kissed, had we?

I felt all light, dreamy, and hungry for him. Jimi reached down and took my hand, lacing his fingers with mine just briefly. He squeezed my hand before letting me go, and then sighed. It was the kind of sigh that suggested he was trying really hard to restrain himself.

Then another sigh, the kind that says, *I really shouldn't be doing this.*

'What about your boyfriend?' he said.

I didn't know how to respond to that.

'Now you're the one asking the questions,' I said after a moment had passed between us.

I turned towards the table and picked up the bottle of wine, realising it was empty.

'We'd better not have any more,' I said unconvincingly, alluding to the fact that I could be very easily persuaded if he were to magically produce more wine. Although I couldn't be responsible for what might happen if we did.

Jimi smiled and in a new tone of voice said, 'Tomorrow is a big day, with the launch.'

He's right, we should call it a night.

We held each other's gaze for a moment, and I felt an energy between us.

'I had a lovely evening. Thank you for confiding in me,' I said softly.

We hugged and when he walked away, I wanted to follow him.

That night, Jimi was stuck inside my head, pulsing through my veins. I felt a physical ache for him to be holding me again; to look at me with those bewitching eyes, with anticipation of what might come. When I fell asleep, I dreamt about his lips meeting mine again – this time getting lost in the softest kisses that would get more firm, more intense, more urgent with each twirl of his tongue against mine, until he was physically pushed against me – and I felt a wet hotness between my thighs. I now understood what Star had meant by 'Thinking Off', as I came in my sleep.

The next morning, when my eyes opened with a jolt, I immediately thought of Jimi. I got up and opened my curtains to reveal the terrace and the panoramic view of the city below me – a view that could never get old; a view I could very easily get used to. Then I batted this thought aside and focused my mind on Rob. He and I had dated in the conventional way – meeting at work, dating in pubs, cinemas, and restaurants. We held hands on walks, met each other's families over congenial dinners, and moved to a new city together. Last night with Jimi, life felt so different, a crazy whirlwind of desire and romance. Our wine glasses and the finished bottle were still on the table. Incriminating evidence. *Is this really happening?*

CHAPTER TWENTY

It felt great to be in the same city as Vicky and I knew she would give me clarity on the Jimi situation, so I texted her a brief update and she called immediately.

'Oh God. Don't tell me you had sex with him?' she asked.

'Of course I didn't!'

'Did he try?'

'No, I don't think so.'

'Did you?'

'I don't think so.'

'*Think?* You either did or didn't.'

'We were drunk. I know I didn't, silly.'

'How do you feel about him now?'

'I'm not sure. I know I feel bad.'

'I feel bad for you too.' She sighed.

'You do?'

'And Rob. Have you spoken to him yet?'

'No, but I'd like to. If he ever phones me back.'

'Oh, Am, perhaps you should try to talk things through with him before you jump into bed with a hot Brazilian.'

'He's American.'

'Similar thing. What are you doing today?'

'Prepping for the Baby Mom launch this evening.'

'You must have an hour to spare. I'm going to kidnap you for a coffee date. Send me the address. I'll ring when I'm parked outside.'

'I'll get an Uber to meet you, it'll be quicker. I need a plan.'

Vicky and I arranged to meet for breakfast at Urth Caffé in downtown LA. I managed to leave the house in an Uber before anyone else, especially Jimi, was up. My mouth was dry, head spinning, stomach rumbling, and I couldn't wait to see my best friend. It had been six long months since we were last able to be together IRL.

The second I spotted Vicky at a table inside the café my spirits lifted. She looked exactly the same, except more tanned, and with a pink Prada Spectrum Bag across her body which I'd bet was definitely real and not one of the designer knock-offs I had bought her from Manhattan's notorious Bag Man.

We hugged each other tightly for a whole minute and the woman who ran the place asked if we were long-lost sisters.

'We may as well be,' Vicky replied excitedly. 'I love her like a sister.'

'Chosen family!' I seconded.

Over lattes and fresh blueberry muffins, the conversation turned to Jimi. 'So, who is he?' Vicky asked.

'He's Jose's younger brother. He's from Miami, he's a DJ,' I replied.

Vicky rolled her eyes. 'I don't mean his Instagram bio. I mean who is he *really*?'

'He does Mandy's social media; he's into meditation and practising gratitude.'

'And?'

'He's nice to talk to, and he's a calming influence compared to the whirlwind Mandy has become. He always seems to be there when I'm feeling lonely, and recently that has been quite a lot. It's begun to feel as though so much time away from Rob is putting a distance between us. Oh, and he's unbelievably sexy and probably the most beautiful man I have ever seen in the flesh.'

'Oh Christ. This is bad.'

'Bad? Do you think I'm a really bad person?'

'Honey, you know me well enough by now to know I would *never* judge you. Secrets to the grave, right?'

'Cross my heart and hope to die.' I crossed my chest to belabour the point.

'Let's analyse this further. You didn't actually snog him, it was just a kiss. Are you married?'

'You know I'm not.'

'Good. But even if you were, you've not done anything that bad, you do know that, don't you?'

'But I thought about it.'

'Thoughts don't count. Do you think you'll marry Rob?' Vicky asked.

This was a big question. Just a few weeks ago I would have immediately said yes. But now I needed to pause. I tried to picture it, as if I was looking down on myself from an unknown place, somewhere in the future.

There is me and there's Rob. We look the same, only

there are rings on our fingers because we are married. My hairstyle is shorter as all hairstyles seem to become the older you get. We are wearing sensible clothes. We have a house, a terrace on a London street. It's in Zone Five and at least a fifteen-minute walk from the closest Tube, because that is what we can afford. There's a buggy parked in the hallway, a baby gurgling on its playmat. Music is playing, a bottle of red is open, and Rob's lasagna is cooking in the oven. It's still his signature dish.

'I guess so.' I sighed.

'You don't sound convinced.'

'But I'm not *un*convinced.'

'You don't sound particularly enthusiastic about it.'

'I think I am.'

'*Think?* Babes. It all sounds very adequate to me.'

'It's adequately happy.'

'Amber, you're twenty-six years old. These are the days. Don't you think you deserve a little more than *adequate*?'

'Says the person who ran off to LA with a film director she barely knew, no job, and a hundred quid in the bank. It's okay for you, Vicky, you're adventurous. You're a risk-taker. I'm not the same as you. Maybe it is enough for me.'

We were interrupted by my phone pinging as a succession of WhatsApp messages arrived from Blair. Seeing their name pop up startled me as it was really late in the UK.

Where are you?
Mandy's just woken me up – she's looking for you.
She says she wants to try the dress.

Seriously Amber – where are you?
Go back to the house asap!
She's about to file you as a missing person. And I want
to go to sleep.

After Vicky and I hugged goodbye, vowing to meet up again as soon as Vicky could get to London for a proper holiday, because one brunch really was not enough time together, I thought about our conversation a lot. I thought about what *adequate* meant. Specifically, whether *adequately happy* is happy enough. Even though it did feel as though that vignette in my mind about life with Rob might have seemed a little dull to her, it was comforting to me. It was calm and I was happy. I mean, I could have been wearing better clothes, but it wasn't all bad. So, I kept coming back to the same conclusion: Rob.

When I got back to the house I crept inside, hoping not to bump into Jimi. The house was quiet, which made me panic. Surely Mandy wasn't conducting her own search party for me?

Blair messaged: *She's gone to get a pedicure, back in an hour. I'm going to try to get some sleep now.*

After all that.

I knew I had to speak to Rob. It was my sole mission for the rest of the day, and I would make sure it happened, even if I had to contact the Divorcee in the flat above and ask him to bash the door down. It would be morning in the UK and there was absolutely no excuse for Rob not to pick up his phone on a Sunday.

'Hey you, how's LA?' Rob's voice was husky, as though he'd not long been awake. He gave me a fright because I was ninety-nine per cent sure he wasn't going to pick up.

'Oh. Hi!' I hooted in surprise. 'How are *you*, most importantly? I've been worried about you.'

'Worried about me?'

'Not answering your phone, going AWOL . . . I think I had reason to be a little concerned,' I replied.

'I'm sorry.' He paused. 'I knew you were busy with work, and I didn't want to burden you with my woes.'

'Woes?' I asked concerned.

'Oh, just work stuff, but it can wait until we're together. Anyway, your soon-to-be brother-in-law made sure I was still alive last night. He took me to the pub.'

'Rory?'

I had forgotten about that.

'He gets out even less than I do. Let's just say neither of us is feeling too sprightly right now. He's on the sofa.'

'The sofa? What did Lucy say?'

'She's the one who told him to stay! Something about "checking up on me"?'

I stayed silent.

'I think she made a wise decision. Lucy's got enough nausea to cope with,' he said.

I giggled. 'You have a point.'

'Anyway, how are you doing? How's LA?'

I filled him in on work so far, seeing Vicky, Mandy's news, the shoot, and the clothes prep, intentionally ignoring any mention of Jimi. Then we discussed plans for the weekend

I would finish this job, and how he would book somewhere nice for us to go for dinner as soon as I was released. Unbelievably, I was already a third of the way through the three months, though in some ways it felt as though I'd been living this weird existence for much longer.

It was lovely to hear Rob tell me he missed me. We were just about to end the conversation in my mind, when he said, 'What are you wearing, baby?'

'What?' I asked.

There was a glint in his eye as Rob repeated the words. 'I said, what are you wearing?'

'Just a dress,' I replied. 'It's warm – sorry about that! – I'm in sandals and this dress.'

'Show me.' He smiled.

'Really?'

'Now, please,' he commanded. It was exciting to hear him order me to do something.

As instructed, I reversed the camera and used my arm as a selfie stick to show him head to toe. I was wearing a basic black shirt dress from Zara – nothing particularly special, which I slightly regretted.

'Open a button for me,' Rob said, with a sexy smile.

'Okay,' I muttered, embarrassed.

His eyes watched me closely. It was both presumptuous and thrilling at the same time. I knew how horny Rob could be on weekend mornings, especially with a hangover, and this was a good sign that he was missing my physical company.

I slowly moved my hand to the top button. It was a

simple outfit in anticipation of fading into the background as I tended to Mandy's fashion needs at the Baby Mom event later.

'Now the next one,' he stated, 'and keep going.'

I now wished I was wearing something sexier, plus I couldn't remember whether I had my 'good bra' underneath, let alone which knickers I'd put on this morning, though I was very sure they were unlikely to be a matching set.

This is Rob. He's seen all of my most grannyish, comfy knickers before and he loves me regardless. Yet somehow it was as though we were looking at each other with eyes full of lust and wonder for the first time.

In silence, holding eye contact, I continued unbuttoning my dress until it was completely open, revealing my black lace bra and red knickers. It could have been a lot worse. My breathing deepened, as did his, as he carried on looking at the screen. His big green eyes moving around my body, his lips so kissable, as I showed him as much of myself as I could.

'You look so beautiful. Now take off your dress and move over to your bed,' he ordered, his voice soft and reassuring.

My skin had become covered in goosebumps. I felt vulnerable and sexy.

'What shall I do now?' I asked, enjoying the scenario, as I lay on the bed in my underwear, my head propped up on two pillows.

'Place the phone down and take off your bra,' he said. 'Let me watch you.'

I propped up the phone on another pillow next to me,

and did as I was told, slowly lowering each strap in turn, allowing one breast and then the other to show over my bra. They felt round and voluptuous. My nipples were hard.

'Now lower your knickers slightly so I can see you,' he continued.

I complied with his wish, losing my inhibitions because I felt so comfortable about letting go with him. This was Rob, *my* Rob.

'Now look at me as you touch yourself.'

I held my breath, my pulse quickened, and I tried to keep my eyes on his as I pushed my hand under my knickers and began touching myself. I felt so turned on, so soft and silky.

'I wish I could kiss you,' Rob murmured, his face filling the screen as he slowly moved his tongue to his top lip. 'I have missed the taste of you.'

'Me too,' I purred into the screen, desperate to be able to kiss him back.

I closed my eyes then, ready to float off on my way to reaching orgasm. The only problem was that Jimi's face kept popping into my mind. He was so close to my face, and then he was kissing me. He was so real in my mind, I could almost feel him, smell him, taste him.

I tried to bat away the image of Jimi and replace him with Rob's sweet, familiar face. I opened my eyes and could see that Rob was now touching himself too. Maybe if Rob was here with me, I would feel differently. I really wanted to. I squeezed my eyes shut again.

'I love you baby,' Rob murmured. 'I want you.'

'I love you too,' I whispered.

After I had come, and he had too, we said a tender goodbye and I lay back on my bed. I was half elated and half in shock about the intensity of the call.

I just wanted to fall asleep wrapped tightly in Rob's arms. The warmth of his body against mine. Yet my mind was tricking me again. I kept imagining the brush of Jimi's curly hair against my face; his strong arms holding me close.

Tears crept up and spread to the back of my eyeballs in quick, hot succession. *Why is my mind doing this to me?*

It was only a matter of seconds before the floodgates opened. I wept like I hadn't for a long time, as the enormity of what I was doing hit me. I felt horrible for Rob; even if it was mostly in my mind, it still felt like a betrayal. None of this was fair on him.

If my feelings for Jimi were getting stronger, I couldn't carry on like this, being unfaithful, even in my thoughts.

I toyed with the idea of telling Rob about Jimi. *Maybe honesty is best?* I was still wrestling with this thought as I noticed it was getting late. Mandy would be back. I needed to get her ready for the event.

CHAPTER TWENTY-ONE

The Baby Mom launch began with the glow of flash bulbs, from the waiting bank of paparazzi who greeted us at the entrance to the fashionable 1 Hotel in West Hollywood. An oasis of green foliage, tasselled umbrellas, and green-and-white-striped seating appeared, with jaw-dropping panoramic views of the LA skyline. Mandy greeted members of the press and influencers, as she extolled the virtues of wearing Baby Mom. The air was heavy with the heady scent of the fragrance, which was being described as 'the softest petals of white roses kissed by morning dew, combined with an undertone of warm milk enriched with vanilla'. Baby Mom by Mandy was a fragrant celebration of eternal love.

Mandy had invited a cosmic doula called Ebony to join her in conversation, and there was a surreal moment where Ebony addressed the guests about the powerful scent of amniotic fluid, and how she would be present at Mandy's birth to whisper encouragement, as the newborn child emerged from her mother's cosmic portal. As the conversation turned to the virtues of turning the placenta into a potent drink after the birth, I kept stealing looks at

Jimi, who was busily capturing content for Mandy's socials with a phone on the end of large selfie stick.

The room burst into appreciative 'awwws' when Mandy revealed she had requested the scents of milk-drunk dreams and moonbeams be added to the perfume. Unfortunately, the laboratory in France hadn't been able to oblige, so she had settled on white rose and vanilla milk in the end.

'We love you, Mandy!' someone shouted enthusiastically.

'I love you too!' she replied, elated. Watching Mandy come to life in front of an adoring audience was like witnessing a butterfly emerge from a chrysalis.

'Do you know the sex of the baby?' an influencer called out.

To which she quipped, 'Not yet – but I'll make sure you're the first to know when I do!'

Camera phones were pointed at her all the time, with videos and photos uploaded to platforms at lightning speed.

All the while I kept Jimi in my peripheral vision, wondering whether I should address what happened last night. But we barely had a chance to exchange any words, he was so busy, and I was constantly shadowing Mandy, checking the peach Hervé Léger dress was hugging her in all the right places and no martinis were getting accidentally spilt on it. I watched in awe as Mandy bobbed around the room, flashing her megawatt smile, chatting happily with all the guests, posing for selfies, spritzing perfume everywhere she went, a seasoned pro at this kind of work. Her baby bump had really popped out and was cocooned beautifully in the dress, with one protective hand on her bump most of the time, she was clearly revelling in all the attention it got.

That evening, after a flurry of loving WhatsApp messages from Rob about how great it was to 'see' me and how he couldn't wait for me to get back home, I was feeling really guilty about what I'd got up to just twenty-four hours earlier with Jimi. I needed to say something. I didn't want things to feel weird between us.

Impulsively, I saved Jimi's number from our WhatsApp group with Mandy and wrote a message to him. *I really like you, Jimi, it's been great getting to know you, but I thought I should say that I definitely have a boyfriend, and I don't think we can see each other like that anymore. I hope you understand. Amber x*

I deleted that immediately, it was far too formal. Then I wrote: *Hi, Jimi, thanks for a lovely evening last night. I'm feeling a bit weird about things today because of my boyfriend. I was hoping to talk to you about this, but meanwhile I wondered if we could perhaps go back to being just work friends? Thanks for your understanding. Ax*

I deleted it too. *Maybe I'm overreacting. Maybe it was nothing?* Instead, I switched to Instagram and then to TikTok and scrolled through Jimi's posts. On viewing his stories, I discovered that Jimi was currently in the West Hollywood nightclub The Viper Room, with what appeared to be some stunning women, quite possibly hangers-on from the event, all around him. I couldn't really blame them, who wouldn't gladly take up a night on the town with one of America's fittest, most well-connected, commitment-phobic bachelors? This was Jimi doing exactly what he had told me he liked to do – enjoying women without any commitment. I felt a little silly for imagining I might be anything more than just a colleague to him anyway.

Impulsively I replied to one of his stories on Instagram, keeping it short and light, showing him there was nothing to worry about when it came to me. *It's lucky I have a boyfriend! See you tomorrow. Ax*

The next day, I woke up to a message from Rob. He still came up as 'Rob Walker (Handsome)' on my phone, an ode to the very first time I punched his digits into my contacts, when Vicky and I had nicknamed him Handsome Rob.

I opened his message and smiled as I read it.

I love you, Amber, more than I've ever loved anyone before. I can't wait for you to come home. 8 weeks and counting . . .

It felt as though something deep inside me had been rejigged back into place, as I thought about Jimi and Rob. Two very different men. One that pulsed through my veins like a canoe down rapids, the other representing a love that was steady and kind.

A day later, as we made our way to the first-class lounge at LAX, a few people glanced in our direction, recognising the famous traveller in our midst.

A stranger commented, 'Aww, hi, Mandy! Such a pretty bump – you are glowing!'

Mandy grunted. She was having one of her off-days, possibly due to a lack of sleep following all the excitement of the launch event. 'I know they mean well, but *please*.

Being pregnant at forty-five, it's like I have a Post-it Note with, "What do you think about this? Tell me your opinion immediately!" stuck on my bump.'

'At least it's all positive, baby,' Jose observed, sipping a coffee. 'It feels like people throw all decency out the window when they're online. Keyboard warriors, trolls, cyberbullying, it's like the Wild West out there. At least people are courteous here in the real world.'

'But what is real?' I muttered sarcastically, shocking myself by saying it out loud rather than in my head, as I had intended.

'What do you mean by that, Amber?' Mandy asked pointedly, turning to me.

I had to think fast. 'I was just thinking,' I replied, buying myself a bit of time. 'I was thinking about whether the same rules of behaviour exist online as in the real world. I mean, sometimes negativity gets higher stats. Surely that's why the trolls do it?'

Jimi, who had been walking alongside us, sniggered. 'You couldn't imagine anyone being negative because they are actually not a very nice person, could you, Amber?' He said it in a slightly nasty tone, which took me by surprise.

I felt myself shrink. And then I felt cross. How dare Jimi humiliate me in front of my boss.

'What's up with you?' I asked. 'Late night?'

'No. Bed early, actually.'

I know that's probably a lie.

I shrugged, before replying assertively, 'I just don't think it should be acceptable to say something online that you would never say to someone's face. In the same way that it's not okay to create a digital persona that isn't the way you live in the real world. Doesn't it perpetuate false standards and unfair expectations? Personally, I think that's harmful.'

'That sounds beautiful, if we lived in an ideal world. Or should that be a Self-Love Utopia?' Jimi said it jokingly, but it was laced with cynicism. 'Everyone falsifies everything online. That's just the way it is.'

'And this from the social media expert,' I replied, with venom. 'How reassuring. I thought we were trying to be real here?'

My eyes bore into the side of Jimi's face. Far from leaping to my defence, he sounded bitter. I'd never seen this moody side of him before and I didn't like it.

Jimi considered his response for a moment, and then replied, 'So, Amber, would you say it's like sometimes we're leading *double lives* – one in the physical realm and another in a parallel universe?' He raised an eyebrow.

My heart picked up speed.

Leading double lives? Is he referring to us? My paranoia about what was, or wasn't, going on between us made me feel anxious. I remembered the message I had sent him last night.

'But what about freedom of expression?' I replied, digging further into what Jimi might be getting at. 'Sometimes it isn't clear cut.'

'I just know that some people behave very differently when they're face to face than when they can hide behind a screen.' He said the last sentence in such a way that I knew exactly what he meant.

I looked Jimi in the eye, hoping he might give me a sign that everything was okay, and I was reading too much into this, but he just looked ahead and said, 'I think I need another coffee.'

CHAPTER TWENTY-TWO

WEEKS FIVE AND SIX

In the weeks following the LA trip, most of Mandy's time was spent in meetings with Jose or going for prenatal appointments, and I witnessed Philippa shepherd a stream of beauty therapists back and forth to her bedroom for at-home wellbeing treatments. When I saw her for fittings and at mealtimes, Mandy enjoyed telling me about the cold feeling of the gel and sonographer's wand on her belly, and the miracle of seeing the baby on a screen, 'grooving around' in her uterus. She was five months pregnant now and there was no mistaking her bump. The amount of freebies Mandy received from baby brands was doubling by the day, and unopened boxes of nappies, clothes, cots, and pram paraphernalia were piling up in one of the spare rooms in the house. Julie-Ann and Blair would wander around, swatches of fabric and colour charts in hand, making plans for the nursery makeover in the LA home, for which they had enlisted a top interior designer for free, in return for some branded content on Mandy's channels.

Jimi and I resumed our gym sessions and I told myself I was cool with it, although I was more flushed than usual around him. I found it harder to compartmentalise what was going on with Jimi in my working life, and the real me who was living with Rob. I was in awe of how Jimi could seemingly just switch on and off our attraction to each other, and it made me constantly question whether the kiss in LA had been real.

'He's playing you,' was Vicky's verdict when I raised this with her. Although my rational mind suspected this when Jimi gave me a charming smile, or our arms accidentally brushed in the house, something would ignite within me, and my heart was so taken by the excitement of it all. I wanted to live in the moment and not worry about the future. In my limited experience of relationships, I wasn't naive enough to think that Jimi was anything more than a bit of tantalising fun. But then something else would happen – a look, a touch that would throw it all up in the air again and make me think this was so much more than just a flirt.

I questioned my own prejudices, thinking it wasn't Jimi's fault he was blessed with perfectly symmetrical looks and plump, kissable lips.

If he wasn't so good-looking, would I be feeling the same way?

The West Wittering trip was postponed twice due to bad weather, but I continued to fill my days arranging Mandy's clothes, prepping for the shoot, and organising a trip to the Surrey Hills Spa for Lucy's pared down hen do with Mum.

For West Wittering, Mandy set her sights on pieces from the lauded latest collection by British designer David Koma. It took its influence from the Greek goddess Aphrodite, a symbol of beauty and femininity, and gave her an ultramodern makeover, using transparent water-like sequin fabrics in aqua green and soft pink, body-contouring crop tops, gowns with sensual cut-outs, and mesh dresses. It wasn't easy to get my hands on many of the pieces from the collection, so I put in a call to Jasmine at Smith's boutique to see if she could enlist her best fashion contacts to help me. Another morning, Coco taught Blair and me how to make date, coconut, cacao, and chia seed balls that tasted so similar to chocolate, everyone in the house was giddy with happiness when they were served as a regular after-dinner treat. As Mandy was no longer on a strict fertility-inducing diet, but something more substantial for a woman carrying a child, we were offered bread with some meals, which lifted all of our spirits. Even Philippa seemed more relaxed, as though she might actually quite like our presence in 'her' mansion. It felt as though our unlikely squad had finally bonded.

I was on my way to meet Blair one morning, when I walked straight into Jimi in a pow-wow with Jose in the hallway. They both looked serious and stopped speaking the moment I was within earshot.

'Is everything okay?' I asked.

Lately I'd become paranoid Jimi was talking about me every time I saw him with Jose. *I wonder if he's told his brother anything about us.*

'There's been some negative commentary on Threads about Mandy not giving enough back to her UK fans despite living here,' Jimi said. His concerned expression was akin to someone reading the latest news from a conflict zone.

Sometimes it was hard to keep a sense of perspective when living in this celebrity commune.

'It means we need to do something special and exclusive to mark being five months pregnant,' Jose replied to us both. 'Whatever the British weather throws at us tomorrow, we go to West Wittering and get the beach shots. We just need to do it,' he commanded. 'You can make that work, can't you, Amber?'

'Yes, she can,' Jimi interjected.

'Right.'

'Talking of which, Mandy's mentioned a David Koma dress,' said Jose. 'She's obsessed with it, it's straight off the runway. If I find a photo, you can get it, can't you, Amber.' There was no question mark at the end of this statement.

'Of course. Send me the exact one, I've already been looking into his collection, and it won't be a problem,' I said with a certainty I didn't yet feel.

I sprinted back to my laptop in my bedroom.

Minutes later the dress image came through from Jose. It was a stunning white, body-contouring, sheer midi dress with a cut out front, and hand-embroidered roses, bejewelled with silver crystals and stitched onto the finest tulle. In the photo it was being worn by Jennifer Lopez.

I could see why it appealed to Mandy. This was the kind of dress that was sheer enough to make her curvaceous body the focus, to hug her baby bump, and to ooze sex appeal at the same time. Some quick online investigating revealed there were two in existence, one had been worn by Jennifer Lopez, and the second was last seen on the runway at London Fashion Week in February. I frantically located it on David Koma's website, where it was marked SOLD OUT.

Who can get me the David Koma dress probably hanging in Jennifer Lopez's wardrobe right now? My brain was buzzing. I called Jasmine at Smith's, but she couldn't help. I messaged Vicky to see if one of her old colleagues in the fashion department at *Glamour* magazine might know, but hit a brick wall. My finger hovered over Mona Armstrong's number, I seriously considered it for a moment, but thought better of it. Even though some time had passed, my PTSD from working with her was still unresolved. Then it hit me like the bouncing medicine ball had smacked me in the face. Joseph! That was it, Joseph, my old boss at Selfridges, had mentioned he was mates with David Koma when the subject came up for a window display. I WhatsApped him straight away.

Oh mate, it's great to hear from you! came the reply within minutes. *I've been following your work with Mandy. Loved her look at the launch in LA, she looked blooming gorgeous! How's it all going?*

It's great, I replied. *Do you think you can help get me this dress?* I WhatsApped the image to him. *It's urgent, and I'm kind of desperate. It's the only thing Mandy wants to wear for our latest photoshoot. It will go viral for sure. The shoot is tomorrow* 😨.

Babe, I haven't spoken to David in a while, but I'll give it a try, you never know.

I will literally be your slave forever. Anything you ever need. Crossing everything and thanking you so much. Ax

And then I took my phone off silent and waited.

An hour later, a message came through from Joseph. *It turns out David is a big fan of Mandy's. You owe me big time, mate! Meet me outside Selfridges at 6 p.m. I'll have the dress. Jx*

I actually punched the air.

The pursuit of the perfect viral moment was the plan for West Wittering beach this blustery Sunday morning. It was an unseasonably rainy and cold April day. Our team of six was primed to shoot a social media moment to show off Mandy's bump to her British audience. It was to be candid, raw, and real, without an expensive crew. Our new stance around authenticity seemed to be sinking in at last, and we set to work capturing Mandy's pregnancy in all its beauty, against the dramatic, rugged, distinctly British landscape.

I sank a little deeper into my camo Dryrobe, glad for its warmth. On the other side of a sparse, grassy verge, perched on the highest point of a sand dune, a beautiful, voluptuous woman was standing in a skimpy dress, barefoot, looking out to sea, her expression wistful. Except for her billowing hair, she could almost be a statue. Her white dress had become see-through, thanks to the heavy rain, and was barely covering her bottom, her thighs fully on show. The dress was clinging to her body in all the right places. The instant tan carefully applied earlier was trickling down her calf and her mascara was smudged.

As the rain poured down on our famous subject, many onlookers stopped to gawk at the surprising vision before them – like a figure from aquatic mythology – her hands on her burgeoning bump, which looked perfectly smooth and round as she posed for the photos being taken by Jimi.

Most passers-by gave her a double-take, some with a look of curiosity, most with visible disdain, perturbed by this blot on the picturesque landscape. Yet, if a bystander happened to be under the age of thirty, the double-take was swiftly followed by the elevation of a camera phone, followed by, I imagine, an upload to TikTok, Snap, or Insta. Soon, a few others had noticed, and this led to a murmur of excitement along the beach as more people wondered what could be causing this much fuss before nine a.m. on a soggy Sunday. Before we knew it, like bees to a hive, a little crowd of spectators had formed around the Queen. It had become startlingly apparent that this freezing-cold figure, in pursuit of the perfect social media moment, was not your average local.

As the morning progressed, still the winds came and the rain fell in sheets, and we could see this wasn't the easiest assignment for Mandy, who seemed to be posing in an awkward way; her hands wrapped around her middle, as if she was trying to hold the dress together, as well as find the most flattering angles.

'I know it's hard, but can you try to relax a little?' Jimi was shouting, as he moved around on an adjacent sand dune capturing her best side. We had no mobile phone reception on the beach, so he was using a megaphone we had brought along to communicate with Mandy.

After a whole hour of standing in various poses in the

biting winds, she picked it up and yelled, 'Just tell me you got it? I'm freezing all my cellulite off over here!'

Jimi signalled with a feeble thumbs-up, followed by a moving flat hand.

Mandy looked stressed. 'What does that *mean*? You're not sure? I told you to keep your finger down. It's meant to look candid. Did you get the video too?'

She turned to her left. 'Jose! Will you check if he's got it? I can't stand here all day, I can feel hyperthermia starting.' Then, clocking some bystanders with phones raised and pointed in her direction, she added, 'I'll either die out here, or someone will get the exclusive before me!'

They smiled uncomfortably and backed off.

When Jose reached Jimi, he also looked unconvinced by the images.

'Well, I can't feel my fat anymore,' Mandy called back. 'Let's call it quits. We can always tweak things in Photoshop later.' That comment made me bristle. Yet I felt for Mandy, being such a trooper in unforgiving conditions.

'We're so nearly there, just a few more shots and I think we'd have it in the bag,' Jimi shouted into his cupped hands.

Mandy began sounding-off about how she needn't have bothered paying for the cryotherapy sessions, when she could have just come here instead.

Jose looked back towards Julie-Anne and asked, 'What do you think?'

Julie-Ann urged calm. 'We need to think about the baby too. Mandy, why don't you take ten in the trailer? Let's see how you feel when you've warmed up.'

'Finally, someone speaking sense!' Mandy stormed. 'Amber, where's that Dryrobe?'

I leapt into action, tossing the other Dryrobe over my arm, and rushing over to fling it around her shoulders, which were glistening with rainwater. I was always prepared, even on our 'candid' shoots. Then I led her to shelter – the Winnebago Julie-Ann had hired as our transport for the day, and for Mandy to use as a dressing room.

As we passed Jimi, he muttered, 'What is it you Brits say, "No such thing as bad weather, only bad clothes"?'

Jimi. Making every day more exciting purely by his presence; his ostentatious bright white puffa jacket at odds with the scenery, but he still looked gorgeous. As the wind picked up, the sharp, fresh aroma of his citrus aftershave made my nostrils zing. *On paper, I should not find it attractive. On paper, he is absolutely not my type. On paper, this is wrong for hundreds of reasons. But the problem is, the paper got torn up and burnt somewhere along the way.*

'Any eagle-eyed fashion fan will know this dress,' I replied, unperturbed. 'There are only two in existence and Jennifer Lopez has the other.'

'Well, you Brits sure are teaching us about resilience,' he quipped, slipping me a sideways glance laced with affection. I wonder what exactly he meant by this.

Could he be referring to the chemistry between us? The night of the kiss had been playing in my mind, over and over, like the opening credits of the telenovela I seemed to have found myself accidentally starring in. Each time the memory was embellished in places; more passionate than the last. Jimi was the human Rubik's cube I was struggling to solve.

'These photos better be worth it,' Mandy muttered belligerently, as I opened the door to the Winnebago and ushered her inside. She was shivering.

My phone pinged with a message, it was Rob. *Are you okay?*

Not really, I thought.

'Give me a minute, I need to sort myself out,' Mandy said, indicating I should leave, so I dutifully closed the door behind her and waited outside like a bedraggled sentry.

I used the time to text Rob back. *I'm focusing on the bonus.*

'Coffee run!' Blair announced from behind me, which was the best thing I had heard anyone say all day. It really was raw-cold, and the sooner we could get this shoot done, the quicker I could get back to the warmth of the house and call Rob.

'Check if Mandy wants a decaf Americano, would you?' Blair called out to me.

I turned back towards the Winnebago and opened the door just wide enough to poke my head inside and take her order. 'Mandy, would you—'

The sight which greeted me made me stop in my tracks.

CHAPTER TWENTY-THREE

Inside the Winnebago at East Head viewpoint, Mandy turned towards me. Our eyes locked: mine, wide with astonishment, hers narrow with fear.

'Oh shhhit,' she said slowly, in a tone that made my throat tighten.

I took in the sight before me. This was a private moment clearly not intended for me to see. It crossed my mind that I should just leave, pretending I hadn't noticed anything. But it was too late. There was no mistaking what I was looking at.

'So now you know,' said Mandy, quietly.

'I, I don't know what to say,' I stammered.

An awkward silence hung in the air for a moment, as my brain tried to compute what this meant.

'Does Jose know?' I asked.

'Of course.'

'Julie-Ann?'

'Yes. Sit down.'

I walked towards her.

The sheer David Koma dress was pulled up around Mandy's waist and she was holding what was obviously a fake pregnant belly in her left hand. It looked like it was made of silicone, the skin tone matching hers perfectly. It was attached to a band of stretchy fabric, which was presumably what was causing her discomfort around the waist as she posed for the photos.

She turned and sat down on the upholstered bench seat just behind her, placing the bump next to her. It was quite dark in there, as the curtains were all closed to give privacy while she got changed, and the lights around the vanity mirror in the middle of the space were dim. It was a melancholy sight.

'Are you sure you don't want me to go?' I asked, feeling the grip of nervousness. 'I can pretend I—'

'Please sit,' she commanded. 'I need to explain.'

I joined her, sitting on a chair close to where she was positioned.

'There is a baby,' she said softly.

I breathed a sigh of relief.

'It's being carried by a surrogate. She's called Natalia and she's been incredible. She's an earth angel, to be more precise.'

I swallowed the lump in my throat.

'I'm really happy you're going to be a mother, Mandy,' I said.

'I had been using a surrogate before, but she miscarried twice, the last one at twelve weeks.' Her face dropped. 'But Natalia fell pregnant at the same time, although we couldn't be sure of anything until Jose had gone out to New York to see the baby for himself on a scan at sixteen weeks,' Mandy continued. 'I didn't want to believe it could be possible until then.' I looked at the side of her face. 'It's common for people to use two surrogates,' she said, 'to double your chances. I couldn't go to New York with him because we were so busy here with work. They FaceTimed me through the whole thing, and when I heard that little heartbeat' – her eyes were moist with tears – 'it was magical. It's really hard to explain, but I felt as if I was now complete.'

'I'm so happy for you, Mandy, genuinely, I am,' I said softly.

'It happened that evening, after the first photoshoot in the house,' she revealed. 'All day I was waiting for the call. It kept getting later and later and still nothing from Jose. I really thought my dream was over.'

My mind ticked over, remembering how bizarre Mandy had been that day. Her mood was all over the place, it made sense now. It wasn't only the effect of the magic mushrooms. She must have been wracked with anxiety waiting for Jose to call; to know everything was okay with the pregnancy. And it also slotted into place why they announced the news to us straight after Jose was back from New York.

She continued, 'Up until that point I hadn't dared to believe it might actually happen for us. Now we're nearly five months, I'm finally starting to relax and believe this is going to happen. It's taken us years to get to this point, Amber. You can't begin to understand how painful it's been.'

'I'm sorry you had such a struggle. It sounds really hard,' I said quietly, as a tidal wave came crashing over my head, bringing with it a number of things that now made sense.

The cryo chamber, the ovulation stick, drinking champagne, dancing on tables – all the things you'd be unlikely to partake in during the early weeks of pregnancy. And, thankfully, the magic mushrooms would not have caused any harm to the unborn baby.

'The bump, though?' I asked.

'When you're as famous as I am, people feel they have a right to scrutinise every aspect of your life,' she said. 'But you have helped me, Amber, more than you know.' Mandy turned to face me, her expression was sincere. 'Do you remember that moment, on the shoot, when you asked me who I am?'

I nodded cautiously. 'No one has asked me that before. They all assume they already know. At that moment, all I wanted to do was scream, "I'm a mother!", but I didn't know for sure if I was or not. We couldn't be sure of anything until we saw the scan. You helped me to see that whatever happens, I don't need labels – I am enough. The universe has a strange way of working at times, but I feel it's all going to be all right, no matter what life throws at me.'

'That's a huge thing to come to terms with,' I said. 'I'm so proud of you.'

I hadn't been aware of having a protective instinct before that moment. I didn't see my role as a stylist as being about rescuing people, but there was something about Mandy. As her large brown eyes gazed into mine, her honesty, and the revelation of her story, made me want to solve all of her problems and stop her from feeling pain. I didn't see her as a global superstar in that moment, I saw her vulnerability – just the same as anyone else.

'By the time that day was over, I was shattered,' she continued. 'I stormed off after dinner because all I could think about was whether I was about to become a mother or not.'

I bowed my head. 'And there I was, banging on about a "self-love utopia". I feel so stupid.' I blinked, feeling tears emerge in my eyes.

Mandy smiled and put a hand on my shoulder. 'It's okay, Amber, you didn't know. It was brave, your little speech, you are so passionate about what you do. You are so much more than a stylist – you give people a belief that they can do difficult things; that it's not really about the clothes, but the wearer who makes them come alive – don't ever lose that. But it's not always as easy for your clients as you might think.'

'I was naive,' I said, hanging my head. 'I'm sorry if I was too direct and I hurt you.' I felt so much compassion for her.

We both found our eyes resting on the silicone bump, lying on the seat between us – a surreal mound of disembodied flesh. Mandy tenderly traced its curve with her fingers, as if it genuinely was carrying something as precious as her unborn baby.

She sighed heavily. 'Surrogacy is a deeply personal process. Wearing the bump felt like a good way to maintain boundaries and avoid speculation. You see, society expects a pregnant woman to exhibit the physical signs, and wearing a fake bump means I can conform to those expectations and avoid awkward comments.' She smiled wryly. 'Although I have discovered that prying questions come thick and fast when you have a bump too. Women's bodies are so rarely our own property. We're objectified and commented on the whole time. It's not right, is it?'

I shook my head. I thought of some of the other prominent women I have styled, Beau Belle, Jennifer Astley, Liv Ramone, even Wonder Winnie – all objectified in some form.

'The bump allows me to control the narrative at least, and maintain privacy around the true circumstances.'

'Will you continue to wear it?' I asked.

'I don't know,' she said quietly. 'As you've just seen, it's not the easiest disguise to keep up, especially in my line of work.' She looked up and met my gaze. 'What do you think I should do?'

This was the first time Mandy had directly asked for my opinion. It made me stop. I looked straight into her eyes. I considered how, until this moment, I had tried to be a patient voice of reason, gently goading her to try out some new looks and own her body, instead of wishing it looked like every other filtered image online. Until now, I had bitten my tongue every time she discarded one of my carefully curated looks and swapped in something else. It had been hard, but I did it, because she was the client, and I was just the stylist. But this time, I couldn't let it go.

'You really want my opinion?' I checked.

She nodded.

'Well,' I began, 'the fake bump allows you to create a certain narrative, I can see that.' I paused, taking my time to find the right words, because this felt like a really important moment in our relationship. 'But would you consider revealing the true story? Imagine how powerful that could be.'

'It's not that easy,' she muttered. 'I feel a responsibility.'

'For what?'

'To be a certain way, to uphold an image.'

'To pretend everything happened in the conventional way?'

She nodded. 'To appear perfect, I guess.'

'Perfect is rarely how life actually is,' I said. 'We all struggle, no matter who we are. I think there is real power in admitting that.'

Mandy looked at me. I tried to read the expression on her face, but struggled. She was quiet, reflective.

A loud knock at the door broke the silence between us.

It was Blair. 'Coffees are here. I got you a decaf, Mandy!' they called cheerily through the door. 'I'll leave them on the step. Good news, the weather's clearing.'

'Thank you – be out in a minute!' Mandy yelled back.

Then she reached across for my hand – a physical gesture I had only felt from her once, after we had the first spat on the at-home shoot. This time it felt more genuine. It was crazy but it seemed as though we were becoming friends.

'You think it will go down well, the truth?' she asked, looking directly into my pupils.

'It's your decision, Mandy, of course. But I'm sure it will. Do you want to go viral, to influence others, for all the *right* reasons?'

We were disturbed by another knock and then the door opened. Jimi peered around the corner. His curly brown hair looked windswept and framed his face, his restless dark eyes sparkling. I sat bolt upright, conscious the bump was sitting on the seat beside Mandy.

'Is everything okay?' Jimi asked.

She didn't flinch.

'We're just talking about the photos and a potential new angle,' said Mandy. 'Will you grab Jose please, Jimi, then come back. We need him here for this.'

Jimi disappeared down the steps and we heard him call for Jose to join us.

Within seconds they were both entering the Winnebago and Jose joined Mandy and I in the seating area.

'You both look serious. What's happened?' Jose asked. 'Do I need my lawyer?' Then his eyes lowered, and he took in the discarded bump. 'Oh.'

'It's more what's *going* to happen,' replied Mandy. 'Amber knows, and she's had an idea.'

'Another one,' he said sardonically.

Mandy's nose twitched. There was a feverish intensity about her now, I could tell she was almost sold on the idea. 'Pregnancy is a symbol of creation and new beginnings, right?'

Jose replied, 'Yes, of course, what are you getting at, baby?'

'Well, I originally thought it meant I needed to wear a fake bump in order to conform to the expectation that being pregnant equalled making a baby and carrying it in the traditional way. But why bow down to the pressure to maintain that façade? Amber has encouraged me to see that there is no shame in sharing our true experience. In fact, in doing so, we will help others to relate and engage.'

'Authenticity builds trust,' I added, 'and trust is essential for building a loyal audience over here in the UK, as well as globally. Your truth will have a much deeper impact and stand out in a sea of polished content.'

I paused, giving Jose a minute to get his head around what we were asking. Jimi was holding back, standing by the door.

I turned to him. 'Did you know?' I asked.

'About what?'

'Come on, Jimi. About Mandy not carrying the baby herself.'

'Of course, I did, Amber. Who do you think started the pregnancy rumours?' he replied.

'That trending video from the party; with me dancing like an idiot – it was you?'

'Who else? I was initially capturing you, to record those epic dance moves you were throwing.' He shot me a cheeky smile. 'But then we thought it was the perfect clip to start the rumour mill turning.'

My heart rate quickened.

'Who else was in on it?'

He shrugged, glancing across at Mandy and Jose.

'*Everyone?*' I turned to Mandy.

'Blair and Coco didn't know initially,' she said. 'But they

do now. I couldn't bear being banned from eating sashimi for the next few months.'

'Remember, you're the newcomer, Amber. It was a huge secret, a personal secret. And we didn't know whether it was going to be successful or not.'

'I can be trusted,' I said. I swivelled and muttered this comment in Jimi's direction.

'So, are we agreed?' Mandy turned to Jose. She seemed brighter, an energy returning to her limbs.

'If it's what you want,' Jose said and squeezed her knee. Then he turned to his brother. 'Do you think it will go down well with Mandy's fans online, Jimi?'

I held my breath as we waited for him to speak. 'I agree with Amber. There's a huge opportunity here,' said Jimi. 'Posing without the bump, while releasing the news that your surrogate is carrying your baby, it will grab people's attention, that is for sure.' His eyes lit up, thinking about the engagement figures she would get for this.

'You will show there is no right or wrong way to fall pregnant,' I added. I felt desperately passionate about this point. 'There is absolutely no shame in that. You have nothing to hide, Mandy and Jose. Being unapologetically you – it is the greatest way to be.'

'Plus, that strap-on was really starting to chaff,' Mandy conceded. 'I have no idea how actresses do it.'

Her eyes seemed to regain their sparkle in that moment. I could tell something had clicked. Jimi had found the right way to present this to her. *And if there is one thing Mandy Sykes loves, it is engagement.*

'Come on,' I said, standing up, ready to leap into action. Jimi peeled back one of the Winnebago curtains to reveal sunshine breaking through the dark clouds.

'I'll see you outside,' he said, opening the door.

Mandy stood up and I watched with pride as she adjusted her underwear and gazed at herself in the full-length mirror. I tweaked her dress and hair, and watched as Lola was called inside to hurriedly touch up her make-up. Her eyes nearly popping out of her head too when she saw the discarded bump.

'It's a long story. I'll tell you later,' said Mandy.

'I'll be right beside you,' Jose reassured Mandy when she was ready to leave the Winnebago.

I paused for a moment to take her in, the Koma dress looked so much better without the fake bump squeezed underneath it. It wasn't designed as a maternity piece and hadn't really worked that way. This was meant to be. Mandy's hair was still a little damp and extra curly from the rain, but it didn't matter. She was a strikingly attractive woman, and even more so slightly undone.

'Hey there, hot mama-to-be.' I smiled, as I placed the Dryrobe back around her shoulders.

Outside, the rain and winds had eased.

Mandy passed Blair, to retrieve her coffee from Jose who had brought them in.

Blair looked down to the place where her bump once was and urgently waved their index finger above it, a figure of eight in the air.

'Erm, Mands, have you forgotten something?' they asked, eyes wide.

'No, I haven't. And there's no need to pretend it's a decaf either, Blair. Amber knows the whole story.'

As we headed back towards the sand dune we identified earlier as the ideal spot for Mandy to pose, I hung back from the group. In the hurry to leave the trailer, I'd left behind my kit containing bulldog clips, tape, and a few other bits I might need to ensure the dress stayed in place on Mandy in the unpredictable weather conditions.

'One second, I'll catch you up!' I called.

Turning back, I took a moment to look out to the horizon, where something caught my eye.

The multicoloured arc of a rainbow had appeared, its faint hues reflecting on the sea's surface. It felt like a symbol of hope, just like the image of Mandy we were about to capture.

A familiar voice spoke from behind me. 'What a gift. We need to get that in shot too.'

Jimi had decided to wait for me. He turned away from the rainbow and smiled at me, in the way that was guaranteed to make my heart flip.

At that exact moment my phone rang. I lifted it out of my pocket and looked at the screen. Rob. I paused before answering.

'Someone's calling you,' Jimi prompted, looking over my shoulder. It was possible he saw Rob's name on the screen. 'Ignore it,' he added.

'I was picking up my kit, but I can do without it I guess,' I replied.

'Come on, you two.' Julie-Ann was on a fast trajectory towards us. 'The rainbow – we need that!'

Jimi peeled away from me. 'Come on, Amber, let's go!'

So, this is how we found ourselves watching Mandy atop a sand dune, being lashed by the wind, designer dress hugging her natural curves, cellulite on show, fake tan running down her leg, black mascara smudged, silicone baby bump discarded on the ground beside her. Her gaze was fixed out to sea where the celestial arch of a rainbow was fading before our eyes.

Jimi captured her from all angles using his phone on a tripod – her beautiful imperfection, every last flawed detail, the rawness of her reality mixed with the pride of being an expectant mother, although not in the traditional sense. The act of throwing down her fake bump was a symbol of female liberation akin to the concept of a bra-burning feminist, or a Victorian woman abandoning the corset to free herself from the constraint of societal expectations. It was bold, beautiful, crude. It was real. Because *that* was exactly the point.

A second after Jimi pressed 'post' on Mandy's favourite image, her surrogacy news was announced to the world on Insta, TikTok, Snap, and YouTube in tandem. Barely a minute had passed when Julie-Ann received a phone call from the editor-in-chief of *Wonderland* magazine. She burst into the Winnebago to deliver the message to Mandy, as I was packing up the excess clothing.

'She wants to know if there are any unseen shots they could use as a front cover of the next edition. You're invited back on page one, Mandy!' she exclaimed excitedly. 'She's a big fan – said she wants to personally applaud your bravery in speaking out as a voice for all the people around the world on a surrogacy journey too.'

Mandy's chest puffed up with pride.

'I've also had calls from the *Daily Mail*, *The Telegraph*, and *The Times*, all delighted to be ahead of the curve because you announced the news here in Britain. Once America wakes up, they will go crazy too.'

I looked at Mandy with a big smile and breathed easy again. We had delivered the objective of giving something back to her UK fans, and in a really big way. Plus, the goal of achieving the financial bonus at the end of my stint in the Sykes household seemed back on track. But, more than any bonus, it was so rewarding to see Mandy find peace and grow in confidence right before my eyes.

'Of course, we can give them more images!' Mandy squealed, eyes shining. 'But I think we could do one better. Natalia, our surrogate, will be visiting in a week, so I can talk to the baby and be present at the next scan – Ebony thinks it will be great for our cosmic bonding. Why don't we offer a *new* shoot to *Wonderland*, of the two of us together? You can make the styling work, can't you, Amber?'

'Absolutely,' I replied, enthusiastically, 'and I think I know how we can make it even more impactful.'

CHAPTER TWENTY-FOUR

WEEK SEVEN

The next week was my most enjoyable working for Mandy. I'd go so far as to say I loved my job. There were busy days when we welcomed media and influencers to the house to view Mandy's latest product launches, to days when I styled her for a premiere or party in London, and quieter times when I could get on top of paperwork, send back returns and call-in items by new designers or rental agencies. Mandy had also become involved with a charity set up to support women facing unexplained fertility issues, and seemed to be really invested in raising awareness about this aspect of her life, and the challenges other women were facing. She spent a couple of hours each day replying to the direct messages she received on the subject. She seemed to be flourishing in her new-found confidence in herself.

I spent the evenings on the phone to Rob or Vicky, or hanging out with Coco and Blair. Jimi had returned to Miami for a bit, continuing to facilitate Mandy's social media requirements remotely, whilst launching his new DJ residency at a fashionable South Beach nightclub. I kept an eye on his movements through Instagram and he never seemed short of female company. I felt glad that I had managed to protect my heart from getting hurt by him, yet felt a fondness for the brief time we had shared.

Anticipation in the house was growing for the arrival of Natalia, the surrogate carrying Mandy and Jose's unborn child, and I was glad for a day off on the date she was due to arrive. It felt like such a personal moment for Mandy, and we were all granted leave to give them some space. Plans were in full swing for the *Wonderland* magazine cover shoot which would take place the following week, when Jimi would be back to shoot the video content. The magazine had commissioned a top photographer who was flying in from New York especially.

I intended to make full use of my holiday and had been granted special permission to meet up with my sister and Mum for Lucy's small hen do. Philippa had connected me with her contact at the Surrey Hills Spa, and within minutes of arriving, Mum, Lucy, and I were sipping mimosas and happily padding around in fluffy white dressing gowns and matching slippers. There was a strict no-plastic-willies, or masks with Rory's head on them, directive from Lucy, and I heeded my sister's wishes.

We were treading water in the outdoor pool, which was warmed to a pleasant twenty-nine degrees, looking out on a vista of the Surrey Hills, when Lucy dropped the bombshell. 'There's something I want to tell you both,' she said seriously.

Mum looked immediately petrified. 'Oh, Jesus. Do I need to be in my depth for this?'

'It's okay, no one is dying, but this isn't really a hen do,' Lucy announced.

There was a commotion as Mum started splashing, so we all swam over to cling on to the side to hear this.

'I just wanted to see you both, and somewhere lovely – thank you, Amber – to share a bit of news.' Lucy stared at us pensively. 'Rory and I—' Mum and I turned to each other with wide eyes, holding our breath as she continued slowly, 'Rory and I have decided to postpone the wedding until after the baby arrives.'

For once, we were quiet as we took the news in.

'Is everything okay between you both?' Mum asked, concerned.

Lucy's face relaxed. 'Oh yeah, of course we are! I mean he pisses me off on a daily basis, especially when he leaves his plates beside the dishwasher, instead of in it, and sleeps like a starfish, but after fifteen years, I have learnt to accept his shortcomings.'

'Oh, thank God for that.' For someone who claimed to be an atheist, Mum was doing a great job of blaspheming today.

Lucy took a deep breath. 'We just feel it's all got too big, too overwhelming, and too damn expensive. Plus, I don't have a dress.' This was like a stab in the heart for me. 'Sis, I know you're working really hard on the Pronovias option, but I just don't know that it's me,' she continued. Her eyes lowered. 'Plus, I don't want to be a pregnant bride. There, I've said it. I feel like I'm *meant* to want to be one, but the truth is, I want to enjoy the champagne which we're practically having to remortgage our house to afford. I want to be back to my pre-baby body shape as I walk down the aisle. And I want to be the last woman standing on the dancefloor! Not the first one off to bed because my ankles have swollen so much, and my waters might break if I don't.' She sighed.

'Oh sis, I hear you,' I said. 'I mean, who else will I perform "Single Ladies" with if you're in bed early? No one knows the full routine like you do.'

This made her laugh. *Making someone laugh after they've been close to crying is one of the greatest joys in the world.*

'Thank you for understanding. I was so worried about telling you both. Sometimes it feels as though you're not allowed to admit these things. But it's how I feel. It's okay, isn't it?'

I put a slippery arm around her shoulders. 'Of course it is. I get it,' I soothed. 'What matters, more than anything, is that you and Rory are doing what feels right for you.'

Mum had remained silent until now. Being a lawyer, she regularly took a moment to process her opinion on something, whereas I couldn't help but dive in.

'How has Nora taken it?' she asked.

'We haven't told her yet. I'm planning to wait until we have a new date confirmed,' Lucy replied.

'As long as you're not splitting up. I love Rory, like a son,' Mum said to Lucy. 'And seeing as I still haven't found the right outfit' – she turned to me – 'it gives us longer to have another shopping trip, doesn't it?' This was a statement rather than a question.

'Unless Amber is first up the aisle,' Lucy added, with a wink.

'Unlikely,' I stated. 'I've barely seen Rob this year. I need to check if everything still works between us.' Then I stopped myself.

'She's not against the idea then!' Mum teased, straightening the strap on my swimming costume.

I diverted the attention from me by kicking off from the poolside. 'Come on, let's do a few lengths.'

'I'm so grateful to you both for not making a huge deal out of this.' Lucy smiled, looking relieved.

'It's not like our family to make a big deal out of a wedding, is it?' I added, ironically. Thankfully they both laughed.

As I launched myself into a gentle breaststroke I thought about the photo and how I had accused Rob of flirting with Emily behind my back. I felt ashamed about how hasty I'd been to accuse him of being unfaithful. It was as though I had been intent on causing an issue between us. Yet I was the one flirting with someone else. I didn't feel particularly good about this, but seeing as that particular episode was over, I decided not to bring it up for discussion.

'Did you always imagine you'd get married, Mum?' I asked.

'Lord, no,' she replied without hesitation. 'I actually said no the first time your father asked me to marry him. I thought it was too soon.'

I had heard this story many times before, but always loved listening to it again because it ended so well – with the fact that she was certain neither Lucy nor I would be here if she hadn't said yes – and how we were the greatest gift. When she finished, I thought back to the conversation I'd had with Vicky about whether marriage gave you security.

'When you said yes, were you certain it would last forever?' I asked.

'Till death do us part,' Mum said. 'In taking my vows, I committed to a lifelong marriage. However, the legal system recognises that marriages may not always last forever and divorce rates are increasing in the UK. So, I guess that means you can't be certain, but I definitely wanted it to. I wouldn't have married him otherwise, would I? Anyway, isn't this a bit dreary for a hen do?'

'A *non*–hen do,' Lucy corrected her.

'Just don't tell the maître d', as they've thrown in a celebratory cake for you in honour of it being your hen,' I added.

Mum flipped over onto her back and lifted her lithe arms into a graceful backstroke. I admired how enviably toned she looked. Then I noticed her eyes narrow and follow something at the far end of the pool. I turned around and saw she was squinting at an attendant who was heading towards us at speed.

He was waving his hands trying to get our attention.

Then he shouted, 'Ladies, I'm so sorry, but we need to close the pool – could you make your way to the side please?'

We looked at each other confused.

'This isn't a drill!' he called again. 'Please vacate the pool as soon as possible.'

This couldn't be a fire alarm, surely. And even if it was, presumably everyone should be jumping into the pool.

'What's going on?' Mum muttered, as we began swimming towards the steps near the attendant.

'Thank you so much for your understanding,' he said, sounding flustered. 'I'm afraid we're going to have to close the pool in a few minutes.'

'Understanding? I'm not sure I do understand,' Mum replied in a tone that made me glad I wasn't on the receiving end. If there was one thing Mum couldn't tolerate, it was bad service.

'I'm afraid we have to close the area for an hour. If you could please make your way out, as soon as possible.'

'But why?' Lucy raised her voice. 'You might not be able to tell from up there, but I am six months pregnant.'

'We booked this especially for my sister's hen do,' I added.

'*Non*–hen do,' Lucy whispered.

I pinched her thigh underwater. 'We've only been in here for ten minutes,' I continued, 'and there was no notification about the pool closing when I booked. Why do we need to get out?'

I briefly considered whether staging an occupation of a spa pool was an arrestable offence.

'I appreciate this, and I am *so* sorry,' the man said urgently. 'We *really* hate to do this, but I'm afraid the directive has come from the top.' Lucy and Mum looked unamused. He sensed this and knelt down, closer to our eye level.

In a hushed voice he said, 'You see, a big celebrity has arrived, and she needs the space. It's for a *ceremony*. I really hope you'll understand. Maybe we can treat you all to afternoon tea in the main house by way of apologising for the inconvenience? The pool will be open again in an hour.'

'Ooh a ceremony? Maybe someone's getting married out here,' I said excitedly, looking around.

I had started to climb out, but Lucy felt affronted. 'Who could warrant—'

Then she stopped speaking.

I almost stopped breathing.

At the exact same time our collective jaws dropped, as we all noticed who had come into view through the spa door.

CHAPTER TWENTY-FIVE

'Oh God,' I squeaked.

'Oh, *God*,' said the attendant.

'Oh Gaaaad,' repeated a familiar American voice belonging to a dressing gown-clad glamorous woman who had appeared in full view.

Two people, also in dressing gowns, stepped out from behind her, near the entrance to the pool area. All three were presumably unable to wait any longer for the signal that the riff-raff had been cleared out.

Mum looked embarrassed, while Lucy broke into a peal of quiet, resigned laughter. There was no mistaking who it was.

I pulled my wet body out of the pool and stood on the side. At least I had waxed my bikini line, it could have been a lot worse. I instantly began to shiver as my wet skin met the cool air.

'Oh hi, Mandy!' I shouted, brightly, displaying an excitement that I didn't really feel.

Her eyes narrowed and for one horrible moment I thought she was going to pretend she didn't know me. My pulse quickened.

Then her face opened up in recognition. 'I barely

recognised you, all soggy. I thought you were a fan about to ask for a selfie.'

'No such luck!' I replied.

'You remember Ebony from LA, my cosmic doula?' Mandy said, encouraging Ebony to step forwards.

'Of course, hi, Ebony,' I said, shaking with cold and feeling very naked. Ebony and Mandy had fully made-up faces, which had discoloured the collars of their white towelling robes.

'And this,' Mandy continued, turning to a woman on her left – her eyes were sparkling as she proudly announced, 'this, is someone *very* special.'

She took the woman's right hand in both of hers. 'This is Natalia. Our surrogate.'

'Natalia, this is Amber Green, my stylist.'

Although she was encased in a robe, you couldn't miss the large, round shape of Natalia's midriff. She was a fairly short woman, with dark brown curly hair and olive skin. She looked at least a decade younger than Mandy.

'Natalia doesn't speak great English, I'm afraid. She's from Mexico originally, but lives and works in Florida. She's our angel.' She smiled at the woman, who had a kind and friendly face, yet seemed nervous. Natalia stepped forward, smiled, and shook my hand formally.

'It's a pleasure to meet you,' she said politely.

Mandy looked across at my mum and Lucy, and I introduced them all.

'I'm sorry we had to clear the pool,' Mandy said, at last making reference to what had happened.

'It's my fault,' Ebony interjected. 'It was all getting a little tight, timing-wise.'

'Timing-wise?' I looked at her puzzled.

'Today marks a full moon, so we're planning to honour its energy and guidance for the unborn child, whilst harnessing the power of the elements.' She said it so matter-of-factly, I wondered if I had missed something. 'Earth, water, fire, and air,' she continued. 'We're going to tap into cosmic forces by honouring the elements and seeking their guidance to explore our own inner cosmos. The pool is our water. Think of it as a birthing pool for all of our souls.'

I nodded slowly, noticing Lucy do the same. Mum gave me a sideways look which suggested she did not buy into any of this woo-woo nonsense. I didn't feel any less confused, but Ebony had a way of speaking with such authority, none of us dared question her.

Undeterred, she lifted her face upwards, towards the sky. We all copied her, lifting our chins to peer above us as if waiting for a divine entity to give us a sign. Ebony pointed out the daytime moon, it appeared pale against the blue sky. 'You see it? It doesn't shine as brightly as during the night, but it's just beginning to appear, and it's critical we get the timing right. It's such a majestic and serene sight, let's all rest our eyes for a moment and take a breath here.' She closed her eyes, Mandy and Natalia followed suit. I kept one eye open. 'That's beautiful. Now try to visualise yourself as a cosmic being, connected to the vastness of the universe. You may like to imagine stardust flowing through your veins, or maybe you are a celestial body, weightless and free, orbiting the moon with an umbilical attachment to it.'

This was too much for Lucy, who made a snorting noise next to me.

'I'm sorry, I think I need to sit down,' she muttered.

'How far on your pregnancy journey are you, my cosmic sister?' Ebony asked, guiding Lucy towards a nearby sunlounger.

'Nearly six months,' she said.

'Snap!' Mandy said excitedly, as she gently patted Natalia's middle.

Natalia looked sympathetically at Lucy. 'How are you feeling?' she asked softly.

'Well, the sickness has passed, but I feel tired a lot of the time. Otherwise, pretty good. You?'

'I feel good,' Natalia replied. 'I feel so blessed to be able to do this for Mandy and Jose.' She smiled shyly at Mandy, who squeezed her hand.

'That's beautiful,' Ebony purred. 'We're planning a small ritual whilst submerged in water to align the inner world of the growing foetus with the cosmic rhythm that surrounds us,' she informed us. 'It is a formative step in the cosmic journey of motherhood. You're welcome to join us, Lucy, if you'd like to?'

I nudged Mum in the small of her back, not intending to make her yelp, but she let out a high pitched 'Ooh!'

Ebony turned to her. 'You are the cosmic grandmother of the unborn child, I presume?'

'That's partially correct. Hannah Green.' Mum held out

her hand. She said it in the official voice she reserved for new clients, rather than new friends, aka the 'don't mess, I'm a qualified lawyer' tone which instantly made me feel everything was under control.

'You form a link in the unbroken chain of ancient ancestors who have enabled this unborn child to exist today,' continued Ebony.

Mum looked offended and also baffled, she had never thought of herself as an ancient ancestor or had to exert authority over a cosmic doula before. 'And you are—?'

'Think of me as an astrological midwife.' Ebony politely took Mum's hand and laid her other hand on top, sandwiching it tenderly. Mum raised an eyebrow, this kind of overt affection from a stranger was way out of her comfort zone.

'You could do with relaxing,' she muttered.

'If Ebony's okay with it, you're all welcome to join us for the celestial bathing ritual, if you would like?' Mandy offered.

'Of course, the sisterhood welcomes everyone,' Ebony replied smiling, her wide face framed by white hair braided in cornrows close to her scalp. She looked a similar age to Mum and was stunningly beautiful. There was a pause as the two women gauged our reactions, expectantly.

'Does it help with blood pressure?' Lucy asked, surprising me.

'Of course, it's one of the best antenatal classes you can do. It will make you feel renewed,' Ebony said calmly.

'I could do with that to be honest,' Lucy mumbled, rubbing her back.

'Please join us.' Ebony put a gentle hand on her back. 'Let the full moon guide you. Just as the moon goes through its phases, our lives and experiences follow a similar pattern of growth and change – and there is nothing more symbolic of this than a pregnancy. The full moon is also associated with the release of negative energy and letting go of what no longer serves us during this time – emotional baggage, high blood pressure, that kind of thing.'

'Cancelled weddings and related admin?' asked Lucy, one eyebrow raised.

'If that is what you need from it, yes,' Ebony replied. 'By embracing the energy of the full moon, we can surrender and make space for positive transformations.'

'I'm in.' Lucy nodded.

'I'm out, if you don't mind,' Mum added, and I linked my arm with hers in solidarity.

'Let's get started, Cosmic Beings.' Ebony smiled.

Then she placed a bowl of crystals by the side of the pool and lit some incense. 'To create our sacred space.'

Mum and I took this as our cue to back away from the poolside, put on our dressing gowns, and cover ourselves in towels, as we lay back on the sunloungers to quietly observe the ritual from a ring-side seat – or pretend we were dead – we weren't sure which way it would go yet. A neat waitress came past to offer us coffee, though it seemed like a ruse to rubberneck the spectacle unfolding in the pool before us.

We watched closely as Mandy, Natalia, and Lucy held hands with Ebony, making a circle in the centre of the pool. At least twenty candles floating on lotus flowers were bobbing around them.

A low humming sound emanated from Ebony who had closed her eyes and was chanting something indistinguishable. Every now and then she would break the circle to place her hands on the midriff of one of the women, and the humming would get louder before subsiding into a whisper.

She then encouraged Mandy and Natalia to turn to face each other, and Lucy looked to be on the periphery. At one point Lucy became distracted and engaged in a game of air hockey above the water, batting away lit lotus flowers with her hand every time one floated too close to her bump for comfort.

After every chant, Ebony turned and threw her hands towards the moon dramatically as she called upon each element to honour their presence within the woman's body.

Lucy shot a dark look at Mum and me, as if we should throw her a lifebelt. She seemed to be regretting taking part, but, just like us, felt too scared of Ebony and disrupting her cosmic vibrations, to say or do anything out of turn.

'Do you think she's okay?' I muttered to Mum, behind my hand. 'Should we do something?'

Mum was silent for a moment, then she smirked wickedly. 'Lucy will be fine. This is much better than any show I've seen recently.'

Ebony began to move through a series of affirmations which involved a womb blessing where she placed her hands gently on each woman's belly, to 'channel cosmic mother energy', as she blessed the womb and the growing life within.

She then encouraged the women to take part in a series of affirmations, encouraging them to 'speak their truth' by repeating mantras after her: 'I am a cosmic vessel', 'I birth galaxies within' and 'My body dances with constellations'.

Suddenly we noticed things turning emotional in the pool, as tears streamed down Mandy's cheeks. Instinctively Natalia put her arms around her, hugging her and soothing her.

We could hear her saying, 'I'm here for you, Mandy, we both are.'

And then Ebony joined in, placing her strong arms around the two women.

'It's like the reality of becoming a mum is just hitting me,' Mandy snivelled. 'And I don't know if I deserve this.'

'Of course you deserve this, heavenly Mandy,' Ebony comforted her, drawing Mandy's damp head towards her large bosom in a motherly hug.

'But I bought my baby on my Amex,' Mandy whimpered.

'There are lots of ways to become a mother,' Ebony continued. 'You tried many of them, and this decision was not taken lightly by you. You were destined to be a mother, and the universe brought Natalia to you at exactly the right time; it was written in the stars. Remember when we worked on your cosmic birth chart?'

Mandy sobbed, 'Yes.'

'This was in your cosmic blueprint. It is your destiny. There is no right or wrong way to become a mum.' She looked across to Natalia and Lucy, drawing them back into the ritual. 'I understand this can be a deeply emotional activation, and this is because your soul is remembering your cosmic origins. Let's do some breathwork together.'

Mandy composed herself, and the women's hands joined again, as Ebony guided them through a series of breathwork exercises, chanting, 'Inhale stardust; exhale fear.'

This seemed to calm Mandy, who smiled, but still looked sad. As Ebony whispered gratitude to the stars, the full moon, and the women's cosmic lineage, she placed both of her palms on Natalia's bump. Her eyes fluttered shut, and she seemed to surrender to the moment, perhaps leaning in to the mystery of creation itself. As Mandy watched, her expression now looked serene, peaceful, as if a shift had occurred and she could be invested in this pregnancy.

Natalia, who had displayed the patience of a saint throughout, encouraged Mandy to cradle the curve of her baby bump. Both women smiled as the baby made its presence known with a well-timed little kick, or 'cosmic dance' as Ebony referred to it.

When the ritual drew to a close, we were all left speechless for a moment.

The moment of contemplation was broken abruptly by a loud bubbling noise emanating from somewhere underneath Ebony. She pressed her lips together into a thin, restrained smile.

'Was that what I thought it was?' Lucy exclaimed, moving backwards in the water, away from a warm patch of bubbles around Ebony.

Natalia twitched her nose, suggesting her highly sensitive sense of smell due to pregnancy had detected something other than the earthy aroma of sandalwood and cedar from the incense.

Ebony let out another sound from her undercarriage, this time louder, sending a bubble plume to the surface with some speed. This was enough to make Lucy audibly snort, before breaking into hysterical laughter.

'She farted!' she howled, almost choking on the words because she found it so funny. Mum and I gripped our sides and burst into laughter too.

'The exhalation of a cosmic gas perhaps?' Lucy giggled uncontrollably.

I held my breath for a second, waiting for Ebony to come out with a spectacular cover-up for what was blatantly flatulence.

Even Mandy was giggling, and Natalia was unsure where to look.

The cosmic doula was impressively composed for a moment, perhaps relieved to have exorcised whatever gases were causing her discomfort, and then the corners of her mouth rose to form a wide smile.

'There are some things, ladies, only Mother Nature controls. I give you the fourth element – air!'

'Whether you believe any of it, or not, she's good. *Very* good.' Mum sighed, as we relived the ritual from the safety of the hotel restaurant, after the trio had left in Mandy's blacked-out Mercedes.

Lucy was nursing a weak bellini. 'I don't care if I'll be drinking Gaviscon all evening, I need something to get over that,' she howled. 'The cosmic farting!'

Even Mum had tears in her eyes. 'Oh, I needed that. There is nothing like a bloody good laugh.'

'Do you think flatulence is a planned part of the ritual?' I asked.

'I love you, but you're *sooo* gullible sometimes, Amber!' Lucy exclaimed, before cracking up again.

'I don't know how you deal with this kind of madness day-in, day-out,' Mum remarked.

'It's not boring.' I smiled. 'And there's only another few weeks until I get the bonus. I've actually enjoyed this experience far more than I initially thought I would.'

We paused as a waiter delivered our afternoon tea on a pretty cake stand. We listened closely as he described in detail the filling of every sandwich and cake, and we salivated over the spread before us.

As we filled our plates, Mum asked me if there was anything I had learnt while working with Mandy. It was an interesting question, and it made me stop to think.

'I've learnt that at the end of the day, we all have struggles because life is rarely linear, it's a squiggle. And there is beauty in that,' I replied.

Mum smiled affectionately. 'Don't ever lose this outlook, Amber,' she said. 'I'm so proud of you.'

I felt my mouth fall open.

'That means a lot – thanks, Mum.'

'And how about learning that even cosmic doulas are prone to windy-pops sometimes?' added Lucy, and we all cracked up again.

CHAPTER TWENTY-SIX

WEEK EIGHT

Over the eighth week at Gables Manor, the energy felt different. I'm not sure whether this was down to Ebony, and the continued presence of joss sticks and chanting around the house, the calming influence of having Natalia and an unborn child in our midst, or perhaps it was because Jimi was back and with him a sense of humour and a lightness that I missed when he wasn't here. We resumed our schedule of Pilates sessions in the gym, and I had finally mastered not blushing every time my eyes met his during sit-ups. I didn't even dream about stealing a whole bar of cooking chocolate from the kitchen anymore, because I felt happy.

Last night Jose shared some news, which saw a sense of relief spread around the occupants of the house. Gathered in the drawing room, as we had been so many times over the last weeks, Jose dropped the bombshell that the family would be returning to LA a month early, in preparation of having the baby there.

'We have more space and staff in the States,' he explained, 'plus, it's closer to Mexico for Natalia to be supported by her extended family.'

Blair, Coco, and I exchanged looks, wondering what this meant for us. 'Blair, if you're up for the move to LA with us, your contract will continue as normal,' Jose continued, at which Blair jumped on the spot and punched the air.

'Move to LA? Y.E.S.!' they shrieked. 'If you'll sponsor my visa?'

Jose nodded. Then he turned to the two of us. 'Coco, Amber, we're happy to finish your contracts a month early. You'll get your bonus, without needing to complete the term. You've been a huge support to Mandy, and we are so grateful. We would love to continue working with you whenever we're back in the UK, and you can rely on us for glowing references.'

'Wow, that's kind.' I grinned, feeling a warmth for my bosses. Coco seemed pleased with the outcome too.

As Philippa entered the room holding a tray of champagne, she seemed to have a sense of joy about her too – as much as Philippa could ever exude gaiety. She handed us each a glass, which Jose duly charged.

'Here's to Frida!' he said, raising his glass into the air, as did Mandy, and all of us followed.

'To Frida!' we echoed, as I whispered to Blair, 'Who is Frida?'

'Their nickname for the baby,' they whispered back. 'I wouldn't be surprised if it's a girl and they keep it. Think Kahlo, Mexico, art, identity. What a name.'

Jose was then joined by Julie-Ann who confirmed we were still pressing ahead with the final photoshoot this week for the cover of *Wonderland* magazine, featuring Mandy and Natalia together. It was to be entitled 'The Tapestry of Motherhood'.

The clothes call-in for this shoot was my easiest yet – I made just one phone call. There were no fine jewels with bodyguards required, no favours to ask for one-of-a-kind straight-off-the-catwalk samples, or rows of extra shoes. The colour palette was neutral; the brief: less is more. In this assignment, it wasn't the clothes that were going to do all the talking.

After planning the items for the shoot, I began packing up my bedroom. Rob was intending to collect me from the house and drive us home together, straight after we had finished on set, and I wanted to be ready to go. I hadn't made this room feel particularly homely during my time here, but I would miss the peace of the Surrey countryside, the birdsong in the mornings and blossoming trees in the garden outside my window. I looked out of the window across to the walled garden, where I could just about see the pond area, the gnome, and the toadstool seats where I had been sitting the first night I felt something for Jimi; how his dark eyes looked at me in a way that was so different to Rob. I thought about how different the two men were, but it didn't make me feel confused. I wouldn't miss the feeling that Rob was a long way from me, not only on the other side of the M25, but a world away in my mind for that period of time. It had only been a matter of weeks, but it felt as though so much had happened. I thought about how maybe Jimi was brought here to help bring me closer to Rob.

The next morning, the call sheet for people on set – which was to be in Mandy and Jose's bedroom – was kept to a minimum. There was a top female photographer with one assistant, two reps from the magazine, and just me in wardrobe, with Lola doing hair and make-up. No men were permitted in the room during filming, and that included Jose and Jimi, who was shooting behind-the-scenes and social media footage. Preparations were in full swing for Mandy and Natalia to get ready. I laid out the items they would be wearing on a marble dressing table in the large en-suite bathroom, which doubled as our changing room for the shoot. The same one I had seen Jimi creep out of on the night he confessed to the mushroom mix-up.

Everyone had stepped outside for a moment, to make a call, vape, or get an extension lead, and I went over to an ornate wooden sidetable in a corner of the bedroom, on which Coco had delivered some of Mandy's favourite protein balls. I shoved one into my mouth and poured myself a glass of water. I looked over towards the bed and grinned as I remembered the night Jimi and I had practically bumped noses in the dark while Mandy slept; and how my assumption they were having an affair was wide of the mark. It had nearly been the other way around.

Mandy came in. 'Caught you!' she exclaimed. 'Those balls are my weakness, and it turns out Natalia loves them too. Don't eat them all.' Her eyes lowered. 'What do you think of this slip?'

A thin, silk spaghetti-strap on the plain black dress she was wearing dropped below her shoulder. 'It's ancient Chanel, I wondered whether I can still carry it off?'

I studied her, seeing a fleeting glimpse of the Mandy

of twenty years ago, a little more chiselled perhaps, but a naive version of the beautiful, strong woman she was now. Mandy was one of those lucky people who seemed to grow into their looks, looking more attractive with each life experience etched on her skin.

'It's pretty,' I said. 'I love silk, but I think it could be more fitted.'

She grinned then. 'I agree. No one is this honest with me. Thank you for always telling me the truth, Amber.'

I felt my body tingle. More than the bonus, this had made my time with Mandy worthwhile. If nothing else happened to me in my styling career, this would be enough. It could be written on my gravestone – *Amber Green, The Stylist: Always told the truth.*

With photography underway, I caught Mandy's eye as she turned her head momentarily away from the camera to find a new angle, one she knew would give the photographer everything she needed. *She knows how to make their work easy.*

Mandy beamed at me, ear to ear, her eyes sparkling. It was a kind smile. She looked happy, but more than that, she seemed at peace. She was commanding the room in a way I'd witnessed many times before, but today there was a new layer to it; something more authentic, something incredibly strong and real. She moved again, this time her eyes stopped on Natalia's huge bump. She paused there for a while longer. A contentment written across her whole being. It was more than a look. It was an energy, palpable in the air between them.

'Hold it right there. This is beautiful,' purred the photographer, going in closer to the two women as the lens opened and closed with a quick succession of soft clicks.

Natalia was a natural in front of the camera too, her soft smile and features complementing, but in no way overshadowing Mandy's incredible beauty.

'Is it still raining out there, Amber?' Mandy called over to me, catching my gaze again.

'Of course, boss. It wouldn't be England if it wasn't drizzling, would it?' I replied. 'It's meant to be sunny this afternoon.'

The corners of her mouth turned upwards. 'Four seasons in one day again. Well at least it's cosy in here.'

The two women were practically naked, bar large 'nude' knickers which blended in with their skin tone. Each had an arm strategically placed over their bosom in homage to the iconic Demi Moore *Vanity Fair* cover which became one of the most culturally influential media moments ever. The 2025 version was more edgy and thought-provoking. It was not a highly polished, full-on glamour shoot, like most of Mandy's magazine covers to date, but it was sensual and provocative, intended to convey the natural beauty of pregnancy and the poignant relationship between the egg mother and her surrogate; a motherhood journey that had not been shown in the fashion press before, certainly not in such daring detail. Celebrity surrogates are normally hidden away. Spoken about rarely, if ever, let alone shown practically nude in photos alongside an A-list star, that will be posted all over the internet. It was guaranteed to make front-page news around the world. In giving Natalia a voice, Mandy was also giving a platform to all surrogates; to show how appreciated they were, and to be a friend to other people on this motherhood journey, so they knew what to expect and that they were not alone.

The editor-in-chief of *Wonderland* was on the photoshoot – a tall, lithe woman called Simone, wearing an asymmetrical black dress, chunky jewellery, her eyes lined with kohl and poker-straight red hair. She was speaking excitedly on the phone to a colleague, as I overheard her tell them, 'It is more major than I imagined. This shoot is going to get people talking. Just wait!'

We all knew we were in the presence of something very special.

Later, during a break from shooting, Mandy called me over.

Her eyes held mine. 'I feel like I've come home, Amber,' she said. 'And I don't mean the physical location – I mean at home with myself. Thank you for everything you have done for me.'

I felt genuinely happy for her. 'You've got everything you wanted from your list.' I smiled.

'Just pray it goes to plan,' she murmured, looking across at Natalia, who was sitting in her dressing gown with Lola massaging her feet.

'This is amazing!' Natalia cooed, enjoying the pampering on the shoot. 'I feel so empowered to be showing the role a surrogate can play.'

'And you will both inspire millions of people in the process,' I said, smiling.

Mandy was destined to be famous. She had the magic formula in abundance, those hard to pinpoint attributes that collide in a way that is so spellbinding it makes everyone stop and pay attention. I don't just mean her killer body and picture-perfect face, she's always had that, but now it was something deeper. I looked around me at the team who were all in the room, equally spellbound by the scene before us. Jose had popped his head around the door to check on his wife. For once, he was lost for words too and his eyes filled with tears as he took in the scene before him.

Mandy had finally, openly, become the person she was always meant to be, and this new inner confidence was contagious, electric, magnetic.

Fairy tales don't happen very often in real life. Not all stories end with picture-perfect wedding days, proposals, or a baby arriving smoothly in the traditional manner. And if I ever felt that a person was transformed by a certain look or a designer outfit, now I knew differently. Fashion, as with life, is complicated. It is nuanced, and it doesn't follow the instructions.

When Simone called, 'That's a wrap!' at the end of the photoshoot, Mandy came over to me.

'Thank you, Amber,' she said warmly. 'This is all down to you. Thank you for helping me to believe I am enough.' A look passed between us, as subtle yet significant as a heartbeat. 'What will you do next?' she asked, before either of us could feel too emotional.

'I'm not sure,' I replied. 'Find a new job, I guess.'

'Keep styling,' she said. 'It's your calling.'

'Thank you,' I replied softly. 'You're going to be an amazing mum.'

Instinctively, we hugged.

CHAPTER TWENTY-SEVEN

That evening, the last bags from my room in my hands, I walked towards the front door of Gables Manor for the last time.

My heart leapt into my throat as I found Rob standing on the porch, deep in conversation with Jimi.

Rob and Jimi, face to face, this wasn't the plan.

The two were chatting easily and something had obviously tickled them, because Jimi threw his head back and was laughing heartily at something Rob had said.

Were they laughing at my expense?

Cautiously, I approached them.

'Oh man, you picked a funny guy,' Jimi said as I stood side-by-side with him in front of Rob. 'Rob was just telling me about what happened when you two worked at the Angel Wear show. An incident with a glitter cannon?' He giggled again. 'I would have *loved* to witness that.'

'I think it was one of the most stressful nights of my entire life,' I said, deadpan.

'Oh baby, that story never gets old.' Rob was chuckling.

There he was, my boyfriend, handsome as ever in a white T-shirt and jeans. He looked really good. And that warm smile which engaged his twinkly green eyes made me want to rush into his arms and nuzzle his neck.

'It sounds like Rob, your *boyfriend*, has done some amazing work,' Jimi said coyly. 'We've had a great chat.'

I looked between them nervously, trying to read both of their faces at the same time. 'There might be some filming Rob can help me out with, especially if some of the TV pitches we're working on get commissioned,' he added.

I shifted my weight between my feet uncomfortably. I hadn't realised Rob had arrived, he was meant to call me when he did. I felt bad for putting him in this position.

'Well, this is it, I guess.' I nudged Rob in the arm, hard. A clear signal that I was keen to get going as quickly as possible.

'I guess it is,' Jimi said, turning to me. 'I hope I'll work with you again, Amber. You're brilliant at what you do.' Then he added to Rob, 'Let's go for that beer sometime.'

It had started raining outside and, assessing the luggage I had piled up by the door, Rob said, 'I'll go and bring the car closer.'

'I'll come with you!' I announced.

'No, you wait here.' He was already moving. 'I'll be back in a sec.'

Then it was just Jimi and me. He gave me a churlish look.

I thought back to the night of the kiss on the lips.

'So, were you going to pretend Rob isn't your boyfriend?' he asked, when Rob was out of earshot.

'I wasn't,' I protested weakly.

'You so were.' He smiled. 'And you're blushing, so that confirms it.'

He raised an eyebrow. 'Did you forget you showed me a photo of him? When you were telling me about how you accused him of being unfaithful?'

I shrugged.

'I'll forgive your amnesia because you were drunk,' he continued. My mind flipped back to the night of the party at the house.

'I forgot about that,' I mumbled.

'Don't worry – I raised it with him, and you have no reason at all to be worried.'

'You *what*?' I felt a hot fear spread through my body.

'I asked him about it. As a friend. You wanted to know, didn't you?'

'You're joking, aren't you?'

'I'm not joking. But there's no need to panic—'

'Jimi! You broke my confidentiality.' I collected myself, not wanting to draw any attention to us. 'Well, what did Rob say then?' I whispered.

'I can't tell you. But you have absolutely nothing to worry about. In fact, the opposite.'

'Well, this is weird,' I said.

'What's weird?'

'You. Knowing something about my boyfriend that I don't.'

He looked straight at me. 'Relax, Amber. He seems like a great guy. I'm happy for you. You don't want to let that one go.'

'I don't intend to. What else did you talk about?'

I kicked a loose pebble on the stone beneath us and it just missed hitting him on the shin.

'He told me about his job, and I think I can give him some work. We had a chat about what he does – he's got great experience and is available to start straight away.'

'What do you mean, his job?' A new wave of fear rose inside me.

'The fact he doesn't have one. You didn't know?'

I was floored. And especially hearing this news from Jimi. *How long have they been standing here chatting for? He's learnt more about my boyfriend in five minutes than I have in eight weeks.*

Jimi looked awkward. 'I'm heading back to Miami for DJ gigs, and I'll need someone to take on more of the content over here whenever Mandy comes back. Rob could be perfect. How would you feel about that?'

I tried to act cool, not wishing Jimi to know how confused I was.

'Rob knows what it's like working with talent. If he's up for it, that sounds good.' I smiled weakly.

'Rob had some cool ideas too – he suggested making a documentary about Mandy's surrogacy journey, it will make a refreshing change from the same bullshit celebrity shows. Netflix is looking for exactly that kind of content at the moment. So, we can be work friends then?' He smiled at me with those amazing lips, but this time I didn't want to jump right into them and get acquainted. Instead, I felt affection towards him in a platonic way.

'I always said we were friends,' I replied dryly.

Right on cue, Rob shut the door of our Mini Countryman.

Philippa, Blair, Coco, and Jose had come to the front door, and now stood in the sunshine outside the house, to join Jimi in waving us off. As we drove past the privet orbs and reached the outer gates, I looked back at the manor house, now partially covered by a cascading wall of lush lilac wisteria, its heavy blossoms hanging like miniature chandeliers. Parts of the façade were highlighted by the sun's rays, beaming down like spotlights through blossom-heavy trees. The house looked so much more alive than it had when I first arrived here on a freezing March morning, with no idea what to expect. A top window flung open just as the gates glided apart and I heard Mandy call out, 'Bye, Amber, thank you!'

I looked up at her and waved.

As we turned onto the road, my parting image was of Jimi, his back turned as he walked into the house behind the others. If I wasn't mistaken, he looked around at the last moment to where our car had been, just as the gates closed. And then he was gone.

You see, sometimes, you can be just friends, even with a really, really hot single guy from Miami.

When Rob and I left the house, we didn't drive straight home, but stopped off at a country pub Rob had booked for my release; where I ordered a dinner of fish and chips and devoured it as though I hadn't eaten anything so tasty in a long time – because I hadn't. Over a pint of shandy,

I found myself laughing with Rob and talking with ease about the whole crazy experience. It felt just like our Saturdays on Portobello Road. Only there was a nagging voice in my mind – there was something I needed to ask him.

'Why didn't you tell me about your job?' I asked. 'It was a bit of a shock to hear that earlier.' My eyes searched his face for a reaction.

He looked resigned. 'I didn't want to bring you down.' Rob sighed. 'You had enough going on with Mandy and it was the day you had the party in the evening. I didn't want to tell you over the phone.'

'I knew it,' I whispered. 'I had a feeling something was up with you that day, it was weird.'

He hung his head. 'I didn't think you needed any extra worry.'

'But it's *you*,' I stated. 'I always want to know your news, and I'll always support you. You know that, don't you?'

He nodded.

'So how do you feel about it?' I asked.

'Okay now, I guess.' He sighed. 'You know how much I was hating it recently. In some ways, being made redundant was for the best. I've got enough money to keep us going for the next few months while I find new work. I've got my head around it, and I'm okay.'

'As long as you understand it's no reflection on your skills, because it really isn't,' I assured him. 'It's just a shitty time with the market. It's the same in retail and across loads of industries.'

'I know. I just hope I get as lucky as you with a shiny new opportunity sooner rather than later.'

'You will,' I said encouragingly. 'You'll get snapped up.'

'If you haven't used up all of our good luck quota that is.' He chuckled. 'You've done so well getting the bonus. I'm proud of you, Am. Really.'

'And I didn't even have to do the full term,' I said, beaming.

He took my hand in his and looked at me intently.

'There is something else I wanted to talk to you about,' he said.

My eyes widened.

'It's about that photo, the one from Christmas. I was—'

'Shhh.' I put my index finger to his lips. 'You don't need to say anything. Honestly, it was silly of me. I'm over it.'

'But I do,' he replied. 'I want to. I was in touch with Emily. We exchanged a few messages just before Christmas.' I gulped. 'I wasn't going to tell you why, but I thought you should know. I asked her for the engagement ring back. So I can pawn it.' The little hairs on my arm stood on end. 'I didn't like the thought of her still having it. And,' he looked at me shyly, 'I might need a new one, one day.'

'So, did you get it?' I asked, trying to sound calmer than I felt inside.

'Yes, after a very awkward conversation on Facebook Messenger, I got it back.' His dimple appeared when he smiled.

When Rob said this, a tense feeling I didn't even realise I had been holding in my body seemed to melt away.

'That's good,' I said, trying to make light of it, whilst wondering where the ring was right now. I bit my lip. As I took this news in, I noticed a strange, visceral reaction in my body, it was as though butterflies were emerging from cocoons inside my tummy.

I pictured Rob on bended knee, asking me to marry him. *We are back in New York when he's doing this, not on the top of the Empire State Building, where I thought he was going to propose at the end of our time there, but on the big rocks in Central Park. It's golden hour and the sun is warm on my skin. I feel happy, really happy.*

The butterflies quietly fluttered when I had this thought. But it wasn't an anxious or overwhelming sensation, it was a peaceful feeling – it felt as though I was just where I was supposed to be.

'Are you okay?' Rob asked. 'You've gone quiet.'

As I looked back at him, a feeling of love flooded my brain. I wanted to keep looking at him more than I wanted to do anything else – even to order dessert.

'I'm great, Rob. Thank you for telling me,' I said. 'I'm sorry I jumped to the wrong conclusion, it was really unfair of me.'

'Not all secrets are bad, you know, Amber,' he said.

I thought about Jimi and the kiss then, wrestling with the question of whether it was okay to keep a locked safe within yourself, to which only you were allowed access.

'Aren't they?' I asked, hanging my head. The pitch of my voice must have given something away.

'Any secrets you need to tell me about?' Rob probed.

It didn't feel right to say nothing, especially after what he had just told me.

'That guy Jimi,' Rob said, reading my mind. 'What's his story?'

Is it weird that he's brought him up? I turned to Rob, my eyes silently pleading with him; trying to tell him by osmosis to leave it. He must have read something into my failure to have mentioned Jimi at all during my time at the house. I was at a crossroads. He knew me so well.

'He's a bit of a player I think,' I said, still toying with not telling him anything.

'Did something happen between you?' Rob asked me straight. He was sitting more upright, the air between us had thickened. Although he had never been a jealous person, Rob was intuitive.

'Why do you ask that?'

'Just something I sensed. You were being jumpy,' he said.

I took a deep breath. 'There was a kiss,' I said. 'I'd drunk lots of wine, we were in LA. It should never have happened. I've been beating myself up about it every day since. It was brief and I'm really sorry.'

I rested my eyes on the table as I waited for his response. The table seemed to blur at its edges, my chest tightened, ribs constricting around my heart.

Is he going to walk out of the pub?

Instead, Rob took my hand.

'Is that really everything?' he asked measuredly.

'I promise, that's it. It made me realise how much I love you.'

I blinked away a tear and when I raised my head, this time his face was blurred. I didn't want to cry, I just wanted Rob to forgive me.

'It's okay.' He stroked my hair with his hand. 'I was distant, I know that. I should have told you what was going on.'

'I should have been stronger. I was weak, falling for his flattery. I'm so sorry. He had bad clothes too.' I hung my head.

'So, no more secrets between us?' he asked.

'None. You?'

Rob leant forward and pulled me closer, whispering, 'Only that I love you more than ever. I'm going to have to keep close tabs on you these coming weeks, Amber Green.' Then he planted a tender kiss on my lips, and I succumbed to the French kiss that followed.

When we got back to our little Ladbroke Grove flat it was late. It felt smaller than ever after the vast proportions of Gables Manor, but I didn't care. I enjoyed making herbal tea in our initials mugs, and Rob went to the garage for emergency Maltesers. We played music and talked about the opportunity of him working with Mandy. I saw an energy return to his bones as his mind lit up with ideas. We laughed about how we had worked together twice before, so why not a third time, and that spun into grand ideas about starting our own production company one day.

It didn't take long before his lips were pressed onto mine again, and my heart was fully in it, as we kissed and fumbled and giggled and cuddled up.

'I've missed you so much,' he whispered each time we parted, only to pull me back for more.

I was so happy and at ease in his arms.

That night, as Rob and I spooned in bed wearing absolutely nothing but the scent of each other, my gaze turned to his feather tattoo. This time I saw it with new eyes. My interpretation of it now was less about representing the freedom of flight and Rob taking off into a future without me, but a symbol of keeping me safe, and navigating life together. As I was thinking about this, I realised Rob was still awake too. He rolled over and propped his head up on his elbow.

'There is something else I wanted to say to you.' His free hand drifted towards mine, and our fingers laced together gently and instinctively.

'Oh no,' I murmured sleepily, 'I don't think I can handle any more revelations.'

A bang on the ceiling made us both jump.

'The Divorcee and Girl Friday.' I sighed.

'Welcome home,' he said.

'So, what? Did you forget to put the dishwasher on?' I looked at him quizzically, suddenly fearful. 'Or do I need to be properly awake for this?'

He looked upwards for a moment. *And now he's thinking twice.*

'That's better, they've stopped.' Then his eyes met mine again and they were soft, loving, and sincere. 'I've been thinking,' he said, 'how about we use your bonus and my redundancy money for another trip to New York?'

'I guess we're never going to get a mortgage until we have secure jobs anyway.' I sighed.

'Does it really matter if it takes a bit longer?' he asked. 'I'm in no hurry. Are you?'

I shrugged. 'I guess not.'

'Let's get solid foundations in place first.' He smiled.

'Oh God, help me now, I've fallen for a man who uses building metaphors as a way to express his love.'

His eyes sparkled as he mirrored my grin. 'You're the only scaffolding I need, Amber.'

Then his arms enveloped me, and we pressed our bodies together again. I felt warm and safe. And there was nothing adequate about it. He was everything to me.

EPILOGUE

Dear Destiny,

Thank you for your response to my question. I have come a long way since then. I have realised I actually had the answer inside me all along. You might be interested to learn that my recent work as a fashion stylist has helped me to answer some of the wider questions I had about my love life. I have always been mesmerised by the power of clothes. Let me explain . . .

For me, fashion is about celebrating people. And that includes everything about them – the negative self-talk, the feeling like we're constantly striving to fit in and failing, and learning to accept the squishy bits we're conditioned to find hard to love. You see clothes, just like relationships, can break hearts because they initially promise so much; clothes can also mask the truth. But the real beauty is when you are able to peel back the layers and work on what lies beneath – only then can a person truly shine.

As a stylist, you have to be careful. You wield enormous power, not just to create a pretty image, but to curate an honest picture of life, and with that comes great responsibility. *When you get it right, when the client steps forward into the spotlight and shows off their authentic self – and is able to use that truth to inspire others – that's when I know my job is done. They could be clothed, unclothed, in a designer dress, or wearing some flesh-coloured knickers, it doesn't really matter. Even if you're an A-list celebrity with all the money, fans, and followers you could possibly desire, this can be the hardest task of all. Fame is meaningless if you don't understand who you really are.*

This principle can be applied to relationships too. When you are able to authentically connect with a partner, and they still love you for all your fuck-ups, frustrations, and bad decisions, that's when you know you've struck gold. And as for knowing whether it will last forever . . . just like the best-loved pair of shoes, sometimes they will go on, treading the streets and spinning on dancefloors for a lifetime, and other times it reaches a point when they have worn out, or you grow tired of the style, and they become someone else's new discovery in a vintage store. That's the way life goes.

I have learnt to be happy amongst all of that uncertainty.

If there is one thing I would offer your followers to take away from my experience, it is something an old lady on the London Underground once said to me: Don't just exist – live.

None of us know what is around the corner, not even you. But you must always, always take care of your favourite shoes.

Love,
Amber Green x

ACKNOWLEDGEMENTS

There were more than a few moments when I thought this novel might never see the light of day – burnout, career reinvention, home renovations, family life, hormones – you name it, it slowed me down! So, I am eternally grateful to my literary agent Jenny Savill for being in my corner when requesting extra time, and to the brilliant and patient team at HQ, especially Lisa Milton, for allowing me the space required to birth this book. To my fantastic editor, Priyal Agrawal, thank you for your willingness to wait, your gentle guidance and belief in my ability, it means the world, and this is a much better novel as a result.

I have always considered Amber Green to be a therapist as much as a stylist, as she understands that to truly make a person shine in the finest designer threads takes a deep understanding of their inner self too. This theme has always been present in The Stylist series, and it comes to the fore in this novel, marking a parallel in my own life. During the writing of this story, I have reshaped my career for the next chapter, and I have done this through a desire to help others find their purpose, and this experience definitely inspired Amber's actions in *Bad Influence*. I would like to thank the people who have been instrumental in my personal growth over the last couple of years while I was writing it. To my family and friends, especially the core six, Chrissie, Kate, Debbie, Becka, Zoe and Jane – our 24/7 dialogue pulled me through many anxious moments. And to Ally whose friendship and working partnership has been such a brilliant reinvention moment. Female friends are the other great love in my life, and I love you all so much.

The other huge, steady guiding force behind this novel is my husband Callum, whose love is unconditional as he champions my endeavours and occasionally pulls me back from tipping into 'hyper-cluck mode' with calm assurance and love. I couldn't have done this without the support and encouragement from you and our two beautiful boys, Heath and Rex, true creative forces who motivate me to make you proud.

My biggest thanks goes to you, the readers of my books. In a world where there is so much choice, your decision to pick up one of my novels is so precious and I am extremely grateful.

It feels bittersweet to say goodbye to Amber Green on these pages, so instead I will take the view that because she exists so vividly in my mind, our lives are entwined, so Amber will always be with me in some form.

Amber and I would like to remind you to always believe that you are enough. You are not defined by a societal expectation – be proud to be the real you and wear whatever makes you happy.

Discover Amber Green's previous adventures!

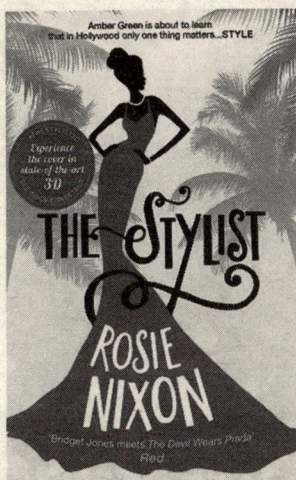

Amber Green loves her job at Smith's, the exclusive London boutique frequented by the rich, the famous and the stylish – and with stylist to the stars Mona Armstrong as a customer, there is never a dull moment.

With the Oscars approaching and yet another assistant walking out on her, Mona needs help, and she needs it fast. Before she has time to say *Rodeo Drive*, Amber finds herself agreeing to get on a plane to L.A. as she is expected to work with the increasingly volatile stylist and dress some of Hollywood's hottest (and craziest) starlets. Awards season turns her life upside down as designer gowns and dazzling jewels are matched to a steady stream of A-list stars, and are paraded on red carpets at the year's most glittering events. Meanwhile Mona is unravelling faster than a hemline . . .

And as Amber starts to enjoy rummaging through the ultimate dressing-up box, she finds herself in the limelight as she catches the attention of two very different suitors. How will she keep her head? Which man will she choose? And most importantly, what will everyone wear?

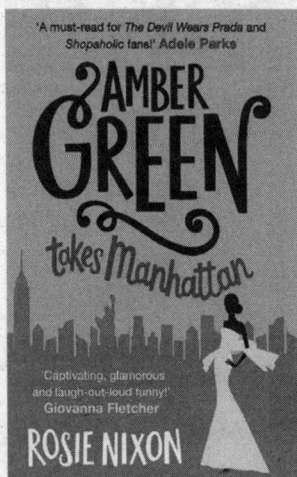

When her TV producer boyfriend Rob announces that he's been offered a job in New York, filming with the infamous Angel Wear lingerie models, Amber knows it's her perfect chance to take the New York fashion world by storm.

But Amber wasn't counting on unruly toddler photo shoots, clandestine designer handbag scams and a Hollywood star who is determined to wear as little as possible on the red carpet. Until she meets a disgraced former designer who could turn her career around . . . or leave it all in tatters.

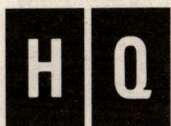

ONE PLACE. MANY STORIES

Bold, innovative and
empowering publishing.

FOLLOW US ON:

@HQStories